STRIFE'S BANE

Also by Evie Manieri

Blood's Pride
Fortune's Blight

STRIFE'S BANE

Shattered Kingdoms Book III

Evie Manieri

TOR

A Tom Doherty Associates Book
New York

STRIFE'S BANE

Copyright © 2018 by Evie Manieri

All rights reserved.

A Tor Book
Published by Tom Doherty Associates
175 Fifth Avenue
New York, NY 10010

www.tor-forge.com

Tor® is a registered trademark of Macmillan Publishing Group, LLC.

Library of Congress Cataloging-in-Publication Data

Names: Manieri, Evie, author.
Title: Strife's bane / Evie Manieri.
Description: First U.S. edition. | New York, NY : Tom Doherty Associates, 2019. |
   "A Tom Doherty Associates Book."
Identifiers: LCCN 2018045358 | ISBN 9780765332363 (hardcover) |
   ISBN 9781429960151 (ebook)
Subjects: | GSAFD: Fantasy fiction.
Classification: LCC PS3613.A5453 S77 2019 | DDC 813/.6—dc23
LC record available at https://lccn.loc.gov/2018045358

Our books may be purchased in bulk for promotional, educational, or business use. Please contact your local bookseller or the Macmillan Corporate and Premium Sales Department at 1-800-221-7945, extension 5442, or by email at MacmillanSpecialMarkets@macmillan.com.

First published in Great Britain by Jo Fletcher Books,
an imprint of Quercus

First U.S. Edition: February 2019

Printed in the United States of America

0 9 8 7 6 5 4 3 2 1

For my mother, Joanne

Dramatis Personae

The Shadari

ALKESH, a Red Guard

ANAKTHALISA, ANI, an asha

BIMA, a widow

BINIT, an agitator

DARYAN, the daimon

DRAMASH, a boy with asha powers

FALIT, son of Erdesh

HAROTHA, Eofar's lover, mother of Oshi, deceased

HESH, a resurrectionist

JEMMA, daughter of Shemoth, an asha

LEM, a Red Guard, Daryan's bodyguard

MEENA, Daryan's aunt, deceased

OMIR, Captain of the Red Guard

SEDENA, a wealthy Shadari woman

SHAIRAV, an asha, Daryan's uncle, deceased

SHEMOTH, an asha, deceased

TAL, Daryan's chief steward

TALBAK, a farmer

TAMIN, Lieutenant, a Red Guard

TESSA, a laundrywoman

VEYASH, a Red Guard
ZAMAR, a Red Guard

The Norlanders

CYRRIN, a healer
EOFAR EOTAN, King of Norland
FALKAR, a lieutenant
FREA EOTAN/THE WHITE WOLF, Eofar's sister, deceased
ISA EOTAN, Eofar's sister
LAHLIL EOTAN, Eofar's sister, formerly known as the Mongrel
OSHI EOTAN, Eofar and Harotha's son
RHO ARREGADOR, a former soldier
TARA PELTRAN, head of the Imperial garrison at Prol Irat
TREY ARREGADOR, Rho's brother, deceased

The Nomas

BEHR, Jachad's wagonmaster
CALLIA, Nomas queen-in-waiting
GRENTHA, first mate of the *Argent*
HELA, a sailor on the *Argent*
JACHAD NISHARAN, JACHI, King of the Nomas
MAIRI, a healer
MALA, a sailor on the *Argent*
NISHA, Queen of the Nomas
SABINA, second mate on the *Argent*

Others

ALLACK, a member of the Mongrel's crew
ARNO, an Iratian fisherman
CLARE, a young woman
DIDI, a barmaid
DREDGE, a member of the Mongrel's crew

FELLIX, a strider
KILS THE RELIABLE, an urchin
NAV, Clare's friend
NEVIE, a member of the Mongrel's crew, deceased
SAVION, a strider

STRIFE'S BANE

Chapter 1

Unlike the rest of the ferry passengers, Lahlil didn't lift her boots when the water sloshed to their side of the boat. She was too busy reminding herself that ordinary people did not threaten to impale ferrymen when they wanted them to pick up the pace.

The woman with the tousled hair sighed and wriggled out of her jacket, revealing a patched chemise and delicate shoulders. The rest of the passengers had already stripped down as far as conventional modesty would allow, but Lahlil didn't want to expose her mismatched eyes or her scarred forearm, so she had to content herself with tugging her collar away from her neck.

"Last winter 'twas warm, but it ain't ever been this warm afore the harbor fes'val," said the woman, fanning herself with her hat.

"We usually have snow up in the hills long before now," said the young man with the wolfish smile. The way he kept touching the heavy purse around his waist, it might as well have had the words "Steal Me" stitched on the front.

The mother paused picking at a knot in the collar string of her little boy's shirt to wave her hand at the water. "It's the fog I don't like: day and night, it's been. Look out there. We should be able to see the watchtower at Bodun by now. Daybreak, but you'd never know it."

Daybreak. Once again the sunrise had come without Lahlil knowing. More than a decade of blood-boiling pain had given way not to peace, but to emptiness. The Nomas sun god Shof and the moon goddess Amai had finally stopped squabbling over their claim, so either Jachad had brokered an accord on her behalf, or they'd realized the treasure they'd been fighting over had been nothing but dross all along. She wouldn't know until she found him again.

"'Tis unnatural, that's what'is," said the old man to Lahlil's right, the elided cadence of the outer islands making his words a drawl. His grown daughter lifted her hand from the basket of limp vegetables to wipe the sweat from her forehead. "This plague out'a Norland—all o' them soldiers cut loose, makin' trouble: the signs'r'all there, for them who c'n read'm. S'goin' t'get worse afore't gets better."

The mother shot father and daughter a dark glance as the child, a tiny thing with a mane of ginger curls, pressed back against her knees.

"It's like you was saying, Clare," the girl at the far end of the bench broke in. She and her friend were both decked out in enough cheap finery to pass for idols in the market square. "About the plague—you said it all along, din't you? Something unnatural al-lus comes out'a the empire. Remember?"

"*You* look like you came from up north," said Clare, turning around to face Lahlil. Her eyes, dark and challenging, rested on the silver triffons on the hilt of Lahlil's sword.

"A while back," she muttered, speaking Iratian with the blunt accent of the mercenaries she had known from that region. "Afore the quarantine."

"Well, o' course," said Clare. "I couldn't've meant *after*, could I?"

"You could've," put in her friend. "They let in those with coin, I bet. Like with errything. Coin buys errything these days."

"Tain't right," the old man declared, stomping his foot and splashing salt water over all of their feet as the other passengers voiced their agreement.

"So, did'y'see it? The plague?" asked Clare. She dropped her voice to a dramatic whisper mid-sentence when the mother made a sharp clicking sound in her direction.

"No."

"You *sure*?" Clare pressed. Her face was taut with the thrill of someone who had never experienced real danger. "I hear it sends you mad afore you die, sets you *tearin'* at erryone. Like a beast, I hear. And then blood comes out'a your eyes and you fall down dead—*just like that!*"

"Clare!" hissed her friend.

"Oh hush, Nav. I'm not sayin' ennything people don't know already."

Lahlil had seen plague victims dripping silver pus from their eyes and mouths. She'd packed snow into their wounds until the cold killed the infection. *Those* people she'd managed to cure, but these, sweating through their light clothes, would have no chance if her brother Eofar's quarantine failed to stop the plague from spreading past Norland's borders. Just one splinter or scrape would turn that woman with the tousled hair, the old man, the little boy, into monsters. She knew exactly how they would look as they screamed in pain, how their limbs would twist as they clawed at themselves and each other, spreading the infection . . .

<Please tell me we're almost there,> said Rho Arregador. <Or kill me. I'll leave the choice to you. Oh, and never, *ever* let me eat again.> A few of the other passengers glanced up. She'd warned Rho not to assume the islanders wouldn't be able to hear him speaking Norlander, but as usual he hadn't listened. He shifted a little in his corner; from the greenish hue of his skin, he was going to be sick—again—and she really didn't want a second look at the sausages they'd eaten on the last quay.

<Breathe through your nose.>

<Good idea. Because the smell of fish is what I need right now,> he snapped, but he was too much on edge for his sarcasm to bite. It was always like this when they approached the next new place, bracing themselves for news neither one of them, even on their

best days, expected to be good. Every creaking boat, jolting cart and muddy trudge brought them a little closer, but she could feel time sputtering like a lamp sucking up the last few drops of oil, with no way of knowing when the light would snuff out for good.

"Fog's getting thicker," the ferryman grumbled.

The boat crawled down the inlet to the west side of the island, vying for space with the other small crafts trying to navigate through the increasing murk. The ramshackle pier gradually took shape, followed by the usual boxy silhouettes of taverns, brothels, moneylenders and jails. Five ships bobbed in the deep bay. The wind wasn't strong enough to lift their flags, but one look was enough to tell her that the *Argent* wasn't there. Lahlil could taste the sourness of Rho's disappointment as strongly as her own.

"Papers," an official bellowed as he settled his bulk at the top of the gangway, scratching his beard. The ferryman held out a tattered card; the official grunted and gestured the passengers out. "Come on, come on, let's be 'aving you."

Lahlil followed the two girls up the gangway. The inspector's glance dipped under her wide-brimmed hat without interest but lingered on the heavily tarnished hilt of Strife's Bane. She hunched her shoulders a little and sulked while she waited: another cheap mercenary washing up like garbage in these backwater islands. Finally he waved her up the slimy gangplank. The old man and his daughter came behind, followed by the wolfish man, the mother and son and finally the woman in the chemise.

"You! Norlander! You stay there."

Rho. Of course. Every time.

"No Norlanders get in without a pass. You got a pass or not?"

<He wants to see your quarantine pass,> she translated for Rho, in case he hadn't understood. She made sure to keep her shoulders at the same indolent angle and crossed her arms in front of her as if her sword was the last thing on her mind.

"You two together, then?" the inspector asked her.

A jerk of her shoulder, noncommittal. "Headed in the same direction."

"Yeah, and where's that?"

"Prol."

"So you ain't staying here?" the official asked, producing a little cheat-glass to take a closer look at the stamp on the damp paper Rho took from his pocket. Clare's friend was right about one thing: a fistful of coin could get you just about anything, including a forged stamp saying you were already in the islands before Norland closed its ports. "Hm."

Kill the inspector first, then the ferryman: two quick strokes, no noise; kick the bodies overboard. Someone sees from another boat, calls out, gets the attention of the people on the dock, so then you make a run for it, tell Rho to go a different direction, divide the pursuers. You'll be surrounded before you get to the end of the pier. Fling off your hat and jacket, let everyone see your scars; someone shouts "It's the Mongrel!" Good. Now they're afraid. They'll stay back. Then they haul Rho across the deck toward you. They've already started beating him bloody and they're holding a knife to his throat, telling you to give yourself up.

"You look like a soldier," said the inspector, handing the pass back to Rho. "You a deserter? Someone coming to haul you back? We still have the garrison here. Don't want that kind of trouble at my port."

"His garrison disbanded," Lahlil supplied. "They closed the border before he made it back."

"He can answer for himself, can't he?"

"He can also spew all over you," she warned. "Better you than me, Worthy."

The islander curled a protective hand over his beard and stepped back out of the way.

Rho picked up his cloak and wobbled to the gangplank, bruising his shins on the benches as he went.

<Come on. We've lost enough time already,> said Lahlil. She picked out the filthiest tavern within sight and started toward it, weaving around the crates, boxes, barrels and nets piled up on the jetty. In the center of a pier stood a statue of a local goddess with

a fish's head and an impractical arrangement of tentacles. The locals had hung tributes of little bits of colored glass from her appendages.

<You didn't need to interfere,> Rho told her, walking so close behind her he would likely bowl her over if she stopped suddenly. <I had the situation in hand.>

<Was that your plan if he figured out the pass was a fake? Vomit on him?>

<We all have our talents,> he said magnanimously, draping his cloak across his arm with a flourish. <I'm sure yours will come in handy someday.>

They stopped to let a man trundle by with a wheelbarrow full of coal. <You should have been quicker getting off the boat.>

<He would have stopped me anyway.> Rho stalked ahead as soon as their path was clear. Two fishmongers gaped at him, their expressions the same as the fish in their baskets, and a stevedore failed to notice he was about to tip over a stack of crates until one of his comrades cursed at him. She hadn't wanted Rho tagging along; it was Eofar who had pointed out how much more damage he could do blundering around on his own. Not that she'd admit it, but the qualities that made Rho a lodestone for trouble meant very few people noticed *her*, which was just how she wanted it. <Besides, someone like that isn't going to spot the forged seals— not unless his beard has some magical powers other than retaining the stink of last week's stew.>

<I'm saying we don't have time for games.>

Rho stopped in his tracks in front of the tavern door. Even if she hadn't felt his emotions turn to a flat, hard white she would have noticed the blue flush on his throat. <Games?>

<Later,> she warned him. <Someone will notice us standing out here.>

Rho's back remained rigid but he went up to the tavern and pulled open the door, holding it for her with mock civility. <By all means, let's get a drink first and figure out how soon we can get

off this shit-heap of an island, since we've obviously missed the *Argent*. Again.>

The Black Whale looked like every other dockside tavern she had ever been in, right down to the pair of old-timers blinking through a fog of bitter cigar smoke. Three drunken Iratian sailors slumped over a table, rolling a set of dice, while behind the square bar in the center of the room, a barmaid with a deformed ear drummed her fingers on the counter.

"Beds upstairs, communal only, no baths and you slop for yourself," the barmaid recited like a bored priestess. "Chops at midday, roast in't evening, less it's a feast-day, which it ain't. Sausages anytime but I wouldn't if I was you, Worthies."

"Just a drink," said Lahlil, fishing out a coin and noting the need to obtain more money soon. Their plan to sail straight to Prol Irat had fallen apart when their Gemanese ship had been held for quarantine at the first port in the Broken Islands. Bribing their way island by island had ripped a sizeable hole in their purse.

"So whatch'as want?" The barmaid yawned into the back of one hand and waved at a collection of brown glass jugs with the other. "Got jackwater here'll burn your eyes right out'a your head."

"Ale."

<Ask if they have Norlander wine,> said Rho.

"Does this look like the fecking Triumverate's palace?" the barmaid answered straight back, scowling at Rho and pulling at her bad ear. "You'll get the local stuff and like it. Or not. Feck if I care."

"He'll take it."

The girl snagged a mug and a flagon, set them under different casks and flipped the taps, then swung both filled vessels onto the counter without spilling a drop. <What's wrong with you, then, Handsome Jake?> she asked Rho in Norlander. Her hungry leer revealed sharp little teeth and looked surprisingly good on her. <Too busy being pretty to talk to me?>

<No,> Rho answered, lounging against the bar like a regular, <only I haven't completely recovered from my ferry-ride yet.>

<Aw, is it like that? Poor lad,> said the girl, sliding the flagon toward him. <Tell Auntie Didi all about it.>

<Didi, from what I've seen of this establishment, I'm sure you know all there is to know about vomiting.>

The girl shrieked with laughter and Lahlil's fingers tightened around the handle of the mug. <You're right there, Worthy, and that's the truth. What you need is the sea air, a little cool wind on that pretty face, not being shut up in this fecking place. Come out back with me and I'll show you—Aw, feck me. Don't you go nowhere, eh? Next one's on me.> This last as the door opened and half a dozen well-armed mercenaries came roaring into the tavern, laughing and hailing the barmaid by name as they tipped money on to the counter. They'd cleaned off the blood and grime but Lahlil saw the fresh cuts and bruises and recognized the post-mission joviality.

Rho had already taken their drinks over to a table, leaving her the corner seat because he knew she would demand it anyway. <Finally, a floor that doesn't rock,> he groaned, sinking down onto a stool with a pleasure that was almost obscene.

<Don't get too comfortable.>

<Meaning?> He flipped the single word at her like a stone.

<You've got to talk to the barmaid again.>

<That's not what you meant,> said Rho. <You think it's my fault we missed them again, don't you? You think I'm slowing you down.>

Lahlil's first mouthful of ale slid over her tongue and down her throat. <That's not what I said.>

<What you said is that we don't have time for games. Do you think this is a game to me? That I came along with you, why—for my love of sea travel? That old woman tried to make Dramash—*a little boy*—murder hundreds of people. She put some kind of spell on Isa that made her turn on all her friends and now she's sweet-talked her way onto the *Argent* and is heading for the Shadar

to do who knows what to it. I left behind the only family and friends I have in Norland to stop her. I even left Dramash behind. There is nothing more important to me than getting to that ship and killing Ani before she hurts anyone else. I'm going to make sure Dramash has a home to go back to some day. So I'd appreciate it if you didn't treat me like a toddler pulling at your sleeve.>

<Finished?> Lahlil asked when he stopped talking. She leaned across the table and pushed his flagon toward him. <I apologize. Now drink your wine and calm down.>

He was right, and he wasn't the one playing games. That would be the game of hide-and-seek she was playing with Jachad—the one he was winning.

Rho tipped his head back to get the last few drops from the flagon and then set it down. *<Am* I slowing you down?>

<No. We've been unlucky, that's all.>

<Be honest, Lahlil. This partnership was your brother's idea, not mine. If you believe you have a better chance on your own, then you should go on without me. Only swear you'll kill Ani when you find her.>

<Drop it, Rho,> she warned him. <We're staying together. For now.>

The door banged open as a man in a thick jumper with a cap pulled down low over his eyes burst in. Lahlil's hand reached for her sword but his gaze swept past her and Rho and landed on a man drowsing at a table near the back. "Arno! Get off your ass and out the boat!"

"Whassit?" the man grumbled, opening one eye.

"Salvage, ya drunk bastard!" barked the man in the cap. "Spotted her soon as the fog lifted. She's loose out past the harbor and not a soul on deck. Whoever gets to her first'll have the claim of her."

Arno flailed to his feet and sped from the tavern as if it was on fire. The other patrons had taken note as well; Didi's high-pitched voice was cutting over the general noise but Lahlil couldn't make out much over the throb of her own pulse until icy fingers dug into her wrists and Rho's silver eyes locked with hers. His fears twisted up with her own, two ribbons of the same bloody hue.

The Argent.

Rho had already disappeared into the street, but Lahlil stopped to hook her fingers through the handle of one of the jackwater jugs and ignored Didi's threats as she hurdled the step. She followed the growing crowd until her footsteps went hollow on the pier.

As she crowded up to the railing beside Rho he told her, <It's not the Argent.>

The prow of the vessel slid through the calm water, drifting with no sign of anyone at the wheel. It was a small, single-masted short-range merchant ship, moving parallel to the shore and too close for comfort to those already at anchor. Lahlil thought the sails were furled until she saw the bits of cloth flapping from the yards. She couldn't see much of the main deck over the high rails and the upper decks were all deserted. One of the launches was missing, but the other was still there.

Water splashed down below them and several vessels of various sizes raced away from the pier, their oars slapping madly while the crowd cheered them on. Two boats collided and their occupants instantly began trying to wrestle each other overboard. She spotted Arno and his friend making headway, two sets of oars pumping like mad.

A triffon swung by low overhead: as Lahlil had expected, the commotion had attracted the attention of the Norlander garrison still deployed on the islands.

"Salvage! It's salvage!" a woman behind Lahlil screamed up to the rider. "You can't touch her! That's the law!"

Lahlil grabbed Rho by the crook of the elbow and hauled him back from the railing, keeping one eye on the triffon all the time. <Come on,> she said as the animal tilted into a tight circle over the ship and then headed back again. She let go of him and, anticipating where the triffon would land given its current trajectory, broke into a run.

<Why are we running? It's not the Argent,> Rho said.

<Grab that man's cigar. And don't let it go out.>

<What? Why?> asked Rho, but he did snatch the thing from the startled old man shambling along in their path.

<There's no damage to that ship. Her crew didn't abandon her; they're still aboard. Most of them, anyway.>

He stuttered a little as he put the facts together. <Why—No. You think it's the plague?>

The triffon dropped to the ground up ahead, its bulk shaking the decking hard enough to make her trip into Rho's side. The lone Norlander rider grappled with her harness and as soon as she was free, disappeared on the opposite side. Not even all the shouting behind them could block out the sound of her retching.

<You fly. And give me the cigar,> Lahlil ordered Rho, grasping the jackwater jug more securely as she swung herself up into the saddle. She jammed her feet in the stirrups and looped one arm through the harness but didn't bother with the rest. <Go. We can't let anyone get aboard.>

<You're not strapped—>

<Go!>

He obeyed, overcoming the triffon's reluctance to head back out toward the rogue vessel with a firm kick to her sides. Swooping low, they could see their tavern companions had overtaken the other scavengers. Arno was standing in the prow of his little boat and had already stripped down to his undergarments. As they watched, he flexed his ropy muscles and dived into the water.

<Faster,> Lahlil urged Rho as the man swam toward the ship with steady, powerful strokes. Clenching the jug between her thighs, she got out her knife and sliced a swatch from the tail of Rho's shirt.

<What are you doing back there? Oh, no—>

Arno scrambled up the netting on the side of the ship and flopped over the rail onto the deck with a cry of triumph. They could see him rubbing the water out of his eyes as they closed in— then he threw himself back up against the rail and grabbed it with both hands, as if he feared being swept overboard.

The sailors, their bodies now twisted and rotting, had obviously torn each other apart while in the grip of the plague's madness. Blood mottled the deck in rust-colored patches and her hatches had been left open to the rain and sea. And beneath the shadow of the heavy clouds, the silver plague shimmered like a billion stars as it continued to feast on the death it had created.

Arno tried to throw himself over the side but got tangled up in the ropes. He flailed there, unable to climb up or down, as if terror had sapped his ability to reason.

Lahlil uncorked the jug and stuffed the piece of fine cotton lawn into the opening. One whiff of the contents was enough to tell her many a sailor must have wandered home blind after a visit to Didi's tavern. <When I tell you, make a pass across her bow, as low as you can.>

Rho tugged on the reins and whistled, getting the triffon into position for the dive. Lahlil drew on the cigar a few times until the tip glowed bright red. She spat out as much of the bitter smoke as possible, then held her improvised slow-match to the fuse, blowing on it until the damp fabric caught.

<Now!>

The horizon tilted up as the triffon pulled in its wings like it would in battle so they wouldn't scrape the mast. Lahlil finally remembered she wasn't actually strapped in and jammed her feet down into the stirrups, tightening her legs against the saddle. They rushed toward the silver-streaked deck with her sheltering the smoldering cloth from the wind, and the moment they bottomed out of the dive, she hurled the jug. The jackwater splashed out over the wooden planking and ignited in a rush of flame, licking up the wood and torn sails, even the tattered clothing on the bodies.

<Turn us around. Make another pass,> she commanded. As soon as they veered around she could see that the fire had taken hold. No one else would be able to get aboard now.

Arno had finally managed to disentangle himself from the rope netting and had jumped off the ship. When he surfaced, he began swimming frantically for the dock, but Lahlil didn't need to tell

Rho what she needed; he was already bringing the triffon around in pursuit, so low the water splashed up over its tail. As soon as they flew past Arno, Lahlil twisted around and threw her knife, hitting him cleanly in the chest. He managed a single cry before the water poured into his mouth.

Rho turned the triffon again, this time heading south along the coast; heading for the next port—the next failure.

<They might pull the body out of the water,> he said eventually.

<They won't. They know it's plague now.>

<I keep thinking about that missing launch.>

<Anyone who left that ship died before they reached land.>

Rho thought about that for a moment. <Still.>

Lahlil finally strapped herself into the harness, but not before sparing a look back over her shoulder for the burning ship. Those flames were the massacres of her own making: villages she'd set alight to keep the opposing army from supplying itself, besieged castles she'd attacked with fire until the thatched roofs caught and drove the inhabitants out like rats. The bodies turning black on the deck of the doomed ship were the dead of a hundred different armies she'd destroyed for coin and for the pleasure of it; the flames were the pyres raised when the corpses were too numerous to bury and the air burned with the stench of her victory. They wore the faces of people she had known. Frea, Isa, Eofar; her father and mother, Aunt Meena and Uncle Shairav; Nevie, Dredge and Allack and the rest of her crew; Nisha, Callia, Mairi and the rest of the Nomas; Cyrrin and Trey. Jachad.

She waited until the burning ship had shrunk to a fist-sized ball of flame before she turned back around.

Chapter 2

Lahlil and Rho spent three days flying along the coast, avoiding patrols, scrounging information and supplies and getting on each other's nerves. At dawn on the fourth day, they ended up in an alley by the docks breathing through their mouths to avoid the smell of piss, stale beer and rotting cabbage. To avoid the harbor's watchtower, they'd left the triffon tied up in a field; they had to hope it would still be there when they got back, since neither of them would agree to stay behind to guard it.

Lahlil pulled her hat down a little further as a boisterous group of dairymaids skipped by, their arms linked. The one on the end aimed a baldly invitational look at Rho, sticking the tip of her finger in her mouth and sucking it in what she clearly thought was a seductive gesture before her friends pulled her away.

<She's a little young for that,> Rho mumbled.

<She's no younger than Isa,> she said. And then came that little silvery flare: the reaction Rho always had to her youngest sister's name. It was there and gone in a flash, but it was enough to add to Lahlil's suspicions.

As they emerged from the end of the alley onto a cobbled street, a barefoot boy of about ten in a floppy knit cap bounded out from somewhere with a crisp salute. "Warm day, in't it, Worthies? Find you a bed? Empty, or not, as you will. Don't listen to them lying proc'resses. I knows all the best houses. Or a drink? I knows all the taverns—and which ones overcharge fer'ners. Or maybe I c'n carry a message for you? I can find anybody. Make a purchase? Hire a berth? Next tide goes out afore noon."

Lahlil dug a snipped quarter-eagle out of her pocket. "Information," she said, dropping the gold into his hand, "about a ship. The *Argent*. A Nomas ship. You'll get another of those if you come back with something." She tilted her hat up a little so he could see the worst of the scars around her mouth. "I'll know if you're lying."

The boy swallowed. "You'll get no lies from me, Worthy, I swear. Ask anyone. Kils the Reliable, they calls me. I'll find out all about it. Nomas—them's the ships that's all girls; see, I know that! The *Argent*. You wait here—won't take no time."

Rho flopped back against the wall, careless of the hilt of Fortune's Blight scraping the wormy wood, but his feigned boredom fell flat. Lahlil pulled her hat down a little further over her eyes and lounged next to him, trying to keep the tension thrumming under his skin from ratcheting up her own.

The door of the two-story house across the way creaked open and a woman sauntered out with a stool under her arm. She placed it beside the entrance and paused to wriggle her breasts more comfortably within her bodice before sitting down.

"Feck if it's not hot as a switched ass," the procuress offered conversationally. A curtain slid back on an upstairs window and offered a calculated glimpse of the doxies preparing for the day. Lahlil had some pleasant memories of smooth limbs gliding over each other, perfumed sweat and a release that might not amount to the blank transcendence of the battlefield but would nonetheless ease her into a dreamless sleep: a purely transactional relationship in which she owed nothing but coin and ended with no farewell except a knock on the other side of the wall.

The woman waggled a finger at Rho and spoke to him in jerky Norlander. <Now I'll bet you left a few sore hearts behind, haven't you, Worthy? Why don't you come in out of this bad air? I'll give you half-rates on account of that pretty face. We could do you a cold bath even. Don't that sound nice?>

<Some other time, Auntie,> Rho answered with genuine regret, though Lahlil suspected that was more for the bath than the company.

<Well, don't you wait too long,> said the procuress, her tone going dark. <If there's sickness abroad, they'll shut up all the houses and leave us to starve.>

<You're not afraid of catching it?>

The woman threw back her head and let out a loud snort. <Never been sick a day in my life.>

<No?> asked Rho. <What's your secret?>

She smiled triumphantly. <Never drink water, nor tea, nor nothing else but ale, morning, noon and night. It's water as kills you, mark me on that. Besides,> she added, patting one of her wide hips proudly, <ale gives you a figure.>

Rho's agreement went unvoiced as Kils the Reliable dashed back into view at the end of the street. "Worthies!" As they closed on him, he lowered his voice discreetly. "The *Argent*, Nomas ship, flag a full moon, silver on a black ground, captain Nisha daughter of Melissandra, six tonnes, give or take, heading south."

Lahlil's heart skipped. "How long ago?"

"She sailed three days ago."

Three days. That meant the *Argent* was still somewhere between here and Prol Irat. "What about the people on board—a man with red hair?" She stalled Rho's interjection by adding quickly, "And an old woman? A Norlander girl with one arm?"

Kils eyes widened. "Dunno about them. Inspectors found sickness aboard so they didn't let none of 'em come ashore. Some was too scared to take their coin, even, when they found out she came from up north."

"What kind of sickness?" Lahlil asked, blocking another onslaught of distress from Rho before shoving him out of her mind.

"Dunno." The boy held out his hand. With a sly smile, he said, "There's more."

She pulled the second snip from her pocket and passed it over. "Go on."

"They're saying Ugly Farrell's son took coin to let one of her boats come in. They're saying *somebody* got off."

"Man or woman?"

"Dunno," said the boy, "but I'll show you where they went."

Rho practically bowled Lahlil over in his haste. They slipped through the streets together, following Kils through the kind of tight-knit warrens only a street urchin would know how to navigate. Alleys switched back on themselves and ended abruptly, testing her sense of direction, until they ended up facing a shack on yet another street stinking of mud and rotting wood.

"Over there. The yellow house," said Kils, pointing to a single-story building with no windows or chimney; there were a few flakes of yellow paint still clinging to the front.

Lahlil dropped another snip into the boy's waiting palm. "Stay close in case we need you."

The boy's eyes shifted nervously toward the end of the street and back, but he closed his hand over the coin. "As you say, Worthy."

<Before we go in, we should—> Rho began, but his words snapped off when she ignored him and marched to the door.

The room smelled of mold and held a chill despite the heat outside. A thick wax candle on the table flickered in the draft; the only other light came through the half-open door behind Lahlil. A skinny cat crouched by the wall and glared at her before darting outside. The occupant, a Norlander with strands of white hair drifting from the confines of a single braid, sat propped up on the sagging bed. She was rigged up in a back brace of leather straps and bone stays, its brass buckles pulled tight across her torso to keep her spine from collapsing.

Her pain . . . her pain was like another presence in the room, an unrelenting pulse of agony as deep as anything Lahlil had ever witnessed on the battlefield.

<It's Cyrrin,> she said to Rho, blocking the door.

<The healer? The one who saved Tr—my brother?>

<Yes. I'm going to talk to her—you wait out here.>

Rho grabbed her shoulder and pulled her back out of the doorway. <You are *not* my commander. I'll go in there if I want.>

<Kils "the Reliable" probably sold information about us to a dozen people before he led us here. There's no time to argue.>

He stared at her as if trying to bore a hole through her with his silver eyes, then he released her and stepped back. As he turned around to survey the street, she shut the door behind him and the room sank into near-darkness.

<Lahlil,> said the healer after a long moment.

<Cyrrin.>

<Where's your eye-patch?>

Lahlil moved a little closer to the bed. <I don't need it any more.>

<You don't look right without it. Too much face.> Cyrrin fumbled under the ratty blanket and pulled out a flask, which she uncorked with her teeth. Her hands were shaking badly but she managed to pour a few drops onto a spoon. The liquid was clear and smelled like rotting flowers but Cyrrin swallowed it without hesitation and then lay back with her eyes closed. The thick fog of pain in the room ebbed, but only a little.

Lahlil pushed aside a cane chair and stood at the side of the bed. <Are you here alone?>

<One of the Nomas came ashore with me but I sent her away.> Cyrrin had never put her comfort or safety above her pride; Lahlil had no reason to be surprised.

<I wasn't sure if you were still on the *Argent* when she sailed from Norland.>

<How would I have got off?> Cyrrin huffed. <You and that strider boy brought me there against my will and then left me there with no way back; and no home to go back to, since thanks to you, Valrigdal is abandoned. I hope you haven't come for forgiveness. I don't have any.>

<I don't want forgiveness.>

<Good.> The iron-gray resolve that had kept Cyrrin alive all this time twisted around Lahlil and pinned her in place. <You're going

to take me back to Norland, back to Valrigdal. To the place I clawed together from nothing until *you* ripped me away from it. I want to feel snow again before I die.>

<I can't.>

<You can and you will. You owe me that much at least. You destroyed everything I built when you came back to Norland. You sent my people into the forest with no one to protect them. You let Trey die and he's the only one . . . > The healer trailed off, still unable to admit to the one selfish thing she'd ever wanted.

<I can't take you back. All the ports are closed because of the plague.>

<And yet you got out well enough.> Cyrrin's emotions fell around her like a sigh and she shut her eyes. Lahlil felt her pain like a steady keening in her ears, shrill as a grinding-wheel. <Go ahead, then. Ask me about Jachad.>

Lahlil felt the blanket beneath her fingers. <Is he still alive?>

<He is,> said Cyrrin, <but he shouldn't be.>

Lahlil finally sat down. The chair creaked as it took her weight, but the noise was nowhere near as loud as the pounding of her heart. <What does that mean?>

<My "cure" is turning him into a god: a god trapped in a mortal body,> Cyrrin explained, lifting her eyes to Lahlil's for a moment before letting them fall shut again. <It's only a matter of time before the process runs its course. If he makes use of his powers it will happen even faster.>

<And then what? Then he dies?>

<I don't know. Maybe. Maybe he'll leave an empty body behind. Maybe he'll burn up from the inside out. Who knows?> Pain rolled up from the bed like a thick mist as the medicine began losing its effect. <At that point it won't be a problem any more. Now—right now—it's a problem.>

<Tell me what to do. How do I fix him?> asked Lahlil.

<You're not listening to me, girl. He has too much power for a mortal—he's straddling both our realm and the realm of the gods, which makes him dangerous. I warned his mother, but those

damned Nomas won't see it. I'm not telling you to *fix* him, Lahlil. He can't be fixed. I'm telling you to *stop* him.>

<I won't kill Jachad, Cyrrin. I *can't*.>

<Don't you dare say that,> said Cyrrin with all her old fire, even as every breath rasped in her throat. <With all the killing you've done before now? Don't pretend you're not strong enough for this.>

That wasn't strength, she wanted to scream, *that was emptiness.*

Cyrrin's pain sliced into Lahlil's nerves like shards of broken glass. The healer's back arched as her whole body began shaking with convulsions. <Water,> she pleaded, <on the table.>

Lahlil grabbed the jug and the bowl sitting beside it, splashing water over her fingers as she hurriedly poured. She turned back to the bed just in time to see the empty flask fall from Cyrrin's hand and skitter across the brace buckles. A drop of liquid clung to the corner of her lips.

<You took it *all*?> said Lahlil, putting the bowl down so she could scoop up the empty vessel and thrust it in front of Cyrrin's eyes. <What did you *do*?>

<You're not stupid, Lahlil.>

<You've *killed* yourself—after all those people like me and Trey, everyone you wouldn't let die when we wanted it—and you kill yourself right in front of me. Do you hate me that much?>

<For Onfar's sake! You still think everything is about *you*, don't you?> Cyrrin asked, a bitter curl of amusement cutting through her pain. Her pupils had already blown wide in her silver eyes and a blue flush mottled her cheeks. <I've never hated you, Lahlil. Not really.> Cyrrin grabbed her forearm and pressed down on those old, old scars.

Lahlil flinched but didn't pull away. A raw and unfamiliar helplessness clawed up from somewhere inside her. <Cyrrin, what do I do? I don't know what to do.>

<Get out of my way, Lahlil,> Rho demanded, his indignation lapping at her in waves of indigo. She had no idea how long he'd been standing there or how much he'd heard. When she didn't

move, he circled around to the other side of the bed. <We need information about Ani.>

Cyrrin had started fumbling with the buckles of the brace, trying in vain to undo the leather straps. <Get it off. Get if off me,> the healer begged. <I hate it—I don't want it on me.>

The leather was stiff and the buckles hard to manage, but Lahlil pushed and tugged, forcing them through as she watched Cyrrin's chest jerk up and down. When the last of the fastenings finally came free, she carefully lifted the frail form so she could pull the tangle of leather and brass to one side. Cyrrin's respiration gradually fell into a steady rhythm, even if the breaths were too shallow and too far between.

<Were Ani and Isa still on the *Argent* when you left?> Rho pressed. <Is Isa still alive?>

<You came back,> Cyrrin said to him. Lahlil shut her eyes against the frantic swell of her friend's hope, but the darkness did nothing to block it out.

<Came back?> asked Rho. <From where?>

Cyrrin took several more wheezing breaths before she answered, <Isa told me you died at Ravindal. She lied to me.>

<Isa,> said Rho, seizing on the name without understanding anything else. Lahlil could have explained it to him, but that would have required speaking and somehow she had lost that ability.

<So Isa's all right?>

<Where are your scars?>

Some of Rho's urgency dissolved into confusion and Lahlil wanted to dig her fingers into his neck and throttle him. She'd *told* him to wait outside. <Cyrrin thinks you're your brother,> she finally explained. <She thinks you're Trey.>

The bed creaked as Rho sank down on the edge, black grief unfurling around him like a mantle.

<I was so angry at you for leaving,> Cyrrin told Trey's ghost. Her presence was so much lighter now, gentler than Lahlil had ever felt her; like the aftertaste of something sweet. <But that's what you always wanted, to fight again.>

33

<I was an idiot,> said Rho. <I should have stayed with you, where I was safe.>

<But you weren't happy. I wanted to make you happy, but I didn't know how,> Cyrrin told him.

Lahlil sank even deeper into herself at the plaintive note curling through Cyrrin's words. She wanted to flip the table over and set the whole house on fire.

Instead she said, <Trey never thanked you for saving his life, any more than I did. He could have been happy in Valrigdal if he'd let himself, but he couldn't let go of the past. That wasn't your fault. You did everything you could for him.>

Rho's anger flared hot, but it wasn't for her. <Thank you for saving my life, Cyrrin. I'm glad I got the chance to say it.>

Cyrrin began trembling again, but it was no longer the violent convulsions of before. Rho climbed further onto the bed and put his arms around her, holding her lightly as her braid dropped to his chest and her head rested in the crook of his shoulder. Her shuddering subsided almost immediately and the space between her breaths lengthened even more.

Lahlil backed away until her back hit the moldy wall and she sank to the floor, ignoring the hard lump of Strife's Bane digging into her shoulder. The candle sputtered on the table, the flame haloed in watery shades of orange and yellow. Lahlil pressed her forehead to her knees and slid one hand up into her hair, pulling hard while Rho's meaningless murmurings filled her ears.

Cyrrin died a short time later with no particular ceremony. Her presence simply snuffed out, leaving the room with two occupants instead of three. It was exactly like every other death Lahlil had ever witnessed—and nothing at all like any of them. Rho took longer than necessary before straightening up and positioning Cyrrin on the bed, his emotions tightly shuttered as he folded her hands over her chest. Lahlil waited for him to leave and then followed him out.

The sun had barely moved while they were inside, even though it had felt like hours. Rho adjusted his cape and pulled the hood over his eyes, even though they were still far enough north that he didn't need to worry about protecting his Norlander skin from the sun.

<We'll catch up to them soon,> he said, his emotions still locked behind a blank wall.

He learned that from me.

<At Prol Irat, or sooner.> She whistled for Kils, who popped out from some hidden niche only a few yards away but hesitated to join them until Lahlil took out her purse.

"There's a dead woman in that house," Lahlil told him. "She didn't have the plague and she's not contagious. Find someone to preserve the body. When Norland opens up again, I want it sent to Ravindal, to Eofar Eotan. Tell him 'L' sent it."

Kils eyes stretched wide. "Eofar—An't that the new Emp'ror?"

"She's to be buried in the Eotan crypt."

"Worthy, I—"

Lahlil pulled two full eagles from the purse, ignoring Rho's gasp and his poke at her shoulder: it left them with only a few loose snips for the remainder of their journey. "I'm relying on you, Kils. I'll be back. And trust me: I *will* know if you betray me."

The boy worked his bottom lip between his teeth, shifting his weight from foot to foot before he finally thrust out his hand to receive the money. "Count on me, Worthy. I'll see it all done, just as you says."

Lahlil pulled her hat down over her eyes and headed for what she thought would be the swiftest route back to their hidden trif-fon, but Rho caught her elbow. It was the second time he'd laid hands on her and she knew she should warn him that there wouldn't be a third, but somehow she lacked the energy.

<Lahlil, can I ask you something?>

She waited.

<Why did you go back to the Shadar the first time, before all this started? Before the uprising?>

<I told you this before,> she reminded him. <Ani found me— she gave me the elixir and I had a vision.>

<About Eofar and Harotha's baby needing your help.>

<Yes.>

<But not about Jachad.>

Her breath caught a little but she stripped the surprise out of her tone before she answered. <No.>

<Because I need to know.> Rho's mask of indifference slipped and his anxiety hit her like the smell of ammonia. <If you have to choose between saving Isa and saving Jachad, who will it be?>

<Isa made her own choices.>

A little while later they were slipping back through the close cobbled streets, watching their feet so they wouldn't twist an ankle in the gutters. From somewhere down the street came the sound of laughter, and from somewhere else a bell clanged.

<You can't even see how much alike you and Isa are, can you?> Rho asked her.

<We're both stubborn,> she replied.

<Of course you are. You're Eotans,> he returned. <But that's not what I meant.>

Chapter 3

"Someone's coming," Daryan warned as footsteps scuffled along the street beyond the broken wall. The five Red Guards who had spent the last hour waiting in the weeds with him straightened up and looked toward their captain.

Omir lifted a hand for silence and leaned out for a better look. After no more than a glance, he said, "It's not him."

"Let me see," Daryan commanded, stepping around the big man.

A young woman of about eighteen was coming down the street, swinging a crook in one hand and a dinner-basket in the other: a shepherdess, returning from the hills after spending the night watching over her flock. She had pulled her scarf down around her neck and wore a crown of little blue flowers in her hair. Daryan recognized the papery blossoms; he didn't know what they were called, but he knew their dry scent, and the way the petals crumbled when you rolled them between your fingers. He also knew the way their color deepened when framed against Isa's milky pallor, and how they made the skin of his naked back itch.

The girl disappeared from sight, leaving Daryan with nothing to look at but the house across the street and the scorched walls and rubbish heaps around it. The curtain over the doorway billowed for a moment and then pooled back down over the threshold. The fabric was brown, faded, not blue—there was not even a trace of blue—and yet the blue crept in as Daryan stared at it.

Don't think about it, he warned himself. *That was three months ago. It's not happening now. It's not blue. It's* not *blue.*

Maybe if he'd gone into the house with Omir—if there had been the sound of other people breathing instead of that thick silence—the shock would not have been so severe, but he'd run past all the others to be the first through the blue curtain. So Daryan was the one to stumble over the father lying by the door, his fingers bloodied from dragging himself toward his family. It was Daryan who first saw the mother slumped against the wall with her arms around two of her children, all three of them drooping like cut flowers. Daryan alone had taken in the sight of the old grandparents sprawled across the cushions over by the fire with their disheveled robes and open mouths. He had been the one to find the two small forms crammed into a corner of the sleeping chamber, and he had been the one to lift the baby from her cradle and the first to touch her waxy skin. He had been tracing the black marks over her heart when the others came in, and in a daze he'd swung at Omir and split his lip when his friend had tried to take the infant away from him.

Today, all those people would be avenged.

"Daryan?" Omir asked, pressed in close behind him. "Do you see something?"

"Not yet." The beginnings of a cough tickled in Daryan's throat, but he managed to swallow it back down. "This has to end today."

"It will. Veyash believes the informer is trustworthy," said Omir, looking toward the guard with the gray streak in his beard.

"As soon as we've caught the murderers, I want everyone searching for the missing daughter—Jemma, the girl with the yellow scarf. We know she's an asha; we need her."

"I wouldn't be too hopeful, Daimon," Omir cautioned. "If she was still alive, we would have found her by now. I'm afraid I failed you."

"You've never failed me," Daryan reassured him. "We'd never have come this far without you. The whole Shadar owes you a debt."

"I'm doing my duty, just like you."

"Don't make this about me," Daryan scolded. A quick smile moved Omir's lips before he turned to look back out at the street. "You built the Red Guards up from nothing. You armed and trained the militia. You keep people safe; you keep *me* safe."

"If this Hesh person doesn't show, we should search the house anyway," said Omir, deflecting the praise as usual. "We'd have the poison and proof of his guilt."

"You're sure the poison is in there?"

"Our informant was certain of it," Omir assured him.

Daryan glanced over at the waiting guards and saw Lieutenant Tamin tug at his uniform jacket in the rising heat of the morning. "If we do that, he'll go to ground and we'll miss our chance to root out the whole gang. He can't have killed dozens of potential ashas on his own; the poisoning part, maybe, but not spiriting away all those bodies without anyone noticing. We don't even know how they're finding their victims, when we haven't been able to find a single asha in all this time."

"But Daimon—"

"Listen," Daryan hissed as he caught the thread of a tuneless whistle coming from the bend at the end of the street.

Omir waved for silence again and pushed down on Daryan's shoulder, making sure the wall shielded them both. The whistling grew louder and then a man came into view, dragging a long early-morning shadow. He had come straight from the pyres by the look of him—a resurrectionist, just as they'd been told: one of the people who had taken it upon themselves to pull the dead Shadari from the Norlanders' tombs and give them the proper death-rites. Daryan hadn't thought it possible for one of their vocation to be substantially grubbier than the rest but this one, with his filthy robe, poppy-red eyes and black-edged fingernails, had somehow managed it. He was far younger than most of the resurrection-ists, maybe twenty or twenty-one. His prominent collarbone and bony wrists made him about as threatening as a kitten, but poisoning people didn't require strength. Poison was a coward's weapon.

The man—Hesh was his name, according to their informant—ambled down the street and went straight into the house.

The captain straightened up beside Daryan and gripped his shoulder with one of his huge hands. "Please reconsider and let us go in first."

"No, Omir. I'm the daimon. I failed to protect all the people who've been killed. I owe them justice." The hilt of Daryan's black-bladed sword practically leaped into his hand as he reached over his shoulder. He'd refused to give the sword a name, but it had taken on a personality anyway: a creature clinging to his back, throbbing with his own blood and whispering promises of power. "I can take care of myself. You've made certain of that."

"I know, Daimon. We're ready to follow you."

Daryan took to the street at a run, heading straight for the door, while Omir ordered two of the guards to remain outside in case of ambush or escape. He didn't mean to rip the curtain down but the whole thing came away in his hand, rod and all, when he tried to yank it aside. He flung it away as Omir and the remaining three guards crowded up behind him. The only light came from the silver disc of the chimney hole and for a moment Daryan couldn't see much else. Then a woman's high-pitched scream rang out and something crashed to the floor. Once his eyes focused in the semi-darkness, he saw an underfed woman pressed against the far wall with her arms crossed over her chest, too terrified even to comfort the naked little boy whimpering into her thigh.

The resurrectionist stood in the middle of the room, a curl of mild bemusement on his lips and unfazed by the presence of five armed men. Daryan scoured his gaunt face for some mark or blight, some sign of the evil within, but couldn't see anything other than dirt.

"Hesh, son of—" Daryan didn't know his lineage. "We're here to arrest you."

"What for?" the young man squawked when one of the guards grabbed his arms and pinned them. Up close, he barely looked eighteen. "I haven't done anything."

"You're suspected of poisoning a family of nine and aiding in the disappearance of thirty-seven other innocent people."

Hesh let out a low whistle. "How did I make them disappear? Am I magic?"

"Watch yourself," Omir rumbled in fury. "You'll speak to the daimon with respect if you want to keep your teeth."

"Search him, and the house," Daryan commanded, keeping his eyes on the young man. The guard held Hesh's arms in one hand while he patted down his chest and bony hips, holding his breath against the reek of ashes and death. Daryan reminded himself that the poison was supposed to be in the house, not on Hesh's person, and refused to take it as a bad sign when the guard came up empty-handed.

He turned to watch Tamin and Veyash tromp through the room, turning things over, tracking ash from the fire pit over the rug, slashing the cushions. Shadows from the lamps they'd lit followed them into the kitchen area where they pawed through every basket and emptied every jar; even flipped the table on its side. When they found nothing, they took the lid off the cistern and tipped it over, sending water gushing over Daryan's boots and releasing a gut-churning stench from the hem of the resurrectionist's robe.

"Are you looking for something? Because this isn't even my house," Hesh informed them as he balanced on one foot to let the water run out of his shoe. He gestured to the frightened woman. "It's hers. I'm only visiting."

"Do you always visit people at dawn?"

"Do *you*?" Hesh asked in return, drawing himself up like an outraged ambassador. "At least *I* was invited."

Omir threw a punch and the young man dropped like a stone. Daryan drew in a quick breath: he had seen enough bones crack under those huge fists to worry about whether Hesh would get up again. But the resurrectionist rolled onto his back and sat up, probing his mouth with his filthy fingers to check for loose teeth.

"Well," Hesh said wetly, pausing to spit out some blood, "you *did* warn me."

"If you don't live here, where do you live?" asked Daryan while Omir calmly wiped his knuckles. "Where's your family?"

"I don't live anywhere in particular, and the last I saw of my father was two years ago, the day before he was buried alive in the mines along with twenty-seven of his friends and neighbors."

That would explain why someone so young would take up with the resurrectionists. It might also explain the misguided zealotry of someone scheming to systematically murder all the potential ashas in the Shadar.

A jar in the kitchen shattered and the woman let out a frightened whine.

"At least let Bima take her boy into the back," Hesh cried out. "Can't you see how scared they are?"

The woman stared while the Red Guards tore apart her home as if she could barely comprehend what was going on. The boy, who looked to be about four, was shivering so hard that Daryan realized the faint clicking sound he'd taken for insects was the chattering of the child's teeth.

"Here," he said to the pair, unhooking his short cape as he moved closer. "You can wrap this around—"

Without warning the woman shrieked and flew at him, aiming her fingernails at Daryan's eyes. She showed no fear or even recognition of the black sword in his hand and for a horrified moment Daryan thought he was going to impale her by accident, but then one of the guards—the new one, Lem—grabbed her around the waist and swung her back. He held the woman close, muttering something into her ear until her screams died away and she sagged into his embrace, her eyes glassy. Daryan had seen that look too many times before: the numb despair when the strength needed for rage was gone.

The guard ushered her back to her still-shaking child and removed his own cloak.

"Lem?" Omir called.

"She's fine now. She won't do it again," he assured them as he wrapped up the boy and then placed the mother's hands on her son's shoulders as if to ground her. "I'll stay with her. No need to worry, Captain."

"Daimon, I—" Omir began.

"Leave them. They're frightened, that's all. These things happen," Daryan reminded him, as if the pink-edged scar cutting through the older man's beard wasn't reminder enough. If Omir had been a little slower that day, Daryan would have taken that fish-gutting knife right in the throat.

"Daimon! I think there's something under here!" Veyash called out from the kitchen.

Daryan raced over to see the guard digging at the dirt floor with the heel of his boot, then kneeling and prizing up a flat piece of stone. His skin prickled as if a thousand needles were trying to poke their way out. "Move aside. I need to see."

"I—Daimon, wait, I—"

It was empty. The hole itself looked new and carefully prepared: straight sides, not yet crumbled in, the bottom lined with a scrap of cloth dotted with dark stains; whether they were new stains or old was impossible to tell, but they were dry when he swept his fingers over them.

Daryan stalked back to Hesh, grabbed his robe with both hands and yanked him up off the ground. "You found out we were coming and did something with it. Where is it? *Where's the poison?*"

Hesh's mouth split into a bloody grin. "What poison?"

"Why do you want to kill all the ashas?" Daryan demanded, jerking the resurrectionist close enough to map the veins in his bloodshot eyes.

The young man gasped as his collar bit into his neck and he scrabbled against Daryan's hold with his ash-stained fingernails.

"*Why?* Do you understand how defenseless the Shadar is without them? Do you understand what's going to happen once word spreads that we're no longer under Norland's protection?"

"You're wrong about me," Hesh wheezed, his face turning purple. "You're wrong about everything."

Daryan shoved the man away from him. He needed out of the

house. He needed air that didn't stink of failure. He needed a drink. "Arrest him," he said to Omir.

"You can't arrest me," Hesh sputtered as he massaged his throat.

Daryan didn't face him; he no longer trusted his self-control. "You forget that I'm the daimon."

"You made a law that no one can be arrested without an accuser and evidence of a crime," Hesh called out as Daryan's boots squelched down into the wet carpet. "You don't have any evidence, do you? That's what you came here looking for: the poison."

From the corner of his eye, Daryan saw Omir's hand come up. He whirled round and seized the captain's arm with both hands. "Wait, Omir, stop. I need to think."

But the familiar scratching in his throat started—temple lung, they were calling it, because the people who'd been nearest the temple when it fell had it the worst. He made a few counter-productive attempts to stifle it, but finally released Omir and left the house, stopping in the street to brace his hands on his thighs as the coughing racked him.

"Here," said Omir as he came up behind him. He pressed an open flask into Daryan's hand. The sweet smell of the wine loosened some of the tightness in Daryan's chest even before he swallowed.

"Thanks," he said, when the coughing finally stopped.

Omir leaned closer and said in a low voice, "You made that law to stop people from trying to settle old scores, *not* to protect murderers."

"I know—but he's right. We have to find another way. Find a law he's broken—*any* law—and I'll let you take him. But I can't put myself above the law to suit my own convenience."

"Laws shouldn't stand in the way of justice. When word gets out about this, people will think you're—"

"What?" Daryan prompted when the captain broke off. "You can say it."

"Irresolute. Weak. They'll say you let an indigent, beardless boy make a fool of you."

Daryan took one more swallow of wine and handed back the flask. "Then I'll trust you to remind them that being an arrogant, disrespectful little prick isn't a crime. And a good thing, too, or our new jail would be teeming over."

Omir made a noise that sounded like him swallowing back a curse. The morning light picked out the patches of gray in his beard and accentuated the purple swags under his eyes. They'd pushed themselves hard for days leading up to this moment, thinking there would be rest for them at the end. "Daimon, be reasonable. You can't let him go. More ashas will die."

"If he's guilty—"

"He is."

Daryan saw the rock-hard certainty in his friend's hooded eyes and wondered how, in the world they lived in, he could be *that* sure of anything. He found it strangely unsettling. "I don't know why you don't understand this, Omir. You were a temple slave like me; you know exactly what it's like to live day and night at the mercy of someone who can beat or maim or kill you on a whim. Laws *have* to be the same for everyone. It's the only way we'll be free of fear."

"Maybe freedom isn't what we need," said Omir.

For a moment Daryan couldn't believe he'd heard him right. "Of course it is," he protested. "What else is there?"

"There's order," said Omir. "Safety. Faith."

"Faith won't do us any good. Our gods have made it very clear they don't care about us. I thought you agreed with me on that."

"Faith in their leaders," amended the captain. "People need someone to believe in."

Omir had never put it so baldly before, but it wasn't news. Daryan's people were succumbing to a new kind of hopelessness, and a couple of coats of whitewash and a few hollow words of encouragement weren't going to change it. Today, catching the poisoner was supposed to have changed all that. He'd just have to keep trying. No one would be able to move forward until he proved he could excise this murderous tumor.

You can't, Isa had said to him on the day she left the Shadar. *You can't, and you never will.*

"Daryan?" Omir called to him.

"Have your men put that woman's house back together and then get them of there, Captain," he said, swallowing back the urge to start coughing again. "I want a watch kept on Hesh, every hour of the day and night. Use as many men as you need. And tell Veyash I want to see his informer, because either he lied or they found out we were coming."

"Yes, Daimon."

Daryan wiped the sweat from his forehead; the air felt thick even with the sun barely up. There'd been talk of rain, though the rainy season wasn't supposed to begin for a month or more. The sky stretched over like an unbroken sheet of glass, blue and shiny and hard. Maybe it *was* glass. Maybe the rain clouds were hiding right above it, waiting for it to crack.

"Wait a moment," he said as Omir turned back to the house to obey his orders. "You know how you keep pestering me about getting a bodyguard?"

"Yes. You've never considered it," the captain answered in surprise.

"I've changed my mind. I think Lem is the man for the job."

"Lem has only been with the Guards for a few weeks," said Omir. "He doesn't have enough training."

"I liked the way he handled himself in there. He was as much concerned for that woman's safety as mine."

From Omir's scowl, Daryan guessed that he had noticed the same thing but come to a different conclusion. "As you wish, Daimon. I'll see to things here. You should go back to the palace and get some rest. You've been up all night."

"That's a good idea. I think I'll do that," he answered, glad that Omir had apparently forgotten that he was holding court this morning, or he'd be subjected to a lecture about taking better care of himself. "Send Lem out to me. He might as well start his new duties now."

Daryan headed down the street toward the well-yard where they'd left their dereshadi. The sun had risen high enough to slice its way down into the streets and Daryan twisted his scarf over his forehead to shield his eyes. He hadn't got far before Lem pelted up beside him.

"Daimon," began the soldier, breathing hard, "I mean, I'm honored, but shit—Sorry! Don't you want somebody better? I only joined up a couple weeks ago and I'm not much with a sword yet. The captain and the others, they don't think much of me."

"If you can do the job like you did in there, you'll be fine."

"I—All right, Daimon, if that's what you want. I swear I'll do my best."

They followed the street until it ended by the boarded-up well. The Andrasha district had suffered more than most during the liberation and was still nearly deserted; Daryan and Lem were the only living creatures in sight besides the dereshadi and a trio of very dirty children watching from behind one of the burned-out houses. Lem followed behind Daryan as he walked around Trakkar and checked every buckle and strap, popping open some of the latches and refastening them securely.

"My uncle made me learn everything about dereshadi—or trifons, as the Norlanders call them," Daryan told his new bodyguard. "I never thought I'd be riding one myself. What about you? Tell me about yourself."

"Not much to tell," Lem answered, grinning suddenly. "Name's Lem, son of Lem. Da always says it's because he likes to keep things simple."

"Wise man," Daryan said, smiling back. "Where were you before the liberation? In the mines?" He had already noticed the traces of pallor on Lem's neck and wrists, along with the over-muscled arms and subtle stoop.

"Dead Ones took me when I was twelve," the guard answered, with a quick swallow that spoke more than his words. "I was big for my age so I made it through three cave-ins. I remember the one the kid in there talked about, where he lost his da. That was a bad one." He laughed a little. "Ma said I had no hair when I was born and that's why I'm so lucky. Never thought I was lucky, really—until today."

"It's not luck." Daryan gestured for Lem to mount up, then vaulted up into the saddle himself and buckled on the harness. As soon as he was sitting down, the after-effects of no sleep, anticipation and disappointment hit him like a brick. The yard felt like it was spinning and the sensation worsened when he tried shutting his eyes. "It's hot, isn't it? Humid, even. I've heard people say the rains might come early."

"They do talk. One less helping of fish-eye soup, is all I'll say."

Daryan shook himself back to full wakefulness. "*What?*"

"Shit," said Lem, suddenly flustered, "oh no—shit. Sorry! Damn it, I did it again. *Shit*—I'm sorry, Daimon—"

Daryan's smile felt like the first genuine one in ages. He twisted to look over his shoulder. "Calm down, Lem. Did you say what I think you said or am I going crazy?"

The soldier's face had gone as red as his uniform and he bent over until his head thunked down on the saddle. "It's my ma— she's got this way of knowing everything. Signs and such, y'know? She always says, if you catch a fish with one eye, it means early rain that year. The rest of us like to tease her and say you're more like to get—"

"—one less helping of fish-eye soup," they finished together.

Daryan was grinning as he took up the reins and whistled Trakkar into the air. The street fell away and the sun picked out the delicate web of cartilage as Trakkar stretched out his wings and caught an updraft. Streets lined with little domed houses swung by below them, clustered around the well-yards and market streets. The people on the ground ducked into doorways or hid their faces when Daryan and Lem passed overhead. *Old habits*, Omir liked to say, but these were wounds, not habits, and they were still bleeding half a year later. All that gleaming whitewash might as well have been daubs over an ash-pile. Sooner or later, the ugliness underneath would bleed through.

Daryan listed their defenses in his head, which didn't take long, given their inadequacy: twenty-seven dereshadi that hadn't gone feral, fifteen hundred armed guards and an untested militia. Nothing else. The Nomas had abandoned them without any reason or word of warning. Eofar's plan to form an alliance between the Shadar and the Norland Empire must have failed or they would have received word months ago. They'd not found a single asha. And Isa—

No, the Shadar couldn't expect any help from outside, and if Daryan didn't find some ashas soon—if they weren't all dead already—they would fall to the first serious invaders who came after the black ore that had started all the trouble in the first place. All to make weapons that obeyed thoughts as well as muscle, as if the ability to kill people faster and easier was something to be desired.

Rain and fish-eye soup. Rain and fish eyes. Raining fish eyes. Daryan imagined the eyes hitting the ground and bouncing around like corks and he laughed as they wheeled around toward the palace.

Chapter 4

Daryan wiped his face clean of all traces of the morning's débâcle as Trakkar dug his claws into the dirt of the stableyard and the grooms swarmed around to take care of his mount. "I want to know the moment Captain Omir comes back," he told them. Lem tried to look imposing as he jumped down and took up his post at Daryan's side, but his windblown hair and the delighted gleam in his eyes rather ruined the effect.

"You know your way around back here, of course," Daryan said to his new bodyguard, smacking his gloves against his thigh to get rid of the dust and kicking up the musky smell of dereshadi hide. "Did you know this whole end of the palace used to be a garden? There were beds of flowers right where we're standing, and a reflecting pool over there." He gestured toward the training ground, where soldiers were running drills aimed at learning to control their ore-infused swords. The black blades were whispering through the air with a speed his eyes could barely follow. "I don't remember those days, of course, but my mother described it to me. Your barracks over there, and the jail, are built on top of an orchard. We had to dig out the old roots to lay the foundations."

Lem whistled in appreciation and toed one of the cracked paving stones. "My da brought me here once, when it was just broken stuff and dirt. I think he wanted to teach me something but I don't remember much, except a lizard bit my thumb and it swelled up and turned purple—my thumb, not the lizard—and Da told me not to let Ma see or we'd both be in for it."

Daryan joined in his laughter and they headed into the sun-bathed village of sheds and stalls set up among the broken pillars of the old great hall: men manning the kilns and brick ovens; children carrying water from the palace well to fill the cisterns; women at the spinning wheels and looms; district officials with wagons taking sacks of grain and barrels of salted fish and oil back to their people; women bent over a big laundry basin that reminded him of the tub Isa used to bathe in.

"Whoa, there you are, little ba—I mean, fellas. What do you want, as if I didn't know?" Lem crooned to the palace's little herd of goats as they came skipping up to the edge of their enclosure, raucously bleating.

"They're spoiled. You'd better watch your fingers," Daryan warned as the soldier paused to scratch their woolly heads. Daryan kept walking. He didn't like to linger so close to the spot where Faroth had been buried. A plain stone marked the site now. Faroth's old crony Binit had insisted they dig up the body—part of his plan to turn Faroth into a martyr of the revolution, and himself into a hero by extension—but they'd never found him. Little Dramash had buried his father too deep for that. "Let's go, Lem. I need to get court over with as quickly as possible so I can concentrate on the Hesh problem."

The soldier caught up to him before he reached the short tunnel connecting the backyards to the main courtyard. Their footsteps crunched down on the shards of a broken roof tile as they passed into the darkness, and then they were in the courtyard.

"Daimon, look!" Lem shouted, rushing over to the fountain and putting his hand into the water spraying from one of the fishes' open mouths. "When did you get it working?"

"The day before yesterday," called out Tal, the chief steward, advancing on them with a wax tablet in one hand and a stylus twitching in the other. "It took five months, all together. It took almost that long to track down the one old granddad who still knew how it worked."

"It's beautiful," said Lem. "The whole place is. Never thought I'd see anything like it."

Daryan wished he could take it all in with Lem's uncomplicated appreciation: the red clay shingles covering the porch roof; the graceful arches heading through whitewashed walls into cool, spacious rooms; the wide staircase sweeping up to the throne room with its airy archways and the stately balcony overlooking the forecourt; four towers rising up from the corners, only the northeastern one still wreathed in scaffolding. Lem didn't notice the cracks in the façade or how the paint on the porch columns was already beginning to flake away; he couldn't understand how Daryan felt like a hypocrite for restoring a structure that represented an age of deception and willful ignorance.

"They're waiting for you in the throne room, Daimon," Tal informed him with obvious regret. "Binit, of course, and this time he's brought a few dozen others with him—all of them barging in, braying like a wet herd."

"Binit can't void his bowels without an audience," said Daryan.

Lem's snort of laughter earned him a look of rebuke from Tal, who'd taken it upon himself to see that the palace maintained a certain level of decorum.

"Oh, and this is Lem. He's going to be my bodyguard," Daryan told Tal belatedly. "I'll go and deal with Binit, but I want to know when Omir gets back from Andrasha."

"Yes, Daimon." Someone shouted a warning and a tool of some kind crashed down onto the roof of the east gatehouse, shattering a whole section of clay tiles. Tal shut his eyes and muttered a prayer for patience. "If you'll excuse me a moment, Daryan. And you, Lem, you look sharp, eh?"

Lem tried to school his expression to something serious but it didn't do much good with water still dripping from his hair. "I won't let anything happen to the daimon."

"Good. Don't let him hit anyone, either."

"That was *one time*," Daryan called after Tal, who was already stalking toward the red-faced and conspicuously hammer-less workman climbing down from the scaffold.

They never made it up to the second-story throne room. The people with appointments to speak to him today had caught sight of him through the archways and now came jostling down the wide stairs.

"It's all right," Daryan called out to the guards who were making a tardy attempt to herd them back up. He reset his smile to its most implacable version as he jogged up the steps to meet them. "It's bracing to see so much civic-mindedness so early in the morning."

"Daimon, we—" Binit called out, already pushing his way forward.

"Talbak!" Daryan called out, gesturing to the wizened old man on the topmost step nervously rubbing his palms against his hips. "I'm glad to see you up and about again. Why have you come today?"

Binit's jaw clapped shut.

"It's the rains, Daimon," replied the elderly man. "If they come early and we've not planted, well, there it is. We gathered up all the seed that didn't burn up and, well, tain't enough. Not without that as the Nomas was supposed to bring us."

"I see," said Daryan, ignoring the whispered "sand-spitters" from some in the group. "We're trying to find some way to contact the Nomas. I don't believe they've abandoned us completely. And it should be another month at least before we need to worry about the rains."

Talbak nodded through Daryan's speech but his eyes stayed fixed on his shoes. "As you say, Daimon. I still think it best we start planting now, just in case . . ."

"We'll get started on it as soon as we can," Daryan promised as he continued up the stairs, with Lem now forming a formidable barrier against Binit, who was dancing up and down, looking for a way to get through on the other side.

"Daimon!" called out a female voice entirely too close to his ear. Sedena had managed to sneak in under Lem's guard and now hooked her arm around his elbow. Gold jewelry dangled from every available part of her and her sweet perfume made Daryan's throat itch again. "I've been waiting for you since dawn. I was hoping for a moment with you in private."

"You'll have to speak here or not at all," he said, gesturing at a scowling Lem to leave her be. "Impressive earrings, by the way. You must have a strong neck."

Sedena's saccharine smile could have sliced bone. "These are dangerous times, and people are concerned about the succession. It would ease their minds greatly if they were to have a queen. A *suitable* woman, from a *respected* family. I'm sure you understand. Your dear wife Harotha would not have wanted you to mourn her forever."

He wished his friend and *not*-wife Harotha was still alive so he could yell at her for burdening him with her lies, and because he still missed her every day. "I'm not in the market for a bride, thank you. I'll let you know if I change my mind."

"Then I can reassure people on your behalf there's nothing to the rumors?"

"Rumors?"

"About you and *that woman*?" she asked stiffly.

The air in Daryan's lungs turned to ice. It couldn't be . . . *No one* knew he and Isa were lovers, not even Omir. "*What* woman?"

"That *laundress*," Sedena whispered, as if the occupation itself were some kind of contagious disease.

"Laundress?" he echoed, dumbfounded.

"She's been seen going in and out of your chambers at all hours."

"You mean *Tessa*?" he asked with a bemused laugh before he remembered the insinuation. "Tessa," he repeated, stopping short on the top step. "She has a name, and it's not 'that laundress.'"

Sedena arched her kohl-thickened eyebrows. "Then I can pass along the reason she's been seen in your rooms."

"I do not owe *you*—or anyone else—an explanation," Daryan

said, lowering his voice to hold back his fury. "However, you might like to know that *Tessa* is not only one of the school's best students, but she is also the only person I trust to clean my chambers without disturbing or destroying my work. Would you like me to leave the bed curtains open tonight so that you can come and check for yourself?"

"That's not—"

"That will be all, Sedena," he said softly.

Whatever she saw on Daryan's face made Sedena change her mind about responding. Her face flushed and she didn't try to follow when he continued up into the throne room. He breathed a sigh of relief as he passed into the cool shade and found a spot to stand where he could feel the breeze from the open arches. His legs were beginning to ache from crouching outside Bima's house and he would have liked to sit, but the massive throne of polished red stone looked even less inviting than usual.

"Daimon," Binit called out again, having finally successfully worked his way to the front of the crowd. The self-appointed representative of Daryan's critics pursed his lips in an affectation that made him look like a fish. "Your people want the Dead Ones out of the ashadom."

Normally Daryan would have objected to the pejorative slang term for Norlanders, but today he didn't have the time. "Your request has been noted. And denied."

"They're sick," Binit persisted. "Anyone can see it—people are saying the plague started with them—they're saying that's why the Reds are taking away the bodies, so no one can prove it."

Something behind Daryan's right eye twitched and sent a bolt of pain straight through his head. "There is *no* plague. If your 'friends' want to help the Shadar, tell them to stop wasting my time and find whoever is *poisoning* our ashas."

"But—"

"The ashadom is the only place we have that's big enough to house them all and protect them from the sun. Those Norlanders are our *allies*," he reminded everyone in the room. "They turned

55

on the White Wolf and fought against her *for us*—can you really have forgotten that? We are going to honor our promise to Eofar Eotan to leave them alone while he's in Norland brokering peace with the emperor."

"He left six months ago," Binit announced, angling his head so that the people behind would be sure to hear him, "and for all we know, when he comes back—*if* he comes back—it will be with an army of Dead Ones to make us slaves again."

"If you're so worried about Eofar betraying us—which he *will not* do—then you should be doing everything within your power to prepare to defend the Shadar against her enemies. If you would—" Daryan broke off as a neat little man with unusually large, drooping eyes came darting into the throne room, a pair of Red Guards in pursuit.

"Daimon—you must help me, please! They're trying to kill me— Save me, please!"

Lem charged forward, caught hold of the old man by the back of his robe and hoisted him up like a kitten. The prisoner yelped and scrabbled at the air with little rodent-like hands.

"Daimon," the man begged again, "please—don't let them hurt me!"

"Put him down, Lem," Daryan said quickly. "What's wrong, uncle? Who's trying to kill you?"

"They want to kill me because they *know*," the old man whispered.

"Know what?"

The man's eyes bulged as he scanned the staring crowd around him, then he jerked his chin a few times to gesture Daryan closer before hissing, *"I'm an asha."*

Blood roared in Daryan's ears. "The audience is over," he announced, waving everyone away. The guards took the hint and began herding them down the steps. Daryan circled a comforting arm over the old man's shoulders.

"You have asha powers?" Daryan asked, trying to keep his voice low and calm. "You can move rocks and sand, like they did?"

"They put poison in my food—I can taste it. And they're always watching me, watching, watching—they follow me everywhere. You know, that's what happened to the others—that's why they're dead. All dead."

A Red Guard appeared at the top of the steps. "Daimon, there's a man here says he's the grandson."

"Good, send him up," Daryan called back, then returned his attention to his precious charge. "How well can you control your powers? Can you show me?"

"Oh, no, no, I can't do that. Not *now*." The man dropped his voice even further, until he sounded like a kettle with a broken whistle. "I have to wait, you see. He only comes to me at night. That's when he gives me the power."

"*Who* comes to you?"

"The boy. Dramash. He comes and touches me, here, and gives me the power." He tapped his own forehead. "He makes me destroy the temple, over and over again. He keeps putting it back up and making me knock it down again—don't you see? That's why they want to kill me! They're trying to stop it. But it's not me, it's the boy: he *makes* me do it. Don't you see? *Don't you understand?*"

A slender man with an obvious resemblance to the old man ran into the throne room, his shoes slipping on the tiled floor in his haste, hands already up in supplication. "Please don't hurt him— he's harmless, just confused, is all."

"Is he an asha?"

The young man laughed nervously. "Is that what he's been telling you? No, there aren't any ashas in our family. Never have been. Yesterday he thought he was the daimon; he kept saying they were waiting for him at the palace—that's why I came here when Ma said he'd run off again."

"You'd best take him home," Lem interjected while Daryan was still trying to breathe through the disappointment, "and don't let him wander off again. He could get hurt."

"We'll keep a closer eye on him, I promise."

The grandson already had a protective hand on his grandfather's shoulder to lead him away. The old man's eyes had gone dull and distant, as if the delusion had abandoned him all at once.

"That was—" Lem broke off, then, "Poor old thing. Shit, that's too bad. Still, nothing much you can do when they get like that. Leastways, he's got someone to look after him. Ma always says, if she goes like that to put her in a skiff when the tide turns and give her a good push. As if we'd ever, after all she's done for us."

Daryan coughed a few times into his fist. "I'm going to rest. Tell Tal I don't want to see anyone except Captain Omir."

"You want me to stay with you? I've got nothing better to do," Lem offered, following Daryan as he pushed his way through a door in the west wall and into the short passage that led to his private chambers. "Truth be told, the other guards are kind of stand-offish. Most of 'em got picked by the captain early on, so I guess a volunteer like me has to prove something to them."

He darted in front of Daryan to open the door for him, then whistled appreciatively as he took a look inside at the curtains, lamps, rugs, sofas, tables and decorative objects littering the surfaces. It was more opulence then most people in the Shadar could even imagine. The bed was a marvel on its own: cool linen bleached to flawless white, every wrinkle ironed out until the pristine expanse looked like the paintings of snowfields in Isa's picture-books. But Daryan only cared about the area underneath the courtyard-facing window, which held his desk, stacks of papers, a few Norlander books and his inkpots and pens.

"I'll send for you if I leave the palace again," he told Lem. "You could probably use some sleep, too."

"If you say so, Daimon. Pleasant dreams!"

Daryan bit back a laugh. Sleep for him meant thrashing around on the bed or drinking wine until the walls swayed, or pacing around the room with his mind spinning, thinking, *Isa's dead. She's hurt and dying and alone. She's found someone who can touch her Norlander skin without hurting her. She's found a place with people who never took her arm, or her home or her family away from her.*

The papers on his desk were still scattered the way he'd left them before the raid. Now, with the compulsion of someone picking at a scab, he sat down to paw through the map of disappearances, the list of suspects with every name struck through, every scrap of information he had collected.

They all had a mark over their hearts, said Isa's ghost. *Like ink.*

The chair legs squealed as he grabbed one of the inkpots and hurled it against the wall, where it shattered with a crunch. Shards of pottery skittered over the floor and ink splashed back over his desk and papers, and bled into feathery plumes over the cushions.

He sat back down and got to work, ignoring the wet stain on the wall shining like black glass.

He remembered resting his head on his arms for a while when his eyes began to burn, but he didn't remember falling asleep. He woke to a rhythmic scuffing and looked up to find a woman scrubbing at the wall with a brush.

"You don't have to do that," he said, clearing his throat after his voice came out husky from sleep. "It's my mess. I'll clean it up."

Tessa made a disapproving little humming noise. "You will not. You'll let it dry there so it never comes out and shames me every time I come through that door. Deny it not, Daimon."

"When are you going to start calling me Daryan?"

She made that humming noise again; she was not pleased with him. "Mystifies me why you'd sleep in those stiff riding clothes when you've a perfectly good robe in that chest over there," she remarked before going back to her scrubbing.

"It's not there to be worn; it's there to remind me," he said as he stood up and stretched out his sore back. "That's a new scarf, isn't it?"

She sniffed and reached up to pat the blue scarf as if she'd forgotten it was there. The color suited her; it made her eyes look darker and brought out her freckles. "A gift from my sister," she said with a little laugh. "It's supposed to be a hint, I'm thinking. She wants to marry me off again."

"Again? You were married before?"

She leveled him with a look that said she knew he was surprised she'd found anyone to marry her in the first place. Certainly she met none of the typical criteria for beauty. Her broad, flat face bore the scars of old pockmarks and a dense patch of freckles lay like a smudge across the bridge of her nose; a vain woman would have tried to cover them. Her hair neither curled nor lay straight and had a tendency to sneak out of her scarf. She had a wide mouth and average brown eyes fringed by thin eyelashes and heavy brows. Her clothes were clean and skilfully mended, but drained of color from years of washings. And she was thirty years old if she was a day. He thought back to Sedena's accusations and stifled a laugh. It must have galled her and her friends beyond belief to think he'd chosen *this* woman for his bed. He almost wished it were true.

Tessa was still eyeing him with that assessing look. "I'm a widow, you know. My husband was killed in the mines, in one of those big cave-ins. They never found him."

"That must be very hard for you. I'm sorry."

"So am I," she said, scrubbing all the while. "He was a good man. You would have liked him."

"Will you? Get married again?"

"No." There was no bitterness in her answer; she was just stating a fact.

He watched her bend down to rinse her brush in the bucket; she moved with the exaggerated grace of one of those big wading birds. "So, tell me the latest news," he asked, leaning back in the chair. "No one ever tells me anything interesting."

"Word's going around the Reds showed up in Andrasha at sunup and barged into the house of a poor widow, tore up the place and then left."

"You sound angry."

"I don't much like it, I don't mind saying," said Tessa. "What business do the Reds have in a place like that? Those poor people ought to be left alone." She dropped the brush into the bucket and stepped back to admire her work. The stain was mostly gone, though a faint trace of an outline remained. "There, that's not so bad. Have you had your fill of mayhem for the night or should I leave the bucket?"

He couldn't help a little chuckle as she gathered up her things to leave. "Tessa, do you think it will rain early this year?"

"Now how in the world would I know, Daimon?"

"Somebody told me today that if you catch a fish with one eye, it means early rain that year."

"Superstitious nonsense. How do these things even get started?" She tried to remain stern but one corner of her mouth twitched. "But if you see a gull with a black feather in its tail, you haul the tarps out quick."

Chapter 5

Isa had no sense of the number of weeks that had passed since she and Ani had boarded the *Argent,* or how many days the ship had been stuck like an insect in a glob of sap. The view through the thick glass of their cabin's porthole was nothing but a flat horizon and bottle-green waves. There was no sign of land, not a gull or whale spout; not even a cloud.

A shudder spasmed up Isa's spine and she pulled her knees up to her chest and curled over, her breath stuttering. The medicine was wearing off. Next would come the shivering pains in her legs and the heaviness like a lead weight around her neck. Then her throat would close up and her muscles would burn from the inside out, as if they'd been slit open and stuffed with coals. Finally those invisible icy daggers would slice into the stump of her left arm, stabbing and cutting at the puckered scars until they scraped the bare bone.

"Ani?" she rasped softly.

Ani glanced up from her little desk and away from the possessions she had brought from her prison cell in Norland: the bottles, jars, finely crafted instruments for weighing and measuring, and a sheaf of notations and charts. The scratch of her pen had become as familiar to Isa as the *Argent*'s rattles and groans.

"It's not time for your medicine yet," Ani responded.

Isa dug her fingers into her thigh and swallowed back an argument.

Ani didn't stop working or turn around but she leaned back enough for the sunlight to make a halo of her gray hair. "It's a trick of your mind, child. You're imagining the pain now, because you fear it. You know the consequences if I were to overindulge you, yes?"

She did: her body would grow accustomed to the medicine and it would lose its effectiveness. She'd need to take more and more, like an alcoholic trying to get drunk on weak beer, until she ended up slumped over and vacant-eyed, lost to the mist like Ani's guard outside her prison cell in Norland. On endless days like this it was hard to see that as a bad thing.

The Shadari woman returned to her work with renewed focus while Isa sat on her hand to keep from prying splinters from the planking with her jagged fingernails. If only she could doze; that would pass the time—but the only way she could sleep now was to lose herself in the first flush of the medicine's embrace. She shut her eyes anyway, trying to ride the rocking of the ship and the *scratch scratch scratch* of the pen into the mist, seeking out memories of Daryan that weren't tinged with pain or the fear of discovery. She'd already worn the few she had to threads, so she glided into the future instead, to her triumphant homecoming, bearing a savior for the Shadari and a key to the shackles binding Daryan to them.

Another wave of pain shook through her. *No, not pain: a trick of the mind.*

She couldn't sit still any longer; she needed some kind of distraction, even if it was just pacing the deck while the Nomas sailors gawked at her. Gingerly, so as not to make a noise and distract Ani from her work, she raised herself to a crouch and crept to the door. In a moment she had her sun-proof cape slung over her arm and her hand on the bolt.

"You mustn't go up there," said Ani, her sibilant voice falling like a sigh.

"I'm going to find out how much longer it will take to reach Prol."

"By asking the captain, yes? Even though you know she'll lie to you?"

Isa ran the pad of her finger over the iron bolt. "Why would Nisha lie about that?"

"She's Nomas. It's in her nature. Why did their so-called healers lie about the worthless medicine they gave you? To enjoy your suffering. They proved their duplicity to me two hundred years ago when they betrayed me in the asha rebellion."

The thought of it still made Isa's skin warm; how the Nomas healers must have laughed behind her back when she thanked them and begged for more. At night she could hear the sailors in their hammocks laughing at her still, not even bothering to lower their voices because they thought she didn't speak Nomas.

"Besides," said Ani, "I need you here."

Isa turned around into the path of Ani's steady gaze. "You do?" she asked, her sluggish heart already thumping.

"I have a solution to my Dramash problem and I need to test it before we see him again."

Isa dropped her cloak in a heap by the door. "What can I do?"

"Sit down on the bunk."

Ducking her head under the beams, she sat down where Ani directed, while the old woman reached for the special casket where she kept her most important supplies, including the ingredients for Isa's medicine. It also contained a little box made of onyx, latched and double-sealed with wax, that Ani had warned her never to open or even touch.

"It fascinates me how little you Norlanders know about the black ore you coveted enough to enslave the Shadar for so many years," Ani commented as she lifted out a brass vial and poured a glob of colorless syrup into a bowl, prompting a throb of anticipation to start up at the base of Isa's skull. "My own people foolishly believed it contained its own latent power and that we ashas somehow had the means to awaken it. I was the first to discover the ore has no power of its own; it is uniquely responsive to intent, but the power comes from the wielder. An asha's power is part of their nature, do you see?"

A shiver ran down Isa's legs. She rammed her knuckle into her mouth, caught the skin between her teeth and bit down. "Ani?"

"Patience, child." The Shadari sprinkled a tiny pinch of black ore into the bowl and Isa breathed in the warm aroma, swallowing against the dryness in her throat. Ani pulled a long, sharp pin hidden somewhere in her borrowed Nomas robes and pricked her palm, squeezing the wound until a few red drops joined the other ingredients in the bowl. Isa clenched her muscles to control her shivering while Ani added less familiar ingredients, consulting her notes and measuring carefully. "But there is another side to our natures: the mortal side. The divine side is power. The mortal side is the control; the anchor, if you will."

The first icy stab shot through Isa's arm and she clutched at her shoulder, trying to stay focused. Ani had never taken the time to explain any of this before and she didn't want to miss anything.

"I've used my wits to keep my body alive for two and a half centuries, but I could not prevent myself from aging entirely. While my power has grown stronger, my mortal body has weakened to the point where I no longer have the control necessary to wield it the way I wish. And that's why I need Dramash."

"The little Shadari boy," Isa confirmed, trying hard to follow while her head was pounding.

The old woman nodded, but her smile had gone tight. "Dramash, who would have followed me willingly if not for the pernicious influence of your friend Rho. Now I believe I have a way to compel the child to come to his senses, but I need to test it, and since you saw fit to leave him behind in Norland, you're going to serve in his place."

Ani brushed the hair out of Isa's face with her delicate fingers and Isa leaned into the touch, craving the attention. But then Ani pressed a little harder and suddenly the stroking was more sensation than Isa's screaming nerves could take. She found herself on the floor looking up at the ceiling beams with her limbs twitching and her head aching from where it struck the planks. Then everything went from gray, to black, to red. *To fire.*

In her mind she was still burning, lying across her mother's tomb while the sun seared her arm into a blackened, bloody mess. There had never been anything but the pain. Everything else was a lie. She would never see Daryan again. There was no Daryan; there never had been. No one was coming to help her. The pain would swallow her whole and leave nothing behind, and no one would care. Everyone knew she was wrong inside, not a real Norlander. They were ashamed of her. They'd be glad when she was dead.

A hand circled around the back of her head and lifted it up. "Take this now, like a good girl," said Ani, pressing the edge of the bowl to her lips. "This will take the pain away. The base ingredients are the same as your medicine."

Ani's sympathy was as much of a salve as the relief Isa knew was coming. The sweet syrup glided over her tongue and she swallowed, licking her lips afterward to make sure she didn't waste a drop. She fell back again when Ani removed her hand, breathing in short gasps between the spasms. Respite came first as a warmth in her extremities, then the tremors ceased and her body unwound as waves of relief lapped over her. When the drowsiness came she embraced it, slipping without regret into the sweet languor of the mist.

"The medicine loosens your connection to your body." Ani's voice floated somewhere above her.

Isa knew she should be listening, but she was too dazzled by the colors: oranges and pinks, all the hues of dawn and twilight, the iridescence of insect wings and mollusc trails. And then Daryan was there, waiting for her, like always. His fingers skimmed down her arms like drips of melting wax and the heat of his touch sank deep into her muscles, spreading outward before converging between her hips and lingering there, aching and insistent. In her dream she could press up against him, lean him back against the wall and stand between his legs so he could take her weight as she pushed in closer, until no space existed between them; he could run his hands around her thighs and then pull her to him, tormenting her with the friction as he nuzzled into her neck, dragging his beard across her collarbone before sinking his teeth in and drawing her flesh into the furnace of his mouth.

"I believe that when an asha like Dramash is given the right mixture in sufficient strength, the mortal and divine halves of his nature will split apart. Then I can reach in and take what I need. You should be feeling that now, Isa. You should feel the bond to your mortal body dissolving."

The vision of Daryan melted away but the fog still cushioned her and soon all awareness of her body dropped away. She soared up, so high that all the details below blurred and faded away. She wasn't alone here; she could sense others around, but the only person near enough to recognize was Jachad, the Nomas king. He too was somewhere on the *Argent*. Everything else around her was soft and blunted, but rage lit him up so brightly that it hurt to look at him, even as it intoxicated her.

She and Jachad had connected like this before when she'd witnessed his "cure" by the healer Cyrrin. Occasionally, when she was drowsing in a slack-limbed haze after taking her medicine, she could see what he was seeing. Most of the time he fixed his gaze on his beloved desert beyond the western horizon, watching from so high up that all the details merged into a single swath of color. But now he was looking down on the Shadar, his fury so hot that the little dots moving around on the ground must surely be able to feel it. Jachad wanted to punish the Shadari: they had poisoned Callia, who was to have birthed Jachad's half-brother and the next Nomas king. They had poisoned *him* and turned him from a demigod into an aberration. He would send a fireball down from the sky to obliterate all those little dots. He would have the power to do it soon; once the few remaining ties to his mortal life snapped, when nothing would be left to hold him back.

"Isa. Stop fighting it."

But Daryan wasn't responsible, Isa thought frantically, as if

Jachad could hear her. *He doesn't deserve to be punished. One of Ani's acolytes made a mistake; they were supposed to poison the ashas to prevent them from starting another war with Ani, like last time. They should have never given the poison to the Nomas.*

"Isa!"

She forced her eyes open and tried to sit up, but managed only to lift her head a fraction off the floor. "Jachad," she gasped, "he wants to burn the whole Shadar."

"He is not your concern," said Ani, her voice brittle, too quiet, even as her fingers brushed against Isa's hair with a feather-light touch she couldn't feel. "He's dying in every way that matters. He won't stop me. Now remain calm, yes?"

Isa saw the pin slip into her palm but didn't feel it, nor the wetness of the drop of blue blood that swelled up around it. The old woman placed their palms together, blood to blood, as she had done with Dramash in Ravindal.

"What's going to happen now?" Isa whispered.

But Ani shushed her, so she lay back again, cocooned from all sensation. She didn't want to see Jachad again, so she kept her eyes open and focused on Ani's little hand curled inside hers, and only then did she realize that it shouldn't have been possible for them to touch so easily. Even if the medicine was keeping Isa from feeling the heat, the coldness of her Norlander skin should have stung Ani beyond endurance.

"How—?" she tried to ask, but neither her lips nor her tongue would move; nothing came out but a wet choking sound. Panic tightened in her throat and she tensed her stomach muscles, trying to sit up, but nothing happened. Her mind seized up in confusion. It was just like the times she tried to pick something up with her left hand before remembering she didn't have one.

"The rabble will always seek to destroy what they envy," Ani murmured above her. "If you could have seen the Shadar before the ashas rebelled . . . I gave them peace and beauty; they gave me war and destruction. They have been chastised and I have forgiven them, but I have learned the price of leniency."

Isa searched Ani's eyes for any sign of the warmth that she knew had been there only a moment ago, but she was looking into the blank eyes of an effigy. A memory kicked up, of waking in the dark after her mother's death and crying out in terror, only to have the Shadari servant sitting beside her bed take no notice. She had thought the whole world had abandoned her, because she had forgotten the Shadari couldn't hear her Norlander cries.

"My people will have their god in me: a god who walks among them, who cares for them, who will listen to their prayers and accept their offerings," Ani vowed.

A phantom impact slammed into Isa's chest and knocked the breath out of her. Then the air turned to mud when she tried to fill her empty lungs and she choked, coughing until her eyes swam with tears she couldn't feel. Physical pain couldn't penetrate any deeper than muscle and bone but *this*, this *ripping* and *clawing*, this violated a part of her so elemental she'd had been unaware of its existence until the teeth sank in and sucked it out of her. A hole opened up in her that she already knew would never close again as long as she lived—and that wouldn't be long. And through it all, she remained so horribly conscious.

"The world has never seen my like, nor will again."

Isa could still see Ani clutching her hand with a beatific smile, while the jar of ore rattled and danced on the desk behind her.

"Stop!" Isa screamed. She hadn't been aware of her paralysis lifting so the sound of her cry vibrating through the brass fixtures of the cabin shocked her as much as it did Ani. The tiny hand clutching hers fell away and the jar of ore came to rest with its lid askew—but more than that, the *ripping* stopped.

The relief was so sharp, it was like a new pain all its own. She felt *used up*, the hole inside her so ugly that she wanted to get the blanket and pull it over her and hide underneath it, if only she had the strength to do anything except shudder on the floor with her arm wrapped around her.

But Ani unfolded the blanket for her and tucked her in. She said something about Isa being good and helpful and dried Isa's tears with a soft cloth and smoothed back her hair. The sunset-hued mist crept around Isa again, lulling her with a promise of oblivion, and to her shame, she listened.

The color of the sky had deepened when Isa next awoke. Shadows swayed along the walls as the brass lantern swung from the beam over her head. Ani sat at her desk, as always, with her back to the rest of the cabin and her silver-haired head bowed over her work.

Isa swallowed, moved her tongue, wet her lips. "You're going to do that to Dramash?"

The scratching went on for a moment longer and then paused. "If I must, with a few adjustments. All redemption requires sacrifice, yes?" The old woman turned around and favored Isa with her gentle smile. "I will be able to protect the Shadar, thanks to you. Once I reclaim it, your Daryan will no longer be needed and you can be together. You should be very proud at what you've accomplished."

Isa sat up, still holding on to the blanket wrapped around her. "What if Dramash stayed in Norland? What if he isn't in the Shadar when we get there?"

"He will be. I saw it in my vision."

"Rho would never let him go back to the Shadar."

The benevolence faded from Ani's face. "Come."

Isa unfolded her aching legs and managed the three steps across the cabin before kneeling beside Ani's chair. The soft scrape of the old woman's fingers over her hair eased some of the tension from Isa's limbs.

"You must continue to trust me, Isa," said Ani, her voice like golden dunes rippling away toward the horizon. "I know the people you trusted in the past have betrayed you, but I have never deceived you, or told you less than the truth."

"I know."

Ani stopped petting Isa's hair, lacing her thin fingers together on her lap instead. "Being aboard this ship no longer serves us. Jachad will succumb soon and it would not be wise to witness his transformation from such close quarters."

"I'll take you to the striders when we get to Prol Irat. We'll get to the Shadar before anyone can stop us," Isa promised, earning herself an encouraging smile.

She was sure she remembered enough about Fellix's house to find it again without Lahlil. The striders hiding there were the only ones to have survived the previous emperor's purge; it wouldn't be difficult to threaten them into cooperating. Savion, the strider Lahlil had half-bribed, half-threatened into bringing them to Norland, was sure to have returned home after the battle at Ravindal. If he'd survived. And if not, there was his guardian, Fellix—although last time the fear of being discovered had brought on a fit of madness. But still, there were all the other children. None of them had been old enough to stride the last time, but children grew up.

"I'll get us to the Shadar," she promised again. "Everything will be all right."

Chapter 6

No one noticed Isa climbing up through the hatch even when her sweaty hand slipped on the rail and she bumped down three rungs. No one had cared enough to come down to the cabin to tell them they'd arrived at Prol Irat. Isa only knew because the scrape and clank of the chain had pulled her from her mist-laced sleep in time to see the anchor plunge past the porthole and splash into the dark water.

They'd anchored in the harbor instead of continuing on into the sheltered bay, so the view was mainly ramshackle boardwalks, low buildings and dark alleys of the Outer Ring. Still, Isa could see the spires of the banking houses, temples and mansions of the Inner Ring poking up into the lavender sky. Their braziers lit the heavy clouds in shades of rose and pearled blue and made them glow.

"The harbormaster?" Captain Nisha called out, leaning over the railing on the stern deck outside her cabin.

Grentha, the *Argent*'s first mate, kept her spyglass trained on a boat with a single lantern at its prow crawling toward them. "Two Iratians, a Norlander toff and a Jajiri at the oars. Ain't the manifest they're after," she announced finally and collapsed the spyglass against her thigh.

"No, I didn't think so. Back to your duties, girls, but look sharp." The sailors broke ranks and returned to their posts, but Isa paid no attention to them. Only the boat mattered. She and Ani needed to get ashore as quickly as possible, so she needed that boat. But her view was cut off as Grentha not only stepped in front of her but pushed her hard enough with the butt of the spyglass to knock her down off the edge of the hatch.

"Get below," said the first mate, her voice as hard as a bucket of rocks.

Isa only just kept herself from shoving Grentha back. "I don't take orders from you."

The sailor's dark eyes glinted with the light of the lantern rocking beneath the wheelhouse porch. "On *this* ship you do, and will."

"Get below, my girl," sighed Nisha, pointing a ringed finger toward the open hatch as she swept across the deck. "I could sell oysters to a merman before I could explain who you are and what you're doing here."

Isa stepped between the two women, standing close enough to feel the warmth emanating from Nisha's sun-crinkled skin. "I'm taking Ani ashore. Tonight."

"Good riddance," Grentha said behind her. "The sooner that one's off the ship, the better."

"Stow it, Gren," Nisha said without any heat. The captain tucked a few loose strands of hair into her scarf. It was the same style as those worn by all the sailors, but made of some shimmering blue fabric stamped with silver moons, marking Nisha as the Nomas queen and high priestess to the moon goddess Amai. Her brow furrowed, but before she said what she was thinking her expression relaxed again and she blew out a quick breath. "You're not in the brig and can do as you like. But for your sister Lahlil's sake, I'm going to say my piece first. Whatever that Shadari is giving you for the pain, it's got hold of you. I've seen its like before, and it won't end well."

Isa's jaw clenched up so tightly she could barely speak. "Ani helped me after your healer lied and tricked me."

"Mairi let you believe what you wanted, that's true, but she meant no harm." Nisha pursed her lips. "Far from it. Your arm was healed. You didn't need medicine for the pain and you don't need it now."

"The pain is *real*. Ani helped me—she's the only one who's helped me."

Nisha stretched a hand out toward the missing arm, but Isa jerked back out of her reach and the captain curled her fingers into a fist over her own heart instead. "I've met her type before, you know. She'll break you down into pieces only she knows how to put together again so you won't be able to leave her, but she'll drop you without a thought once you've served your purpose. You don't mean *anything* to her, Isa."

"She said you would do this. She said you would try to drive us apart. You hate her because she can see through your lies."

Nisha had the gall to squeeze false tears into the corners of her eyes. "This isn't you, sweetheart. Those aren't even your words."

"Captain!" Grentha broke in, and gestured toward the prow of the ship as four sailors draped the rope netting over the port side.

Isa slipped into a corner between the rail and one of the *Argent*'s boats for a better look as the captain and her first mate strode away. The larger of the local men was some kind of official; he wore a thick gold chain and kept smacking his lips above his stiff black beard; his companion was obviously a subordinate. The shirtless Jajiri stowed the oars, moored the cutter to the Nomas vessel and stretched out with his feet up on the rail. He produced a handful of seeds and began feeding them to the pink-beaked bird on his shoulder. But Isa's eyes lingered longest on the Norlander, with her intricate braids and her sword-hilt gleaming like whorls of spun sugar.

<I hope someone on board speaks Norlander. I have no intention of shouting,> the noblewoman said. Her studied boredom reminded Isa of Rho, but without the self-deprecation.

<You'll have to forgive my accent, then,> said Nisha pleasantly, <or come aboard so no one needs to shout. I'm Nisha, Queen of the tribe of Amai and captain of the *Argent*.>

<Tara Peltran of the Imperial garrison, and my coming aboard

would hardly be prudent, as we've been informed your ship left Norland prior to the quarantine.>

Quarantine. Images of flailing bodies, fetid cuts and slimy silver tears swam up through Isa's watery memories of Norland.

<There's no sickness here,> said Nisha. <Come aboard and see for yourself. We've nothing to hide.>

<The Triumvirate has closed the port to anyone coming from the north. You will not be permitted to sail further south. You're to turn around and go back where you came from, or remain here until the order is lifted.>

<And while we sit here,> said Nisha while Grentha growled something in her ear, <we can depend on your Iratian friends to sell us what we need to keep us from starving, eh? At double their usual prices?>

<I'd expect triple,> said Tara, straightening one of her already immaculate gloves with a little tug, <but that's hardly my concern.>

"Who's gonna stop us?" asked Grentha in her own language, which the Iratian quickly translated. "Never been a blockade yet a Nomas ship couldn't run."

Tara's annoyance flooded Isa's senses like the smell of vinegar. <Why don't you ask the captain of the *Bold Jenny*? You might recognize that charred black lump out there as her hull. Perhaps you don't know we still have a full garrison here.>

Isa reached out for the rail as her stomach cramped, feeling suddenly like a snake had uncoiled somewhere in her and was now looking for a way out. She and Ani were getting off this ship tonight and no smug Peltran was going to stop them. Her hand found the cool comfort of the hilt of Blood's Pride and she asked herself what her sisters Lahlil and Frea would do, as if she didn't already know.

The tension on the deck shifted to the stern deck as Nisha gasped, "Jachi, no!" and Grentha instantly sprang for the ladder.

Jachad had appeared outside Nisha's cabin and stood with both hands resting on the rail. He looked dreadfully ill: shadows in the new hollows of his cheeks, robe hanging off him in baggy folds, beard untrimmed; only the brightness of his flame-red hair remained the same. He was eroding like the sand dunes in the desert, losing all the edges that made him uniquely himself. But his eyes were the worst. The warmth had seeped out of them, replaced by something righteous and uncompromising.

"We're going on," said Jachad.

The sound of his voice made Isa's jaw clench: it was too calm, too deep to belong to the man she knew. The smell of hot metal cut through the sea breeze as the brass rail turned black and then red under Jachad's hands. "You will let us pass."

<If you mean this to impress me, you're wasting your time,> Tara replied. <I've seen better tricks at the fair in—>

Plumes of flame roared in both of Jachad's hands but his expression remained blank; Isa might have thought he was sleepwalking if she hadn't been able to see the focus in his eyes and the tiny trails of flame circling his pupils.

"Go," he commanded. Isa wasn't sure if his mouth even moved; the word might have been spoken by the flames themselves.

<I don't take threats from Nomas swindlers,> Tara fumed, drawing her fancy sword and setting her stance as the boat rocked beneath her. She was plainly irritated, but Isa sensed a quick drumbeat of fear as well—or that might have been her own, pulsing somewhere beneath the medicine's soft blanket.

<No, don't do that. Put that sword away,> Nisha told Tara, but her frantic alarm did nothing to tamp down the tension. <Stand down, please. My son doesn't speak for us. I'm the captain of this ship and there's no need for this to—>

The first flames burst from Jachad's hands, forcing Grentha back as she closed in on him. Tongues of yellow and orange wound around his arms, blackening the sleeves of his robe and sending motes of charred fabric floating on the heated air. The varnish around his bare feet bubbled up and Grentha shied further back, grimacing as her skin reddened and dripped with sweat.

"You will let us pass," Jachad repeated.

Nisha loped across the deck and vaulted up the ladder, dodging Grentha's grasping hands to get to her son as Jachad joined the streams together in front of him into a spitting ball of flame. She fought through the heat as if she were pushing her way through molten glass, shielding her face with her arms even as sparks showered down on her headscarf and errant flames snuffed into smoke under the soles of her boots.

Isa tore herself away and made for the hatch, spurred on by the absolute certainty that she and Ani would be getting off the ship in the next few moments or not at all. The darkness of the hold shifted like oil as she tripped down the ladder, only to find Ani already waiting at the bottom with her bag at her feet and scorn flickering in her eyes.

"There's a boat," Isa told her, breathless for no reason—unless the medicine was wearing off again. "I'm going to get it for us."

"Isa," Ani called her back when she already scaled the ladder, "you'll need someone to row. You can't do it with one arm."

"I know," she answered with a flush of shame, although the truth was it hadn't occurred to her.

She regained the deck in time to see the fireball in Jachad's hands burst like a bladder. A rippling ring of hot air spread out from him until the sky shimmered behind it. Isa drew herself into a ball to protect herself as scraps of flame darted and zipped in all directions: into the water, into the Iratians' boat, onto the deck and into the sails. Isa could feel Jachad trying to anchor himself back into his body, but it was no use; he was no longer controlling the fire, which was being fed by the limitless reserves to which he was now bound; he was its vessel and it was burning through him as easily as the sparks were burning black-rimmed holes in the sails.

Screams of pain and horror and the stench of burning chased Isa toward the prow. Sailors hurried by in a blur of pale faces, some to help Nisha with Jachad, others to put out fires all over the ship. Nothing felt real: all the faces were hollow-eyed carnival masks. Flames were gushing straight from Jachad's chest and up into the clouds, feeding them until they glowed. Isa swung herself over the rail and dropped straight down into the cutter.

She landed right in the center between the benches, falling hard to one knee as the boat pitched from the sudden weight. The Jajiri had been in the process of untying the boat; he pressed himself backward against the flat stern, big hands still fingering the knot. One Iratian, the functionary, jumped or fell overboard and started swimming for the distant shore. The other shouted something at her, his face beet-red and his hands scrabbling in the air as she advanced. He tripped trying to get over the bench and fell like a sack of rocks, rocking the boat wildly again. Isa braced her knee on the bench and tore the gold chain off his neck before jamming her shoulder under his chest and heaving him into the water. He quickly disappeared under the flame-streaked swells.

The Jajiri cocked his head at her. His whole body was coiled to spring out of the boat if necessary, but at her nod, his tension eased and he made himself as small as possible as he worked at the rope. Isa drew Blood's Pride and turned around to face the Norlander.

Tara Peltran ignored the chaos playing out on the ship above them and focused all of her attention on the knotted shirt sleeve swinging below Isa's left shoulder. Her revulsion stained everything a bright sapphire-blue. <I don't know what you are or what you're doing here, but I'm going to send you to Lord Valrig where you belong.>

Isa didn't wait for her to finish speaking before attacking, churning out blow after blow even as she fought for balance. Tara Peltran fought with the predictability of someone who had never been in a real battle and Isa countered her easily, blocking a few blows, then pausing to watch as her opponent's fingers caught in the fussy hilt when she tried to change her grip. Isa left an opening and the woman predictably came at her left side—stupidly assuming she'd be more vulnerable there—and ended up on her knees when Isa blocked the blow. Isa used the momentum to swing around and kick the Peltran square in the chest, knocking her into the rail at the prow.

<You're disgusting,> the Norlander woman said as she got up, humiliation pouring off of her like sweat. <A disgusting *thing*. If I were you I'd kill myself.>

Isa feinted and a cool wave of satisfaction seeped into her as her opponent flinched. <You think you can judge me?> she demanded of the Peltran. <You, who were born into a privilege you did nothing to deserve; you dare judge *me*? > She ripped open her collar strings and pulled the shirt down from her left shoulder so Tara Peltran would have to look at her stump. <So you can describe it,> she told the Norlander, <when you get to the afterlife and have to tell them who sent you there.>

The Norlander launched into a pointless attack—and then Isa was stabbing her, over and over again. It bothered Isa that all the rocking made it hard for her to really *feel* the blade sinking in; she wanted that resistance of muscle and the bite of bone; she wanted to experience the flesh tearing apart. Blood spat back at her and spotted her hand, but she couldn't really feel that either. At some point she heard Ani calling her name, but the rhythm of her stabbing had taken hold of her now and she didn't want it to end.

A second, harsher call from Ani jolted her out of her trance and she looked up past the slope of the *Argent*'s side to the rail above to see the old woman watching her.

"I want to go home," Isa told her, too wearied now to bother about the catch in her voice.

"I know, child. I know."

Isa wiped her sword on her trousers and sheathed it again so she could climb up to fetch Ani. The netting swung as she climbed and her lungs were burning when she finally reached the top, but she accepted the bag Ani held out to her and then held still so the old woman could slip over the rail and on to her back. The climb down was a lot faster, but the bag felt heavier than Ani herself, so that Isa had barely enough energy to dump Peltran's body into the water before collapsing on the bench.

Ani composed herself on the second bench in the stern and spoke quietly to the Jajiri, who promptly unshipped the oars and

79

began rowing in powerful strokes toward the southeast, away from the main harbor.

"Can we trust him?" Isa asked. Smoke tickled her throat; she only now noticed the air thickening with it.

"He knows what will happen to him if it's discovered he had contact with a quarantined ship," Ani assured her with one of her sanguine smiles.

The lights of Prol Irat had dimmed, but it was only the fog settling in lower. Isa heard a whistle from somewhere out in the darkness and thought she saw a streak of the hot light from a torch or lantern: triffons, out there in the dark, likely flying to the *Argent* to find out what had happened.

She turned around to see the ship on which she had spent the last three months floating in a terrible bubble of heat and sound.

"We'll find the striders," she promised as she fished the gold chain out of the bottom of the boat; that would pay their way. By morning they'd be in the Shadar with the sun baking the air to a dry grit and the sea sparkling like a carpet of fallen stars. When she turned around to look back at the burning ship it had no definition, no individual parts or features. She expected she would see it again soon, in her nightmares.

Chapter 7

The Mongrel kept her sword up as the guard unbarred the cell door, then had to push forward against a wave of heat like nothing she had ever expected to find in Norland. It took only a moment to inventory the small room: desk in the corner crowded with objects, instruments and writing materials; bed heaped with furs in another; a maw of a fireplace taking up most of one wall; ventilation slits up near the ceiling that provided no relief at all from the stifling heat. No other door besides the one at her back. One occupant, a small, elderly woman sitting by the desk.

"Come in, Lahlil, and shut the door," said the woman in Shadari. "The draft, yes?"

The Mongrel hadn't heard the language of her birthplace or her real name spoken for decades; her surprise was the only explanation she could give for why she obeyed. "What do you want with me?" she asked, her throat clenching around the language.

The old woman, perfectly at ease in a locked room with a world-famous mercenary and murderer, took a glass vial from the desk in front of her and held it up in her thin little hand. "I have something for you. Divining elixir. My own invention."

"Is that how you knew my name?"

"I know a great deal more than that. I know you were betrayed by the very people who should have loved you: your parents; your brother and sisters; your Shadari guardian."

The Mongrel had slashed her way through mêlées and massacres without anything like the sense of danger screaming at her now. She needed to flee, but already the heat of the fire had wormed its way into her muscles, leaving them slack and useless.

"I know the things you've done, Lahlil. I know you came here to assassinate Emperor Gannon and that you don't intend to survive," the old woman went on, her soft voice relentless, grinding Lahlil down. "I know you still want what you've always wanted: to go home."

"You're wrong. I'll never go back there."

"Take the elixir, Lahlil." The woman pressed the glass into Lahlil's palm with a touch as light as a bird's, a smile crinkling across her cheeks and something in her eyes that looked terrifyingly like fondness. Memories Lahlil had bottled up came trickling out, like her Shadari nurse sitting by her bed and the sway of her mother's snow-white braids.

"I don't need it. The future means nothing to me."

"It will, once you've seen it," the old woman assured her. "I understand how it feels to be feared, Lahlil. I understand the loneliness that comes with being exceptional. But you are not alone any more. You must understand, I know you as well as I know myself—and I love you for it."

A deep shudder passed through Lahlil's whole body and she finally sheathed her sword.

<How can you even fly in this?> Rho's cool breath ghosted across Lahlil's neck as he leaned in close to peer over her shoulder. The fog was so dense that even following the coast had become a challenge; she doubted they'd be able to see Prol Irat's beacon fires until they were right on top of them. They'd been riding hard for three days and she'd found herself dreaming with her eyes open more than once. If they didn't catch up with the *Argent* at Prol, they'd have to stop to rest.

She kicked her heels into the triffon's rib cage and urged the jittery beast on through the black clouds. <The fog isn't a problem. It will hide us from patrols.>

<Until they crash into us,> he grumbled. <We'll have to stop when it gets dark.>

Lahlil walled herself off from him after that so his jangling nerves wouldn't keep distracting her. They passed a rocky bit of coast and a few fishing villages large enough for them to find a night's lodging without raising too many questions, but she decided to push on a little further. She was craning forward, peering at a few winking lights that might have been Prol's beacons when Rho's flailing arm hit her in the back. She grabbed his wrist by reflex and only just managed to stop herself from snapping it.

<She's there,> he said, <look! It's the *Argent*, all the way out in the harbor.>

Lahlil twisted around until the harness bit into her chest but she still couldn't see past the triffon's wings, so she wheeled around. Rho gripped her shoulder with one hand and pointed with the other, but it wasn't until she covered her Shadari eye that she spotted the three pinpoints of light. <Are you sure that's her?>

<Of course I'm sure,> he answered. The tired triffon growled a little when she drove it to pick up speed but obeyed once she guided it down lower. The points of light, lanterns at prow and stern and mainmast, brightened once they'd breached the fog bank and were facing the ship straight-on. Lahlil traced her familiar lines as the bell in the crow's nest rang out—and a sudden dread filled her veins like sludge.

<Can you smell that?> Rho asked as they circled the mast, waiting for the sailors to clear the deck.

<Yes.>

<Like they've had a fire.>

She focused on the delicate task of landing a triffon on a ship not made to accommodate such beasts, keeping her eyes straight ahead until they'd rattled down onto the planking and slid to a stop. She picked out a few familiar faces as the sailors gathered around while she unbuckled, but she didn't find the ones she sought.

"Where's Nisha?" she asked as she jumped down. She had to see Nisha first; she knew she wasn't ready to face Jachad yet.

"Grentha's cabin," one of the sailors said finally.

"Hela . . . what happened?" Rho asked the girl with the round face and little snub nose who rushed to his side. She shook her head, scattering the tears that had welled in her eyes.

The stern deck had seen the worst of the fire. Grentha's cabin on the port side looked all right except for some blackened streaks across the wood, but the door to Nisha's cabin hung crookedly on half-melted hinges, banging against the frame with every roll of the ship. Most of the brass railing was gone and the ends of the decking dripped bits of charcoal onto the wheelhouse awning. Lahlil remembered sitting there with Jachi, their arms over the lower bar of the railing and their feet dangling, watching seabirds wheel where the waters churned with fish.

"Where is Isa? And the old woman?" asked Rho.

"They stole a boat and left," said Hela, her voice dripping with venom. "We're quarantined."

The door to Grentha's cabin opened and the first mate's craggy features slid into the lamplight. "Come up, girl. Nisha wants to see you."

Lahlil walked past the wheelhouse and climbed the ladder up to the deck while Grentha leaned against the wall to fill her pipe. The first mate's changelessness made Lahlil want to cling to her for all she was worth. If she'd still been a girl, she would have hugged her tight while everything flowed past, wave after wave rising and falling, leaving no trace behind. But Grentha made an impatient noise and held the door open before following her inside.

Entering the cabin was like stepping into Cyrrin's surgery all over again: the pungent odor of medicines, blood, burned skin; a table crowded with jars and rolls of lint; a bed with a bandaged occupant; a silence that couldn't be broken without shattering something. Sabina sat beside the bed threading her fingers through Nisha's hair while Mala, the ship's healer, stood behind the table. Stained bandages swaddled Nisha's hands and arms and a greasy ointment covered the blisters on her face.

No one looked at Lahlil, or greeted her.

"They wouldn't let us land, 'cause of the Norlander sickness. Wouldn't let us go on," Grentha explained. "The boy didn't like it. Once he started in on them, he couldn't stop."

"So why didn't *you* stop him?"

Sabina angled her head far enough to spear Lahlil with a furious glare. "She *did*—why do you think—"

"Belay that, sweetheart," said Nisha. Her voice sounded forced and horribly dry, and Lahlil desperately wanted someone to give her a drink of water but she couldn't find the words to say so.

"Jachad would never have—" Sabina cut herself off this time and bit down hard on her bottom lip, blinking back tears.

Nisha stirred a little on the bed, turning her head so she could see Lahlil. "Sit where I can see you, girl." She was silent for a long moment and Lahlil couldn't tell if she was gathering her thoughts or in too much pain to speak.

"We were selfish," said the captain finally. "We made Jachad into this when we let Cyrrin work that cure on him. She tried to warn me. She knew it would kill the son I knew."

"We had no other options. Cyrrin saved his life."

Nisha flinched. "We kept him alive. We didn't save him."

"You think we should have let him die? Why, because he lost control?"

Nisha hissed and raised herself up, holding out her bandaged arms. "I'm his *mother*. I'd stand in fire until I burned every inch of my skin if it would help him. I'm saying we were wrong because he's *suffering*. He's becoming something he never wanted to be and he can't stop it. So tell me again how we *saved* him."

Sabina murmured something to her and gently urged her back down again. The second mate was weeping openly now, tears running down her cheeks and dripping from her chin.

"I want to talk to him."

"Hm." Grentha took a long pull on her pipe until the bowl glowed, then puffed a cloud of smoke into the cabin. "Why?"

"Let her see for herself," said the captain. "He's in my cabin."

Grentha stepped out of the way as she left the cabin, bubbled varnish crunching under her boots.

The edge of Nisha's door came apart where she grabbed hold, leaving a handful of black grit in her glove. She yanked what remained from the broken hinges and tossed it down. The fire had licked across one side of the cabin, destroying the bunk and the priceless charts pinned to the walls. A layer of sand from the fire buckets covered the floor and the remaining furniture. A large hole in the bay window bristled with glass shards and torn strips of lead, but the rest of the diamond-shaped panes still refracted the light from the stern lantern into colored shards. That's where she found Jachad.

"Jachi."

"You shouldn't have come."

His voice sounded the same . . . unless it didn't. Unless the undertones resonating in the broken glass meant it was deeper. Unless it was flatter, too, with all of its normal affectionate loops and teasing percussion tamped down.

"I wanted to see if you were all right."

"I'm alive," said Jachad. "That's what you wanted."

"That's not all I wanted."

"I know." He should have said it softly, with a sigh, or with a cocked eyebrow and a provocative lilt. But instead, it was just two words: a proclamation. "You're too late."

"I never wanted to leave you." Sand slipped under her feet as she moved further into the room. She needed to *see* him. She wanted to know he was still a person and not a *thing* with breath in lungs it didn't need, wearing Jachad's face like a mummer's mask. "Cyrrin wouldn't have helped you unless I went back to Ravindal to get Trey."

"She regretted it." There might have been a hint of sympathy there for a dying woman's guilt. "But it's done now and it can't be undone."

"I don't believe that." The voice she used came straight from the battlefield, the one that people obeyed without question. Her leg brushed up against the window seat and suddenly they were standing side by side. "I'll find a way."

"My mother thought the same thing. I don't want you here, Lahlil. I want you to go." Finally he turned and met her eyes for the first time and she understood what it felt like to be flayed alive. There wasn't a nerve in her body that didn't feel exposed. But for once she didn't try to hide the ugliness of muscle and bone under her clothes, the scar tissue twisting it all up in knots, or her heart, bleeding through the slashes in its coal-black crust. Her trust was the only thing she had left to give him.

"You only want me to leave because you're afraid you'll hurt me."

"Lahlil," he warned her when her fingers brushed the back of his hand. Sparks trailed along the path of her fingers but she didn't let go and he didn't pull away.

"Look at me, Jachi. My eye-patch is gone. The attacks are gone. You did that."

"I prayed, that was all. I told the gods to leave you in peace."

"You won't hurt me," she promised, moving her fingers up until she was caressing his wrist, touching the tips of her fingers to his pulse to reassure herself he was really alive. Warmth burrowed down into her and the knot in her chest unspooled a little as she shifted her body closer. His fingers caught in her sleeve, white-knuckled and trembling.

"Lahlil. Stop." Her heart skipped at the way his voice broke and her first impulse was to cling harder, but the desperate way he'd pressed himself back against the wall was enough to make her break the connection between their bodies. His breathing slowed gradually and the sparks in his eyes pooled in the corners and then snuffed out, leaving after-images floating between them like a curtain. "You don't understand what's happening to me. I can't make sense of anything close to me now; I can only see clearly from a distance, from above, where it's quiet and calm. You want me to remember how I felt about you but I don't, and that *hurts*, because I know that once it was more important to me than anything else. And now I've lost it."

Lahlil remembered the ugly tears streaming down Sabina's face and wished she was capable of that kind of relief. Denials and re-assurances tilted with the slow roll of the ship but those things were not enough after everything they had done to each other. So she went back to the beginning. "You know why I went back to the Shadar."

The change in topic eased the pain lines bunched up around his eyes and mouth. "Your vision: you saw yourself holding Oshi and you were happy."

"Not happy," she said. A breeze filtered through the broken window and kicked up the smell of ash. "Happiness is nothing. This was more." She struggled with herself for a moment, seeking some way to express something she had avoided examining too closely. "You told me once I needed to have faith in something. Now I do. I have faith that you'll be there, with Oshi and me, when that moment comes."

Jachad lowered himself down onto the bench, his spine too straight and his face too still for her to pretend he was still the same man. "The Shadari gave us that poison. My people have already lost their next king thanks to Callia's miscarriage, and soon they'll lose me. Before that happens, I will see justice served. I must get to the Shadar."

"Then I'll go with you."

He watched her for a moment with that same blank expression. "The Iratians have quarantined this ship. Can you get us to Prol on your triffon without getting captured?"

"Yes."

"Can you make the striders take us to the Shadar?" he asked.

"Neither you nor I have any blood connection to the Shadar. But if we find Savion or another strider to take us, we could try using my connection to Oshi. He's only my nephew, though. It may not be good enough."

"It's the only way I'll get there in time," he said. "I'll take the risk."

"So we go together?"

"If you will accept two conditions. First, you won't try to save me. I may have to use my powers to get justice and if I do, I won't last long. If you interfere in any way, I will leave you and you will never see me again. Do you agree?"

"I agree."

"Second," he went on, "at some point, the rest of my mortality will burn away. Cyrrin believes I will be a danger to innocent people. When that happens, you will do your best to kill me before I hurt anyone the way I hurt my mother."

The words sent cracks through her until she was like a glass pane ready to shatter with one little tap.

"Lahlil. Do you agree?"

"I agree."

He came to her then, hand held out. His robe still hung loosely around him and the lantern light teased the spray of freckles on his shoulder. "Then it's a bargain."

"It's a bargain."

He led her through the broken doorway, then went to tell Nisha what he'd decided.

Rho, pacing on the deck below and leaving vapor-trails of distress in his wake, craned his neck up at her the moment she appeared. He flapped an arm at the round-faced girl, now leaning up against the rail. "Hela said they left hours ago—they could be anywhere in Prol by now. We'll never find them."

"No, never," Hela drawled. "An ancient Shadari woman and a one-armed Norlander—think how they'll blend right in."

"I know where Isa's going," Lahlil said, sliding down the ladder. "She can't risk trying to get passage on another ship, not after what happened here. She's going to take Ani to the striders."

<Striders!> He gaped. <There are striders at Prol, and Isa knows them?>

<Yes.>

He shoved her, hard, while she was still blinking away the on-slaught of his distress. <Then why are we still standing here? They could be gone already—>

<We're waiting for Jachad. He's coming with us.>

<Wonderful. A city built of wooden sticks is the perfect place to bring a fire-wielder.>

She ignored him; he always skittered off into facetiousness when he was anxious.

Jachad emerged from Nisha's cabin and made his way down to them.

Lahlil was about to swing herself up on to the saddle when a cloud of pipe smoke engulfed her and Grentha seized her by the arm.

"You take care of my boy," said the first mate, leaning close to growl into her ear.

"I'll do what I can," said Lahlil, not sure how much Jachad had told his mother and her friend about his plans.

"Thinks he's a *hero* now," said Grentha with a disdainful snort. "Like enough to end up in a ditch with no one looking out for him. Never had no sense. You stick by him, girl, hear me? Else I'll lash those lilywhite hands of his to the wheelhouse and haul him back to Norland where he belongs. Idiot."

Rho. Of course. Every damned time.

Chapter 8

Daryan tapped his fingers on the balcony's balustrade, counting the number of students entering the school across the forecourt. He stopped at eight, after concluding that the three teenage girls talking to the guards at the door were only there to flirt. Of the eight, at least five were palace staff and required to attend. But three voluntary students was better than none at all, and smiling guards weren't worried about a torch-wielding mob coming to burn the place down.

"Start again," said Daryan, turning back to the throne room where Lieutenant Tamin had come to make his report after a week observing Hesh. The balcony was otherwise empty except for Lem's unobtrusive presence.

"He gets up at noon, then goes to dig corpses out of the mines with the other rezzies. They put the bodies the carts and take them to the pyres, and burn them until dawn. The widow goes to the market but they all know her husband was an overseer so no one talks to her. She hasn't had any visitors."

"And Hesh? Who talks to him?"

"People come to the pyres to donate food and fuel for the fires, but no one's given him anything that could be the poison."

"Because he knows we're watching him," Daryan said, mainly to himself. A grit-filled breeze swept over the balcony and set him coughing into his hand. "What about Veyash's informant?"

"Still missing, Daimon."

"Thank you, Lieutenant," said Daryan, dismissing the guard with a wave before heading back inside, wiping his watering eyes. "Lem, I'm going inside to work for a while. You don't need to stay."

"I'll wait out here, if it's all the same to you, Daimon," Lem answered predictably, and made himself comfortable against the wall outside the door.

Daryan went back to shuffling the scraps of paper on his desk and arranging them in a different order, trying to trick the sinister intent buried in all those mundane details to reveal itself. After another fruitless hour, the vein below his right eye began to throb with the same rhythm as the incessant hammering in the courtyard and he stopped to rest his head in his hands. He heard the servants' door click open but didn't look up; the servants didn't need to ask his permission to enter if the door was unlocked. The tread was familiar, as was the rap of a tray being set down and the swish of a duster. It wasn't until a thump landed on his desk that he looked up.

Tessa stood in front of him, one hand pressed down on his manuscript, *The History of the Shadar,* and her eyebrows arched in an expression he couldn't decipher. Her complexion had lost some of its ruddy good health and her eyes looked dry and sore, like she hadn't been sleeping well.

"I need to talk to you," she said.

He was about to ask if it was important, and then thought better of it. "I'm listening."

"First I need to ask you something," Tessa started. "This writing, here. I remember you told me how your uncle breathed down your neck in the temple while you were writing it. You *stole* ink and paper from the Dead Ones, like some kind of maniac. And then you dropped the whole thing in a puddle and spoiled it, and instead of getting drunk and forgetting all about it like a sensible person, you sat yourself down and started over again from the beginning."

"I—" Daryan cleared his throat, tugging his jacket collar open as he remembered shredding the ink-streaked pages while Isa watched, her silver-green eyes wide and bright in the darkness, water from her bath still dripping down the white column of her throat. "Yes. That's all true. Why?"

Tessa drummed her fingers on the paper. "You said it was because people forget. You said stories change with whoever's telling them, so there's no way to know what really happened, because if people always wanted to hear the truth, they wouldn't have invented lying. You said you wanted those who'll come after us to know the truth of what happened here."

"Tessa—"

"I need to know if you meant it, is all, and if you feel the same way still."

An odd flutter kicked up in his chest and he pushed back to stare at her, almost expecting to see that she'd changed into someone else, but she had not. Her eyes were the same unremarkable shade of brown, still a bit too small and too far apart, but with a frankness in them so foreign he wasn't sure what to do with it. "You need to tell me what this about. Right now."

"Fine, I will then," said Tessa. "That resurrectionist boy you have the Reds plaguing, peeping at him all hours of the day and night? He's not done a single thing wrong. Someone's been telling you what you want to hear and I know you well enough, Daimon, to think part of you must know that."

Daryan half-rose behind the desk, arms braced on the edge. "Are you saying you know something about the ashas?"

"I do, yes," she acknowledged, folding her arms across her chest. "Now you've been waiting and waiting for an asha to come here and make themselves known to you, haven't you?"

"You know I have. No one's ever come."

"Oh, the ashas came," said Tessa, "only they never got so far as to meet you. Oh, for the love of mercy, sit down again please before you break your fingers, holding on to the desk like that."

Daryan sank back down into the chair but suddenly the cushion felt like it had been stuffed with splinters.

"Now think hard about it, Daimon," Tessa went on. "When someone comes to see you, they can't stroll in like they own the place. They have to tell the guards their business first. So if an asha came, they'd have to tell the guards *why* they wanted to see you. And of course, they'd tell their name, and where they came from. And if they were told the daimon wasn't there, or was too busy, and to go home again and come back tomorrow—"

"Stop. *Stop there,*" Daryan interrupted. "I know what you're insinuating. Do you think I'm so incompetent that I would let a murderer into the *guards*? The Red Guards are all above suspicion. Captain Omir hand-picked—"

"—them all himself?" Tessa finished for him, and then left the implication dangling there, bloody and broken-necked.

Daryan felt his gorge rise and it lifted him out of the chair again until he was looming over her. "Omir is my closest friend," he warned her. "There's no one I trust more completely. He's done more for the Shadar than I or anyone else. If you're going to spread gossip like that about a true patriot like Omir then I want you out of this palace, today."

He expected her to either dissolve into entreaties or storm out, but she stayed planted in the same spot, with the expression in her eyes inexplicably softened. "I'm sorry, Daimon, but no, I couldn't live with myself."

"I'm not joking, Tessa. Unless you have some proof, get out of my sight or I'll call Lem and have him drag you out."

A frown creased the patch of freckles above the bridge of her nose before she tugged the blue scarf from her head and placed it on the desk. Every movement was purposeful, precise. Daryan leaned in as she pulled the knot apart to reveal something tucked up in the folds: a tiny bundle wrapped in cloth. It was all he could do not to snatch it from her while she picked at the string until finally a vial rolled out from its little cocoon. The glass was badly scuffed, but the cork had been sealed under a fresh coat of wax.

Daryan's heart stopped beating completely for a moment, and then gave a dull, heavy thump. The dark liquid slipping inside could have been any number of things: headache oil; perfume; a cure for wind. But it wasn't any of those things, and he knew it.

"Where did you get that?" he whispered. *Smash it. Pour it out. Throw it on a pyre.*

"Here, take it," she said, setting it down on the desk and sliding it across toward him. "See for yourself. It's the only way you'll believe it."

"Divining elixir," he confirmed. That stuff was at the heart of everything that had gone wrong for them, showing people visions that spurred them to do the unthinkable. For instance, he would be stuck until the day he died with Harotha's lie about their fake marriage, all because Eofar couldn't keep his distance when the elixir told him she was in danger. And that wasn't nearly as bad as all the previous generation of ashas throwing themselves from the roof of the temple because the elixir made them think— *wrongly*—that they would be saving the Shadar. So they died, the Shadar endured thirty years of slavery at the hands of the Norlanders and in the end, the temple fell anyway.

"There wasn't supposed to be any more elixir," said Daryan, hoping his voice didn't betray his near-panic. "The bottle Harotha found—that was supposed to be the last."

Tessa nudged the bottle a little closer. A drop of liquid rolled down the inside, leaving a smear of deep red behind like a bloody tear.

Daryan blinked at it. "Where did it come from? How do you know it's real, or even safe?"

"I made it myself," she said, her voice muffled as she pulled her scarf down over her face to adjust it, "and I used it this morning. I couldn't stand by while you persecuted that boy."

"You—?" He lunged across and grabbed her wrist, keeping hold of her as he came around from behind his desk. As soon as he could reach, he grasped both of her arms and turned her to face him. "What are you saying?" he asked, shaking her hard enough to draw a little gasp from her. A knock sounded at the door but it barely registered over the thumping of his own heart. "Are *you* an asha, Tessa? Do you mean to tell me you've been coming in and out of this room every day for *months*, knowing all the time I was looking for people like you and saying *nothing*?"

"Daimon?" Lem's voice called from the other side of the door. "Are you all right?"

"I'm fine," he called back, wincing as his voice cracked. "Don't—"

But the great wooden door swung open anyway, and it was not Lem's but Omir's heavy footsteps in the antechamber and his huge shadow in the doorway. Tessa took advantage of Daryan's distraction to twist out of his grip and flee. He sprang after her but caught his foot on a stool, giving her enough time to disappear through the back door while he shouted after her.

"What's happened?" asked Omir, his hand already on Daryan's elbow to help him up.

He shook his head. "You won't believe—"

And the next moment froze in time and he knew, he *knew* with absolute certainty, that it would remain fixed in his mind forever. This was the instant a tiny particle of doubt, like a drop of dye in a tub of water suddenly spreading its color everywhere, stopped his words at the top of his throat, where they disintegrated into chalk until he coughed them out.

"I won't believe what?" prompted the captain, heavy brows drawn together.

"How sensitive some people can be," Daryan finished, trying for a rueful smile. His empty hand found a cup of wine on the tray and he downed it in one swallow, but it didn't take away the taste of his lie. "I just asked if she could make less noise while she cleaned and she ran out of here crying."

"She'll get over it," said Omir. "I need you. There's trouble at the ashadom."

An iron spike of rage went straight through his gut. "Binit again? I've told him over and over again, we have an agreement with Eofar to protect those Norlanders until he returns."

"I know. I thought he'd contented himself with making a fuss, but I'm told he's got about two hundred people with him. They say they're going to drag the Norlanders out if you won't lock them up. I've got more guards on the way."

Daryan didn't know enough words foul enough to express what he was feeling. Binit had just enough charisma to turn a crowd into a mob and nowhere near enough to stop one. "When our guards show up, Binit will say I don't care about the will of the people. It'll end in blood on both sides."

"What do you want to do?"

Daryan tried with all his might not to look at the vial sitting in plain sight on his desk. "I don't know."

"Did I ever tell you about my father?" asked Omir.

"No," said Daryan, looking up. Omir rarely shared anything about his personal life.

"I was about the age you are now when the Dead Ones invaded. By the second night, we knew we couldn't make a stand, not when they could come at us from anywhere. All we could think was to get up high. You remember the market streets in Chama?"

Daryan visualized the few forlorn shops and dirty taverns still standing on the shattered foundations; alleys delineated by ropes and rusted metal racks, leaning outbuildings, broken doors and cracked wine jugs, rats' nests and fish bones and over it all, the ammonia smell of piss hanging above the sun-warmed piles of bricks. He had made a note to himself to raze the place as soon as he got the chance.

"Abahar's bakery was two stories high, so we went up on the roof. Me and my dad, a few others. We couldn't do much more than throw some rocks, a spear or two—then someone threw a net at one of the dereshadi, got its legs tangled and brought it down—that got their attention. They came down and smashed through the roof, then set everything on fire. My dad fell through. I never saw him after that."

Omir rubbed his chin with the back of his hand but his eyes stayed dry and hard. "The strange part was how the air smelled, even after the fire. Good, like honey cakes. I couldn't get the taste out of my mouth for days after."

"I'm sorry. That must—"

The big man curled his fingers over the sleeve of his jacket: he wasn't finished. "When I got back home, after it was all over, they told me they'd found my wife in the street. There was not a mark on her—we never did find out how she died. She was pregnant. It would've been our first." He drew in a long breath through his nose and met Daryan's eyes.

"Why are you telling me this now?" Daryan asked after he swallowed against the dryness in his throat.

"I know the Norlanders in the ashadom are our allies, but that's what I think about, when I look at them."

Daryan squeezed his eyes shut for a moment, then rapped his knuckles against his desk. "Have them saddle Trakkar and I'll meet you in the stables. We can't let this go on any longer. And send in Lem on your way out."

Lem bolted in a moment later, hooking the top clasp on his uniform jacket. "The captain said we're heading to the ashadom. I'm ready," the guard announced.

"You're not coming. I have something else I need you to do. Do you know a woman named Tessa? She's a laundress here. She's the one who cleans my rooms."

"Tall, with freckles? Sort of . . ." Lem circled his own face with his finger as he stretched his mouth out in an exaggeration of her smile. "Sure, I know her. She gave me the once-over when I first came. Said I'd better look after you good or she'd tell my ma on me. I believed her."

"I need you to find her. She left my room through the back door right before Omir came in. She can't have got far."

"The back door. Right. I'll find her," Lem vowed, dashing past before stopping, swearing when he knocked a vase to the floor. "Er . . . what am I supposed to do with her?"

That was an excellent question. If Tessa really was an asha with control over the ore, then Lem and his black sword weren't going to be able to stop her from doing as she pleased. "Watch her—

don't say anything to her, just keep an eye on her. I'll talk to her myself when I get back."

"Daimon, I don't like you going to the ashadom without me. I'm supposed to be looking out for you."

"I can look after myself," Daryan told him. "Hurry up, before she leaves the palace."

"Right, I'm off—Just take care of yourself out there, Daimon. I'd never forgive myself if anything happened to you."

The patch of sunlight that had been sliding across his floor for the last hour had finally reached Daryan's desk, skating across the objects there and streaking the surface with shadows. The bottle Tessa had left behind looked so innocuous among all the other items.

So if an asha came, they'd have to tell the guards why they wanted to see you. And of course, they'd tell their name, and where they came from . . .

This was how it always started with the elixir: this bleak temptation, this need to *know*, even when you knew you wouldn't be able to change anything. This was the path that had led the old ashas, Eofar, the whole Shadar to destruction. The glass warmed his hand like living flesh as he rolled it back and forth along the length of his fingers, as beguiling and sinister as a magic potion in a children's story. He didn't even remember picking it up.

He felt like he'd been scratching away at a door with a blunt spoon and someone had just handed him the key. If he took the elixir, he could prove to Tessa there were no traitors in the Red Guards; that she'd misunderstood what she'd seen in her vision; that Omir loved him like a brother and would never betray him. He could discover the real murderers and finally set the Shadar on the path to independence, to peace. He could lie down to sleep at night without the voice in his head reminding him over and over again of his failures. Why would he even hesitate?

A rough laugh forced its way out of his throat.

Because daimon or not, he was a coward. Because he lacked the courage to continue leading his people if he knew he would fail them someday—if he saw the ashas dead, the Shadar invaded, his people enslaved again or burned to ash in one final conflagration. Because if what Tessa believed was true, then Daryan had personally lured the ashas to their deaths, simply by being willfully oblivious to the truth. Because he was still clutching a last kernel of hope that Isa would come back to him, and if he lost it now—if he saw her dead or alone and dying somewhere—he feared the hole in his heart would rip wide open and suck the rest of him in.

The sunlight slid away from his fingers while he stood there holding the bottle, trapped in a moment of indecision and shame.

Omir would be waiting at the stables, probably on the verge of sending someone up to fetch him. Finally he made the only decision possible right then: he slipped the bottle into his pocket and left the room.

Chapter 9

Daryan kept an eye out for Tessa or Lem during the hurried march to the stables, but neither of them appeared. The tiny bottle of elixir weighed him down so heavily that it was a wonder he didn't limp. An irrational fear that it might fall out had him pressing his arm to his side from time to time, feeling for the hard lump. He was starting to think he should have stashed it somewhere, but he couldn't imagine letting it out of his sight.

Omir greeted him at the stables with his usual reserve and a few moments later they took to the air with a full wing of six Red Guards wheeling around to face the last curve of the sun below the pearled twilight skies.

The city lay like a carpet before him on its flat little strip of land, dark except for the dancing candle-flames of the funeral pyres along the beach. The city couldn't have looked much different in his father's time, before the Norlander invasion, with the dying light glancing over the domes and the air perfumed with charcoal smoke. If Daryan let his focus soften he could imagine the temple was still there on the northern horizon, dominating everything around it. He remembered those brief boyhood years hiding from the Dead Ones with his mother, when he would look up at a sky like this at the dereshadi launching out and she would say, *That's where the ashas used to live.*

No one remembered that the ashas had not been the ones to

build the temple or the first to occupy it. No one remembered the tyrant who had tried to enslave them, or the civil war that nearly destroyed them. If they had, when the Norlanders came three centuries later, the ashas would have fought back and it would have been the Dead Ones with their broken bodies on the ground and their ships on fire.

Omir led them toward the mountains. Torchlight marked out the space in front of the ashadom where the crowd had gathered, penned in by guards and their dereshadi, with yet more guards blocking the entrance. Daryan saw no sign of the Norlanders themselves; he doubted they had any idea of the danger they were in. Trakkar was making for the open ground well away from the crowd, but Omir swooped down over the pile of red rocks Binit had climbed on to give his speech. The wind drowned out most of Binit's scream but Daryan took a little satisfaction from watching him flop down on his face with his hands over his head when Omir's triffon streaked through the air right above him.

Omir put the dereshadi down between the crowd and the ashadom and stood up in the stirrups while Daryan landed beside him. An unpleasant smell hung in the air, the exact nature of which eluded him until he saw the shattered wine-jugs, dirty rushes and rotting scraps. Without Shadari slaves to do their picking-up for them, the Norlanders had turned the area around the entrance to their sacred space into a rubbish heap.

"Go back to your homes now, all of you!" the captain roared. "The Norlanders are under the protection of the daimon."

"Do you not understand that these people are worried about their families?" Binit called out to them as he climbed down from the rocks. He was having a difficult time with one hand cupped under his bloody nose. Daryan nodded for the guards to let him through. "People are dying of plague and you and the Reds are covering it up," Binit announced.

"That's a lie," Daryan said calmly.

"A lie?" Binit shouted back, but had to wait while one of his friends tried to wipe away the blood from under his nose with a dirty rag. "No, you won't put me off this time. They're *sick*. They have the plague. *You're* the liars!"

Omir cuffed him on the back of the head and Binit cried out in pain and outrage as fresh blood flowed from his nose, some of it dripping on to Daryan. An angry shout went up from the crowd and a man with a pointed shovel made a break for the line of guards at the entrance until they tackled him to the ground. A rock whizzed past Daryan's head and bounced off the wall next to the doorway. Some of the crowd broke into a derisive cheer and Omir gave the guards the order to draw their weapons.

"Stop!" Daryan shouted, drawing his own sword and using it to tip up the blade of the nearest guard. "We didn't make these swords to turn them on each other! We came together to defeat the Norlanders. We mustn't let them divide us now. I'm going to prove to you there's nothing to fear."

"How?" called Binit.

Daryan pulled Omir close and murmured, "Stay out here and keep everyone calm. I won't be long."

"You're not going in alone," Omir growled. "Why isn't Lem here?"

Daryan's hand went reflexively to curl around the bottle in his jacket pocket. "I told him to stay behind; he's not a good enough flier to handle a crowd like this yet. I'll take six guards. You may need the rest out here."

Omir glowered, but he rattled off six names and told them they would be accompanying the daimon.

The crowd hushed when Daryan started down the boulder-lined path toward the doorway. He was horrified to see the amount of rubbish increasing the nearer he got, as if their "guests" couldn't be bothered to walk even a few steps before flinging their waste away into the rocks. It wasn't just trash, either; his years as someone's personal slave had made him intimately familiar with the smell of a slop-bucket.

"And they called us savages," muttered one of the guards behind him.

"Conquered half the world but can't wipe their own arses," said another before Daryan's curt reprimand ended the exchange. Once inside the tunnel, he paused to let his eyes adjust to the darkness. The stench of dirty clothes, unwashed bodies and the rotten-fruit smell of spilled wine permeated the cool metallic bite of the cave air. He should have been prepared for it, but the moment he came out under the domed ceiling and entered the cave proper he had to stop and give his stomach a moment to stop churning.

Six months: that was all it had taken to reduce the once-indomitable Norlanders to this level of degradation—and they had no one but themselves to blame. Eofar, the commander they had chosen to follow, had conscripted them into a cause they found abhorrent and left them in the hands of people they believed to be their inferiors in every way.

The only lamp burning was set on one of the tables, and the invisible margins of the vast cave made Daryan feel like he was walking into a void. He could see nothing of the mural of the gods over his head, which was just as well; he did not want to think too much about the pollution he'd brought into this once-sacred place.

For a moment his eyes came to rest on the dusty hump of the triffon saddle Isa had used to wall herself off from the others when she'd lived here. She could have told him sooner how Falkar and his friends had ignored her, demeaned and threatened her, but she hadn't. *I didn't want to worry you*, she'd said, meaning she'd had no faith in his ability to do anything about it.

Some light came from the bluish glow of the Norlanders' skin where they languished on the benches or sprawled out on pallets. All seventeen of them were stripped down to the waist. The glow might have been the only thing holding them together: they were skeletal, all bony arms and legs, muscles withered until their skin hung in slack folds like wax candles set too close to the fire. Lank white hair snaked past protruding shoulder blades; most had given up tying it back. The dark patches blotching their skin might have been dirt, but Daryan feared it was something less benign. His father's generation had called them Dead Ones, and

104

no wonder. Creatures like this could not possibly be alive, not the way they understood it.

Daryan swallowed the bile rising up in his throat and called, "Lieutenant Falkar." The Red Guards fanned out around him, fingering their weapons, as Falkar walked toward him until Daryan could see the webbing of dark veins around his silver irises and the bags underneath like a pair of fat bloodworms. The Norlander wore his sword across his back, but his shoulders were trembling under the weight of it.

"There's a mob outside out for blood," Daryan announced, purposely using short words so all the Norlanders would understand him. "My guards are keeping them back. For now."

Falkar's blank expression remained fixed but he swallowed several times before he forced out a reply. "We need nothing from you."

"No?" Daryan's sharp laugh broke the hush and he took some satisfaction from the way the Norlanders recoiled. "You all need baths, but I can't spare the water—nor can I spare my soldiers to guard you day and night. So I've come to a decision. Once we've broken up the crowd outside, I'm moving you into the jail, for your own protection."

"Give us back our triffons," Falkar demanded, using the Norlander name for the dereshadi.

"No."

"They're ours," the soldier muttered, his eyes gaining a little of their old luster.

"*Yours?*" Daryan laughed. "Did *you* breed them? Did *you* feed them, bathe them, slop out their berths, look after their tack, take care of them when they were sick or hurt? Because *I* did."

Falkar continued to loom without so much as twitching a white eyebrow. "We don't answer to you."

"No, you don't. You answer to Eofar. And in exchange for giving you food and shelter and *not murdering you*, you were supposed to help us train and defend ourselves. You're going to start doing your part."

Falkar finally moved, but only to turn away toward the nearest table and lift a jug of wine. A trace of liquid spilled down his chin and neck as he drank, renewing the pungent smell of old sweat. He choked, then heaved into a coughing fit, sinking down onto the bench with one hand braced against the table for support. "Lord Eofar will not return."

"If I believed that, I'd have no reason to stop my people from coming in here and dragging you out into the sun to burn. Luckily for you, I still have faith in him."

"He's damned. He allowed his sister to live."

Daryan swallowed the lump of fury in his throat and fixed his eyes on the lamp's steady flame until his eyes began to water. "Isa Eotan is a hero."

Falkar slammed his fist down on the table with a thump that bounced right back from the rock walls. "She's cursed. Corrupted."

Several of the Norlanders climbed out of their pallets and Daryan motioned behind him to keep the guards from rushing to his defense. Ice prickled through his chest but he knew when he was being baited. He had no more reason to stay. He turned back to the tunnel but hadn't taken more than a dozen steps before he heard the scrape of a sword behind him. His own joined the chorus as he swung around to find all the Norlanders on their feet now and the Red Guards standing ready, blades twitching.

Daryan drew in a breath to warn off Falkar, but the fetid air stuck in his throat. The truth was, he'd *wanted* this fight ever since he'd found out how they'd treated Isa. He wanted to punch Falkar in the face and feel the bone crack under his knuckles. He wanted to see Falkar on his knees with blue blood swelling up around his wounds. He wanted to hurt Falkar because Isa wasn't there to do it herself. But he didn't want it like this. This was beneath him.

In the end, one of the other Norlanders moved, some nameless, lank-haired skeleton on the fringes of the darkness, making the choice for him, and that single step kicked everyone else into motion.

Daryan blocked Falkar's first blow before his mind even caught up to the fact that this was *actually* happening. Falkar may have had only an ordinary steel sword and veins full of cheap wine, but the Norlander had a lifetime of training and experience on his side. Daryan staggered back under the surprising weight behind the blow, flinching when his back foot skidded on something slick, threatening his balance. He had to block two more hacks before he found a moment to circle away.

"Call them off," he shouted to Falkar over the stomping and clanging ringing through the cavern. Bodies and blades flashed all around him in the dim light. "Or the death of this alliance will be on your head."

"*You* cursed Isa Eotan," Falkar spat at him. "She hated you for not letting her die."

Daryan's black blade swung around in a sweeping blow aimed straight for Falkar's neck; the speed and accuracy was something he could never have managed with his muscles alone. The concussive force of the parry reverberated deep in his bones and the sweet synchronicity of his sword sang out to him: *again again again.* He drove Falkar back, relishing the stretch through his shoulders as he swung, smirking as a near-hit sent a swatch of yellowed linen shirt fluttering to the floor.

Daryan aimed a cut at the lieutenant's leg, expecting to feel the blade sink into flesh or slam up against another parry, but Falkar somehow skirted the blow, leaving Daryan slicing through empty air. He overbalanced and crashed into the table, but recovered quickly enough to snatch up a jug and hurl it to buy himself some time. The jug flew over Falkar's crouched form and struck the Norlander fighting behind him square in the back. Daryan rushed forward to get a thrust in before his foe had time to straighten, but again ended up with a stinging jolt to his arms. Worse, his feet had gone wrong again—Omir was always warning him about his footwork when they sparred—and he found himself teetering helplessly to his right. The edge of Falkar's sword sliced toward his left side and he made a desperate lunge to block it, but his back foot slipped on soiled rushes and he went down, hard.

It was his mistake that saved him: Falkar had committed to the blow and couldn't pull back in time. Daryan scuttled away from the white sparks as the steel scraped over the rock; he managed to pull himself back onto his feet with the help of an overturned bench.

In the dim light he thought he counted one Norlander and two Red Guards down; the rest were still fighting. The Norlanders had encircled him, preventing any of the Red Guards from coming to his aid. Eofar had once told him that separating the leader from the troops was a common battle tactic, meant to sow disorganization.

He shoved the bench across the floor toward Falkar—not much of a deterrent, but it gave him enough time to vault up and over the table behind him, scattering dice and cups in his wake. Someone swiped a blade over his head and he ran in a half-crouch until he found an empty spot to gather himself to meet Falkar again. The Norlander stalked forward, wasted chest heaving, blue veins distended, and Daryan imagined standing on the beach that night in place of the father he'd never known, watching a creature like this destroy his whole world.

As if the vision had overtaken him, the need to protect himself and the people he loved shut down his conscious mind; there was nothing left of him but arms and legs, steel and sinew. He and Falkar traded blow after blow until Daryan's muscles were screaming for rest and his eyes burned from staring through the darkness. The lamp's flame disappeared and reappeared as they chased each other in circles, even as the fight raged on around them in a spiral of bodies, steel and blood.

He charged again, this time managing to drive Falkar back, one heady step at a time. Every clash of the blades shifted a little more of the control over to him as he struck, blocked, struck again, forcing Falkar toward the back of the cave. The lamplight died away to nothing, but that made it easier to track the Norlander's movements by the glow of his skin. He feinted to the left and sent Falkar shifting the wrong way before he rocked his hips and struck from the other direction. The sword snicked through a fold of the Norlander's loose trousers; Daryan didn't see any blood on the dark blade when he swung back but a little stain blossomed around the rent. Falkar stopped and slipped gracelessly to one side. He caught hold of something, scrambling to stay on his feet, and Daryan realized he had backed him straight into Isa's saddle. The Norlander couldn't get a good enough grip on the humped leather to get his feet back under him but he refused to drop his sword, even though the point of it was scraping the ground.

Daryan gripped his hilt with both hands and leveled his blade, shoulders back, legs braced, strength pouring into his arms for one final thrust. He looked into those dead silver eyes and peered through that emptiness until he discovered a speck of triumph lurking there.

"You were close," he whispered. He took the tip of his sword away from Falkar's laboring chest and stepped back. The lieutenant's gasping breath caught, hitched up in a peculiar noise and then rasped back into its frantic rhythm. "You're not going to stand on my shoulders to win yourself a place in the afterlife. You provoked this fight; there's no honor for you here. If you want to die in battle, you can wait until someone takes up arms against the Shadar and fight by our sides." He knocked Falkar's sword out of his hand, then brought his boot down over the hilt and kicked it away. "Now call off the others."

The other Norlanders broke off fighting and moved back at once, presumably at Falkar's command.

"Make sure they're disarmed and let them treat their wounds," Daryan ordered the nearest guard, hoping no one else could hear the tremor in his voice or the grunt as he raised his arm high enough to get his sword back in the scabbard. By tomorrow his muscles would be so sore he was going to need someone else to scratch his nose. He tried not to break into a run as he left, even though his lungs were begging for fresh air. But when he finally saw the mouth of the cave framing a sky the color of mold and a rumble trembled through his skull, his steps slowed.

"It can't be," he said, repeating the words under his breath like an incantation as Omir caught sight of him and strode forward. "It's too early for rain."

"Never seen it come in this fast," Omir agreed as another roll of thunder swelled, steadied and then dissipated. A gust of wind cooled the sweat on Daryan's face. He looked up in disbelief at the sharp dividing line between the blue sky directly overhead and the bank of gray storm clouds barreling in from the sea.

Then the first fat drops plunked down in the sand around him. One struck his forehead and slithered down his nose, leaving a chill trail even after he'd wiped it away. They weren't ready. The planting hadn't been done; they had moved none of their precious stores of food into waterproofed shelters or dug out the drainage channels to keep the streets from flooding or covered all the chimneys and skylights with tar-cloth . . .

"We've got to get back to the palace!" The rain was already steadying into a heavy downpour. Binit's mob was dissolving as people bolted back toward their homes and families. Daryan winced, his muscles protesting as he slung his arm over his head to keep the water from dripping into his eyes as he ran for Trakkar. Then one of the other dereshadi snorted and launched into the air, dragging the guard holding his leads until the panicked man finally let go and crashed back down into the dirt. The people who still remained scattered wildly.

"Dereshadi don't like thunder," said Daryan under his breath as another one rose up on its back legs, then thumped back down hard enough to shake the ground. He ran faster, determined not to be left stranded.

"Get down!" Omir yelled behind him, and before he could even turn around the big man had pushed him down under the reach of the claws and tail of another dereshadi sweeping down for a hurried landing. Daryan wiped his stinging palms on his trousers and watched the new arrival butt up against Trakkar for comfort. There was a white ring around her black eyes and her ears were flat against her head. She had no rider or saddle.

"Careful, Daimon," Omir called out over the steady drum of the rain as Daryan drifted toward her. "She's feral."

He heard Omir call his name again, but now he was jogging. The beast was a little on the small side, the hump of its back a bit more graceful than average, and as he came closer he could see the lighter patches of new-grown hair on her hide where the edge of a saddle had previously rubbed it away, meaning she had been ridden hard and without proper grooming, but not recently. He ducked under the sweep of her tail as she turned around to face him. Then she lowered her massive head and rumbled a deep hum of recognition.

"Daimon," Omir panted, a heavy hand landing on Daryan's shoulder.

"It's Aeda." He could feel his heart pounding. "It's Isa's dereshadi—it's come back without her."

Lightning sizzled down into the sea, followed by a still-distant thunderclap, but right now the little bottle in his waterlogged pocket had all of Daryan's attention. One sip, and he would know if Isa was alive or dead, healthy or injured, wandering alone somewhere or knotting her fingers in the sheets of someone else's bed. His eyes fixed on the captain's broad back as Tessa's accusations came rushing back.

"What is that?" Omir asked. His tone implied that he already knew.

He didn't look up from peeling away the wax seal of the tiny bottle, not trusting himself to use his knife, not the way his hands were shaking.

"Where did you get it? Daryan? *Answer me!*"

Daryan gave up and put the cork between his teeth to bite it off—until a hard shove from behind jerked the bottle out of his mouth. He stumbled and before he could catch himself, his legs were swept out from under him and he went down again. As he pitched forward, the bottle jarred free from his clutching fingers and went bouncing over the sand.

"You can't do that!" Omir insisted, already fishing for the bottle, but Daryan spotted it right in front of him and snatched for it. Omir tried to grab his wrist, but Daryan rolled away across the wet ground and clambered to his knees, trying to find his knife under his soaked shirt while the captain—*his closest friend*—called out to him to stop.

"You don't know that's real," said Omir, his face a blur behind a curtain of rainwater. At least he was no longer advancing. "It could be poison—where did you get it?"

"From someone I trust."

Omir's gaze shifted for a moment; the list wasn't long and Daryan could almost hear him ticking off the names. "You know the problems that stuff has caused. Think about it, Daimon. Could you lead a battle you knew you would lose? Could you reassure someone you knew was going to die? People need the daimon to give them hope. You can't do that if you don't have any. Now put the knife down and give me the bottle. *I'll* take it."

"No. I need to see for myself."

"Daryan," said Omir, water streaming from his beard, "I can't let you do it. It's my job to protect you."

Omir seized his wrist and tried to force his hand open, but as Daryan tried to break the hold, he gripped the slippery glass too tightly and it shot through his fingers and into the mud several feet away. Without even thinking he dived after it, ducking under Omir's arm and landing on his belly with the bottle trapped beneath him. He could feel the glass against his shin and he pushed his leg over it possessively as the rain pounded against his back. Fingers gripped his hair and yanked his head back, then slammed it forward. His head swam as he was flipped up over onto his back, too addled to fight back.

When Daryan's vision cleared he saw his gold circlet sticking up in the dirt beside him. He scrambled to his feet in time to see Omir hack off the neck of the bottle with his own knife and pour the liquid out into the dirt, shaking it to make sure every last drop had been destroyed.

Daryan lifted himself to his knees and then stayed there,

arms hanging at his sides, rain dripping down his forehead and pooling over his cheekbones. His knees sank a little further into the sodden ground. He wouldn't have minded too much if it had sucked him down to death, the way Faroth had died at his son's hand. Only for Daryan, it wouldn't be magic but the weight of his own heart pulling him down.

"I couldn't let you do it," Omir said, still breathing hard.

"I know."

"I was protecting you."

"Yes, I understand."

Omir nodded, apparently satisfied his non-apology had been accepted. "Let's get out of the rain. You need dry clothes."

Daryan didn't argue; only took the forearm on offer to pull himself the rest of the way to his feet. That's when he noticed it.

"You're hurt," he told Omir, his tongue thick and numb. "You're bleeding."

"I'm not hurt."

"You're bleeding—Omir, *your hands*. Look at your hands."

"There's no blood," said the captain, but he held up one dripping red hand, then the other, and his mouth twisted up in confusion. He fell back a step as if he needed more distance to see his own body and held his arms out, looking for the wound. "I'm not bleeding. It's not my blood."

"No, you're right," said Daryan, pointing to the captain's red jacket before turning around and heading for Trakkar. "It's only the dye running."

Chapter 10

Isa ground her teeth as she considered the dozens of boardwalks leading away from Prol Irat's southernmost wharf, finally choosing one heading more or less in the direction she thought they ought to go. Faces and forms swirled out of the fog: groups of men and women gathered in doorways or running down the street; people leaving their houses, coming back, going out again. Their whispering filled Isa's head and blunted all the other sounds as darkness erased the details from the buildings she passed. She began to imagine she was back in the temple, roaming those endless blank corridors in the dead of night, hoping and dreading she would see Daryan around every corner. Nothing looked familiar—or rather, *everything* looked familiar, because everything looked the same: rickety boardwalks, makeshift bridges and bowed ramps leading every which way, crooked shacks leaning shoulder-to-shoulder.

And the *spirals*—spirals were everywhere, chalked and painted on the shutters and boardwalks, scrawled on sheets hanging from the windows like flags, scratched into the plaster walls.

Still, when the streets narrowed and the buildings shrank to single-story, weathered slat structures with unglazed windows, she knew they were getting close. She recognized the pylons where Dredge had tied up his boat, then the staircase where she had rushed ahead of Lahlil and Jachad. And there was the street with

114

the taverns, and the doorway where the sweeping woman had glared at them.

"This way," she said at the next steep stairway, holding out her arm so that Ani could lay her little bird claw upon it to steady herself. Isa took the stairs slowly so the old woman could reach the top without struggling, feeling the sagging treads jump beneath her as impatient Iratians skirted them on their way up or down.

The statue at the top of the steps was new, some Iratian deity with dead eyes and a gaping fish-mouth. Everything below the claws and scaled torso was hidden by a mound of offerings: baskets of fish, vegetables, fruit and seaweed. She shuddered as a rat whipped its hairless tail in her direction before it disappeared under the banquet.

"I think my medicine is wearing off," she told Ani, her discomfort drawing her gaze away from her companion and up to the painted eyes of the statue.

Ani hummed in distress. "So soon? I'm afraid you are becoming too accustomed to it. I did warn you. I will have to consider lengthening the period between doses in the future. Now, you need your head clear to find this house, yes? So, you must concentrate for me."

She kept her strides short to match Ani's and walked with a hand behind her elbow in case she stumbled, trying not to let the noxious smells of smoke, garbage and urine make her dizzy. They crossed a small footbridge, then passed down a narrow street lined with windowless shacks. "It should be around the next corner, at the end of the pier," she said, remembering the way Savion had chased his turban when the wind blew it off.

"Striders should not be living in squalor like this. I'm ashamed for them."

"They had to hide here because of Lahlil. She made them do it."

"People with power like theirs should never have allowed themselves to be murdered and subjugated," said Ani. "If they had any pride, they would blame their fate on their own weakness and not on your sister."

A noise from behind them drew her attention back to the street. It sounded like a lot of little bells tinkling. "Someone's coming," she said to Ani, urging her back behind a porch support. The sound of bells crept up on them, jingling rhythmically like harness bells on some trotting beast, and she could hear the susurration of a large crowd. There was a flare of lantern light at the end of the street and most of the doors around them creaked open and people came out, whole families, clutching children and holding bread, fruit, or fish wrapped in leaves.

It was a procession. A young woman and a young man, both dressed in nothing but garlands of flowers and holding lanterns on poles, followed by another pair waving censers streaming with pungent smoke. Next came a troop of children garlanded with necklaces and bracelets covered in tiny bells, and finally the priests, bringing up the rear. The holy men were masked and robed from head to toe, and carrying pots of ash to mark spirals on the foreheads and hands of the people lining the street.

"They're protecting themselves against the plague," Ani informed her.

"But there's no plague here."

"Of course there is, child: envy, hubris, greed; these are all plagues. Fear is a plague. Sadly, this display will do nothing to protect these people. Their gods are too remote to interest themselves in their care."

Isa twisted her fingers into her cape as the procession edged up the street one house at a time. The wind shifted and the thick odor of the incense hit the roof of her mouth, bringing bile up into her throat. Her mind suddenly spewed up all the fears she'd been trying to ignore: Savion had probably died in Norland—and even if he'd survived, he had little reason to return to Prol; or he and the other Abroan refugees might have fled the city by now, or even moved house. A quick thrust of anxiety knocked her back for a moment and she waited for the familiar soft wave of her medicine to come and sweep it away—but it didn't come. Her legs were beginning to tremble, but Ani had intimated there would be no more medicine for her until she found Savion. If she could plot out a route for them to slip through the crowd—

—and there was Savion, not a dozen paces away, with a small child clutching each hand and a basket of eggs over his elbow. He was shorter than she remembered, and he'd grown a thin beard, but he looked well and more importantly, very much alive. The procession inched closer and the people around Isa began to maneuver into place to receive their blessings, suffocating her with their heat and smell. A woman with a spiral of ashes smeared across her forehead and a toddler in her arms turned and walked straight into her. For a moment they couldn't get out of each other's way, then the woman bent over to put down the squirming child and Isa saw Savion looking right at her.

His yellow eyes narrowed and he muttered something under his breath as he backed up, yanking the children with him. The pair protested instantly—and loudly—and tangled themselves around him while he tried to keep the basket of eggs from tipping over. Isa's legs were trembling violently now, but she kept her eyes fixed on the Abroan as she twisted through the crowd, afraid he would disappear if she looked away. Five paces away. Then three. Her foot slipped on the board when something rotten squelched under her boot but she didn't let it slow her down. One more step and she'd be able to grab him; then he couldn't stride away without taking her with him.

A scream cut through the close air and the tinkling of the bells turned frantic as the procession suddenly swirled into chaos. It took a moment for Isa to find the cause: a man with a drawn sword was running down the crowd like he was possessed. Isa's heart leaped into her mouth as she remembered all those frenzied people on the Front in Ravindal infected with the silver slime and screaming as they hacked and slashed at anything that moved.

And this madman *was* a Norlander—but he had no visible wounds bleeding silver and his emotions weren't a disordered splatter of rage but a focused, needle-sharp sense of purpose. A giddy disassociation sealed her off, like she was looking down from a great height at something she was powerless to stop, and three things became clear to her in that instant: the sword was Fortune's Blight, the man wielding it was Rho Arregador and he was going to kill Ani on that dirty street in front of all those Iratians with spirals on their heads.

Then the bubble burst and Isa had an Abroan child pressed in front of her, pinning the girl's fluttering chest down with her elbow so she could hold the edge of the sword against her throat. She may have screamed at Rho to stop; the child may have screamed in fear; Savion may have screamed when she pulled the child away from him—she wasn't sure.

She knew only that Rho stopped in his tracks well before reaching Ani, and the people in the crowd either fled or backed up to circle around them so that no one stood between them.

Rho's features were exactly the same—that angular Arregador nose and chin, the silver eyes with a hint of ice-blue—but he'd sloughed off the wry self-deprecation that had always defined him. No bemusement or world-weary humor diluted his horror as he returned her stare. This was not the same man who had sparred with her in the temple when her own siblings couldn't be bothered to train her. This was the man she had trusted second only to Daryan—until he had twisted up that trust like a slop-rag and wrung it out right in front of her eyes when he'd tried to take Ani away from her the first time.

<Isa, for Onfar's sake!> he called out to her, devastation flaring through his words like heat-lightning. The child's shoulders heaved, but other than that, she stayed perfectly still. The tiny blue flowers embroidered on her little turban reminded Isa of the weeds she had plucked while waiting for Daryan to wake up in their little bower on the mountainside: papery blossoms drifting away on the breeze. <We'll find some way to resolve this. Just let the girl go.>

"No. You'll kill Ani and Savion will stride away." She spoke in Shadari so Ani wouldn't think she was trying to keep secrets from her; the old woman had lived in Norland long enough to sense a conversation happening even if she couldn't hear it.

<This isn't you, Isa,> said Rho, and even though he came no closer he might as well have shaken her by the shoulders. <She's done something to you.>

<She *helped* me. She *cares* about me.>

<Is that—?> He cut himself off, then the sensation changed to something like a weird, angry embrace. <Isa, have I not been enough of an idiot that you thought you needed to fill the gap?>

Before she could make any sense of that statement, the attention of the crowd circling around them shifted and a presence she knew too well poked ugly fingers into her mind, just where she didn't want them to go. *Lahlil.*

"Well done, child. Make him tell you where he's keeping Dramash," Ani instructed her. "He would not trouble himself going back to the Shadar without the boy. He must be somewhere nearby."

"Oh, you think so?" Rho answered archly. Isa could feel his hatred snaking toward the old woman's throat as if he could choke her with it. "Then I appear to have mislaid him. Maybe you'd like to come over here and check my pockets."

"Where is he?" Isa demanded. "Where are you holding him?"

"He's in Norland with your brother, eating his own weight in stew on a daily basis—and I'm not 'holding' him. He chose to come with me."

"You made him turn against us."

<Onfar's balls, Isa!> he erupted, suddenly switching back to Norlander. A strange bubbling rose up from him, so discordant that it took her a moment to realize he was actually laughing at her. A phantom sensation brushed her cheek, as if he were reaching through the incense-heavy air and cupping her face with his cold hand. <In all the time you've known me, have I *ever* been able to make *anyone* do *anything*?>

Stop making me remember. You never cared about me. You didn't take the pain away.

"Let the girl go, Isa." Lahlil stepped out of the crowd a little way past Rho with her sword drawn. It took Isa a moment to recognize Strife's Bane; her sister must have stolen it from Eofar. She didn't know why Lahlil was no longer wearing the eye-patch but her scarred face looked pathetically naked without it.

The girl let out a tiny whine, and Isa realized she'd been digging her elbow harder into the child's sternum. She loosened the pressure a little, but warned Lahlil, "If you do anything to Ani, I'll kill you."

"Don't distress yourself, child. Lahlil won't harm me," said Ani easily. "We mean too much to each other."

"She used me, Isa, like she's using you now," Lahlil insisted.

"I gave you the elixir, Lahlil," Ani soothed, addressing her sister with a warmth deeper than Isa had ever heard before. "I set you on this path. I sent you home. Your vision, Lahlil, you remember, yes? I was there with you. I remember how you wept when I told you I loved you."

Lahlil did not respond but Isa felt a thread of panic weaving through her attempt to maintain control. "You used me," her older sister repeated, but she sounded less certain.

"No, child," Ani told Lahlil, "I *made* you. You belong by my side: my general, my glorious champion. Don't fret. I forgive you this little rebellion. I've yet to show you what it truly means to belong to someone. Once you understand, we'll have no more of these disagreements."

It was happening all over again. Isa had found someone to care about her and now Lahlil was going to take her away like she always did. *Poor Lahlil,* her mother had said. *Don't tell anyone about her, Isa. It's a secret. You're so lucky you're not cursed; you don't have to be imprisoned in a secret room; your arm isn't covered in scars. Poor, poor Lahlil.*

"You *bitch,*" Isa shouted at her sister, blackness roiling up out of her quaking limbs. "You're *not* going to take Ani away from me. You don't belong here. None of this would have happened if

Mother had let you die! You were a baby—babies die all the time. Why couldn't you?"

"Shut up, Isa," Rho pleaded. "Just *stop talking*."

"This is pointless, Isa," said Lahlil. "You can't stride to the Shadar. You don't have a blood connection. There's no one left from our family there."

Isa's blood drained away until nothing was left in her veins but the acid burn of humiliation. Only now did she remember waiting in the rain while Lahlil handed over a page of *The Book of the Hall* stained with Trey's blood. *No one*, said her sister's voice. *No one left.* They were all dead—her father and her sister Frea; her mother buried in the ruined temple.

"My arm is still there in the temple somewhere," she spat out. Each word felt like coughing up a stone. "There's a piece of *me* there. That should be good enough."

"And then what?" Rho hurled at her. "What do you think is going to happen if you get Ani there?"

"The Shadari need Ani to keep them safe. Daryan can't do it; he's not strong enough. He was never supposed to rule; he's not even an asha. Only Ani has the power to save them."

"Do they *want* her to save them? Because according to Harotha, they went to an awful lot of trouble to get rid of her a few hundred years ago, and then took some pretty drastic actions to keep it that way."

Rho's stupidity made her wish she was close enough to strike him. "And the Shadari made themselves so weak that we were able to conquer them with two ships and a few half-dead triffons. Harotha saw a war in her vision, then decided which side was right and which was wrong, based on her own prejudices. The ashas were *jealous* of Ani—that war was *their* fault. Ani's made sure that won't happen this time."

"How has she done that?" asked Lahlil gently.

Isa would have blamed the pain lashing into her for her failing to see the trap in her sister's question, and for not noticing the figure in the striped robes standing off to the side, his bright red hair setting him apart from the Iratians. But at the time she wanted only to prove to her sister and to Rho that they weren't as superior as they thought, and that she knew exactly what she was doing.

"She left behind acolytes and told them to watch for the signs that she'd be coming back. They're making sure no ashas are left to rebel this time—*that*'s why she made a poison that wouldn't hurt anyone except the ashas, even if they took it by mistake."

"So poisoning Jachad and Callia was not part of the plan?" asked Lahlil.

"No, no, that was a mistake! Ani never ordered that. One of the acolytes must have overreached. She's going to find out who did that and—"

A muffled thump cut her off, and then the night around her went darker as two balls of flame curled into being. The child under Isa's arm wailed and pressed back against her, clamping both hands down on her own neck as if she was choking herself. Isa didn't understand what was happening until she saw blood sliding out beneath the girl's fingers and the dark trail on the edge of Fortune's Blight where she'd cut her by accident. She pushed the child away as her goal abruptly changed: *lop off Jachad's hands before he could throw that fire*. Let him know what it felt like to reach for something and never grasp it; let him dream of being whole again, only to wake up and force himself to endure the horror and loss all over again.

She brought Blood's Pride up to her shoulder and attacked, her mind already dispassionately lining up every movement of her body as she cut into the path between Ani and her attacker. Her vision went red as the wild flames ripped straight toward her and heat slammed into her.

. . . blackened flesh flaking away from white bone, thick poisoned blood seeping into carved lines of the tomb . . .

A body slammed her sideways and the planks of the boardwalk

rushed up at her. With no hand but the one holding her sword to break her fall, a nail-head gouged a divot above one eye and she jammed her left shoulder hard enough to dislocate it. Worse, Blood's Pride kicked out of her hand and rattled away out of reach. Rho made a grab for her ankle when she tried to scramble away, but she kicked out at him until she connected with something solid. As soon as he stopped pawing at her, she rolled to her feet and looked to see if Ani had been hurt, but she wasn't standing where she had been a moment ago, nor could Isa find her in the sudden confusion. Dozens of small fires had managed to catch, even in the damp wood, and a thick, greenish smoke spread through the air as some of the Iratians rushed around stamping them out.

"Ani," she cried, her eyes darting around the burning wood near where she'd seen her last, but it was difficult to see with blood running into her eye. She was concentrating so hard that she'd forgotten about Rho until he grabbed her arm and turned her around to face him. <Let me go!>

<I'm sorry, but no,> said Rho, his terrible sincerity pulling her down like a millstone. Rho wasn't *supposed* to be sincere. He was supposed to be flippant and sarcastic and to make everything feel like one big, inconsequential joke the gods were playing on all of them.

<So did Lahlil take you to bed?> she asked him, writhing as he pinned her arm behind her back and wrapped his other arm around her midsection like an iron bar, holding her tight against him. He was stronger than she remembered. <Is that why you're trailing after *her* now, like the good little dog you are?>

<Stop it,> Rho snapped, moving her legs between his and pinning them too when she tried to kick him. <It's not like that.>

<Not like what? Not like when you murdered Dramash's mother so Frea would screw you again?>

Her words sliced through him like a hot knife, just as she knew they would. The moment his grip loosened, she wriggled around far enough to spike her knee into his groin, precisely as he'd taught her. His scream bottomed out into a bone-deep groan and he doubled over, losing any chance of holding on to her.

She sprinted forward and scooped up Blood's Pride and aimed for his back—a coward's death for a liar and a coward—but he lunged out of the way, stumbling on some spilled cabbages, punting one into the swamp. He shouldn't have been able to evade her, but she could feel the buzzing in her head and the pain twisting through her slowing her down. She pivoted on one foot and went for him again, but this time he got his sword up in time to block her. She hammered at him, slashing blows to either side, driving him back to the wormy railings, but he blocked each attack as if they were just sparring in one of the temple's empty, echoing chambers. He never made any real attempt to hit her.

<You remember on the beach, that day?> Rho asked. He meant the day the temple fell; that day didn't need a name. <In spite of everything I'd done, you said you would still be my friend. I want you to know, when you're ready to come back, you've already been forgiven.>

He was lying, pretending to care about her, but it was too late. Nothing he had to say was of any importance—not unless it led them to Dramash. He was late sweeping her next thrust aside and the very tip of her blade ripped through his shirt and scraped along his ribs before falling away. He winced and staggered back, covering up the line of blue blood with his forearm.

. . . *leaning over him as he bled out on the beach, feeling the brush of his lips for the first and last time* . . .

Then a flash froze everything in a stark tableau: Jachad stood curled over himself in the middle of an inferno, fire pouring from his hands and pooling around him. He had lost control again, like on the *Argent*. Lahlil hovered as close as she could get without being consumed. Then, with another thump of pressure in her ears, the fire snuffed out all at once and Jachad collapsed, unnaturally still, although sparks were still flickering between his fingers and tracing around his blue irises.

A triffon swooped by low over their heads, stirring up the smoke and fanning the still-burning fires. The people in the crowd hoisted up their children and their belongings and ran for the nearest doorway or fled down the street. The beast landed where the boards were wider, its heavy feet shaking the deck and its tail tearing through the railings like kindling. Isa needed to find Ani and get her away from here, but the movement of the crowd was confusing her: too many bodies moving around, too many shadows, too much noise, too many people gawking at her like they had discovered some kind of obscene curiosity.

She just wanted to go home.

"Isa." Ani stepped out from the little corner where she'd tucked herself, so well hidden that it looked to Isa like she'd emerged from thin air.

"Are you hurt?" Isa asked as she rushed over, scanning her for blood or bent limbs.

"No, no, child." The old woman breathed out, leaning on Isa's shoulder for a moment. A second triffon landed and the pier rocked beneath them. Any more weight and the whole thing would give way. "But I'm afraid your strider friends will be of no use to us after this unfortunate débâcle and we must get away, yes? Those triffons are from the Norlander garrison here."

<You!> someone behind her shouted. <Norlander! Stay where you are.> A soldier came stomping up the boards, her sludgy mixture of profound boredom and contempt for everything in her field of vision reminding her of Tara Peltran. A perfectly stitched Eotan wolf's head leered out from the front of her tabard. Two more soldiers jogged up behind her and a third triffon swung by overhead. They were heading straight for Rho, who was still bleeding, and Lahlil, who was waiting two paces away while Jachad got back on his feet.

"Ah," Ani breathed as the guards drew their black-bladed swords.

"I can take them," Isa vowed, even as she clenched up against a wave of agony that made her want to drop down onto the boards and curl into a ball.

"I know, child," Ani said gently, pulling out the long pin. "This is a small matter for me. You can help me the way we practiced on the *Argent*."

Isa whimpered as the old woman pricked her hand, "Please, I don't want to drink that stuff again."

"You needn't," Ani reassured her. "The dose you took earlier should still be effective enough."

The sword being held by the nearest guard flew back, taking his arm along with it, jerking him backward across the boards in a helpless stagger. Before he could recover, the guard nearest to him swung around and slashed him across the left side of his neck. Blood showered from the cut, pattering down on the boards when he fell, followed by a hollow boom as the second guard finally thought to drop his sword.

Isa writhed as those phantom, bony fingers dug into her again, but she couldn't make it stop. She remembered Ravindal, and how Ani and Dramash had turned the guards' weapons on each other as they came up the narrow stairway. But this was different, so—

The word she wanted slipped out of reach as the buildings in front of her began to sway.

The third guard had had the presence of mind to drop his black-bladed sword, but the moment he let go of the hilt, it snapped back around and impaled him. The last of the Iratians had already fled as Ani forced the guards to attack each other and Isa felt the edges of the hollow void inside her crumbling away. Voices screamed in her head, along with the clang of steel on steel, the thumping of boots running and bodies falling, the thud as a sword notched into bone. There was blood, blood every-where, and it should have filled up the hole inside her but nothing ever would.

At some point, Ani released her. Isa's eyes wouldn't focus long enough for her to see more than an image at a time: an orange glow; a face with ice-blue eyes; a bloody hand reaching for her; the turning line of a blade in motion. And all the while, whispered words told her where to walk, what to grasp, when to climb, what to buckle. The triffon took off the very moment the whistle passed through Isa's cracked lips and they rose up through the smoke and fog, Isa marveling that her body could continue to function when her mind kept sinking down lower and lower into the comfort of darkness, begging for release.

Chapter 11

Lahlil couldn't reach Jachad in time to catch him before he sank to his knees on the boardwalk, but an instant later she had both hands on his shoulders and was supporting him while sparks circled his blue eyes. The planks around them had caught fire in places, but the damp wood had resisted the worst of Jachad's conflagration.

"Jachi," she called to him when he didn't look at her. She had to get him out of the open. "Jachi, please—stay with me."

"Tell me something you see," he demanded, his voice cracked and smoke-roughened.

"What?"

"Something you see."

He sounded so desperate; she obeyed without trying to understand. She focused on the place she had already picked out as a likely shelter. "A shack."

"More. Something specific."

"The door is open," she answered. The shouting coming from further down the street intensified and she could see the black-bladed swords jerking their owners around like the inmates of a madhouse: Ani's power at work, and Isa standing beside her as blank as a doll. Norlander screams of pain—tellingly short-lived—burst inside her head. "No lights inside."

"What color is the door?"

"Red," she guessed, although she could barely make it out in the fog.

"Show me."

She was about to point when she realized he meant it literally, so she moved a hand up to his cheek and carefully turned his head until the shack was within his line of vision. His stubbled cheek felt feverish, his skin too dry, especially considering the humidity. She pushed her fingers into his hair, smoothing the red strands curled up in front of his ear. When he shifted enough that he was no longer relying on her to hold him up, she circled her arm around his chest and pulled him to his feet, then got him walking toward the shack. People ran by, either to escape or help put out the fires; they all pretended not to see them.

One small room with a chair, two stools and a table encrusted with burned-out candle-ends. He pulled away from her as they entered and stood alone, looking out through the half-open door.

"My mother," he said, "when I . . . drifted. She would describe things to me and get me to look at them."

"I'll remember."

"I didn't have control. If I had kept on, I would have burned down the whole pier." An edge to his voice made her think he wasn't happy with his decision. "They escaped?"

Isa and Ani were gone. She didn't know what had happened to Rho, or Savion. Jachad wouldn't look at her.

"I lost them in the crowd," she admitted. "They got to a triffon."

Rho chose that moment to elbow his way through the door. One look at the pinched line of his mouth and her eyes dropped to the bloody rent in his shirt. <We're supposed to believe "the Mongrel" let them get away? What's happened to you?>

<"The Mongrel" would have had no problem letting Isa cut that girl's throat,> she reminded him. <How bad is that wound?>

He flinched away from her hand when she tried to pull up his shirt. <Never mind that. We've got to go after them. We can steal

a couple of triffons from the guards. We might still be able to catch up to them if you stop dawdling.>

There was no way Jachad could ride a triffon now. If he lost control of his powers while they were flying, they would burn or crash, or both. <Isa isn't stupid enough to fly in a straight line, not when she expects us to pursue her. We won't catch them that way.>

<Then how do you propose we stop them before they get there?> he asked. <You saw Ani kill those guards with their own swords, didn't you? Do you have any idea what she could do once she gets to the Shadar?>

<The ore in those swords is concentrated enough for ordinary people to wield them. Her powers are still limited without Dramash.>

<You don't know that,> Rho snapped. <If you don't want to go after them, I'll go myself.>

<There's no point. You've already proved you won't hurt Isa, and she knows it. She'll kill you before you get anywhere near Ani. Besides, you're wounded.>

<As if that's unusual. I'm indestructible, remember?>

<No, you're not! So next time a sword or a fireball is coming at you, *you get out of the damned way!*>

Savion slipped through the door and kicked it shut behind him, blocking out the light from the street so the only illumination came from his yellow eyes and the soft glow of Rho's skin. Normally Jachad would have conjured a spark between his fingers to light one of the candle-ends, but he didn't do it now.

Savion did snap his fingers at her to get her attention. "You see what she did, *your* sister. To children! Pay for it, and not with gold, follow?" he announced in his thickly accented Iratian before folding his arms and glaring at her. "Won't let her hurt my family. We're going after them."

"You can't stride to them," Lahlil had to tell him.

Savion jabbed one of his gnarled fingers at her. "Your *sister.* Plenty of blood."

130

"She's on a triffon. *Flying.*"

"Eyah," the strider muttered as he saw the problem.

Rho kicked the leg of the table. <Might I remind you, *again*, there are triffons saddled out there and ready to go.>

Lahlil braced her hands on the table and looked down at the blobs of candlewax. <Isa will need at least three days to get to the Shadar by triffon.>

"My caravan is outside the Shadar right now," Jachad quietly informed them. Lahlil hadn't even known he was listening.

"My nephew Oshi is with them," she said, straightening up. "Savion can use my blood to take us to the Nomas. We'll stay in the desert until the timing is right, then stride straight to Ani and Isa. We'll be able to take them by surprise.>

<Do I have a choice about this plan?> asked Rho.

<No.>

Rho pulsed with frustration, but Lahlil preferred his blunt-fisted anger to Jachad's disengagement. <Fine. At least it'll get the smell of the swamp out of my clothes.>

"My nephew, in the desert," she told Savion, passing him her knife. "My brother's child. Will the connection be strong enough?" He rolled his eyes and reached for the blade, but she pulled it back. "Don't lie to me."

"Not lying. My hide, too, follow?" he sniffed, and then made a poor show of carelessness before he squared his narrow shoulders and grinned up at her. "Never been to the desert."

<This is going to make me sick, isn't it?> asked Rho. <No, never mind. I don't want to know. In case I haven't mentioned it yet today, I hate you.>

The stride yanked them away from Prol Irat and the mess on the pier and into the now-familiar black tunnel with its streaking lights and crushing sense of speed. It didn't take long for Lahlil to realize something wasn't right. The pressure in her ears kept changing from a piercing shriek to a bone-shuddering roar, and even in the darkness she had the sense they were weaving like a

131

child trying to carry something too heavy. She couldn't tell if Jachad still had his hand on Savion's sleeve—after refusing the hand she'd offered him—but Rho had gone from gripping her shoulder to wrapping his arm around her neck in a panic, nearly throttling her. If she lost her grip on Savion now they would both go spinning out into whatever they were passing through; ocean, mountain, desert, swamp—the terrain wouldn't matter much after the speed of their descent had ground their bones to jelly.

Her tainted blood: the connection to her nephew, who was only half-Eotan himself, wasn't strong enough. The stride was going wrong and it was her fault.

The blackness blurred a shade or two closer to gray, then the tunnel twitched like a fishing line and threw her to the side. Rho's arm tightened around her neck as the force of their speed tried to rip them apart. He shouted something, but she ignored him, focusing all her attention on stopping the slow slide of her fingers from Savion's wrist. She had no leverage; no way to twist her body around and change her position; no way to use her other arm to reach out for Jachad.

The light shifted much too quickly from gray into a hazy gold, then her grip failed. Savion yelled something, but the wind stretched out the sounds until they were unrecognizable. Rho loosened his arms around her neck at the exact moment she needed him to hold on and the wind tore him from her. She was alone; alone, and falling. The ground rushed toward her, flat and hard and bright. Her body would hardly make a mark in all that sand.

Strife's Bane rammed into her shoulders when she landed, but the force of the impact hardly slowed her speed at all and she found herself pitching over into an uncontrolled roll, tumbling down and down with the rigid sword endangering her neck and spine with every revolution. She grabbed for anything she might be able to hang onto, but there was nothing solid, and the sand just flayed her clawed hands. When the rolling finally started to slow she thought the worst was over—then came the rocks, cracking against her bones and digging their sharp points into her flesh.

Then something hit the back of her head and finally, everything *stopped*.

She might have blacked out. The moment she opened her eyes, bright light speared straight into her skull and she rolled onto her stomach before it blinded her completely, blinking away the colored spots until she could see well enough to check out her surroundings. The rocky field continued on toward the south for as far as she could see. Dunes hemmed her in on the other three sides, one of them cut through with a trench made by her tumbling descent. The way the wind was blowing, her mark wouldn't last long.

A jolt of blinding pain went through her head when she tried to stand up and her probing fingers found a gritty patch of blood soaking the back of her hair and a hard lump underneath. Worse, her eyes wouldn't adjust to the light, even when she squinted and shaded them with her hands. The climb back up the dune was like a slog through cold treacle. Near the top she lost her balance and slid a third of the way down again before she managed to dig in her heels. On the next attempt she managed to pull herself up the last steep bit on her hands and knees.

She was alone. Totally, completely alone.

The most she could make out was a swollen sun, a charcoal smear of what might be storm clouds to the east, and dunes, dunes and more dunes.

There was no Nomas caravan. No oasis. No Savion. No Rho. No Jachad.

"Jachi!" she called out, but the name dropped from her lips like a lead weight. She tried calling for Rho in Norlander, but with even less hope. There was no way he could survive on his own in the desert. That was all she managed before the ache in her head pressed her down to her knees, then kept on pressing until the warm sand was cushioning her head and the wind was hissing a lullaby.

A thumping noise, faint but rhythmic, made its way through the blood pulsing in her ears. The moment she tried to look up, the brightness slammed into her like a fist, but she could still see the dark spot moving in front of the sun. It had no shape at first, but when she wiped the burning tears from her eyes she saw a tail snaking down and the graceful undulations of its wings.

The triffon was still far away, but she lurched to her feet and shouted, <I'm here!> The words ripped straight out of her chest as if they had been swelling there her whole life. <Over here!>

The triffon veered around and she started to run toward it— but no, it would be easier for them to reach her on top of the dune. Shairav had told her to wait right here until he came back for her. It would be dark soon, so he had to come back before then. Meena would be missing her.

<I'm here!> she called out again as the triffon's elongated shadow raced up and down the dunes. She had been out here such a long time and she was so thirsty.

<Lahlil!>

Mother had come to take her home. Maybe she wouldn't have to go back in her room any more.

<Lahlil! Stay there! I'm coming to get you.>

Through the slits between her fingers and past her mother's billowing white cloak, she saw the two smaller figures in the saddle. She didn't know why her mother had brought her sisters. There wasn't enough room in the saddle for all of them.

"Turn back," growled an unfamiliar voice. "Turn back."

The triffon swept closer and closer and her mother's joy wrapped her up like a hug, like a cool hand on her forehead.

"No!" the voice said again, a wild snarl that ached in Lahlil's throat. "Turn back! I'll destroy you. I destroy everything."

She knew what was going to happen next, but she couldn't look away: her mother was leaning out over the side of the triffon, both hands trying to tie the harness around Isa while she slipped further and further; she felt her own terror, and her mother's and her sisters', until Lahlil began to run. She ran until her mother's scream lanced through her; ran until she saw the splash of blood where the body had bounced, the white cape twisted around a mess of pulp and bone. The shadow of the triffon as it turned around and flew away with Frea at the reins, leaving her alone.

Alone.

Her vision whited out and then went black and she thought this was better; this time she would die in the desert. All of those people she'd killed as the Mongrel would have to find some other way to die; she would never drive a wedge between Cyrrin and Trey, never be drawn into Ani's schemes, never go back to the Shadar and rip it apart. This time Jachad would grow up, live a comfortable life, marry Callia and die surrounded by spoiled grandchildren.

Then a cool presence flooded her mind, and along with it came a steady voice, beautifully composed. <What happened here wasn't your fault. You were a child.>

Lahlil's vision cleared again and she spun around, kicking through the deep sand as she sought the speaker. There was no one there.

<You did not cause this, Lahlil. You are not to blame.>

Tears finally soothed her burning eyes and she curled up in the sand, tightly wrapping her arms around herself, as she waited for the wind to wear her down.

<This is all your fault. I really should leave you here.>

Lahlil suspected the voice was actually there this time, but she was still having trouble sorting out hallucinations and dreams from reality.

<Oh, for Onfar's sake, I didn't—Lahlil, wake up. Come on. Wake up.> He was shaking her, one hand on her shoulder and his knee digging into her back. <You can't sleep any more now. Your head

is bleeding and your hair is full of sand. We need to do something about that or you'll get an infection on top of the concussion. How you're not dead already is beyond me.>

<Rho.> Boulders loomed over them; she didn't remember seeing any boulders before. The shadows weren't as long as they should have been, either. No landmarks, no signs of life except Rho's footprints in the sand and a telltale furrow. <What happened? Did you carry me here?>

<Carry, drag,> he mused, watching her pupils for a moment before circling round behind her to start poking at her head. <That's striding, is it? Thank you for introducing me to an even more suicidal way to travel.>

<It's not supposed to be like that; something went wrong. The others?>

Dab, dab, dab. When he started winding the bandage around her head, she realized he was stalling for time. <I'm sorry, but it's just us. What's the plan? Wait until dark and head east?>

<We're not equipped to cross the desert.> Not to mention the way her vision had gone blurry in spots and how she was having trouble holding up the lead weight that had replaced her head.

<We'll die here once we run out of water, so what's the difference?> asked Rho.

<Dying with your skin still attached to your body,> Lahlil answered. His flush colored the air between them for a moment, a twist of warm red in her gut, before he waved it away like he was clearing smoke. <We'll wait here for the caravan to find us.>

He blew out a breath and came around in front of her again, grimacing as he wiggled himself into a crevice between the rocks. Blue veins stood out in his neck and sweat dripped down his forehead and soaked his hair but the blood on his shirt had dried and she could see the darkly cauterized stripe underneath where he'd closed the wound.

<Then you think the others survived?> he asked.

<Yes.>

<Why?>

<Because they didn't have *you* choking them.> The real answer—that Jachad *couldn't* be dead because nothing would matter then—made her head hurt worse, so she closed her eyes and watched the shifting colors behind her eyelids.

The sun slid down and eventually her fatigue overcame the thumping in her head and she fell asleep leaning back against the rocks. At some point she opened her eyes on a black sky full of winking stars and dragged herself back to consciousness long enough to tuck Rho's cape around him to protect him from the morning sun. Grentha had made her promise to look after "her boy," and no one made light of a promise to the first mate of the *Argent*.

After that she dreamed of bells—little tinkling bells—and the sound brought memories of long days and nights surrounded by music and cheerful voices, when no one was ever alone.

"So a rock is all it takes to get through that thick skull?" said a woman's voice. Efficient hands were doing something with her head. "Wish I'd known that years ago. No, no, you stay right there until I've had a look at you, too. I know it's closed but it's a nasty piece of business."

"Mairi."

The woman hummed and moved the lamp back a little bit, giving Lahlil a blurry view of the Nomas healer's messy hair and sharp eyes.

"I didn't save Jachad," said Lahlil. "He's alive, but I didn't save him."

Mairi's face faded back into the darkness. "I know. I've seen to him already. But alive is better than I would have done for him, and a lot better than dead. Come on." A tug on her elbow pulled her up and Lahlil went where she was guided, not really feeling like her feet were touching the ground. The tinkling of bells came again, undeniably real this time, and she ran her hand through the shaggy manes of one of the burcapas as she passed. Then came the wagon, a blanket, the wan glow of Rho's face. Voices all around—soft, midnight voices—and then warm hands pushed her down onto a bed infused with someone else's scent; not Jachad's, but familiar in some other way.

She fell asleep to the memory of King Tobias' rich laugh outside by the bonfire and Jachi pretending to be asleep in the cot next to hers, ready to wake her if the nightmares came again.

Chapter 12

The left palace gate had stuck in the mud on the second day of rain and remained perpetually open while the untreated wood rotted and the hinges rusted. Daryan was just grateful that he could trudge in and out without waiting. He'd spent the last three days touring the worst of the flooded neighborhoods, digging gutters until his hands blistered and comforting farmers weeping over their drowned crops and stranded animals. Fatigue had heightened all his senses to the point of pain some time ago, turning his thoughts as thick and sluggish as the mud squelching inside his boots.

Tal waved at him from across the tunnel on the other side of the courtyard, which the addition of a table and stool had turned into his temporary office. The number of people seeking shelter had dwindled in the last day as word got around that the palace was full, but his staff were still working to make sure as many people as possible had access to shelter, food and clean water. Daryan acknowledged his chief steward before he pushed back his cowl and wiped the water from his face with the dry cloth Lem, appearing at his side, held out to him.

He dropped the cloth into Lem's hand and mouthed, "Tessa?"

The guard answered with a tiny shake of his head.

"By the fountain," Daryan said, leading him through the ankle-high puddles. He stuck his hands in the basin to wash off some of the mud and kept his head down, trusting to the combined noises of fountain and rain to keep his voice from carrying. "Did you find out anything about her?"

"Found out where she lived before the restoration, but she hasn't been back."

"No family?"

"None except the dead husband you told me about," said Lem. "Someone said they thought she'd mentioned a son once, but no one ever saw him. If she ever had one, he's probably dead— or should be, since he's not done a thing to take care of her that I can see."

"How did she end up working in the palace?"

"Tal hired her. I didn't think you'd want me asking him."

Daryan would have loved to have been able to say that Tal was one of the few people he trusted with his life, but right now he just couldn't. "We need a reason for you to ask. I don't think anyone would believe you're in love with her."

"I don't know her like you do," Lem admitted, leaning against one of the stone fish and petting its head, "but why not? She's a little older than me, but she's got those great freckles."

Daryan laughed in surprise. "Yes, she does."

One of the Red Guards caught sight of him from the top of the throne room steps and called, "Daimon!"

"Lieutenant?" Daryan straightened up as Tamin skipped down the steps, his buckles jingling.

"There's a man come, Daimon. Falit, son of Erdesh. Says he has information for you. Won't talk to anyone else."

"Where's Captain Omir?"

"He's been with them at the seawall since this morning."

Daryan tried to stay calm even as Tessa's warnings overwhelmed him. One persistent visitor didn't mean anything. Attention-seekers, lunatics, hustlers and schemers turned up at the palace on a daily basis, all claiming to be in possession of some priceless secret. A quick poke or two at their stories and they invariably fell apart. "Falit? Why do I know that name?"

140

"He leads one of the militias, Daimon," Lem broke in. "Big family, good to the poor. He's not like some of them ars—I mean, he's not like Binit."

"Falit from Andrasha. Thick build. Smokes a pipe." Daryan was remembering him now. "Bring him here."

They didn't have to wait long for the lieutenant to return with the portly man huffing along behind him, wiping the rain from his eyes with the tail of his scarf and biting the stem of an unlit pipe. "Daimon. I'll make this quick because I've got to get back to my people, but I didn't trust anyone else with this."

"Go on," Daryan urged.

"Mm," Falit began, worrying the pipe between his yellowed teeth. "Shemoth was a neighbor of mine—you know who I mean, the family you found murdered, all but one, anyway. Shem had a girl about the same age as my eldest, Jemma. She wasn't there with the rest of them and they never found her."

The girl with the yellow scarf. "Yes, I know who you mean."

"Right, well, earlier this morning, I saw her."

Daryan sprang forward so quickly that Lem reached for his sword in alarm. "You *saw her*? Where?"

"By the temple, where they moved the pyres. Went down there looking for—Well, don't matter. I see a girl by herself, not walking quite right, like she hit her head or something. So I start over to see if she needs help and when I get closer I think, 'If that don't look like Shem's girl—' But I didn't think anything of it really, only the resemblance. And then a rezzy comes tearing up from the pyres, grabs her and starts whispering to her so I can't make it out. And then he takes off with her and I didn't follow, because why would I? But I kept thinking about it because something was bothering me, and a little while ago it finally hit me." Falit slapped his hand against his thigh. "*Yellow.* Shem's girl always wore a yellow scarf. And this girl, she was none too clean, but her scarf was cleaner than the rest of her, like she took pains with it. And it was yellow, Daimon, yellow as the noonday sun, I swear to you. That girl was Jemma."

"And he took her away? Where?"

"Wish to the gods I knew," Falit answered, smiling ruefully. "I wish I'd gone after them. That rezzy meant her no good, I can tell you."

"Would you know him if you saw him again?"

Falit offered up a bitter smile. "Don't need to. His name is Hesh, son of nobody knows. He's been staying with Bima, for what that's worth. Her husband was an overseer, you know. Nasty piece of business," he added, before pointedly spitting into the mud.

Daryan drew his breath in with a sharp hiss and reached for his sword, all set to order Tamin to round up every Red Guard in the palace and get them out to the pyres, until Lem grabbed the front of Falit's robe and nearly pulled the man off his feet.

"It wasn't Bima's fault her husband was an overseer," Lem said, "and shit, it wasn't his fault either—the Dead Ones picked the overseers and if they picked you, you didn't say no. Most of them did the best they could. So," Lem finished, dropping his captive back down in the mud, "stop thinking you know something you don't."

The older man's face reddened with fury and he plucked the pipe from his mouth, lips mashing together while he gathered the words he wanted to spit back. But then, instead of lashing out, he drew in a deep breath, stuck the pipe back in his mouth and smoothed away the genuine rage with something as false as it was amenable. "I'm sure you've got a point there, young man," he said to Lem. "I'll keep it in mind."

Daryan broke the awkward pause that followed. "Lieutenant, assemble a troop under your command. We're leaving for the pyres at once."

"Yes, Daimon."

"Thank you, Falit. I'll let you get back to your family. I'll send word if we find Jemma."

"That's all I ask, Daimon. Good luck to you."

When both men had left, Daryan strode toward the stables

with Lem at his elbow. "Don't apologize," he said the moment he heard the younger man draw breath to speak. "I'm glad you spoke up for the overseers."

"Thanks, Daimon, but I know I shouldn't have. Falit came here to help us—shit, he told us something that could help save lives and I almost punched him."

"I almost wish you had. I would have liked to see him shrug that off, too. Does he seem like the kind of man who'd usually let someone dress him down the way you did?"

"More like the kind who'd kick me in the teeth while his friends held me down."

"It's almost like he wanted to make sure we didn't get distracted from searching for the girl."

Trakkar needed a little coaxing to leave his nice dry stable, but eventually they were skimming over the beach toward the temple ruins, where the pyres had been moved to give them a little shelter from the wind. Thanks to the storms, the high-tide line now ran straight up into the dunes, where the gaps had been filled in with sandbags; Daryan's aching back twinged again at the memory. The eastern edge of the temple ruins had been submerged since they first fell but the water had crept even further in and scavengers were busy picking through whatever had washed up. Daryan signaled Trakkar to land on an empty stretch of sand near the pyres. Only two of them were lit today; a rickety cover had been erected over them to give them some shelter. Omir had urged Daryan to shut down the resurrectionists many times, calling this a wasteful, empty ritual, and he had a point: most of the dead they "freed" went to the fire without a name or anyone to mourn them—and if their spirits *did* rise to join the gods, they were certainly showing no interest in helping those who had ushered them along.

Daryan had seen too many fires: the secret funerals in the temple; the fire in the stables when they had finally stood up against Frea Eotan, the White Wolf; the fires that had leveled whole districts the night the temple fell; the funeral pyre on which Harotha's body burned while the Shadari wept maudlin tears and he tried not to gag on the irony. Too many fires all blending together until they became the *same* fire, one that had been burning since before he was born, flaring up to consume bits of his life whenever it wanted.

Lem coughed into his hand, trying to be unobtrusive but in the end choking himself into a hacking fit. "The smoke," he explained apologetically, wiping his streaming eyes. "Sorry, Daimon."

Daryan signaled a command to the Red Guards and they charged in with their swords drawn, herding the people away from the pyres and carts and keeping them there, ignoring their shouts and ducking the occasional rock. With no one to tend it, the body on the nearest pyre soon toppled down and collapsed into a heap of blackened bones.

Lieutenant Tamin led his men methodically through the encampment, upending the packs lying on the ground and examining the carts and other conveyances. "We've got him, Daimon!" he shouted back as two guards dragged the struggling young man between the pyres. Daryan was about to go to them when Lem coughed again, this time more pointedly: Omir, surprisingly neat after a day spent allegedly doing manual labor, was striding toward them.

"Tamin sent word," the big man said as soon as he was close enough to be heard over the jeering of the crowd. "I see you've got him."

"That's all we've got unless he tells us where he's got the girl," said Daryan.

"We'll make him talk this time."

"Daimon!" the lieutenant shouted, appearing from behind the pyre and gesturing to him. "You need to see this."

"Make way," Omir told the crowd as they approached and the guards cleared a path, not to the pyre itself but to the nondescript handcart sitting nearby. It didn't take much imagination to identify the lumpy shapes beneath it.

"Over here, Daimon. I don't know if—I heard Falit's description so when I looked at the cart . . ."

Daryan stared down at the filthy blanket as the guard tailed off, angry that they couldn't have found something cleaner, even though he knew that wasn't the important point here. Tamin looked to be waiting for him to ask for it to be removed, but Daryan grabbed the corner himself and threw it aside.

The girl's robe had fallen open in the front and the marks were there: a splatter in the center and tendrils reaching out, a little more blue than black, maybe thanks to the dead girl's bloodless pallor. She was filthy: greasy hair, a ring of dirt around her neck, fingernails jagged and dirty, bare feet striated with calluses and dirt. But the yellow scarf around her neck had been kept spotless, just like Falit said. The fabric, soft from years of careful laundering, slid between his fingers when he reached out to touch it.

He tried to stand back up, but the reek of the pyres made him light-headed and clouded his eyes with a silvery mist. "She was on Hesh's cart?"

"She was, Daimon. Right on the top. If we'd got here a little later he'd have burned her right up—I'm sure that's what he did with all the others."

The guards had Hesh on his knees next to the fire, his arms pinned behind his back, tears streaming from a freshly blackened eye and blood welling in a scrape across his cheek.

Smoke clung to the inside of Daryan's throat as he struggled up; he had to cough before he could even speak. Lem mirrored his movements like a shadow.

"Why did you wait so long to kill her?" Daryan asked Hesh.

"They're making a fool out of you, Daimon," the young man lashed out. "Whoever killed Jemma and the other ashas is here right now, *laughing* at all of you, knowing they can do anything they want right under your nose because you're too stupid to catch them."

Daryan grabbed the young man and pushed his face closer to

the pyre behind him. He needed answers that made sense. "Talk to me."

"I didn't kill her—I've been *hiding* her." Hesh explained desperately. "This morning, when I went to bring her some food, she was gone."

"Daimon, let go," said Lem, his face bright red in the firelight. "You don't want to do that."

"Stay back," Omir rasped. "The daimon can do what he likes."

"Gods, why are you so *stupid*?" Hesh shouted. "Can't you see they put her on my pyre to blame me, like they tried to hide the poison in Bima's house?"

Sweat dripped down into Daryan's eyes and he let go of Hesh with one hand to wipe it away. The resurrectionist pushed back hard, breaking his hold, but there was no place to go; they were completely surrounded.

Lem darted between them and gripped the boy's shoulder in one of his big hands, forcing him back to his knees.

"Someone's been telling you exactly what you want to hear," Hesh panted, looking at him squarely. His earlier tears had washed some of the dirt from his face and for the first time, Daryan noticed the dense patches of freckles on the crest of both cheekbones and the shape of the wide mouth, unfamiliar only because it was usually turned down in a scowl. Hesh had never mentioned his parents' names, only that his father had died in the mines. Like Tessa's husband. Tessa, who had been so upset about the raid on Bima's house that she'd taken divining elixir and confessed to being an asha.

"Let's arrest him, Daimon," Lem broke in, "and get him out of here. You've got a lot of agitation going on right now."

Daryan wiped the sweat from his face again as another coughing fit swelled in his chest. He pulled his stomach muscles tight, trying to stave it off, afraid if he did start coughing he would end up vomiting. "Take him back to the palace and lock him up. We have cause now."

"Tamin can take him back," said Omir, and raised his hand to call the soldier over.

"I want him riding with you, Lem," said Daryan. He snapped open the clasps on his jacket one by one, feeling stifled by the damp heat. "He couldn't have done this alone. Whoever he's working with might try to kill him before we can get it out of him. You understand what I'm telling you."

"I do, Daimon. No one'll lay a finger on him."

"Take Trakkar. I'll go back with Omir."

Lem went about the task of binding up the prisoner for flying while Daryan tapped Omir on the back and gestured toward the dereshadi he'd left lumbering along the beach. Shells crunched under his feet when he crossed the high-tide mark and the foamy surf hissed up over the tops of his boots. The sea and sky had darkened to the same shade of ash-gray. A flock of pickwings scurried up and down by the water's edge, pecking up tiny molluscs. He tried to take a deep breath, but the smoke he'd swallowed rattled in his lungs.

"How did you get here so quickly?" he asked Omir. "I didn't even think to have Tamin send for you."

"When I got back to the palace they told me I'd just missed you, so I followed."

"Oh," said Daryan, watching as a big, dark wave crested and broke close to shore. "I know it doesn't really make sense, but I can't help thinking I might have saved Jemma if only I'd taken the elixir. I might have seen where she was hiding before they got to her."

Omir made a noise in the back of his throat, but didn't say anything else.

"You'd better get some rest when we get back," said Daryan. "You're going to be there for the interrogation, won't you? We have to get to the bottom of this, and I can't do it without you."

"Of course, Daimon."

They walked up the slope side by side but Daryan had to

work to keep up with the weight of his sword pulling him down into the soft sand. He felt like he was in a dream, a nightmare, running toward Isa through the temple corridors, already knowing he would be too late to save her from burning.

Chapter 13

On their second day out from Prol Irat, Isa and Ani flew over the plague town.

Isa almost didn't notice; Ani had been regularly administering her medicine since their escape and it had banked down deep among the roots of her nerves, flowing outward to wash away the pain in her arm and the cuts on her face. It had even pushed Rho's duplicity and her sister's betrayal down into the deeps. She had stopped wondering if the edges of the hole inside her would stay fixed, or if the emptiness would bubble up out of it until it consumed her entirely.

She felt no danger or even curiosity when the slender tower appeared in the distance, or when they flew close enough to see the terraced streets wrapped within a winding outer wall. There were birds everywhere: lining the tops of the walls, perched on the roofs, flocking in strange sweeps and swirls, flittering to the ground and coming back up again with tidbits dangling from their beaks.

Later, she would think that Lahlil would have understood about the birds, and she would have noticed right away that the gates had been boarded up from the *outside*, not the inside. But Isa did begin to feel *something* about it as they got closer, although it took her two passes over the town to notice that the smoke shrouding the rooftops was not coming from the chimneys, and another to realize that the silvery glow from within the deepest shadows was not reflected sunlight.

"How did the sickness get out of Norland? And so far south?" she asked Ani the next time they stopped to rest.

"Greed," said Ani. "A few coins in the right hand, a few boxes loaded onto a boat, a few barrels into a cart, a few warm nights."

"There's no way to cure it—it's not cold enough to snow here."

"Cure it? No," Ani agreed, "not yet. But I promised you I will protect the Shadar once we get there. Don't concern yourself, child."

And with the medicine soothing her back into the fog, she didn't.

The terrain the following day alternated between dense woods and rocky cliffs, making it difficult to find any place to set down, but at dusk she landed on a strip of open ground near the snaking black line of a stream, while a flock of shrieking birds poured out of the canopy. She hunted for firewood; the scent of the leaves crunching under her boots reminded her of something—damp paper, maybe?—while the shifting light made her suddenly aware of the fatigue that had been pulling at her eyelids. A vine with a barbed stem and furred leaves kept catching in her glove and she had to keep stopping to pull thorns out with her teeth. She had figured out how to light a fire one-handed by shoving a flint in the dirt and bracing it with her foot so she could strike. By the time the kindling caught, cold sweat had crawled beneath her hairline and her fingers were trembling.

"You've bloodied your face, child," said Ani.

"There were thorns."

"Those scrapes will need to be cleaned."

Isa tried not to hiss at the sting of the pungent mixture, or to stare too openly into Ani's pack. Her next dose of medicine was in there somewhere, but she couldn't ask for it; that always made the time come a little slower.

After Ani finished applying a cooling salve to her cuts, her face softened into its crinkly smile. "You have a comb in your pocket.

Give it to me." She untied the leather strap holding Isa's braid in place and began to ease the knots out of the tangled mess. "We can't have you looking like a beggar when we get to the Shadar, can we?"

"No," she breathed out, settling again at the rhythmic tugging of her hair. A long shudder went through her. "Lahlil will still come after us, but I'll be ready."

Ani sighed. "There's no need. You must allow your sister to act according to her nature."

"She betrayed you! Rho and Jachad tried to kill you and she sided with them."

"I'm afraid you'll never understand her as I do," Ani said gently, running the comb through in long strokes now that she'd managed the knots. "Destruction and death are Lahlil's purpose. To pretend otherwise? That would have been the betrayal. All the ills of this world come from people denying their true natures, Isa."

Isa didn't understand that at all but she knew Ani would just sigh if she asked for an explanation. The fire took hold of one of the bigger branches and the eager, snapping flames leaped up. Isa's neck stiffened and she tried not to look down at the center of herself, at the hole left behind by Ani's experiment. "What about me? What's my nature?"

"Loyalty," said Ani instantly. "Your nature is to serve with your whole heart."

By the time the combing stopped, the sky had darkened to cobalt above the restless fringe of the treetops. Isa lay on her side, hoarding the warmth of the fire until she woke shivering a few hours later with weakness pinning her body down and the taste of rot in her mouth. A vial of medicine lay on the blanket beside her and Ani was fast asleep under her pile of blankets.

She didn't need to take it all. She could take half—or even less, maybe a quarter—to prove to Nisha and the rest of them that she did still have a choice. As if choosing to be in pain was some twisted kind of virtue . . . She would keep the rest in her pocket without saying anything to Ani yet. It would make a nice surprise when it came time for her next dose. Ani would praise her restraint and courage.

A quarter of the bottle would only be a few drops, which would be pointless, really. Better to start with half. The syrup pooled on her tongue as she measured it out drop by drop; it disappeared down her throat with the first swallow. Pain throbbed in her shoulder but the numbness would come soon, rolling over her with its pollen-tinted fog. She lay back and waited, already breathing more deeply in anticipation. A dozen inhales and exhales went by and nothing changed except the cold jutting into her bones as if the fire had started working in reverse, sucking the heat from her marrow. The pain in her arm was getting worse and worse; worse than in Prol Irat; worse than on the *Argent*.

She should have asked Ani—maybe taking too little was as dangerous as taking too much? Maybe the pain would never stop now. Ani would be angry that she'd taken it upon herself to decide how much to take; she'd gone behind Ani's back; she'd been *disloyal*. By the time she got the stopper out again, her hand was shaking so badly she was terrified she'd spill it before she got it into her mouth.

When Ani woke less than an hour later, Isa had filled their water skins, inspected the harness, packed their supplies and doused the fire. Ani braided her hair before they left.

The next time they stopped, Isa dreamed of the sea, her lungs burning, looking for the light to find her way to the surface, breaching only to gag on the fabric of a white cape spread over the water.

On the blanket next to her was the vial, filled again. She drank every drop.

Chapter 14

Lahlil jolted awake to the sight of striped tent-cloth rippling above her and choked on a breath of relief. A horrific plague, her baby sister corrupted, Jachad turning into a god—it had all been a nightmare. But the hand she raised to wipe the sweat from her neck was too veined and scarred to maintain the illusion that she was still a young girl, and when she finally looked beside her, there was no second cot and no ginger-headed boy. By the time she'd drunk some water, washed her face and buckled on her sword, the years and their misdeeds had settled back down on her shoulders.

Rho loped out from the shady space between two wagons the moment she ducked out of the tent, his sun-proof cape buttoned all the way up and the cowl so low she couldn't see his eyes. <Nice of you to join us.>

<How long was I out?>

<A day and a half, and if you're going to scold me for not waking you, don't, because it could have been worse. According to the very rude woman who claims to be their healer—despite having all the tenderness of a rabid bear—you knocked your brains loose on those rocks and I wasn't supposed to let you sleep. So thank you for not dying.>

<That's Mairi. Did she look at your wound?>

Rho actually shuddered and changed the subject. <This is bad, Lahlil. Apparently the Nomas have been preparing to go to war

153

with the Shadari for months now. They have two thousand people here ready to fight. We can't let them do that.>

<A full-scale attack will accomplish nothing; Daryan didn't even know about the poison. Didn't Jachad explain about Ani?>

The veil over his emotions slipped a moment and his ambivalence swirled around her, dusty and dry. <Jachad hasn't said much to anyone. Wait, Lahlil, we need to talk about how we get Isa away from Ani.>

<I told you before: Isa's made her choices and now she has to live with them.>

<And that's the end of it, is it? It's not as if *you* threw her into Ani's arms.> Rho stood his ground in front of her, not giving an inch. <People in the Shadar are going to suffer and Isa will blame herself—if she even survives. For Onfar's sake, you and I know what that's like better than anyone. You would really condemn her to that?>

The clasps on his white cloak lost their sharp edges and she nearly reached up to adjust her absent eye-patch. <Nothing I say to her will make a difference. She made it clear in Prol Irat what she thinks of me.>

<Then don't say anything. Take her away by force.>

<I can't—I have to stay with Jachad.>

<Why?> Frustration swelled around him, pushing at her. <He doesn't need your help to burn things down. Why do you have to stay with him?>

Her answer took shape and then crumbled in her mind before she could make herself recognize the words, much less say them. Because she had promised Cyrrin, Nisha, Jachad himself: she'd promised them all that she would kill Jachad before he hurt any innocent people. But she couldn't tell Rho that because then it would be real; inevitable. <I just do. You don't need to know why.>

He remained in her path, making her wait while he decided whether or not to accept her answer. Finally he stepped out of her way but he gripped her shoulder, squeezed once, and then let her go. She could still feel the coolness of his fingers as she followed him toward the center of the camp.

This was not a normal Nomas camp. The rows of tents and wagons snaked around in a haphazard maze, nothing like the usual neat arrangements. No one stood around talking, smoking or tending cooking fires, and not a single small child could be seen or heard. Rho pulled her through an ally between rows of wagons and out into a gathering space with a bonfire in the center. Behr, Jachad's wagonmaster, sat alone on one of the scattered cushions, tapping his thumb against his lips. Two men she recognized as leaders of other caravans stood close together, talking and gesticulating. The captain of the *Windward*, a woman with a row of silver earrings in one ear and eyes lined with kohl, thoughtfully pared her nails with her knife. The rest were largely strangers to her, except of course for Jachad, who stood with his head tilted up to the sky and his red hair catching the last of the light like strands of copper wire.

The rattling of Callia's bracelets turned everyone's attention to the sight of her sweeping toward them with Mairi behind her like a combination guard dog, nursemaid and very bad lady-in-waiting. In spite of the riot of embroidery, the silk tunic and trousers she wore were much more practical than the voluminous dresses Lahlil was used to seeing her in— but then, she remembered, she had only really known Callia in the last few months of her pregnancy. The scimitar Callia wore in her sash was no less decorative than the rest of her outfit, but the loose way the girl held her shoulders and wrists told Lahlil she knew how to use it.

"So you finally decided to wake up," Callia called over to her. "You can thank Jachad for telling us where to find you. He said he could 'see' you, whatever that means. I haven't decided if you can stay, you know."

It took a moment for Lahlil to realize she wasn't teasing, and another moment to wonder why Callia thought it was her decision—until she noticed the silver moon medallion nearly identical to the one Nisha always wore. So Callia had declared herself queen after all, dead princeling or not. "Are you telling me to leave?"

"I didn't say that; I *said* I haven't decided. Why, did you think you'd be welcomed back with open arms? You said you were going to cure Jachad, but you didn't." Callia spoke about him as if the man himself wasn't standing a few feet away. "He's still dying, only this time because of something *you* did to him."

"He's not dying," Mairi pointed out. "He's becoming a god."

Callia huffed and gave a dismissive wave, jangling her bracelets again. "*No one* would have had to become *anything* if she had stayed away from us in the first place. No one ever asked you to come back—you know that, don't you? I don't mean now, I mean six months ago. All of this is your fault."

The silence roaring in her ears filled the moment when Jachad would have made some objection, offered some witty remark to put Callia in her place.

"None of that makes a difference now," Rho put in. "You want justice, and she can help you get it."

Callia's perfectly arched brows rose for a moment and then furrowed, dainty even when she frowned. She slid her attention over to Jachad for a moment. "Maybe she can, but I don't see why we should trust her. Jachad told us she could have killed that *witch* in Prol Irat and she didn't do it."

Jachad caught Lahlil's eyes and held them for a moment, the pale sea-blue reflected in the light of the fading sky. "We've been attacked," he declared, stopping all side conversations without even raising his voice. "We're entitled to retribution. We're here to decide how best to get it."

"We're going to march in there and tell King Daryan to give us that witch and the people who killed my baby," Callia announced, "and if he doesn't, we'll burn the Shadar to the ground. They're going to pay for what they did."

"Attacking would be a mistake," said Lahlil. "They have triffon patrols and watches set up on the hills, and you have too much ground to cover to get to the palace. Their guards and militia will be ready for you. You'd be fighting your way through streets where they have the advantage of numbers, familiar territory and local support. They'll chip away at you until there's nothing left."

The captains and chiefs all jumped in, offering up their own opinions, until Jachad silenced them again.

"In the morning, the strider will take me to Ani and I will kill her," he announced. "Lahlil will come with me to deal with Ani's conspirators. No more Nomas will die because of that woman."

Except you, thought Lahlil, because Callia was right; maybe it wouldn't feel like dying to him, but he'd be gone, so it would be no different for the people he left behind.

"I thought you didn't do this any more," Callia said, turning on her, hands on her hips and little chin cocked. "Fighting and that kind of thing."

"Not for money."

The girl's eyes widened with something that looked uncomfortably like understanding. "And the rest of us wait here and do nothing?"

"Two days," said Jachad. "If no one comes back to tell you it's done, then you march."

"That's a terrible idea," Rho objected, startling everyone. "Jachad has the best chance against her, power against power. If he fails, the rest of you won't have the slightest chance. Throwing yourselves at her would be suicide."

Callia combed her fingers through a lock of black hair curling over her shoulder. "You may be right, but I don't care: I'm going anyway. But the others here, from the caravans and the ships, representing those who will fight *and* those who will get left behind, they need to decide for themselves. I won't order anyone to fight. That's not who we are. So stand if you're in and sit if you're out."

None of the people already standing sat down, while more than half the people sitting stood up. The *Windward's* captain worried her tongue between her teeth for a moment and then stood up, and as soon as she did, more joined her until everyone was standing, except for one man who remained perched on a rock with his arms folded and his face screwed up in indecision. He looked at the people standing around him, looked at Jachad, then turned and looked over his shoulder at Callia. Finally, he gave the most Nomas shrug that had ever been shrugged and stood up.

Jachad turned and walked away through the cooling sand.

Lahlil went to follow him, then she heard Mairi's frantic hiss and saw the healer beckoning from behind one of the tents. As soon as Lahlil came close enough, Mairi took both of her hands and pressed a bundle between them: from the feel, a clay vial wrapped in a cloth.

"Break the bottle and hold the cloth over his mouth and nose," the Nomas whispered. "Don't breathe it yourself! It doesn't stay potent for long once the air gets to it, so don't dawdle. Make sure he drinks water when he wakes up or he'll have a terrible headache."

Lahlil untangled herself and tried to hand the bundle back again. "There's no medicine that can help him."

"It's not *medicine*," Mairi said, her scowl only barely visible in the dying light. "It's to make him sleep—so you can take him somewhere where he won't need to use his powers until we can find out how to fix him. Do I really have to explain this to you?"

Lahlil stepped back, wanting to push Mairi away but unable to trust herself not to use too much force. "Stop. Stop it."

"Sweet Amai!" Mairi swore. "You can't take him to fight knowing he won't come out again! What was the point of dragging him all the way to Norland looking for a cure if you're going to let him die now?"

"I shouldn't have done that, either. I can't make the same mistake again."

The healer's face darkened to a deep red and she forgot to whisper. "What are you even talking about, girl?"

"He never wanted to go to Norland—he only went because he knew I'd go without him and he'd be dead before I got back."

"And what of it? He'd have died for sure if he'd stayed here. You didn't have a choice."

"I could have listened to what *he* wanted. I could have let *him* make the choice." Lahlil remembered Isa flinging those very words at her when they'd faced off at Valrigdal: another of her sister's perfectly aimed darts. "I won't choose for him this time, Mairi, and neither will you."

The Nomas backed away from her, eyes glazed with unshed tears, wild hair standing up as her scarf slipped down.

"Fine, then," she said, and spat into the dirt at her feet. "Have it your way. It'll be on your head."

Chapter 15

Lahlil wasn't sure how long Jachad had been standing on the other side of the wagon but he was visible now, his robes swirling around his ankles despite the lack of a breeze. When she walked away from the encampment, he followed, and they passed the wagons and the tents and into the open desert together. When he stopped by the curve of a moonlit dune and loosened his scarf, she stopped too.

"How did you find where Rho and I landed after the stride?" she asked. "We could have been anywhere."

His answer took so long in coming that she could feel the air cooling against her skin, the night chasing the twilight hard. "I can see you," he said eventually. "When I look down from above, everyone—my subjects, my friends, my mother—all look the same, but I still see *you*."

A delicate shiver that had nothing to do with the cold spread over her like hoarfrost.

"Why didn't you kill Ani at Prol Irat, after I failed?" Jachad demanded. "She said you belonged with her. Is it true? Do you have some loyalty to her still?"

I remember how you wept when I told you I loved you, Ani had said. "You'd lost control of your powers. I needed to stay with you."

"To save me?" His voice sounded strangely resonant out here, echoing off walls that weren't there.

"To keep my promise."

A little fire zipped up from under his collar and twined around his throat like a lizard's tail before flicking out of sight. She drew a little closer to him, chasing that warmth, until she saw him stiffen. And then the stars above went soft and some kind of strange transposition happened, where she was seeing out of his eyes and looking at her and she knew what it felt like, all those times she had moved toward him and then crept back, keeping him close but always too far to touch; close enough to ache, but too far to comfort.

"You're afraid any crack will break you," she told him.

"You don't know how hard it is, holding on." Then Jachad finally looked at her, blue eyes dark in the starlight, tongues of flame twisting through his hair. "Or maybe you do."

"You never pushed me," she said.

"I didn't think you were ready. I was afraid I'd lose you."

She couldn't tell him he was wrong, so she said nothing. He ran his knuckles along his beard and the gesture made it impossible for her not to focus on his lips. Her skin prickled with the memory of their brief moment at Wastewater before it all went wrong; the feeling of her tongue running over their roughness while he traced brands into her back. "You won't lose me now. I think—I've changed."

"How?" he asked. The word was barely a breath, but she heard it because now they were standing close enough for their arms to brush.

"Now . . ." *Words. She needed words.* "I thought I needed to deserve how you felt about me, but I don't get to decide if those feelings are right or wrong. I'm supposed to trust you when you say you—"

She couldn't say those words, but his mouth met hers and he took them from her anyway. His tongue brushed her lips and then she was drowning in him, her hands climbing up his shoulders until she could sink her fingers into his hair and guide him even closer, cradling his head as if she could physically tether them together. Her back arched as his hands swept around her waist and then slipped up under her jacket, skin against skin; she gave a throaty moan when she felt flames sizzle across her stomach. She wanted him to understand that she *welcomed* the burning; she *needed* it to pierce through the numbness that came from a lifetime of treating her body carelessly, as if she had borrowed it from someone with no intention of returning it.

"Lahlil," he breathed, the sound impossibly close against her ear but also echoing far away, past the purpling sky to somewhere within a river of molten light, wherever the gods went to rest.

Then he broke the kiss and leaned back, something dangerously indecisive playing over his shining lips. She set her jaw and braced herself for rejection—until he grabbed her hips and pulled her down into the sand, on to his lap, with her knees on either side of his thighs. She shuddered from the heat of him pressed up against her, and then she was dragging her lips against his beard and down his neck until he pulled her jacket back from her shoulders. He waited for her to tug it the rest of the way off before he lifted her shirt over her head for her.

A flurry of hands later, and her trousers and boots and his robe were on the ground and they were kissing again, their bodies mashed together as they touched in as many places as possible. All the while, delicate tongues of fire dragged over Lahlil's skin like sharp fingernails, piling on layer after layer of sensation until everything else blurred into insignificance.

She pulled away for a moment and leaned back to look at him, to fix in her memory the sight of his swollen lips, the flush sweeping up from his neck, his eyes, pleading and needy. For this time, at least, Jachad was nowhere else but right here.

Their bodies did not fit easily together—her legs were too long, his chest was too broad—but the *rightness* of it came so close to the feeling from her vision that she felt the tears gathering. The shattering couldn't be stopped now. It started with the crack between her eyes and splintered its way downward, turning her into a pile of brittle shards as she broke apart. With her forehead touching his, her weight settled against him as his thumbs traced sparking circles over her hips, she found the poor starving thing that had been trapped inside her and tried to coax it into the light. Eyes closed, with his breath warm against her neck, she said his name.

He moved his hands to her face, sending fire skittering down her neck but he didn't move and finally she realized he was waiting for her to open her eyes. So she did, offering up to him the last bit of herself she'd been holding back in a kiss, tender this time, and they moved together, falling effortlessly into the shared pulse that had joined them since the nights they'd lain side by side pretending to sleep. She took everything he had to give her, everything she could get, gripping his shoulders as ropes of fire bound them together until what began as tender turned into something fierce and desperate and ended with them helpless and trembling in each other's arms.

Lahlil woke in Jachad's tent, where they'd returned a little before sunrise. An unfamiliar languor pressed down on her like a warm, heavy hand—until she saw the hollow in the cushion next to her head and a chill of apprehension shot up her spine. "Jachi?"

Instead, she found Oshi nestled beside her like a glass ornament packed in straw, kicking in his sleep and making the little stuttering sounds that had woken her up. His eyelashes fluttered and he smacked his lips a few times before blinking up at her. He had Eofar's long white eyelashes and Harotha's full lips, but those golden eyes, they were all his own. His neck flushed, like he was gearing up to cry.

"I'm your Aunt Lahlil," she reminded him. "Don't you remember me?"

His mouth twisted.

She clapped a hand over her left eye. "What about now?"

He grabbed for her fingers with both of his tiny hands and pulled, so she let him move her arm back down. His clear sense of satisfaction in the accomplishment took her by surprise. He might be half-Norlander but she hadn't expected his feelings to come through with such clarity. He smelled like fresh linen; like ripe fruit and Callia's perfume; like wood smoke. He made a successful grab for one of her loose collar strings and held on tight while she sat up and repositioned him on her lap, surprised at the softness of his hair when her cheek brushed against it. He pushed himself up on his chubby arms—that was new since she last saw him—so he could keep looking at her face.

"You shouldn't have brought him with the caravan," she told Callia, who had been watching all the time from one of Jachad's chairs. "You know Harotha made me vow never to take him to the Shadar."

"We're a solid league from the Shadar and it's not like I'm giving him a sword and sending him into battle. He'll stay here with all the others who aren't going to fight."

Oshi had already lost interest in the string and was now trying to turn himself upside down on Lahlil's lap while he babbled nonsense sounds. Callia sighed impatiently and rose from the chair. "Come on, get out of bed and get dressed. I need you to come to my wagon and get out the maps and things so you can show me what to do because I haven't the slightest idea, I'm not afraid to say. Come on, sprat." Oshi squealed with joy as Callia lifted him by his waist and swung him through the air, giggling madly when she let him dangle upside-down for a moment before bundling him back up into her arms.

"Leave him. I'll bring him."

Callia stared at her. "Do as you like," she said, pushing the baby back into Lahlil's arms, her bracelets jangling. "Only don't let Mairi take him, whatever you do. She's always putting him down somewhere and forgetting where she left him. Last time we found him in a trough. There wasn't any water in it, thank Amai, but it was still a trough."

She swept out again, leaving Lahlil sitting up on the bed, her cheek pressed up against Oshi's soft hair and her hand covering the second hollow in the cushion.

Chapter 16

Rainwater showered down through the barred window of Hesh's cell, pattering louder every time there was a gust of wind. The smell of wet straw reminded Daryan of mucking out the dereshadi under his uncle's critical eye, but the resemblance to a stable ended there. Animals didn't need jails; beasts didn't take prisoners. They settled disagreements with teeth and claws and all judgments were instantaneous, based on instinct and not the muddied pretexts of morality and public order.

The jailer let out another grating snore and smacked his lips against the drool trickling out on to the table. Daryan would have thought the man would be more vigilant with his cells full of Norlanders, but their newest guests were nothing if not quiet. Lem made up for it by prowling up and down the long corridor, eyeing the cell doors in case they suddenly burst open.

"Tell us who else is killing ashas."

"Who *else*?" Hesh pushed back his hair to remind them of his bruised face and swollen mouth, not to mention the oozing scrapes on his chin from being thrown to the ground. "Are you trying to trick me into confessing now?"

Omir cuffed him back down against the mattress. The resurrectionist reclined with his fingers laced together behind his head but Daryan saw him swallow a lump in his throat when he turned his face to the wall.

"Tell us the names of the others."

Hesh's answering laugh scraped against Daryan's nerves. "Other *what*? Other innocent men? Other scapegoats? I can give you plenty of those."

"Do you hate them? The ashas?" Daryan asked before Omir could lash out again. He leaned against the wall where he could see both men's faces without turning. "You're one of those people who still believe what we were taught, that only ordained ashas are supposed to have powers. You think the ashas are sinners, some kind of abomination."

Hesh's nonchalant posing vanished in an instant. "Jemma was *not* an abomination. She was a girl who wanted to help, that's all. A nice girl who came home one day and found her whole family murdered. You don't get over something like that. She needed someone to look after her so that's what I did."

"You resurrectionists want to be the new priests," Omir broke in. "You're killing the ashas because they're a threat to your ambitions."

The young man's laughter bounced off the cell walls. "*None* of us want to be priests—and we couldn't kill a netted fish if we had to work together to do it. It turns out people who cart dead bodies around aren't very sociable as a rule."

"Then it's a coup? You want to replace me as daimon—maybe you think I'm weak because I haven't executed the Norlanders or rounded up the overseers?" Daryan suggested, trying to keep any bitterness out of his tone. "Maybe you *want* a daimon who won't mind getting his hands bloodied; one who won't let laws get in his way. Maybe you killed the ashas so I won't have their help when you come for me."

Hesh craned his neck and looked at him in utter mystification, but Omir's broad shoulders twisted away and his eyes skated across the room.

Daryan could hear himself breathing too loudly and chafed his hands together to cover it.

"Daimon," the captain rumbled, tilting his head toward the

open door and leading Daryan out into the hallway so they could speak privately, "we know it's the resurrectionists. We need to move against them now, before they scatter."

"You want to arrest *all* of them?"

"He won't give us any names," said Omir. "He's left us no choice."

"We don't have any place to put that many people. We'd have to build another jail."

Omir's heavy hand landed on his shoulder, pinning him in place. The steady drag of Lem's footsteps came to a halt. "Not if we empty the cells in this one."

Daryan's own words echoed back to him: *Maybe you think I'm weak because I haven't executed the Norlanders.* He said slowly, to buy himself some time to get his bearings, "You never talked about killing the Norlanders before." He worked at keeping his shoulder steady under the pressure from Omir's hand. "What's changed?"

"It didn't matter before. Now we're running out of time."

"For what?"

Omir's fingers dug in and he looked into Daryan's eyes. "Saving the Shadar."

The door to the outside squealed open and a Red Guard poked his dripping face in the doorway. "Captain! They're storming the gates."

"The resurrectionists?" Omir asked as Lem made a nervous grab for sword.

"Binit and his lot, coming for the Dead Ones," said the guard as the door, holding the door open for them into the teeming rain.

"Go!" Daryan commanded, giving Omir a little shove to get him going. "I'll make sure he's locked up. Lem will be with me." The captain hesitated for a moment, then followed the guard outside.

The door slamming behind them finally woke the jailer, who jumped up and grabbed his key ring while his stool clattered to its side. He spluttered, "What's happening?"

Lem's face darkened and he looked ready to launch into a tirade, but Daryan grabbed his bodyguard's sleeve and pulled him into Hesh's cell. "Get him out of here. Find some place safe and wait for me."

"You still think they want to silence him?" Lem conjectured.

"I think they want to kill him—maybe to silence him, maybe because they won't have to prove he's guilty if he's already dead. *Watch him*. He's clever. Don't let him out of your sight."

He expected Hesh to offer some snide comment but the resurrectionist just backed into the corner, his eyes flicking back and forth between the door and the tiny window, for the first time looking like a very young man in a very bad situation.

"What are you going to do?" asked Lem, very obviously restraining himself from demanding to stay by Daryan's side.

"I think I know where to find Tessa."

Suddenly Hesh leaped forward and nearly succeeded in grabbing the front of Daryan's jacket before Lem flung his arm out and knocked him back. "Don't let them get her," he shouted. "You need to protect her!"

"I know. She's coming to rescue you, isn't she?"

"You don't understand," Hesh begged, his voice audibly trembling now. "If they—"

"I *know*," Daryan repeated. "She's an asha, and she's your mother. I'm not quite as stupid as you think. Do you have any asha powers?"

The resurrectionist shook his head.

"All right. Go with Lem. I'll find Tessa and let her know you're safe."

Outside in the rain, Red Guards were rushing to set up a cordon around the jail. Shouting and the clash of weapons were already coming from the direction of the courtyard. Daryan drew his nameless sword and pounded through the puddles, threading his way through the animal pens until he could feel the old paving stones under his feet. He knew Tessa wouldn't leave her son in a jail under attack by an angry mob; she had to be somewhere in the crowd. More guards ran by him to keep the rioters bottlenecked in the tunnel. Most of the mob were only pushing and shoving, but some had armed themselves with weapons pilfered from the militia stores, others with whatever they had to hand. It didn't take long for them to overwhelm the guards and spill into the yard.

Daryan jumped up on a pile of bricks as the chaos washed around him, looking for the familiar blue scarf in the sea of muddy grays and browns. He saw four people tackle a guard from behind, two of them beating on him while the others ran off with his black-bladed sword to keep him from willing it back to himself. In front of him, a guard stabbed a hatchet-wielding woman and then let go of his hilt in a panic, watching in horror as she staggered back and fell with his blade still drooping from her chest. Bricks and stones were flying everywhere, snatched out of the mud and thrown again as soon as they landed. Daryan's sword twitched with his anxiousness to leap down into the fray and stop it somehow, but finding Tessa had to be his priority. He held his resolve until a dozen grim-faced men and women with sharpened mining tools and a few cheap, conventional swords advanced in a loose group. One of them held a lantern aloft, illuminating their faces in its trembling light.

"Call this off, Binit!" Daryan roared through the din.

"You won't stop us, Daimon," Binit threatened, brandishing his sword in a ham-fisted grip; it might as well have been made of wood for the good it would do him against the Red Guards' black blades. "Those Dead Ones have to pay for what they did. This is justice."

"*This* is Shadari killing Shadari. It's not justice; it's a *tragedy*."

"A tragedy?" Binit's voice rose in outrage as water dripped from the end of his red nose.

Daryan was so angry he'd forgotten to keep track of his surroundings, which was why he didn't see the spade coming, or who swung it; he only felt the impact as the thick metal edge sliced into his shoulder until it hit bone. A huge pulse of pain tried to rip a scream out of him, but he managed to snap his jaw shut and stifle it into a tight groan. The ground swelled up as his knees buckled but he staggered to the wall of the potters' shed and clung on, digging his fingers into the grooves between the bricks and using his mental control over his sword to keep it from dropping from his hand. Binit and his friends scattered like cockroaches and Daryan could do nothing but focus his energy on breathing and not passing out.

That's when he finally saw Tessa, staring at him with her hand in front of her mouth—but the moment their eyes met she ran back in the direction of the jail. He squeezed his shoulder to hold back the blood and went after her, clenching his teeth through the shock of every muddy footfall. The crowd of jostling, shouting people congealed around him, but he kept his sword up through the force of his will, and the black blade was enough to clear a path. Meanwhile the Guards had wrested back control of the entrance to the jail but Daryan imagined the tide could turn at any moment. He caught a glimpse of Tessa rounding the back wall and lurched after her, water dripping into his eyes and the ground sliding away underneath him until he finally butted up against the wall and groped along it, leaving a trail of bloody handprints until her gray outline took shape behind the rain. "Tessa!"

A jolt of something struck him and ripped his sword from his hand, disorienting him so badly that he stopped short, fighting against an invisible force determined to tip him over backward. He felt himself falling anyway and steeled himself for the impact, but when his vision cleared he was on his knees with no one else anywhere near him. His body lobbed a dozen different feelings at him, overloading his senses until he distilled it all down to lessening pain in his shoulder and frost creeping into the marrow of his bones. He wanted to wrap his arms around himself for warmth, but couldn't lift either one of them; the best he could do was pull his knees into his body and shudder inside his wet clothes.

"Daimon!"

A warm hand cupped his face and he found Tessa kneeling over him, her face wrinkled up in concern. "Look what they've done to your poor shoulder. Thank the gods, though! A little further over and it would have been your neck." She pulled off her scarf and refolded it into a makeshift bandage before binding the wound as best she could. Daryan found himself staring at her. With the rain soaking her hair into black waves and her cheeks flushed she looked like someone different, someone else.

"I never took the elixir you gave me. I—I lost it." Even now, he didn't want to confirm her suspicions by telling her Omir had destroyed it. As she moved her hands down he grabbed her wrist with the strength he had lacked a moment ago. "Why didn't you tell me you were an asha sooner? Were you afraid?"

"I wouldn't have given you the elixir if I was afraid, would I?" asked Tessa, pulling her hand from his grasp only to pat his knee. "I'm a laundress, Daimon. That's the life I know and it's the one I like, and I think I deserve to keep it. I didn't wanted to be gawked at or paraded around."

"I wouldn't have done that. We could have kept it secret."

"Up until the day you decided you needed me to fight for you," she said. "And I can't, Daimon. I can't do what that little boy did, bury people under the ground. I'd only be able to think of my boy Hesh, digging day after day through the caves, trying to find his da."

He pushed himself up higher on the wall. "You're an asha, whether you like it or not. I never wanted to be the daimon—do you know how many times I've thought about leaving and never coming back? You and I don't have that choice. We are what we are."

Tessa leaned in closer and lifted his chin so he would have to meet her gaze. Her touch was strangely gentle, although her eyes held no softness at all. "I'm not a 'what.' I may be poor and homely, but I'm still a *person*. No one is going to make me into a tool or a weapon. *I'll* decide if I'm going to use this power, and the when and the how of it." Her anger drained away and left behind the hurt he knew he'd caused her. "Now I'm going to get my son out of your jail."

"Hesh is safe," said Daryan. He had to close his eyes as a new wave of dizziness overtook him, so he didn't see her reaction. "I had Lem get him out of there. He'll protect him."

"Do you believe what I told you before, then?"

He almost shook his head before he realized what a terrible idea that would be with it already spinning so spectacularly. "No—I don't know."

"Then here," said Tessa, and held up another vial much like the first. Raindrops pinged off the glass. "You didn't think I'd give you all of it, did you? Not the best time, I know, but we may not get a better one if things go on the way they are. After that speech I made just now, I would be a terrible hypocrite if I poured it down your throat, so what will it be, Daimon? Yes, or no?"

He closed his eyes again. "Yes."

The liquid trickled over his tongue and slid down his throat, thick and warm as blood. He would have coughed it up, but the first jerk of his chest felt like it had pulled his arm clean away from his body and he stifled the rest, feeling the stuff clinging to his throat as it slid down. The empty bottle hit his leg before it fell into the mud.

With a whispered apology, Tessa vanished into the rain.

Daryan clawed his way up the wall with his eyes as open as he could make them, staring hard at whatever he could see around him to keep him rooted *right here, right now*. Maybe if he concentrated hard enough, he could keep the visions under control. So far nothing had changed; everything looked the same, sounded the same—

—until a wall of sand-filled wind pinned him back, flaying his skin, grinding his eyes to pulp, shredding his lungs so that his next exhale came out in a cough of bright red blood. The wind receded, only to twist itself into a maelstrom, snatching up and flinging those running for cover into the walls and down on the ground, or tossing them up high into the air and then abandoning them to crash down in a shattered mess of broken bones. The ground beneath him cracked open and a fissure ran riot, branching as it reached out for the stumbling figures and swallowed them up.

That's when he saw her. He knew in an instant that this was the great tyrant Harotha had seen in her visions, the one who had started the war with the ashas and nearly destroyed their entire civilization. It wasn't that he recognized her—Harotha had never described her, and until this moment Daryan had always assumed it was a man—but the way she walked through the devastation, the anger and aggrievedness as she turned her attention this way and that, knocking down a building here, drowning someone in sand there. He heard a name shouted in terror and rage, breaching the barrier of time as a distant wail: *Anakthalisa.*

The scene in front of him dissolved. The flying sand and the noise disappeared and he looked down from a great height at the bodies in the street, blood everywhere, broken houses, still-smoking fires, the screams of the living and the dying. He was standing on the roof of the temple with the whole city spread out around him. The ashas stood there with him, but not the ashas of his day; there were no white robes, no aura of detached sanctity. These were warriors on the verge of a victory that had already broken them into pieces. He stood with them as a ledge crumbled into the sea and took a drained, powerless Anakthalisa with it.

Why was he seeing this? Harotha had described all of this to them before she died. None of this could help him—

Then, as he turned to look at the faces of the ashas around him, all still staring at the spot where the tyrant had fallen, he realized what Harotha had missed, or maybe hadn't been shown. *None of them—not one of them—saw Anakthalisa's body hit the ground.*

What does it matter? thought Daryan. All of this took place hundreds of years ago. Even if she had somehow survived the fall, she would still have been dead for centuries.

The scene dissolved and for a moment Daryan saw the present again, and was shocked to find himself not propped up against the wall but stumbling through the rain. The riot had got out of control; he saw Norlanders being dragged out of the jail and the Red Guards unsure who to fight. Daryan needed to take control—

—and now he was inside, at a table lit by a single lamp, the margins of the house or cave in darkness. Around this table stood a group of men of various ages, all marked with an expression he remembered on the face of his uncle as he prayed to the gods, a look both pious and self-important, reverent but not humble, sincere but self-conscious. The faces of the men were changing, sliding from one set of features into another, often similar but never exactly the same: generations passing. They were praying: *Blessed Mother, Anakthalisa*, chanting by rote, reciting prophecies, signs to tell them when their god would return and how to prepare for her. The faces whirled round him, faster and faster, until he felt like he was falling—

And then he was in a different room, in a house empty of furniture but not of people. Voices reached him now, garbled, as if the people were moving too fast or too slow by turns, but somehow he could understand them anyway. He recognized every face; worse, he knew the room he was standing in as well as he knew his own bedchamber, having visited it as often in his dreams as he did in reality. *He didn't want to be here*—but the vision had fused him to the spot.

"I told you I could get her any time I wanted," said Alkesh, rubbing at the stumps of the missing fingers on his right hand as Omir lowered himself onto the floor next to the girl with the yellow scarf. Alkesh had been one of Faroth's cronies; Daryan had always hated him. "I knew leaving her where she was would pay off."

"I should get back to the palace," said Lieutenant Tamin, fidgeting with a clasp on his red uniform jacket. Tamin had always been so capable, so reliable. "I'm supposed to be on duty. Someone might notice I'm gone."

"*Your* conclave let her get away," said Alkesh. "And came *this* close to letting Isa Eotan find out everything. You don't get to keep your hands clean now."

"I brought you some water. You must be thirsty," said Omir, offering a cup to the girl.

Her vacant, red-rimmed eyes followed the movement and he

thought he saw a flicker of understanding there; maybe she was not as unaware as she pretended. Maybe she knew what they had planned; perhaps she would spring up and bolt for the door. But, no, Daryan had already seen her body lying on the ground next to the pyre, black poison snaking from her heart. *Yesterday. This had happened only yesterday.*

"Take this, Jemma."

She folded her dirty hands in her lap, leaving him holding the cup. "It was my fault, wasn't it?" she whispered.

"No. Of course not."

Alkesh huffed and muttered, "I couldn't get a word out of her."

"Quiet," Omir commanded.

"I wanted to tell the daimon about . . . something. That's why it happened, isn't it? The gods are punishing me. That's why they didn't let me die too."

"That's not true," said Omir. "It wasn't your fault. Sometimes things have to happen. No one wants you to suffer. Your family is with the gods now."

She bobbed her head in agreement.

"I want you to drink some water," said Omir, this time taking a sip himself before holding it out to her.

Jemma wet her lips and again, Daryan thought he saw something sharp lurking behind that blank stare. Instead of taking the cup from him, she strained toward Omir like an infant, until he held the cup to her lips and tipped it back. Some of the water spilled, dripping down onto her lap, but she swallowed most of it.

"It don't taste right," she said. It was not a question.

When her convulsions began Omir held her against his chest, pinning her arms down to keep her from clawing at her heart. The seizures didn't leave her enough breath to scream, but each inhalation came as a tormented little wheeze. Omir held her tightly as she writhed in his arms, not letting go even when her fingernails tore into his wrists and the blood dripped down onto the floor. Eventually her flailing eased into twitching until that too died away, leaving her limp in Omir's embrace. Then the long sigh of her last breath whispered through the room.

"You can get her on Hesh's cart?" Omir asked Alkesh as he cradled the girl.

"All arranged."

"And Falit, you have your story for the daimon ready when Tamin brings you to him?"

"This is risky," said Falit, knocking his pipe against his knee. "The resurrectionists aren't like the others—threats aren't going to shut their mouths if they see something. And that Hesh—he's a mouthy little brat, but he's sharp."

"The daimon still supports the resurrectionists. This will change that," said Omir.

"It wouldn't matter if we killed the daimon too," asked Falit. "Don't make sense, keeping him alive."

"Don't," Tamin hissed at him.

"Why not?" asked Falit, turning on him. "So I don't end up like Vash? You killed him—one of our own, born into this like the rest of us—for poisoning that sand-spitting Nomas bastard. But Daryan? Oh no, no one's allowed to touch *him*—but how is he any less of a threat to the Blessed Mother than the ashas? Why shouldn't her prophecies include him, too?"

Omir rose with the girl in his arms, holding her like he would a sleeping child. "No one is a *threat* to Anakthalisa," he said, the note of command in his voice Daryan knew so well. "Her commandments are to prevent another senseless war against her. The ashas would start one, and I don't trust the resurrectionists not to do the same. Daryan is different. He wants what's best for the Shadar."

Omir didn't know the first thing about what Daryan wanted. Right now, he wanted to scream—he wanted to draw his black-bladed sword and slash and slash and slash—and then he wanted the house to fall in on him and crush him so he wouldn't have to face anything he had just seen.

And he did scream, finally, but by then the house had disappeared and he was stumbling . . . he was in the back yards, stumbling in a circle of his own muddy boot-prints with blood still coating the inside of his mouth.

"Daimon!" Omir's solid arms came around him and held him up as he toppled over. Daryan tried to push him away, but was unable to get his arms to do much of anything. "You're bleeding badly. We have to get you inside."

He still couldn't *see* it: the betrayal. There was nothing in Omir's face except concern; nothing in the arms holding him up except support. The vision was wrong, it *had* to be wrong: it was some kind of trick; there was a detail he couldn't see. He had stood beside this man every day of the last six months and *endlessly* discussed the asha killings. He would have known. *Unless.* Unless he'd been blinded by his desperation to have someone else shoulder the responsibility he had never wanted; to make the decisions he didn't want to make; to face the things he didn't want to know.

"Everything will be all right," Omir reassured him, dropping each word on him like a weight, pulling him slowly toward the bottom of a dark, dark ocean.

"I hear wings." The muscles in Daryan's neck went slack and his head fell back, tilting up to the weeping clouds. A single dereshadi with two riders on its back swept overhead, wings tilted, long tail snaking behind it as it circled over the palace. The rider in front had her cowl thrown back despite the rain and a white braid slid down over her shoulder as she leaned over the saddle to see below her.

One arm or two? One arm, or two? The chant pulsed behind Daryan's eyes as he started to lose focus. Omir released him, crying words he didn't heed, and ran off, leaving him to lurch around in a loose circle, unable to get his balance while his head lolled back like his neck was broken. *One arm or two? One arm or two?* *One.*

Chapter 17

The storm clouds took Isa by surprise, since she knew it would be at least a month before the rains came to the Shadar. For a while she just sat in the saddle, clutching the reins until her fingers ached, trying to understand what had gone wrong when she'd simply been following the coastline. Nothing looked familiar; the overcast skies turned the sea green and gray by turns, nothing like the azure waves visible from the temple windows of her childhood. She *had* caught herself drifting from time to time, wrapped in the sweet stillness of her medicine—and she was so tired from flying day and night.

The triffon veered up to go over yet another cold fogbank but Isa tightened her grip and kicked, keeping it down under the clouds. If she couldn't see below them, they might end up flying out to sea until the triffon tired and they all drowned. Her sister Frea had drowned. Isa had told her to take off her cape before it pulled her under, but she wouldn't listen.

They had to be getting close now. She made herself imagine the peaceful city Daryan had promised to build, but her mind kept drifting to the dark winding streets and the suspicious looks she had left three months ago. So instead she tried to picture Daryan waiting for her on the walls of the palace, but in her imagination the tower beacons kept turning into funeral pyres.

"There," said Ani, her hand brushing Isa's shoulder. "There's the Shadar."

Lightning flickered above and the thunder rolled in with the waves, a rumble only. They flew into the rain, the palace and the houses that had come into view blurring behind the gray clouds. Isa's heart stuttered when she realized there could be other triffons out there, the feral ones. She remembered the collisions she had seen in the battle against Frea: the frantic tangle of claws and wings, the blood and the head-splitting shrieking.

"What is *that*?" asked Ani, distaste thick in her voice.

"The palace? Daryan is rebuilding it," Isa answered before remembering that the first palace had been built only after Ani had been betrayed by the ashas; of course the sight of it would offend her.

The city always looked so different when it rained. The tarpaulins stretched over the chimney openings made the domed houses look like glistening, disembodied eyes and the cartwheel ruts had turned into streams, the well-yards into dimpled lakes. A woman holding a swaddled infant in her arms looked out over a patch of muck and drowned greenery that must have been her garden; she slipped back inside when she saw the triffon coming.

By the time they'd swung around to circle over the palace, Isa's chest was aching so badly she thought her ribs might crack from the force of her heart pushing up against them. Her skin crawled with the sensation of the rainwater soaking her clothes and the harness hemmed her in like a cage. She needed to be on the ground *now*, to hold on to something that didn't melt away like ice or blow away like ash: something that would cling back, dig its fingers in and not let go, never let go, *never leave her alone again*.

And then she looked down and all her hopes fell into ruins.

Figures were swarming over the ground, dripping with rain and mud and blood, shoving and punching, cutting with metal and smashing with rock. Riot or uprising, it didn't matter; it was a mockery of all her sacrifices, her hoarded daydreams. Every word of encouragement she had ever said to Daryan welled up in her throat, the sharp Shadari consonants scraping and poking like fish-bones. Her body shook with fury, fueled by shame when she thought of Ani behind her, greeted by this havoc at the moment of her triumphant return.

The people in the courtyard ran for cover when they realized she intended to land there; she made no attempt to give them more time. As they spiraled down, the triffon's wing smashed through the porch roof and brought it down in a slow, trickling crash; at the same time, its tail smacked up against the east tower and shook it enough to send bricks crashing down the side, while a foreleg knocked one of the gaping-mouth fishes from the overflowing fountain, leaving water spurting from the broken pipe.

And then they were on the ground and Isa was looking down over a blur of dripping faces as figures in red rushed forward, pushing others aside. Daryan was nowhere to be seen, not under any of those drooping hoods and scarves, but Captain Omir did appear, towering over the others, coming toward them with his black-bladed sword held across his body. Isa drew Blood's Pride and stood up in the stirrups. It didn't matter what they were fighting about or who was on whose side: they were not going to bury everything she'd gone through, all her sacrifices, in the mud with them.

But then Omir was offering his hand up to Ani and she was placing her delicate fingers in his without hesitation, allowing him to support her as she climbed down from the triffon. The moment Ani was standing under her own power he backed away and lowered his eyes, almost as if it hurt to look or be too near her. Ani walked toward him, ghostly in her cloak, hardly rippling the water as she moved through the puddles.

Omir knelt and lowered his head, Ani reached out to rest a hand on his forehead like a benediction and his stoic expression broke, his shoulders sagging as if a terrible weight had been lifted from him.

More of the Red Guards circled around, sealing them off from the surrounding chaos, and all of them were staring at Ani with similar awe. Isa didn't like it. They looked like they wanted to touch her, to claw at her—like she *belonged* to them.

"Yes, I see it," Ani said, lifting Omir's chin. "You have the look of your ancestors."

"Blessed Mother, my name is Omir, son of Paresh," he said. "Your acolytes have prepared the way, as you commanded."

Acolytes. These men were Ani's acolytes—*they* had killed the ashas—and Omir was their leader. "Where is Daryan?" Isa asked. Her Shadari sounded shrill in her own ears and she hated the way the men all looked at her—and Ani did not.

"Now, where is the boy, Dramash?" Ani asked the captain.

Omir's face went blank. "They took him to Norland, Blessed Mother. He has not returned."

"You are wrong. He *is* here," Ani told him. Her voice was smooth on the surface but hard and cold underneath, a boulder covered in sand. "Or he soon will be. Send your men to find him."

"I will, Blessed Mother." If Omir had been asked to cut off a body part, he couldn't have shown more fervor. "We *will* find him."

Rain tapped against Isa's hood, *tap tap tap*, and she could feel herself beginning to drift. Ani had her acolytes now; she might not remember about Isa or her medicine. The pains would be on her soon, tapping at her nerves the way the rain tapped against her head, and she had to find Daryan first.

No one tried to stop her as she left the circle. Someone knocked into her from behind and she turned, jerking her sword up, but whoever it was reeled away. Those scared off by the triffon hadn't returned; the only people there were groaning on the ground or propped against the walls.

She started toward the throne room and Daryan's chambers—but no, he wouldn't hole himself up there if the fighting was down here; he'd have been in the middle of it. So she turned toward the back yards instead, plowing past the fallen bricks, through the darkness under the arch where more groaning figures huddled against the walls. She came out the other side to find the brawl-

ing still going on, although it looked like the Red Guards had re-
duced the conflict to its final throes.

Thunder rumbled across the sky, trembling in Isa's bones long
after it died away. She paused to rest her shoulder against the wall
of a shed, trying to think of some way to find Daryan, but the rain's
tap tap tap on the tin roof bored right through her thoughts.

She didn't remember closing her eyes but she must have,
because one moment the only thing in front of her was the rough
brick wall of the shed and the next moment Falkar was standing
close enough for his unwashed, stale-wine odor to push away the
clean scent of the rain. The three months since her fellow Norlander had threatened to kill her had not been kind to him, going
by his bony frame and the webbing of dark veins around his silver irises. She couldn't guess how he came to be at the palace instead of the ashadom, but she knew the battered sword he carried
didn't belong to him any more than the blood red Shadari
blood—splattered over his shirt.

<You should have stayed away,> Falkar told her, but the relief
pouring off him nearly knocked her back. A little puff of breath
escaped her lips. He thought she was giving him the chance to
die fighting. It was all she could do not to laugh aloud when he
charged.

Rain scattered off her blade as she angled to block his first cut
and then again as she swung around to block the follow-up to her
neck. To her surprise, the jolt of the clashing blades knocked the
encroaching pain back again, so she let him expend his pitiful
strength on her, his presence in her mind whistle-thin as he tried
to goad her into more aggression. When he lost his balance and
scraped his sword against the wall behind her, she lost her taste
for the game and kicked his legs out from under him.

Falkar fell heavily, gracelessly. Mud splashed into Isa's face and
she had to bend her head down to her shoulder to wipe it from
her eyes. Falkar had dropped his sword but he got his hands
underneath him and started to push himself up.

She shoved her boot down against his neck and pushed his face back down in the mud. <Just so there's no confusion,> she told him, <this is not a duel. We are not fighting soldier to soldier. I'm exterminating you like the vermin you are.>

Isa lifted her boot, but only long enough to replace it with her knee. She continued pressing his face into the mud, but he was able to turn his neck enough to get in a choking breath—then she grabbed his hair and shoved his face back down.

A bubble floated up to the surface of the mud and popped as he flailed, trying to throw her off, but he was too weak, and she just pushed him down harder. She was sitting on him now, watching air bubbles bursting in the mud. She knew the exact moment he lost consciousness, when all the straining muscles in his body went limp and it was no longer necessary to hold him down. He might not have been quite dead yet, but he wasn't breathing, so she stood back up and used her foot to roll him over. He had mud in his open eyes.

All of a sudden the pain came rushing back, doubling her over, draining the strength from her so rapidly that she had to jam Blood's Pride into the ground just to stay on her feet. The rain was still coming down and she couldn't see far enough; she couldn't find Daryan.

And Ani might need her—leaving without a word had been a mistake. She needed to get back right away.

"Isa."

Her name: not a question; he didn't need her to answer. The beard pulled her attention for only a pinprick of a moment and then his eyes, wide and dark and soft, pulled her in. She let go of her sword and he sprang forward, folding her into a jerky embrace as she crashed against him. He tugged her into the shed and she barely noticed the shelves of drying pots and the rain hammering down on the roof *tap tap tap.*

"You're hurt." She brushed her finger over the scarf bandaging his shoulder, eyeing the darker spots on the fabric and the way he held his arm pressed up against his side.

"You're all right," Daryan said as if he hadn't heard her, but he sounded all wrong, like someone reciting a speech in a language they didn't understand. Darkness pooled under his chin and in the hollow below his throat and she tracked the lines of muscles: harder and thicker than she remembered, new dips and angles. "Aeda came back without you—I didn't know what to think."

"I had to let her loose. I hoped she'd come back here." Why was she standing here *talking* when she could still feel the ache from when he'd held her only a moment ago. She needed to be touching him, to brush away that curl drooping over his forehead; to know *right now* if that beard was rough or silky and how it would feel against her cheek when he kissed her. And then he slipped his hand against her neck, stroked his thumb along the line of her jaw, and she turned into his touch.

"You're warm," he whispered in a dry voice, his eyes tracking up and down her body. "Where did you go? You said you were going to get Lahlil but—"

"I found somebody better than Lahlil, much better," Isa promised, filling the tiny space between them with her breath.

"Why are you so warm?" he asked, moving his hand up to her forehead while he searched her eyes. "You're trembling. What's going on? Why can I touch you without burning you? Are you ill?"

"I'm fine," she replied, barely parting her lips enough to get the words out. She *was* fine. Three months of torment for his sake, thinking about him every moment, and yet that's all she had to say to him: that she was fine. This was all wrong. "You don't understand—you need to listen. I brought back an asha, the most powerful asha who's ever lived. I rescued her from a Norlander prison. The Shadar will be safe now. She can protect it from everyone."

"That's who came back with you on the dereshadi," he said, his eyes sliding down to the floor. "What's her name?"

"Anakthalisa. I call her Ani."

"And you brought her here?"

She couldn't understand why Daryan was having so much

trouble following what she was telling him, but she didn't know how long he'd been stumbling around with that wound. The blood loss might be affecting him. "Ani is back now—don't you see what that means? The Shadari don't need you any more. We can leave together, like we always wanted."

He pulled her to him and kissed her, ferocious in his intent, and she clung to him, parting her lips and pushing into his mouth with insistence, basking in the closeness they had never been able to sustain before. He wrapped his arm around her and pulled her even closer, clutching her as if he expected a cyclone to come and rip her away from him.

When he finally pulled back, she saw the fresh tears mingling with the rainwater on his cheeks.

"You did this for me," Daryan whispered, his voice broken in a way that sent a pulse through her heart. "I can't believe you did all this for me."

"We need to go and see Ani." A slow, gripping pain had taken root in the space behind her eyes and she tried to blink it away. "You can trust me now, Daryan. Everything's going to be all right."

Chapter 18

"Wait," Daryan pleaded as they limped into the tunnel, Isa supporting him by the elbow of his uninjured arm. He moved away from her too-warm touch and leaned up against the sloping wall instead, trying to blink away the after-images of her holding Falkar's face down in the mud. "My head's spinning. I need some time."

This was the way the gods had chosen to punish him for his lack of faith: by answering his unvoiced prayers and then watching him choke on their gifts. Isa was alive and still loved him, and she'd brought back an asha capable of defending the Shadar, one who had all the knowledge about the past he could ever care to know.

And it was all terribly, *horribly* wrong.

Isa waited beside him with her shoulders sagging, but the slouch was more like enervation than ease and her eyes never rested in any one place for long. Something was clearly wrong with her. Touching her had been like trying to dig his fingers into water, the way she'd responded just a little too late, as if each sensation had to travel a long way before she felt it. And the unnatural *warmth* of her—he'd fantasized so many times about being able to hold her without being bitten by the cold of her Norlander skin, but it just felt wrong. Anakthalisa had done something to her, tricked her somehow; Isa obviously didn't have the faintest idea about the true nature of the woman she had "rescued."

"Can we go now?" Isa asked, already turned toward the court-yard.

"I'm still dizzy," said Daryan, holding up his fingers to stall the man he'd spotted jogging toward them. He wasn't lying, either; his head felt like he had a brick sliding around inside it.

"You need to get clean," said Isa. "And Ani will be waiting."

"You go. I'll follow you," he said, knowing that of course she would argue; she wouldn't leave him alone, not like this—

"All right. I'll come back for you, or send help."

Daryan watched her disappear into the dark tunnel and then reappear in the liminal light at the courtyard end. She never looked back.

"Daimon!" Lem grabbed his jacket to stop him sliding down the wall into the mud. "Those shit-stained maggot-eating—"

The fact that he wasn't censoring his swearing actually cheered Daryan a little.

Lem fished out a miraculously dry scarf from somewhere under his jacket and began unwinding Tessa's makeshift bandage. "Gods! A little further over and it would have been your neck. I swear, I'm gonna find them and chop off every one of their—"

"Where's Tessa? And Hesh?" Daryan gasped as the dressing came loose and a shock of pain sliced through his shoulder.

"Gone—the kid said he knew somewhere safe, but wouldn't tell me where. Stubborn little jackass." Frowning down at Daryan's wound, he added, "You're going to need this stitched up, but you need to clean it first. If it festers—Well, I don't have to tell you."

"Hesh has his reasons not to trust you—or me, for that matter," he said. "The Red Guards and—" He couldn't make himself say the name; not yet. "They've been the ones killing the ashas. They're in some sort of cabal."

"What—? *Why?*" Lem gaped, rocking back on his heels.

"I'm not sure yet." In truth, at this moment he didn't care. First he had to stop Ani and Omir and whatever plans they had for the Shadar, by any means necessary. "What's happening out there?"

"Binit and that lot broke into the jail after the Dead Ones—not sure what happened after that. You've gone real pale, Daimon. We need to get you out of this mess and get that shoulder fixed."

"No. Not yet. I need to—"

"Daimon!" Omir's voice blared through the tunnel and he came in at a run, looking like he was about to shove Lem aside. He had two other Reds at his back and Daryan looked for some visible sign of what they were; but no, they could not have kept their secret for twelve generations by something obvious like a scar or tattoo; not living shoulder-to-shoulder in the mines or the barracks with good men like Lem. "I didn't know you were hurt so badly. I shouldn't have left you."

"I'm fine," he said. He put his hand on Lem's shoulder for support, knowing that he wouldn't be able to stop himself from flinching away if Omir tried to touch him. He thought of all the other times they'd stood like this, how secure he'd always felt in that huge shadow.

"Lady Isa said she told you about Anakthalisa," said Omir. "She's asking to meet you."

He's not your friend; he's a murderer. He poisoned that girl, and so many others. He's been lying to you since the day you met.

"Captain," Lem broke in, with a very poor attempt at composure, "that's an ugly wound he's got. Let me take him to get fixed up first."

"No," Daryan said, taking his hand from his bodyguard's shoulder. "First I want to meet this great asha Isa's found for us."

Omir visibly relaxed, leading Daryan to wonder what would have happened to him if he'd refused; or what Anakthalisa would have done to Omir if he'd come back alone. He steeled himself and moved past the others, leading the way, keeping his eyes fixed on the guards lining the top of the throne room steps. Little details of the scene around him stuck in his mind like darts: a sash lying sodden in a puddle; an unconscious man spread-eagled over a pile of shattered roof tiles; cracks in the paving where Isa's dereshadi—now gone—had landed.

The guards at the top of the steps exchanged a look but they said nothing as he passed; it took him a moment to realize Omir had probably signaled to warn them off. More guards lined the walls, but for the moment they were not his concern: no, that honor went to the petite figure with the fall of gray hair looking out over the balcony toward the blank site of the temple ruins. Even if Daryan could have lifted his arm to draw his sword, which he could not; even if he moved quickly enough to evade the guards, which he could not; he would still have to get through Omir before he could touch a hair on the old woman's head.

Diplomacy, then; smiles instead of daggers. He'd just have to fight the urge to slam Omir into the nearest pillar and beat him bloody, a fist in the gut for every innocent life he had taken. Then he noticed Isa standing beside the throne—*his* throne—with her features smoothed over and an unfamiliar languidness in her posture, nothing like the jitteriness of before. She watched him approach, but the look she aimed in his direction didn't quite close the distance between them. Something about the situation reminded him of being taken to meet his "aunt" Meena on his first day in the temple; the way they'd pushed him in front of the chair where she sat like a statue, her eyes blank except for a spark of hatred reserved for him alone.

"So, you're Daryan," said Anakthalisa.

"Yes, I'm Daryan." His elixir-induced vision had not prepared him for her sympathetic eyes or her silky voice. For a heady moment he wondered if he had got it all wrong—if he had made himself another victim of the elixir's trickery—but then he heard the echoes of the ancient Shadari screaming her name in terror. "Isa must have told you about me."

"Yes, she has. A great deal, in fact." Anakthalisa focused on him exclusively, lavishing him with attention, drawing him in. Effective—but unfortunately for her, Daryan had been raised by his uncle Shairav, one of the Shadari's greatest manipulators.

"She's only had time to tell me a little about you," he responded. He wandered a few steps to his left so he could see Omir out of the corner of his eye, like he had in Hesh's cell. "It sounds like you've had a rough time of it. How long were you a prisoner in Norland? How did they capture you?"

Anakthalisa smiled sadly. "Those days are best left in the past. I'm concerned with the present and the state in which I find things here. A difficult homecoming, yes?"

Daryan smoothed his fingers down the side of his face as if he could actually tilt his placid mask back into place. "Isa tells me you're an asha. A very powerful one."

"That is true, yes."

"I'm sure Isa has told you about the asha murders. It may not be safe for you here."

Anakthalisa raised her chin, in a kind of vague acknowledgment, but not agreement. "I'm concerned about the boy, Dramash. He is in considerable danger. Where is he now?"

"Dramash?" he repeated, not having to feign his surprise. He didn't miss Omir's downcast face or the way he fingered the strap of his scabbard; Anakthalisa had to be upset that such a powerful asha had slipped through her net. Thank the gods Rho had got the boy out of the Shadar. "He left for Norland months ago. We don't know what's happened to him, in all honesty. I didn't want to send him away, but it was hard for him here after he destroyed the temple. People were so frightened of him. They looked at him like he was some kind of monster."

Daryan didn't think he was imagining the way Anakthalisa's smile fixed itself in place or the way her eyes hardened.

"Ah, the rain has stopped," she said. "Come, walk with me on the balcony."

Daryan had to wave Lem back when he started forward, earning himself a narrow-eyed glare that worsened when both Isa and Omir closed in behind him. The balcony had been built so he could address his people outside of the walls; it barely accommodated the four of them. Once his lower back hit the balustrade he was essentially trapped. The rain *had* stopped, but breathing in the humidity felt like having a bag over his head and he was suddenly unbearably thirsty.

"Isa is worried I'll think less of you, coming home to find so much disorder, but I understand. You never wanted any of this," Ani said, touching her fingers to his hand in a brief, sympathetic pat. His skin crawled and he bit the inside of his cheek to keep from flinching.

"I've done my best."

"The ashas abdicated their responsibility to your family out of cowardice," she said. "You've inherited a burden that never should have belonged to you, yes?"

"Perhaps—but the burden is still mine."

"Ah, but now you can be free, child, like you've always wanted. Let me take that burden from you."

So, she expected him to smile and hand over his throne for a pat on the head, like a good little boy. She didn't even respect him enough to kill him and climb over his dead body.

"I couldn't ask that of you," he said, "not after you've already suffered so much."

"Your commitment does you credit, but I'm not thinking of you alone. This is no place for Isa, now, is it?"

"She was born here—she's lived her entire life here, up until three months ago."

"She's a Norlander: she will always be hated by the Shadari. You must see the tragedy that's awaiting her if she remains here."

It was a threat; nothing in her manner betrayed her but he *knew* it. He couldn't believe his impulsive, stubborn Isa was standing behind them and allowing her fate to be discussed as if she wasn't even there—but that was because she *wasn't* really there. From up close, her silver-green eyes mirrored the lack of interest he'd seen in her posture, a passivity that felt so *wrong* he wanted to shake it out of her.

"Is that what you want?" he asked Isa, forcing himself to really look at her flushed face and not focus on the sluggish way she turned to face him. "You want to leave the Shadar?"

"I did this all for you. So we could be together," she said. That rasp in her voice that he'd missed so much made him want to pull her to him again. "We said it from the very beginning: when the Shadari didn't need you any more, then we could leave. I did this all for us."

So Isa was to be his prize for abdicating.

"Daimon," said Lem, appearing in the archway, "I think you should come and see this."

Daryan left the others behind and went with the guard, even though every step risked him tripping over his own feet. The shouting from the courtyard sounded more like a celebration than a re-escalation of the fighting. Most of the guards had abandoned their posts to crowd around the top of the steps, but Lem shouted at them to make way as the clouds opened up yet again.

A wheelbarrow so loaded that it was taking two men to push it clattered into the courtyard. When people moved aside to clear a path, Daryan saw another cart already waiting there. Both carts looked like they were piled high with dirty sacks.

"Binit," Lem pointed out, gesturing to the one figure behind the carts shouting louder than any of the others. A group of three lifted a sack from the top of the pile and raised it over their heads before tossing it down into the puddled water, to laughter and cheers from the crowd.

Bile gurgled and Daryan retched and spat it out on to the steps, where it was quickly washed away by the pouring rain. Whatever reserves of strength he'd been using to hold himself together finally cracked, splitting him all the way down to his gristly heart. Still coughing, he watched the crowd swarm the wheelbarrows and drag the rest of the corpses off, tossing them around in a macabre dance. Every dead Norlander soldier had a long blue line where his throat had been cut; most of them still had their hands bound behind them. They hadn't been killed in the fighting; they'd been executed.

It wasn't until he started down the steps—to do *something, anything*, even though it was too late—that he realized that Lem was holding him up.

"No, Daimon," the man whispered: a plea. "You're hurt bad already. There's nothing you can do."

He heard Omir's heavy treads behind him and turned. "This didn't just happen, did it, Omir? You gave the order to execute them." It was a statement, not a query.

"They tried to escape."

"That's not true." He stopped to cough again, leaning more heavily on Lem. "Binit broke into the jail and dragged them out. I saw him do it."

"Their deaths were necessary to restore order," said Ani, walking up with her hand on Isa's shoulder.

"I put them in jail for their protection," Daryan fumed. "They were our allies. I promised—"

"Eofar Eotan has made himself Emperor of Norland. By their laws, he can't leave Ravindal," said Ani. "The bargain you struck with him is over. No one is coming to protect the Shadar. Do you see now how fortunate you are that I came back?"

He turned to Isa in shock. "Is that true? Your brother is the emperor?"

"Frea was right all along," Isa replied. "Emperor Eonar lied about our family. He had us banished so we wouldn't challenge him for the throne; there's nothing wrong with our bloodline. Eofar won the throne in fair combat. He's not coming back."

It was too much to take in—but there was still more. Staring down into the courtyard, he saw the extent of the damage for the first time: the top sheared off of the east tower; the porch roof in ruins; his precious fountain spewing water everywhere. So much effort destroyed in so short a time.

"Lem," said Daryan, pulling back, "send someone to my chambers to stitch up my shoulder."

The guard looked like he had asked him to stab him in the gut. "I can't leave you now, Daimon. I'm your bodyguard, remember? You need me."

"I have all these people looking after me; I'll be fine. And after that, I want you to go and visit your mother, like we talked about," he said, praying Lem would pick up on the cue. "Someone needs to make sure she doesn't try to *wander around* on that broken leg of hers. It's important for her to *stay safe*."

"Oh no, Daimon—I don't need to go. She'll be fine. She's a sensible woman, *my ma*."

"And what if that *little dog* of hers runs away again? You know she'll chase after it. No, you need to go be with her and keep her from getting into any trouble. Don't make me argue with you about this. I'm giving you an order."

Lem swallowed hard and swiped a wet glove across his mouth. "If you say so, Daimon." He bolted down the stairs like he'd been shoved, not looking back.

"You really believe Isa and I should leave the Shadar?" Daryan asked once Lem was gone.

"I do," said Anakthalisa.

"If you're not here, our people won't feel like they have to take sides. You'll be saving lives," said Omir. He'd probably been telling himself as much every time he lied to Daryan's face. "They can accept the Bl—Anakthalisa as their ruler without feeling disloyal, or fighting each other. We'll have peace and security. That's what you've always wanted."

And there it was: the reason for the asha murders, the reason Daryan had been seeking all these months. They had to be eliminated so they couldn't fight back against Anakthalisa like they had in the last civil war. The Shadari would have peace, and they would pay for it with the blood of anyone who might value their freedom a little bit higher.

"Then we'll leave at dusk," said Daryan, turning to Isa and taking her too-warm hand, "and good luck to us all."

Chapter 19

Lahlil stepped out of the tent to buckle Strife's Bane on her back while she checked the sky for the time. The sword was all she intended to bring with her, except for her knife and some water. Win or lose, this battle wouldn't last long.

"Lahlil!" Mairi called out, flapping a hand to get her attention in the cool, pre-dawn light as she jogged over, "are you going now?"

"As soon as the others are ready."

The healer tried to match Lahlil's strides as she followed her toward Rho's tent. "I wanted to say I'm sorry. I didn't mean what I said the other day, about it being on your head if Jachi—All right, I did mean it, but maybe kidnapping him was going too far."

Lahlil let her silence speak for itself.

"Fine, you were right," Mairi huffed. "Jachad should have the right to make his own choices just like the rest of us. But—Wait, can you stop walking for a moment, please?"

They both stopped, but the wind kept Mairi's wild hair from settling. "No matter what he says, I think you will find a way to save him."

Lahlil's denial stuck in her throat, unable to get past the obstinate faith in the Nomas woman's eyes. "I'll try," she managed at last.

They crossed a line of wagons and headed over to the little tent where Rho had been sleeping, but even before she stuck her head through the flap, she knew he wasn't there.

"Where is he?" she fumed, scanning the quiet camp until the sound of Callia's bracelets drew her attention.

"Over there, talking to the Abroan," said the new queen, using her free hand to indicate the part of the camp where the older children had gathered. Her other arm was keeping Oshi balanced on her hip. The baby curled into her side, blinking slowly once in a while but mainly still asleep. "I want to say something before you go."

"You, too?" Lahlil asked. She didn't like all these people fussing around her; she had to keep her mind on the task at hand.

Callia flipped her dark hair her back before pointing an imperious finger at Lahlil's chest. "You *owe* us. We took care of you when you were a girl and never asked for anything in return, and then you ran away from us and started killing people."

"That happened before you were born," Lahlil pointed out.

"Shhh!" the girl hissed. "It's your fault we got all tangled up with the Shadari again, and because of that we've had the fighting and the poison and all the trouble since. So you listen to me: no matter what happens there—if Jachad lives or dies, if there's war or no war—you come back. That's what Nisha would want, and it's what I want. And Oshi too, even if the little sprat can't say it for himself. This time, you come back to us."

Lahlil stared at her, at a loss. "You said I owed you."

Callia rolled her eyes. "You owe it to us not to disappear again, stupid."

Rho called out to them as he jogged through one of the shallow trenches left by the wagon runners. <Lahlil, what's taking so long? You need to talk to Savion.>

<What's the problem?> she asked, moving forward to join the aggravated man. The two Nomas women tagged along, uninvited.

<He says he won't stride until you tell him what you plan to do about Isa.>

<Oh. I see.>

<I explained that what happened at Prol wasn't Isa's fault,> said Rho. <Well, at least I tried to explain. Turns out none of the eight

197

or so languages Savion and I speak overlap in any way, so I had to resort to gestures to get my point across. The Nomas children laughed at me.>

Lahlil imagined Rho waving his arms and jumping around, and couldn't blame them. <I'll talk to him.>

<So what are you going to do about Isa?> Rho demanded. <You said she made her own choices. Are you expecting to make her pay for that in some way? Because I won't help you do that.>

She spied Jachad over Rho's shoulder. The dark jacket and trousers he'd adopted made his hair stand out like a brand. He bore no weapons except for a knife at his belt. "I'll talk to Savion," she told them all, without answering Rho's question, and then found herself in the middle of the company as they retraced Rho's steps.

They found three dozen young people gathered around the last embers of the fire, most of whom stood up as the adults approached. Savion had acquired an honor guard of six determined-looking Nomas teens, one of whom had taken the Abroan's hand. The Nomas never could resist a stray.

"My friends, here. These Nomas," Savion opened as she squared off in front of him, gesturing to his stony-faced companions, "they say I made a bad bargain with you."

"Do they?"

She accepted a bit of folded paper from the fair-skinned boy holding Savion's hand and discovered a bill laid out in tiny, precise characters, showing the amount of transportation for each traveler as per their original agreement, the interest accrued over time as the first bill went unpaid, then the charges for all the additional strides in Norland, a line item marked "grievous personal danger" and then the stride from Prol to the desert, once again itemized per traveler. The total at the bottom resembled the wealth of a medium-to-large-size duchy.

"I can't pay this," she said, folding it back up. "I have this much, and more, but I can't get to it without people finding out I'm still alive."

Savion's eyes flashed. "This. This is what you did to *us*, follow?

Striders. You made us choose—real death, or pretend. Didn't tell us we would lose who we *are*. Fellix went mad with it."

"I know. But you're not mad."

"I saw my little sister with a knife here," said Savion, pulling a finger across his throat and making his turban slip a little to one side. "I saw the blood. Not mad, Lahlil. *Angry*."

"I won't kill my sister for you. *But*"—she paused to make room for the discontented muttering of Savion's new protectors—"I promise, if she survives I will see that she makes amends for what she's done." Lahlil looked down at the paper again. "And as for this, I propose a trade."

"She doesn't have anything worth that much," the blond boy whispered to Savion.

"My brother is the Emperor of Norland now," Lahlil told them, raising her voice to make sure they could all hear. "I can tell him to cancel all of the contracts on striders and put the survivors under his personal protection. Anyone who harms a strider will answer to Norland. Any striders who are left can come out of hiding."

Savion stared back at her, his turban still askew and his yellow eyes shining, but he didn't answer. His new friend pressed closer and whispered something in his ear. The Abroan answered under his breath but never broke off looking at Lahlil until the boy stepped out in front of him.

"Savion accepts."

Lahlil tore the bill in half. "Then it's done."

The Nomas children broke out in a quiet cheer and then pushed forward to swamp their new friend with congratulations.

<Are we ready?> asked Rho.

Jachad turned toward the horizon, where the sun was spilling its first golden light across the sand. "We're ready."

Chapter 20

At dusk, Daryan and Isa pulled their cowls down low against the pelting rain and made their way to the stables. Omir's discreet orders had seen Aeda saddled and provisioned for their journey. No one else knew about their departure except Anakthalisa, who had airily waved off Daryan's concerns about how she would explain his disappearance.

No one bade them goodbye when Isa took up the reins, or watched from the ground as Aeda pushed up toward the weeping clouds.

The weather cleared after the first hour and the moonlight was bright enough to navigate by, so they flew on toward the first oasis. Daryan started shivering as the night wore on and then couldn't stop; his shoulder felt like someone had wrapped an iron band around it, then tightened it until the edges bit into his flesh. The arm attached to it alternated between numbness and an agonizing thudding. He knew he should have taken the physic's advice not to look while she cleaned the wound and stitched it back together; now the image of two jagged flaps of skin framing a well of blood filled his head whenever he closed his eyes.

He didn't see the oasis until they were spiraling down. It wasn't much more than a few boulders and a brick well scarcely larger than the ones in the Shadar. Relief at the thought of solid ground beneath him crumbled immediately when he remembered he would have to face Isa alone now, with no physics or Red Guards or stablehands hovering nearby to deter conversation and no rushing wind to whip the words out of their mouths. All those months of aching for her to return, and now the chasm between them was wider than ever.

It would take three days for them to reach Wastewater: three days of pretending that he didn't know the truth about Anakthalisa; of pretending he was prepared to start a new life with Isa. Three long days before he doubled back to the Shadar alone, leaving behind the woman he loved—bewildered and friendless—in a disreputable, backwater town.

"Are you all right?" she called out to him, her voice softened to a breezy hiss, the same tone she used to wake him when he fell asleep after one of their hurried trysts.

"Thirsty," he said, turning the bitter laugh into a cough, which then set him to coughing in earnest as he pushed his stiff muscles through the process of unbuckling the harness. Isa got down first and started rummaging through the saddlebags.

"Come and get a drink," he said, brushing his hand across the small of her back and watching her shoulders heave as she pulled in a breath. The buckle jingled loudly when she dropped the flap back down, but at least something had broken the silence. They had to work together to shift the cover off the well and the closeness of her crawled under his skin, itchy and insistent. And with the proximity came the certainty that she was *not* fine.

"Daryan?" she asked, lowering the dipper and sweeping the beads of water from her lips with her tongue. Her skin glowed less brightly than it should have and a film over her eyes held back their light.

"I'm sorry for staring," he said, trying a smile. "You look a little feverish. You're sure you're not sick?"

"No, I'm not sick," she said, rubbing at her left shoulder. "I'm tired. It took me so long to get home—not *home*; to you." Daryan winced at her slip. Anakthalisa had made it clear the Shadar wasn't her home. "You look different, too. You look older."

"It's the beard," he said, smiling a little easier. "Omir thinks—"
He stopped to clear his throat. "He thinks it makes me look more
imposing."

She ran the back of her hand down his cheek, smoothing down
the bristles, tracing his jawline with one long finger. "No, it's not
the beard. It's your eyes."

He *felt* old, looking at her. He felt ancient. "It's cold out here. I
should start a fire."

Not until they'd taken care of Aeda and set up camp did they
say anything to each other that wasn't about the business at hand.
As Daryan laid out a blanket over the cold sand, he could feel his
duplicity scratching at his insides, looking for a way out.

"So tell me everything that happened to you in the last three
months," he said as she came back from the dereshadi.

She settled down on her knees, closer to the fire than she should
have found comfortable, angled so that he could only see the
sharp sweep of her cheekbone and the edge of her jaw. "There's a
lot of it."

"We have time."

She told him a lot, from going to the Nomas and finding
Lahlil, to Jachad's poisoning and their journey to Norland. He
listened, fascinated, as she talked about Cyrrin the healer and
Valrigdal, her enclave of outcasts. She told him how she had rescued Anakthalisa—*Ani*—and brought her back home. Sometimes
Daryan would hear her breath stutter and he'd know that she had
decided to omit some detail or was glossing over something.

He noticed that her body was curling in on itself more and more
as the story went on, and little tics were getting more obvious: she
was scratching her fingers through the sand, biting her lip, tapping her foot.

"So Anakthalisa wants to make amends for having told the
Norlanders about the ore, which led them to invade and enslave
us. That's what she said?" he asked when Isa finished her story
with her arrival back in the Shadar.

"Even though it wasn't her fault," she murmured; he didn't think she realized she'd said it aloud.

"And she's going to use her powers to protect the Shadar against anyone else who tries to come after the ore?"

"Yes, but we don't have to think about that now; you and I have left. It's over for us." She almost sprang to her feet, went back to Aeda and started rooting through the saddlebags again.

That's what he'd told her, time and time again: once the Shadari no longer needed him, they would leave for some place where they could be together openly. He'd said it at first without believing it could ever happen, and he'd kept saying it because he'd needed something to hope for when every step forward drove him back another two. The day he'd begged Isa not to leave him, he'd believed it with every fiber of his being.

She did all this for you.

He couldn't do it. He couldn't lie to her any longer, no matter what the consequences. He loved her and she deserved better. So when she came back to the blanket and settled on to her stomach, he said, "I need to tell you something."

"Later, please," she said, shutting her eyes with a little flutter of her lashes. "I'm so tired."

His resolve drained away in an instant. Why shouldn't they rest, when in a few hours they would need all their remaining strength? For the first time since coming back she looked truly at ease, stretching now and again to lose the tension, sighing softly with contentment, as if the scratchy blanket were a feather bed.

He stretched out next to her and propped himself up on his uninjured arm so he could twist his fingers into her shirt and tug her closer. Her lips parted in anticipation of his kiss but he tilted his head and kissed her tears away instead.

"Why are you crying?" he asked her softly, pushing himself higher so he could see her better.

"Am I?" she asked, scrunching her face a little. "I don't know. I didn't notice. Kiss me again."

"You're warm. Why are you so warm?"

"It's the fire. Kiss me."

It was a chaste kiss, because something was wrong and he knew it, but when she flicked her tongue over his lips, pleading, he opened to her and she poured herself into him. With a rush of abandon he kissed her back in kind, entwining his body with hers in a way that had never been possible before, when the pleasure of every touch had to be weighed against the pain. She tasted of fennel and ripe berries and he couldn't make himself care that that made no sense. He pulled away, but only so he could jerk open the clasps on his riding jacket. Isa rubbed her cheek against his beard like she needed the contact; when he shrugged the jacket from his shoulders her lips brushed his neck and he felt no freezing pain, nothing but a fizzing sensation that had him arching his back to get closer to her.

"Your shoulder," she said, "can you—?" She broke off with a moan when his fingers curled into the hair at the nape of her neck and pulled her in for another kiss.

Soon their clothes lay scattered over the blanket and he slid into the hollow her body had made in the sand, tightening his hand on her hip. A soft noise came from her throat and he circled his uninjured arm around her, looping one leg over hers to pull her even closer. Her hand slid down his side, caressing, a touch that was too gentle, too coaxing, when he wanted to roll over and reclaim her, to make it clear to her that he wouldn't allow her to leave him again.

But he couldn't do any of that with his wounded shoulder, so he stayed where he was, tasting and exploring, finding the spots that made her twitch and moan and clutch him to her.

Finally she murmured his name in a breathy whisper, slipping her hand to the inside of his thigh before he tilted her head back and took her lips again, guiding her until they connected along the whole length of their bodies, the bones of her narrow hips sliding against his, his weight against her, her chin pressed into his shoulder when he kissed her neck again.

And as he kissed her ever harder, clutched her more ferociously, moved with more insistence than he had ever done before . . . it felt like part of her wasn't even there.

After their passion had crested and then ebbed away, he maneuvered her into his arms, resting his cheek against her white hair and splaying his hand across the warm curve of her hip. He thought of all those trysts where they had been forced to retreat from each other, close enough, but unable to touch. He wanted to swaddle this fragile moment and protect it, stash it away and keep it safe.

He slept, but not for long. He woke with dreams crowding in around him: the bad kind, hashed in shades of black and gray and hissing with fear; the dreams where he had failed everyone and his apologies were spat back at him in disgust. He rose to the point of consciousness where he would normally open his eyes and feel the sweetness of reality, but this time he didn't want to face the knot of guilt and dread curdling in his gut, so he went back to sleep.

When he woke up the second time, the fire had burned down to embers and a hollow marked Isa's spot on the blanket.

"Isa?" he called out, reaching for his trousers. Dawn had leached the indigo from the sky but the sun had yet to appear. Aeda still slept by the rocks—thank the gods, she hadn't abandoned him—but Isa was nowhere to be seen. He called again as he hurried toward the dereshadi, forgoing his shirt and jacket but taking his sword instead. Finally she came out from behind the rocks—completely dressed. "What are you doing?" he asked, the question coming out harsher than he intended. "Why didn't you answer me?"

"I forgot something. I have to go back."

"*What?*"

"I won't be gone long." That flat tone might have been normal for the other Norlanders, but it wasn't for Isa. He knew her husky drawl after they had been kissing; the tight strain when she needed to express something difficult; the way her words dropped down at the ends when she was angry; the arch and dip of the phrases when she was relaxed, or happy, or amused.

"What could you possibly have forgotten that would make you go back without me?" he asked. "Were you going to wake me, or leave me here to wonder what had happened to you?"

Her eyes reflected the silver sky, giving him nothing. "I won't be gone long," she said again.

"Isa," he said slowly. At this point he wasn't sure if she could really hear him. "What's that in your hand?"

A little tremor passed through her, not as big as a shudder but still noticeable. "Nothing."

Her wrist hung limply in his grip when he grabbed it, so pliant that the force he applied wrenched her arm, but she gave no sign of pain. Neither did she so much as tense her fingers when he peeled them back to reveal a little glass bottle, its little ridges pressed into her palm in swollen blue lines.

"Is that—Is that *divining elixir*?" he asked.

"No. It's medicine. *My* medicine. Ani made it for me."

"Medicine for what? You told me you weren't ill."

Isa's eyes widened a little, like the question made no sense. "For the pain, in my arm. She gave me all she had to take with me, but then I took some before we left, and last night, and then again this morning, and now this is all I have left."

"What happens if you run out?"

Her body went rigid and her silver pupils widened until they swallowed up every bit of the green. He guessed if he had been a Norlander, her fear would have knocked him straight into the boulder behind him.

"*That's* what's wrong with you—that's why you're warm now. Why you . . . drift, sometimes. She's been *drugging* you."

Her flush deepened and she shoved her fist into her pocket, still clutching the bottle. "She said you wouldn't understand."

"She was right about that," he shot back. "You're not going back to her, I can tell you that much." He hadn't really meant it to sound like a command but it did, and her demeanor changed instantly.

"Ani *helped* me. I was in pain and you did nothing." Her voice scraped, sounding overused.

"No." He was not going to let that stand. "You never gave me the chance to help. You hid it from me, like you hid how Falkar and the others were threatening you when you lived in the ashadom."

"I didn't want to give you another burden—"

"Because you thought I was too weak to handle it—isn't that right? That's what you think—and that's why you left."

"Yes!"

"I see," said Daryan, somehow keeping his voice steady even as jagged claws tore at his heart. "Thank you for being honest. Now, can I be honest with you?"

She stared down at the sand around her feet, clenching and unclenching the fist still jammed into her pocket.

"You've been duped," he told her bluntly. He began pulling his own shirt and jacket back on as swiftly as he could. "Anakthalisa isn't here to help anyone but herself. She only brought you here to get me out of the Shadar so she could take over without a fight. She doesn't care about you. She's not a victim: she's the tyrant Harotha saw in her vision and she's been planning this for three hundred years. I *saw* her, Isa. I took the elixir myself and I saw what she did to the Shadar the last time. Do you honestly believe she told the Norlanders about the ore *by accident*? She *wanted* them to come here—to break us, so that we'd be so desperate for her protection that we'd hand the Shadar to her on a platter. Omir and her other acolytes are the ones who've been murdering the ashas—and it's all been at her command."

Isa never raised her eyes during his speech and he was left panting in silence after his tirade, every muscle taut and trembling, the wound in his shoulder sending pulses of pain shooting up his neck.

"I can explain," she whispered finally, still without raising her eyes. "You don't understand—she *had* to do it. Let me explain."

Horror pushed him back away from her as a rotten seed of doubt burst into putrid flower. "You already knew."

"I have to go back," she said. "I thought it would be all right but I have to go back."

Daryan dropped his head into his hands and pressed his palms to his temples, unable to think, unable to move. Not even the worst of his nightmares had shattered him like this. He didn't want to hear Isa's explanation; his only hope of surviving this moment was to narrow the world down to the patch of sand at his feet.

"Daryan."

"Don't, Isa. I can't."

"Look up."

The tone of her voice had changed. When he did look at her, he saw she was slowly pacing backward with her eyes focused on the northern sky. The sight of the two dereshadi flapping toward them jolted him back into motion.

"They're here to kill us," he said, drawing his sword. "Anakthalisa was never going to let us go. She'd never risk me coming back to challenge her."

One of the dereshadi tucked in its head and dived, sharp talons shredding the dawn air. Daryan seized Isa's arm and bolted for the rocks, yanking her down beside him as the force of the wind pushed them back. He sheltered her beneath his own body when the beast's tail smashed the top of the boulder, showering them with rock.

"Get up," she said, shoving him off, "quickly—they want us trapped."

He sprinted toward the well while Isa lit out for Aeda. Two Red Guards were dismounting from the second dereshadi, which had already landed on the other side of the well. As the second slammed down near Aeda, Isa rushed its riders. Daryan took his eyes off the guards coming at him long enough to see her brace herself on Aeda's foreleg before leaping at the harnessed riders. For a moment he was sure she had managed to cut the leader's throat, but no, he'd got his arm up in time to shove her back down. She fell hard on her back but was on her feet again before the guards had torn themselves free of the leather straps.

But Daryan didn't have time to worry about Isa; he had his own problems. He turned to face his attackers, but he felt his stitches tear the moment he raised his black-bladed sword. His vision swam a little as warm blood seeped from the wound; he switched the sword to his left hand but he knew he'd be next to useless now.

"Who sent you?" Daryan yelled at them, backing up to put as much of the well between them as possible—but they immediately split up and circled around in opposite directions. "Veyash—who sent you to kill me? Was it Omir?"

The guard hesitated a moment at that, then he steeled his expression and kept coming. Someone shouted an order at the other guard—Daryan didn't know him—and he changed direction, running toward the second dereshadi and Isa, but there was nothing he could possibly do to help her in his condition.

"Anakthalisa ordered this, didn't she? You don't have to obey her."

"Yes, I do," said Veyash, circling the well to get to him. "She's the Blessed Mother—I've served her since the day I was born. I'm sorry, Daimon, but you don't understand. We've been preparing for this day for a dozen generations."

Veyash put on a burst of speed and Daryan knew that short of turning around and running into the open desert—and he knew exactly how *that* would resolve—he was out of options.

He turned to face his opponent, ducked under the first thrust and let Veyash's momentum carry him past, then spun around and lashed a kick at the back of the man's legs while he was out of position. That brought the guard down to one knee and Daryan poured all of his concentration into his black blade, willing it to compensate for the awkwardness of his non-dominant arm. He might have had a chance if Veyash hadn't had a black sword as well: instead, Daryan's blade was swatted aside like a wooden toy.

He backed up against the side of the well for support and managed to get his sword up again for a messy sweep, keeping Veyash off him for another precious moment. Bits of brick flew into the air as the Red Guard's blade cleaved the wall, the brick dust making Daryan choke even as he used the opportunity to slash at Veyash's leg. A long, thin line of blood bloomed on the cloth. Daryan pushed himself off the brickwork and barreled right into the startled guard, knocking him down into the sand where he became entangled in the blanket; he followed up with a stomp to the man's wrist that made his sword spring from his grip; Daryan bent down to throw it out of range before Veyash could call it back, but the guard had recovered enough to kick Daryan in the stomach. He toppled backward, doubled over and was still clutching his sword when Veyash's sweat-streaked face swam into view.

Daryan channeled all of his will into raising his sword again.

Then something changed.

It wasn't an earthquake; the earth didn't tilt, but he felt a *pull* like someone had taken hold of the back of his shirt and yanked as hard as they could while his feet remained anchored in the sand. Everything in his field of vision was elongated: the well; the dereshadi; Isa battling two opponents with the third lying vanquished on the ground. He was afraid to look down and see his own body pulled like so much dough.

The sensation lasted only a moment, but that too felt stretched out of shape, so that hours could have passed before everything finally sprang back where it belonged.

A woman in nondescript clothes ran in front of him, kicked Vayesh in the chest to keep him down before bending over to methodically cut his throat. In the time it took her to wipe her blade clean, Daryan decided nothing would ever make sense again.

"Where did you get that sword?" he spluttered, pointing at the silver dereshadi on the hilt.

She held out her arm to help him up. "From my brother."

A laugh huffed itself out of somewhere as he looked up into those mismatched eyes. "Lahlil," he managed to get out before he began to cough.

A new note entered the sound of swordplay and a second caped figure appeared fighting alongside Isa: Rho Arregador.

Daryan broke into a painful run, Lahlil jogging effortlessly beside him as Rho rammed the hilt of Fortune's Blight into the side of one man's head and dropped him like a stone. Isa, breathing hard with exhaustion, backed away from the last opponent and Rho took over. Daryan wondered if she'd been hurt. It wasn't at all like her to let someone else fight for her—

"Rho—*stop her!*" Daryan yelled even before Isa started running to Aeda. He clutched his wounded shoulder and tried to pick up the pace, but Lahlil had already left him behind. She leaped as Isa ordered Aeda into the air, managing to get a hand on the saddle—but Isa kicked her back down again. Isa hadn't even strapped herself in; the harness was looped perilously over her shoulder.

Daryan had to shield his eyes from the flying sand when Aeda swept her tail across the ground and arched her wings, and by the time it was safe to open them again, she was gone.

"She's going back to the Shadar, to Anakthalisa," he shouted to Rho and Lahlil as they hurried over. For the first time, he saw the others who had arrived with her: King Jachad of the Nomas, and a slight man in a turban with rough, dark skin and yellow eyes.

"She's going *back* to the Shadar? So where are *we*?" asked Rho, looking around the oasis.

"Half a day from the Shadar," said Daryan. "We—"

But Lahlil broke in, "You were *leaving*?"

Daryan's attention shifted away as the young man in the turban yawned widely and lay down on the abandoned blanket, looking very much like he was settling in for a nap. "No, not leaving," he answered, turning back to Lahlil. "I was *pretending* to leave, or Ani would have killed me on the spot. I wanted to get Isa away from her first, then I was going back to fight."

"Then you're not on Anakthalisa's side?" asked Jachad.

Daryan stared back at the Nomas king, suddenly struck by how different he looked. It wasn't just the jacket and trousers in the place of his usual striped robes, but something in his eyes—or rather, the *lack* of something.

"Anakthalisa is a monster. She needs to be destroyed," he replied unequivocally. "How do you even know her name?"

"She poisoned me," Jachad replied. "She also poisoned our next queen and killed my half-brother in her womb."

"Is that why your people abandoned us?"

The red-haired man showed no sign of remorse. "Yes, and my army is waiting in the desert just outside the city. If we don't defeat Anakthalisa, they'll attack."

Lahlil came closer and peered down at the bloody stain on Daryan's shoulder. "Can you fly a triffon with that?" she asked.

"No." His pride was the last thing that mattered to him now. "I *can* ride on one."

"Then you and Rho take that triffon and go after Isa. We'll give her enough time to get there, then follow. Savion needs to rest anyway."

"How did you even get here?" Daryan asked, the question finally bubbling up to the surface. "I didn't see any triffons."

"Come on," said Rho, loping off toward Veyash's beast at a pace Daryan couldn't have matched on his best day. The Norlander had already buckled himself into the harness by the time Daryan steeled himself to climb up after him. Pain exploded through his whole upper body as his weight settled into the saddle and he clenched his stomach muscles to ride out the agony, too breathless even to scream, until it faded back to a pounding ache.

"I need you to tell me what happened," he said to Rho while he buckled himself in. "Everything—why you came here. *How* you came here."

"Have you ever heard of the striders?" Rho asked.

"They're all dead. The Mongrel—I mean, Lahlil—killed them all."

Rho whistled and the dereshadi launched into the air, taking Daryan's breath along with it. "So, let me tell you a story . . ."

Chapter 21

Isa closed her eyes, trusting Aeda to fly back to the Shadar without her guidance. She could hear the pattering rain on her clothes and smell Aeda's wet hide but she couldn't make up her mind whether the rain was cold or warm or hard or soft; every time she decided, she changed her assessment again a moment later. Even when she tipped her head back and offered her face to the sky, or darted out her tongue to pull a few drops into her mouth, she still couldn't tell. But it didn't matter; she needed to focus on her one goal: getting back to Ani.

It had been a mistake, leaving while she knew Ani was still being hunted by Lahlil and her cohorts. Now they would play on all of Daryan's misapprehensions to get him on their side. The way he had looked at her—that appalled expression, like she'd had streams of blood instead of rainwater dripping from her chin. He had *no right* to judge her, to drag her down with him and his failures. And to think that before she met Ani, she would not only have let him, she would have thanked him for it.

The rain became a downpour as she reached the edge of the city but Aeda had seen far worse and didn't balk. In the streets down below, Isa could see the Red Guards rousting people out of their houses, leaving them shivering in the rain while they searched inside. They must be looking for Dramash.

Landing in the courtyard of the palace was out of the question now that the Red Guards had herded in a crowd of pushing, shouting Shadari—they must have rounded up the people responsible for the riots. She landed in front of the gates in the forecourt instead, drawing angry looks and yells from the people who had to scurry out of her way. She felt them staring at her while she dismounted, muttering like they always did, but they weren't going to try anything, not when they knew she could cut them down like weeds. It didn't matter. This palace never was and never would be her home. Her home had been the temple; she had its red dust in the back of her throat still. The hole in the horizon matched the one in her heart.

The gates were broken, so once she'd shoved away the guards who tried to question her she just walked in. She drew Blood's Pride in the courtyard and went directly to the throne room. No one tried to stop her, but one Red Guard ran up the steps ahead of her, which meant she could expect to find Ani advised of her return.

The throne room glittered with lamps to chase away the sea-green darkness of the storm. Ani stood near the great stone chair with Red Guards—acolytes, judging by the heady reverence on their faces—lined up in ranks on both sides with Captain Omir at the head. Isa herself nearly dropped to her knees seeing the change in the old woman, now dressed in flowing robes of deep red, a thick gold chain around her neck, dozens of gold bangles on both thin wrists, a ring with a huge faceted red jewel, her gray hair braided and pinned with gold clips. The heavy stone tables were piled high with fruit and cakes, and servants stood by to fetch whatever she desired. This was exactly the kind of magnificence Daryan had derided as pointless and wasteful, and Isa now recognized his greatest mistake: people didn't want a leader who kept making a point of how he was just like them: they wanted somebody *better*. Ani belonged more to this room than Daryan ever had.

"Ani," said Isa as she walked the length of the room, "someone followed us to the desert. They tried to kill us."

The old woman closed her eyes briefly before taking a goblet of wine from a servant's tray and examining the ornate decoration around the rim. She took a sip. "Oh, child," she sighed. One hand pressed the creped skin below her throat. "I hoped you would have had the sense not to return."

Isa's pulse throbbed in her ears. "I don't understand."

Ani's ring clicked against the goblet as she took another drink. "I believed you when you said Daryan would happily leave the Shadar for you."

"He did."

"Of course you realize he intended to return here, yes? To rebel against me?" She sounded resigned, as if Isa's fall in her estimation had been inevitable. She gestured the servant with the wine forward and put the empty goblet back on the tray.

Isa rocked back, searching Ani's face. The warm eyes, the fond smile, the tilt of the head that meant Isa had her undivided attention: they were all still there, but they didn't match the words she was hearing. "I don't understand."

"Look at yourself, child." Ani came forward in a cloud of rustling silk and raised her fingers to Isa's maimed shoulder. Her touch lit a path straight through her nonexistent arm, mirroring the lightning forking beyond the arches. "He could never look at you and forget what your people did here. Can you not see how he kept you like a dog on a chain, parading his mastery of you? He encouraged you to humiliate yourself so he could revel in your shame. I saw as much the moment we arrived."

Isa shrank down under the weight of the sopping clothes clinging to her body. She tried to understand what was happening, but everything was too cold, too wet; the lightning was too bright, the thunder too loud. The medicine shouldn't have been wearing off yet but the feverish shivering and the throbbing in her left shoulder said otherwise. She clamped her hand around her forehead, trying to squeeze everything back in so she could think. "No. That's not right."

Ani brushed Isa's cheek with her fingers before stepping back. "Did he tell you where he's hiding Dramash?"

"No. He's not—He doesn't know. Dramash isn't here."

Ani pursed her lips. "It's not your fault, child. It should have been Lahlil," she said, her soft voice sliding over Isa's skin like the flat edge of a razor. Another gust of wind blew through her robes and a shower of red raindrops pattered around them. "I asked too much of you."

Isa tried to remember how to breathe, but the effort only worsened the pain. She had to ignore the wheezing and the darkness creeping around the edge of her vision, even though thunder was pouring into her, setting everything trembling, loosening the connections.

Your sister.

Isa said, "But Lahlil abandoned you in that tower. *I'm* the one who rescued you."

She was the one—*not* Lahlil!—who went to Norland and braved the tower; she was the one with the snow matting her hair, the one leaving a trail of blood behind her. *I have been waiting a very long time for this—for you, Isa.* The memory sat heavy on her. Ani was supposed to be the mother who had been waiting for *her*, the one who needed *her* help. She was *not* supposed to choose Lahlil.

Somehow Isa's legs began walking, but they had no help from her; not with her eyes half-shut and her head pushed into her shoulder to block out the thunder. The pain came from everywhere and nowhere now, and each step was driving the invisible knives in a little deeper. She didn't know where she was going—where could she go now? She knew only that she had to get out of there.

"Stop her," said Ani, and Isa tensed—but the guards were lunging for the servant with the wine, who was heading toward the steps. The tray flew from the woman's hand as they grabbed her and forced her arms behind her back while she let them, too frozen with fear to struggle.

"It must have occurred to you that I would protect myself against my own poison," Ani said to the servant, her silken voice filled with sorrow. The goblet chimed softly as it rolled over the tiles; fragrant wine poured from the carafe's mouth. "That you could be so blinded by prejudice that you would risk your life this way comes near to breaking my heart. You're an asha, yes?"

"Her name is Tessa, Blessed Mother," said Omir, stepping forward. "I believe she's the one who gave the divining elixir to Daryan."

Ani swept forward as Omir was speaking and stood in front of the visibly shaking woman, her robes settling around her like a bird's feathers. "Why did you try to poison me, Tessa?"

"C-c-couldn't let you," the woman stammered. "I've never killed another living thing, but I have seen who you are and what you have done and I couldn't let that stand. You think we're all gasping to have you take over, but it won't be that easy, I can tell you. The daimon's had more of an influence than he knows. We'll fight you." Then she visibly pulled herself together with a look that Isa recognized; Tessa had decided to use her last moments to get some retribution. "And I wouldn't rely too much on your man, there," she said, pointing to Omir. "He tried to put his murdering ways on my son, but instead we got the poison away from him. Oh, we led him a merry dance. And me right under his nose this whole time."

Ani turned back to Omir. "You had an asha this close to you, undermining you—and yet she slipped through your fingers?"

Omir's face went bloodless and he drew his sword, clearly intending to silence Tessa before she embarrassed him any further—but a tremor ran through the floor and he gave a strangled cry, clinging to his sword with both hands as Tessa used her powers to tug it backward. His muscles strained like he was trying to keep a falling load of bricks in place.

Isa lost sight of Tessa when one of the guards stepped in front of her, but she heard the distinctive thump of knuckle on bone, then Omir stumbled backward as the pressure on his sword abruptly stopped. Tessa's head lolled, bright red blood welling from her split lip and dribbling down her chin.

"No more of that, now, child," Ani said soothingly to the asha, using the end of her sash to wipe the blood from the woman's chin. The warmth in her voice made Isa's chest ache. "I don't fault you for your misguided notions. Your love for our people does you credit."

Tessa sobbed, but Isa wasn't sure if she understood what Ani was saying.

"You were clever enough to survive the purge and I commend you for that. You want to protect our people, as I do, yes?" Ani stroked the woman's freckled cheek with the backs of her nails.

"Yes, I do," said Tessa, her eyes hazy with confusion.

The old woman drew out a vial from an embroidered pocket. "That's very good. Then you, my dear, will be Dramash's proxy until he takes his rightful place by my side."

Isa knew that vial. She could almost feel the stuff slithering down her throat all over again, the way those filthy claws came burrowing down into her chest until they found the hole they'd already dug and then scratched open the scars until they oozed. The thunder sounded like hundreds of wings now, shaking the floor until it fell away from under her and she was dropping down, down and down to the bottom, where a twisted, broken *thing* waited for her, crooked arms hanging loose and wide, ready to embrace her. *This isn't happening now*, she told herself. *It's just a memory. Stop this. Do something.*

And suddenly Isa didn't care if Tessa was friend or foe, patriot or traitor, if she deserved to live or die. She only knew that she couldn't watch what she had experienced on the *Argent* being done to Tessa, or to anyone. The wrongness of it went deeper than any questions of loyalty or power.

"Ani, please," she called out, "don't make her take that. You don't *know*—let me talk to her. I'll convince her to help you."

"Silence that Norlander, please," said Ani, not even looking over as she held the vial to Tessa's lips.

Isa swept Blood's Pride out before the nearest guard had so much as flinched in her direction. He struck out at her in a panic and she batted him away easily, and then kicked him into the nearest column. Her victory was short-lived, for Lieutenant Tamin rammed his heavy fist into her ribs, her legs gave out and he grabbed her wrist as she toppled, twisting it until he'd loosened her grip enough for him to pluck Blood's Pride from her hand. When she reached for it, he backhanded her and sent her sprawling to the ground, gasping against the pain of what was likely a cracked rib.

"Omir," Ani called over, straightening up from where she had crouched down beside Tessa to pet her hair while the woman quivered in silent pain and her eyelids twitched. "Come closer."

"I'm here, Blessed Mother," said the captain, presenting himself.

"You are my First Acolyte. It was your sacred duty to prepare for my return, yes?" Ani asked as she gently pressed her fingers to the man's massive chest.

"Yes, Blessed Mother."

"And yet I arrive to find our people at each other's throats and a man by your side who calls himself a king, with followers willing to fight and die for him."

"Yes, Blessed Mother." Omir swallowed. "I believed Daryan would join us."

Tamin unconsciously loosened his grip on Isa as he watched the proceedings. She thought of making a grab for her sword, but she hadn't yet caught her breath and she couldn't afford to waste what would likely be her only opportunity.

"You recognize your failure then?" Ani asked Omir, raising his chin a little so he would lift his downcast eyes.

"Yes, Blessed Mother."

"And you are penitent?"

"Yes. Yes, Blessed Mother," the captain choked out.

"Good, my child. I will aid you in your redemption," Ani promised. She reached into her pocket and produced the onyx box Isa remembered from the *Argent*—the one she had been so sternly warned never to open—and peeled away the wax seal. The latch clicked. "Draw your knife and make a cut on your palm."

Omir didn't flinch as he slid his blade over his hand. Blood welled from the cut a moment later and dripped onto the floor.

"There's a stone in this box. Take it out now and hold it in your hand."

Omir lifted the stone out of the box. Even in the light of all the glimmering lamps, Isa could see the silver slime crawling all over it.

This was the secret prize Ani had brought with her from Norland: the plague.

"No!" The word ripped from Isa's throat and brought her to her feet, but the floor rocked like a boat; she breathed deeply, trying to keep herself from collapsing again. It wasn't supposed to be like this: Ani was supposed to *protect* the Shadari—*help* them, like she'd helped Isa. "Ani, you can't—! There's no way to cure it here! It will kill *everyone!*"

"Not everyone," Ani reassured her. "The people down there are traitors. I've told you before, child, I've had to learn from my mistakes."

People were going to *die*; people who had stood by Daryan, people who had stood against him . . . and suddenly those factions no longer mattered. What mattered was that Ani was only here in the Shadar because *she* had brought her here.

Isa tried to dash forward, but Tamin kicked her legs out from under her and she crashed to her knees again. He looked uneasy, though, and so did most of the other guards, who were shifting around and exchanging worried glances. But none of them looked ready to break ranks to put a stop to this.

"Ani, this isn't what you promised," she pleaded. "You said you wanted to bring peace."

"Hush now, child," Ani said, gesturing for Omir to put the stone—the silver now mingled with his blood—back into the box. "They have to be purged," the old woman said, her voice soft with regret. "It will teach the survivors that they can count on me to protect them from treachery, invasion or sickness. It will be a difficult lesson, dear ones, but the vital ones always are."

Isa moved, only to be felled by another kick from Tamin—but she was expecting it this time and flipped herself on to her back and lunged up at him, shoving her knee into whatever soft parts she could reach as she jabbed her fist into his face. He fell back, blood streaming from his nose, and this time she made it all the way to her feet before two more guards set on her with drawn swords. She ignored them and ran at Omir instead, catching hold of the back of his jacket before he turned around.

"Omir, she's infected you with the plague!" she cried out. "It will kill *everyone*—please, *please*, go away! Get away from everyone before you turn and infect them too—"

But a hand seized her hair from behind and knocked her head into the pillar. Her vision went blurry and the next thing she knew, she was curled into a ball on the ground, desperately trying to keep from vomiting. She retched until the sounds of the rain outside, of people moving and speaking around her blended into one meaningless hiss and the world went white.

It was different, this emptiness. It wasn't all softness and shimmering colors, nor a void trying to devour her, but plain emptiness. No Daryan, no Ani, no home, no arm. She would never get back what she had lost. There was no mercy for her here. Her fealty to Ani was something spoiled, wriggling with a contagion that had finally swelled large enough to rupture her skin and crawl out.

Isa's eyes snapped open.

A flash of lightning etched the scene around her: Tamin had twisted her arm behind her back and was holding her on her knees at the top of the steps, looking down into the courtyard—except the steps themselves were gone, pulverized into dust. The blowing rain stung her face, washing the vomit from the front of her cloak. Her stinging eyes couldn't adjust to the confusion below: too many people were running or huddling against the walls; too many guards were herding them with shouts and shoves.

And then the screaming began.

A space in one corner of the courtyard cleared like a drop of oil in water, and there was Omir, twitching with fury, drooling silver pus, while more leaked from his hand and dripped from his eyes. She had been unconscious long enough for Ani to send him down into the crowded courtyard and for the plague to take hold of him, doubtless spurred by the wet heat hanging in the air. Already out of his mind with the sickness, Omir drew his sword and charged the crowd, missing the first man he tried to grab and instead throwing a woman to the ground and stabbing his sword through her chest. The people might not yet have understood the nature of the silver slime sliding down his blade, but they had seen enough to panic.

The screaming rose in pitch and blended together: a single sound twisted together from a hundred different nightmares. Isa's stomach heaved again as she watched helplessly from the edge of the throne room. She needed to breathe, but her lungs wouldn't accept the pestilential air and her extremities had gone numb.

A deep groan juddered across the space and the tunnel to the back yards caved in, trapping anyone who might have been frightened enough to charge the armed guards stationed in front of it. Isa didn't have to guess the cause: Ani, still magnificent in her sodden red robes and her glistening gold jewelry, was standing with Tessa's hand in hers as she plundered Tessa's mortality to control her powers.

The east tower rocked, at first refusing to fall, until something shifted and bricks slowly toppled onto the broken gates, cutting off any attempts to flee in that direction. Isa flinched as tiles flew past, but she couldn't tear her eyes away from the people below as the madness spread. The infected had started scrabbling and scratching at each other. One man picked up a brick and smashed in a Red Guard's head. A young woman slit a resurrectionist from his throat to his navel. An old woman wrestled a sword from a Red Guard and slashed an unarmed man's abdomen with such force that his organs spilled out before he fell.

Another flash of lightning lit up the carnage while the simultaneous crack of thunder made Isa feel like she'd been split in half.

"They're your people," she said to Ani, even though she knew she'd never be heard over all the screaming. "The guards down there are your acolytes. They murdered for you—and now you're letting them die."

"They're martyrs," Tamin answered for Ani.

A triffon flew over the courtyard toward the stables, drifting like a black mote against the slate-gray sky, but instead of landing, it banked sharply and came back around.

<Rho!> she screamed, pulling in all her strength to reach him over the distance, <Rho, don't land! She's brought the plague!>

The triffon passed overhead and banked again before she heard his reply, wraith-thin but bright with urgency. <What? What is she doing? She'll kill herself along with the rest of you!>

He was right. The guards in the courtyard were being infected, along with everyone else. Someone would find a way out and spread the plague to the rest of the Shadar. <There must be more to it. She must have known—>

"I know you're talking to them," Ani interrupted. "Plotting, I'm sure. Oh, Isa—how did we get to this point, after all we've been to each other?" The ground in the courtyard below rippled, as if someone had picked up one end and flapped it like a carpet, tossing people up in the air. The fountain shattered, the paving cracked and lifted, sticking up at all angles like broken glass, and bodies came down hard, cracking heads open, snapping limbs. Those who could still walk stumbled around, but there was no place to go.

The west tower fell next, quickly, crushing everyone beneath it, giving no one any chance to crawl to safety. Only the throne room section of the north wing, where Isa knelt in front of Tamin and Ani, remained standing. And still Isa could see silver glowing below, spreading in spatters and streaks, crawling into any open wound or orifice it could find, proliferating.

Then the ground opened up, not all at once, but slowly, like flour through a sifter, dozens of pockmarks sucking in the debris—the stone fish from the fountain, the broken bodies, the paving stones, the porch columns, the weapons, the bricks and tiles—and swirling it down and away. It all went down—the dead and the living, sometimes leaving a hand or a foot flapping behind for a moment before being engulfed.

And it pulled Isa down too, in a way; pulled her head to her knees and the last shred of hope from her heart.

Chapter 22

Lahlil came out of the stride with one arm threaded around Savion's bony elbow and the other around Jachad's; it left her without a weapon at the ready, but Savion was already tired from the first stride and she wasn't going to risk having either man torn away from her this time. The moment their surroundings solidified, she let go of them and drew Strife's Bane. Judging by the columns, long tables and ponderous throne, they had ended up in Daryan's palace. Some two dozen people were gathered in the open archways at one end of the room, all of them with their backs turned. The air thrummed with a particular stillness Lahlil recognized from the battlefield, and the earthy smell of damp brick dust hung in the air.

"I'm ready," said Jachad.

"Wait," she hissed as Savion sagged against her, in danger of falling until she pulled him into a hasty embrace. "Savion? Hey! Look at me," she said softly, then waited until his yellow eyes blinked up at her. "Can you stride away yet?"

He shook his head.

She held on to his shoulder for another moment until a roll of thunder gave some cover to their movements and then half-carried him behind the throne, while Jachad slipped behind one of the columns.

"You should be safe enough here for now," she told Savion, propping him up against the stone, "but listen: the moment you can, you stride back to the desert and let the Nomas look after you until I get back. You've done all you can here. Do you understand?" She held his face and looked into his unfocused eyes until he nodded again.

Back behind the pillar, Jachad had his eyes fixed on the small form of Anakthalisa, almost floating in a sea of red-jacketed soldiers. The witch was holding the hand of a nondescript Shadari woman, who was swaying like she was about to faint.

<They don't know we're here. We won't get a better chance than this,> he said. <I'm doing this now.>

<No, wait—I don't see Isa. We used her presence for the stride, so she's got to be here.>

<Does it matter?> Jachad made the question feel chillingly rhetorical. <We're here to kill Anakthalisa, not rescue Isa.>

The Mongrel would not have hesitated. She would have let every person in that room burn, and then put her sword through anyone who had managed to survive that. But the Mongrel's skin was too tight for Lahlil now; she couldn't squeeze back into it if she tried. <Let me find her first. One more chance, that's all I'm asking. Will you wait?>

<Yes. But not long.>

She slipped away and began making her way toward the front of the room, silent and low. It didn't take her long to find Isa on her knees, with one of the uniformed guards twisting her arm behind her back. Clearly her sister had not had the warm welcome she'd expected. Lahlil didn't know if Isa had suffered enough to turn her loyalties, but there was only one way to find out.

<Isa.>

<Lahlil,> her sister answered, her voice thick with misery, <if you can kill her, do it now.>

<You need to get out of the way first.>

<No.> Weakness dragged at her sister's words, overlapped by jagged lines of pain. <This is all my fault. You and Rho tried to warn me. There's no going back now.>

Lahlil let her head fall back against the column as she strove to keep her urgency from exploding into anger and driving Isa away again. She spared a moment to check on Jachad and found him staring fixedly at Ani. <Jachad won't attack while you're in the way. If you want Anakthalisa dead, you have to *move*, Isa.>

Her sister's presence had faded to a sluggish throb.

<Isa!>

"We're done here," said Anakthalisa to her companions, stepping back from the archway and out of the rain, away from the edge of the ruins of a wide stone staircase. "I'd hoped to find Dramash here, but we'll be together soon enough. I wish to return to my temple. Lieutenant—ah, no—it's *Captain* Tamin now. Have you sent your guards ahead to await my arrival?"

"Yes, Blessed Mother," answered the man holding Isa's arm, releasing her in order to bow. Isa slumped to the ground.

<That's good. Stay down,> Lahlil called out to her sister. <They're not paying attention to you. Now move away from Ani, slowly.>

"And the men your predecessor sent to the desert with my instructions, have they returned with the item I needed them to fetch?"

"I—I'm not sure, Blessed Mother," Tamin stuttered. "The scout who returned said they knew where to find the baby, but it might be hard to get him out. The Nomas have a whole army encamped there."

"Baby? Do you mean Oshi?" Isa gasped.

Lahlil felt the air around her contract and snapped her attention over to Jachad, but he had shifted his position to where she could no longer see his face.

<Isa, shut *up*!>

"Leave Oshi alone!" her sister shouted at the old woman. "You can't use him like you used the rest of us! He's just a baby!"

<Isa—!>

"Lahlil won't let you—" Isa finally cut herself off, which only made it more obvious that she had looked directly at Lahlil's hiding spot.

228

"Ah," Anakthalisa breathed, smiling slowly as she made the obvious connection. "Lahlil, come forward and stop skulking back there like a naughty child. You see? I knew we would meet again. Our destinies are intertwined."

"Oshi," Lahlil spat through gritted teeth as she stepped away from the pillar and walked to the center of the room, drawing all eyes to her. <I'll keep her talking while you get away,> she told her sister, at the same time asking Ani, "What do you want with him?"

The witch regarded her with wearied fondness. "I want to keep him safe, Lahlil. *For you.* Your vision, yes? You will be holding him when it comes true."

"You sound like you expect me to thank you."

"It would be polite, but no," said Anakthalisa, "I expect you to join me. As I have told you before, you are my champion."

Lahlil's throat clenched tight at the feel of those warm eyes on her, the scrutiny of this woman who had won the trust of the Mongrel with a few pitiful words of maternal affection. She could hardly criticize Isa for falling under the same spell. "Why me?"

"Because you are extraordinary, like me," said Ani.

"You think you've been wronged, and you want to make people suffer for it. There's nothing extraordinary about that. Every puffed-up little tyrant who ever threw me a purse wanted the same thing."

Ani's smile stayed in place but her eyes glittered. "The differences will soon be apparent, child. I have already destroyed the traitors in our midst; next it will be the Nomas. I want them to see the cost of meddling in the affairs of the Shadar. But I do intend to allow a few to live, to spread the word that the Shadar is under my protection now—perhaps you'd like your little ginger king to be one of them? Or should I wipe him from the face of creation along with the rest of his mendacious, thieving kind?"

"Don't," Lahlil warned, but the whispered word barely made it past her lips. She heard footsteps behind her and turned to see Jachad step out from his hiding place, flame twisting around his arms and hands and his face shimmering with rage.

There was a moment of stunned silence—and then everyone began shouting at once. The guards surged in closer to Anakthalisa, blocking Isa's escape path. Jachad was about to strike. Lahlil only had two choices: get out of his way, or—

<Isa, stand up. I'm coming to get you!> Lahlil ordered. She charged the guards, slashing the first one in the chest while he was still fumbling with his grip, and then kicking him into the others behind him. Their black blades reflected the surge of light behind her, but apparently Jachad was still holding back. Lahlil swung at the next guard and caught her blade on his parry, pushing back against it and holding it long enough to surprise him with a punch to the face. She stabbed into his chest as he was still reeling back, while another guard's frantic thrust skimmed right past her. With no time to pull her sword out of the first man, she grabbed her knife and stabbed the second man in the neck.

Finally she was close enough to seize her sister's wrist and fling her to safety behind her, while slashing and kicking at anyone who came within reach. They were retreating when one of the guards let loose a nerve-shredding scream.

He was on fire.

A wall of flame sprang up around Jachad, scorching the white-washed ceiling, bathing the columns in ocher and saffron and casting striped shadows along the walls. Lahlil yanked her scarf up over her mouth and nose to protect herself from the smoke and the stench of burning flesh.

Then a sharp crack cut through the noise of the flames and a fissure raced across the floor, followed by another, and another, all of them fanning out from the spot where Anakthalisa stood.

"Jachi, look out!" Lahlil cried, as he thrust out his hands and sent all that fiery destruction straight at Anakthalisa. The men in front barely had time to scream before their skin scorched to ash and they fell where they stood. Tamin grabbed another guard and together they upended the closest table to shield Ani, scattering food, drink and crockery to the floor. Tongues of flame rippled over the stone surface and fluttered around the edges, but nothing caught. Lahlil could feel the heat pushing at her like a wall.

Jachad roared with frustration, gushing flames so fiercely they actually lifted him from the ground. He raged inside his blistering shield, elemental and terrifying, but Lahlil alone understood how unfocused and unintended those wild tendrils of flame really were. His control was already crumbling.

The floor trembled and another great crack whisked up the pillar right next to Lahlil. She grabbed her sister and hauled her out of the way as the column crashed down, but not before a chunk of plaster and brickwork smacked her between her shoulder blades, sending her staggering.

<The woman with Ani—Tessa,> Isa called out to her, her voice faint but urgent. <She's an asha.>

Lahlil looked back at the Shadari woman. Her eyelids were fluttering and her mouth gaping open as if she were trying to suck in a breath that wouldn't come. Rho had described how Anakthalisa had used Dramash's power in Norland; this had to be the same thing.

If she could separate them—

Jachad let out a deep wail that plunged straight into her heart as the blaze roared up even higher. Copying Tamin, Lahlil heaved the nearest table onto its side and pulled Isa behind it. Chunks of burning masonry rained down on Jachad, and Lahlil was certain he would be buried alive—his worst fear—but the debris burned up or was pushed aside by the heat. For a moment she saw the god he would become: the figure in the eye of the inferno, too bright for mortal eyes to look upon—until the roof over his head shattered like an eggshell and an avalanche of brickwork crashed down on him.

"Jachi!" she cried out as he disappeared beneath the rubble, buried completely.

She started to run to him, already mapping out the best place to begin digging him out, when she saw the fire still there, licking up through the crevices, heating the edges of the bricks until they smoked and glowed like coals. Bright spikes of light poked out and lit up parts of the room that had never before seen anything but shadow. He was alive under there, that much was certain.

She was also certain that she would never be able to dig him out as long as Ani had the power to bring the building down around them.

The remaining Red Guards braced themselves as she ran at them again, expecting her to go for Ani, but instead, she charged one on the fringe and grabbed his sword arm before he'd realized what had happened. She used his own blade to hold the others at bay before pushing him bodily off the ledge and into the ruins. The next man didn't have enough training to realize the black sword would respond to his agitation; he waved it around so wildly that she all she had to do was drop down on one knee and let his blade whiff over her head, then thrust Strife's Bane up through his ribs. Warm blood poured down the blade and over her hands as she yanked the sword free.

The two deaths had taken little more than a moment and Anak-thalisa only now shifted her focus away from Jachad and began shouting at the guards to protect her.

Lahlil tried to stop thinking about Jachad buried behind her, looking to slip into that quiet place where instinct ruled, where there was nothing but the fight. But it didn't work. Instead of soulless wax figures falling under her blade, she saw men with fear and courage in their eyes; she saw unique and irreplaceable lives bleeding out. And as much as she longed for the detachment of fighting to satisfy her craving for oblivion, she could not forget for one moment that she was fighting for her family now.

Several of them rushed her simultaneously, which was exactly what she would have expected of soldiers who had never fought in a battle and didn't have the training to keep out of each other's way. Two tripped each other up and went down without any help from her, leaving her free to slice one man across the shoulders and in the same motion, swing back and smash the pommel of

Strife's Bane into another. The floor kept lurching and more bits of the room crashed down, but she was close enough to Anakthalisa now for her very proximity to protect her.

Another soldier attacked, this one with such a disastrous grip on his sword that she disarmed him with a move a Norlander child could have made. She jabbed him in the side with her dagger before shoving him away to join the other bodies piled around her.

Anakthalisa was nearly within reach, but Tamin and the few remaining guards curtained off her small figure—and left her asha proxy unprotected. Lahlil tossed her sword to her other hand and grabbed a chunk of stone from the floor. Tamin swung out at her but she slid out from under him on her knees, emerging in time to sling the brick at the witch's grip on the freckled woman's hand.

<Lahlil, no!> Isa's voice shrieked inside her mind.

Her aim was true. Anakthalisa flinched and pulled back her hand and the Shadari woman immediately slumped to the ground. She was trembling and drooling, but she was alive.

Anakthalisa gave a stifled scream and listed into Tamin's side.

<It's all right, Isa,> Lahlil called back to her sister. <I broke the connection. She can't use the asha's power any more.>

<No, no, that's not how it works!> Isa responded frantically. <She doesn't need the asha for power—she needs her for control.>

Only then did Lahlil see that Anakthalisa's dejected posture wasn't about defeat at all; it was about keeping her energy close to her, lashing down her power to keep it from exploding outward.

Lahlil charged Tamin, trying to get past him to take out Ani with brute force, but she was already too late. A blast of energy tore through the room and tossed both her and the lieutenant into the air like rag dolls. She landed hard on her back, gasping, as a nest of cracks flared out around her; although she immediately sprang to her feet, another crack was rushing from one side of the room to the other, cutting her off from Anakthalisa and her remaining companions. Again the floor lurched, and again she went down onto the sharp bricks. More falling masonry battered her, and a heavy piece to the shoulder knocked her flat before she could get up again. By the time the stuff stopped moving, she found herself with one leg buried up to her hip and flakes of white-wash falling around her like snow.

"Jachi!" she cried out, futilely trying to warn him while she dug herself out. They needed to get out of there before—

The back half of the room tipped like a capsizing ship as the supports on the story below gave way and everything tumbled down on her. Her leg slid out a little as the debris shifted and she used the traction to pull it out the rest of the way. At the end of the room, the throne twisted out of position with a juddering groan and flew backward, smashing straight through the wall and the balcony railing before ramming into the ground below. The roof sagged in the corner and collapsed in one great mess of red clay shards before two more columns broke apart and bowled toward her. She barely had time to jump out of their way before a great slab of the ceiling came crashing down.

She called out to Jachad and Isa in Norlander, but received no response.

The pattern of the rain shifted and a triffon glided into view overhead. Broken stone clattered as it landed up above, unhampered now by any kind of roof. Lahlil craned her neck and could see the witch being helped to mount by the surviving Red Guards, two of whom climbed aboard with her while the rest moved off somewhere. The triffon's wings snapped open and another round of masonry tumbled down the slope. She couldn't do anything but cover her head and wait for it to end.

Then a strange feeling swept over her, suffusing her with warmth like the burn of strong liquor. The feeling rushed into her head and for a dizzying moment she had to fight the urge to faint. Bricks clinked behind her and a kiln-like smell overwhelmed the petrichor—then a burst of light pierced the dust cloud and she whirled around in time to see the center of the pile explode. Chunks of charred brick whizzed out of the flames and Lahlil had to duck down to keep from being bludgeoned, but she kept her eyes lifted and saw the exact moment when Jachad's figure slowly emerged from the firestorm.

She didn't remember making the decision to run to him, but the next thing she knew, she was on her knees beside him. He curled over himself as the last of the flames flickered out, until all that was left behind was Jachad, swathed in the charred remnants of his robe and covered in ash.

"Don't touch me," he cautioned as she reached toward the blood snaking down the side of his face. Only then did she see the flames still racing along under his skin, as if his blood itself had turned to fire in his veins. "I'm not safe."

<Lahlil?> Isa called out.

She found her sister climbing out from underneath the table where they'd taken shelter earlier. <Isa? Are you hurt?>

<No,> said Isa, although the pain gnawing through her words said otherwise. <But come . . . over here.>

A breathy cry in a voice she didn't recognize reached her and she clawed her way over to a spot where she saw a bit of movement, only to find Savion lying there clutching his left wrist and trying to blink away the blood dripping into his eye. Another trickle of blood leaked from the corner of his mouth. He was conscious and his eyes were lucid, but she could see why he hadn't got up: one of the pillars had fallen across his abdomen. There wasn't much blood, but it was obvious his pelvis had been crushed.

"Help," he croaked, as his yellow eyes rolled up to watch her approach.

"I thought you had gone," she said, trying to get close to him without jostling anything underneath him.

"Fell asleep—get this off me and we get out of here, follow?" he said, weakly squirming.

She took another look at the column, but there was nothing she could do. "You don't want me to move it. The pain would be too bad."

"Eyah, you're not going to leave me here?" he wheezed, trying to lift his head before he began coughing. It sounded like he'd also punctured his lung.

"No, I'm not leaving you here."

Savion's eyes widened. "I'm dying. You—You—!" He reached for her hand and she closed it around his rough fingers, squeezing hard enough to make sure he felt the contact. "Help me," he pleaded again.

"I'll stay with you," she told Savion. It was all she could promise.

He began to cry, silent tears running down his face because he no longer had enough breath to sob.

"You pay your debt to me, follow?" Savion asked her, the words barely more than a movement of his lips.

"I will. I swear to it."

"Lahlil," Jachad called to her, "Anakthalisa is getting away." The tone of his voice spawned a hundred memories of her own cold calculations; of all the times she'd won a battle and walked away, leaving others to count the cost. Her forehead broke out in a cold sweat.

"Tired," said Savion, his eyelids fluttering.

"Close your eyes," Lahlil suggested, laying her hand over his chest and feeling the twitch of his gasping breaths. "I'll protect you."

<Lahlil!> Isa called out, adding her urgency to Jachad's.

The sound of Savion's breathing shifted to a thin wheeze and his hand fell limp. She kept her other hand over his heart as the rhythm faltered. When his breath caught and his muscles suddenly seized, she held him down until it passed. Then she kept holding him, waiting for him to start breathing again.

He didn't.

The rain washed some of the dirt off her hands and face as she stood but she still needed her scarf to wipe her eyes clear of grit. When she could see properly again, the first thing she noticed was Daryan and Rho climbing up over the ruins of the balcony to get to them, along with a Shadari teenager and a disheveled Red Guard. Rho broke into a run as soon as he saw Isa, while Daryan headed for Jachad. Lahlil checked that she still had her sword and dagger and made sure she had no injuries that couldn't wait.

The Mongrel had won a hundred battles for nothing more than base coin and a fleeting respite from pain. Lahlil had fought a single battle for love, and lost. There had to be a lesson in there somewhere. She hoped someone would be left alive at the end of all this to explain it to her.

Chapter 23

Daryan paused in blazing a path through the rubble and looked back over his shoulder, but the dereshadi carrying Ani, Tessa and Lieutenant Tamin had already flown out of sight. Lem placed a steadying hand on his back, while Rho broke away on his own and stumbled toward the broken column where Isa was sitting with her head on her hand. Daryan drove on toward Jachad and Lahlil, ignoring the bone-cracking impacts on ankles, shins and knees. Even his shoulder no longer bothered him; the pain from a few torn stitches could hardly compare to bearing horrified witness to the deaths of hundreds of innocent people, including the traitor who until yesterday had been his closest friend. Daryan was deeply thankful that Rho had known what it meant when the people in the courtyard started tearing each other apart, or he would have charged right in among them.

Lem had been swearing non-stop since he and Hesh had met their dereshadi as it landed, and then as they stood beside the fallen throne and watched the palace collapse right in front of them. Hesh, though, had remained locked in a trembling silence as Anakthalisa took his mother away—until now, when he suddenly shrieked and ran straight at Lahlil.

"You let them take my mother!" he shouted at her, but Lem caught the boy's arm and dragged him back. "You could have saved her but you let them take her!"

"I couldn't get to her. I'm sorry," said Lahlil. Jachad, standing beside her, said nothing.

"But we're going after her, right? We're not going to let them keep torturing her?"

"I tried to stop her from coming here, Daimon," Lem said apologetically, even as he kept an iron grip on Hesh's arm. "Tessa, I mean. Never met anyone so stubborn in my life, and I'm including this lad here. She had the poison—the stuff we were supposed to find in Bima's house that day. She was certain she could walk in with the other servants and slip it into the witch's drink."

"She did," Isa rasped, supporting herself on Rho's shoulder as she climbed toward them. Daryan couldn't look at her, not even to see if she looked as wrung-out as she sounded. "Ani drank the poison, but it didn't affect her."

"So my mother tried to save you all and you're going to abandon her," Hesh rushed on, writhing around in Lem's hold until the guard gave up and released him. "We should never have trusted you."

"Of course we're not going to abandon her," said Daryan, trying to stay calm, "but it's been a bloody day and it's going to get bloodier. Killing Anakthalisa has to be our first priority, and that's also the best way to help Tessa. Do you know where she's going?"

"The temple," answered Jachad. "She thinks she'll find Dramash there. She saw something in a vision."

"That's why Omir sent the Red Guards there earlier," Lem broke in, "so let's go get those shit-stained sons of maggots."

Daryan swung around to Rho. "You *swear* you left Dramash in Norland?"

"I've been asked that so many times I'm starting to think I *must* be lying," said Rho. "*Yes*: I left Dramash in Norland. He cried and begged me not to go and I almost didn't, but I knew if someone didn't stop Anakthalisa, he'd never be able to go home again. Satisfied?"

"Wait," said Isa, clinging onto Rho's cloak to keep herself upright. "You need to understand—Ani has kept herself alive for too long. She's too weak to control her power. *That's* why she needs Dramash. She says he's the only one powerful enough to keep her in balance."

"That's what she was doing with Tessa," Lahlil confirmed, "using her like an anchor."

Hesh swallowed noisily. "My mother would never help her kill people."

"Ani made a new drug, after Dramash resisted her in Norland," said Isa, so quietly everyone had to lean in closer to hear her. "She can just *take* what she needs now. She tried it out on me. What it does . . . it's terrible. *Violating.*"

"What happens if she uses her powers without someone helping her?" Daryan asked.

Jachad's shoulders twitched minutely. "First she'll destroy everything around her," he said, "then she'll become a god. She'll ascend."

"She doesn't want that," said Isa. "She wants the power of a god, but she wants to be here, in the Shadar."

Daryan turned his focus to Jachad. Even charred and soaked, the man held himself with the gravity befitting a demigod-king. "I can lead our militia against the Red Guards, but Anakthalisa will kill us all unless someone stops her. Can you do it?"

"Yes," said Jachad, "but I won't be able to control my powers for long. People will die—*your* people. I don't want the Nomas to be held accountable for that."

"*I* will be accountable," Daryan shot back. "After what I witnessed here, I'll take responsibility for *whatever* has to be done to stop that woman." He pointed at Lahlil. "Take the dereshadi and go after them. Do whatever you have to do. I'll rally everyone I can and move on the temple." He stopped to cough, jarring his shoulder, and once again found Lem there to steady him. "If you fail, we'll find another way. The people of the Shadar defeated her once before. We can do it again."

"But they *didn't* defeat her," Rho pointed out. "She only pretended to die, and then she spent three centuries plotting her revenge."

Daryan pointedly ignored him. "Lem, I need you to go and find Binit and get the militia ready to move on the temple under my command. If you can find any deserters from the guards, get them to join up. Get all the dereshadi we have left into the air. You can take Trakkar yourself."

The soldier looked like he'd been kicked. "I'm staying with you, Daimon."

Daryan put a hand on his shoulder. "Listen, Lem, the Red Guards aren't some invading army. We're asking people to fight their families and neighbors, and that means I need someone who can convince them it's necessary. I can't think of anyone who could do that better than you."

"Shit," Lem mumbled, scrubbing a hand over his face. "All right, Daimon. I won't let you down."

"And remember not to hold your sword like it's a pickaxe. You're not in the mines any more."

"You're right about that, Daimon."

"I'll get the rezzies," Hesh offered suddenly. "There aren't many of us, but we're not squeamish. We can fight."

"Good," said Daryan. "Do that."

Isa was struggling to get up again, using Rho's knee for support. "I'm going with Lahlil," she announced.

Daryan choked back a laugh and Isa stiffened.

So did Rho, and then a very specific silence overtook them.

"You're in the Shadar now. Speak Shadari," Daryan thundered.

Rho tipped his hood back, scattering raindrops. "I told her she's not well enough to fight, and I'm reasonably sure she's going to feel a great deal worse before she starts getting better. I've had enough experience from crawling out of a wineskin to know how this goes."

"Fine. Then you can take her away somewhere until this is over." Daryan knew he was being callous, but he had nothing else to offer.

Two days ago he couldn't have imagined anything shaking him more deeply that Omir's betrayal, but Isa's had wounded him so deeply that the full horror of it was still sinking in.

"I'm not your subject. You can't tell me what to do," Isa spat at him before turning on Rho. "And just because you—" She swayed on her feet and bit back a sharp gasp of pain.

Rho caught her before she fell back down, and this time she didn't try to push him away. Her face flushed dark, like she couldn't breathe, and she doubled over, shaking wildly.

Daryan leaned down and lifted her chin. Her eyes were rolling and her lips were turning pale. "She's having a seizure!"

Rho immediately scooped her up into his arms and sat down with her across his lap, holding her tightly.

"The drug," Daryan said urgently, "she still had some in the desert—it was in her pocket." He was already pulling at the clasps on her cloak and scrambling for her pocket when her tremors stopped, but he pulled out the bottle anyway and thumbed out the stopper. "Here," he said, holding it to her lips.

"No," she gasped, turning her head, "I'm not taking that. Never again."

"Yes, you are," said Daryan, his blood boiling. If Rho hadn't been glaring at him, he would have held her down and poured it down her throat. "You could have died—you're going to take this."

"She doesn't want it," said Rho, "and in a few hours that dose will wear off and she'll need more. What are you going to do then?"

"We'll worry about that in a few hours, if any of us are still alive." Daryan tried to get closer, but Rho placed his gloved hand on his chest.

"She said no."

"You can't be serious. Look at her—she's in pain. She can't make any sort of decision right now."

"I was in more pain than this when my arm burned," Isa said, her voice weak but lucid. She pushed against Rho until he helped her to sit up. "I made my own decision then. Remember? You waited for me to decide."

"That was different," he replied, tightening his grasp on the bottle.

But she narrowed her eyes and looked at him with such intensity that he pushed his wet hair back from his forehead to break the contact. "How was it different? Because that time I did what you wanted?"

"Don't be ridiculous. You just said you made the choice yourself."

"What if I'd decided to die instead? Would you have cut my arm off anyway?"

"Of course not!" And Daryan believed that, right up until the moment the words left his mouth, and then the bitter taste of the lie nearly made him gag. He shoved the bottle at them and Rho grabbed it. "Fine. It's your choice and I have more important things to do right now than argue. But if you go into battle in this condition you're going to get somebody killed—probably Rho, who will obviously do anything you want, no matter how stupid it is. That will be your choice, too. I hope you can live with that."

Daryan hated himself for saying such a thing, but it was true. Feeling like a boat heading straight for a reef, he climbed up the slope of his broken home without looking back, turning his burning face up to the rain to wash some of the heat away.

He made his way up to the point where the floor leveled out and from there he could see down into the courtyard. Nothing was left, not even the old foundations on which he had built his new palace. He mourned for his people, friends and strangers alike, supporters and detractors; the Red Guards who had chosen a side willingly and those who hadn't. He mourned the injustice of being robbed of a reckoning with Omir. Most of all, he mourned the suffering Tessa must have endured when her power was used to bury people alive. All so Anakthalisa could erase the legacy of the ashas and the daimons the same way they had erased hers.

What Anakthalisa couldn't understand was that he had never cared about his legacy. He didn't mourn it; part of him felt cleansed to have all the expectations, the pretensions and the outright lies so thoroughly wiped away. He understood now why the daimon's robes never fit him: because they were the garments of a puppet king on a puppet's throne. They weren't good enough. No, the Shadari were going to leave their rotten past behind them. Daryan was going to dig a strong, clean foundation and build something new, something *better*—and Anakthalisa was standing in his way.

Chapter 24

Lahlil found Rho and Daryan's triffon hitched to what was left of the gate, its eyes bulging with anxiety and its tail smacking furrows into the mud. She stroked the wet fur behind its eye ridges until it settled enough for Jachad to mount, then yanked the knot loose and swung up after him. A few moments later they were winging their way toward the temple. Lahlil had to stop herself from digging her heels into the triffon's sides. She ached for speed, but the beast was already tired and they'd soon be needing whatever strength it had left.

<I remember when you were afraid of flying,> she reminded Jachad, testing him to see if her Jachi was still within reach.

<It feels like a long time ago,> he answered finally.

It wasn't much, but it was better than nothing.

As they closed in on the temple, she picked out the figures of the Red Guards' triffons from the heavy clouds behind them. She didn't like what she saw. A sloping pile of debris spread out from the temple ruins, except along the shore where the waves had already taken a bite out of the rubble, pushing it into a sandbar stretching far out into the sea. But the lowest levels of the temple had survived, four, five, even six stories in places, dominating the low land around it. The western half, a tiered maze of corridors and rooms, was awash in red-tinted rainwater and littered with chunks of rock and the ephemera of daily life.

All of her childhood things were still in there somewhere: her toy swords and dolls, the picture books she'd refused to pass down to her younger siblings, the blanket Meena had embroidered with green triangles to represent a forest neither of them had ever seen. The eastern half was pretty much rubble, and what looked to be the bulk of the Red Guards had been stationed all around it.

The chaotic nature of the aerial defenses gave her pause. A fixed position like the temple should be defended with a top-down spiral; properly maintained, it would be nearly impossible for any opposing force to penetrate without intentionally ramming through the lines and incurring heavy losses. But no one had explained this to the Shadari. The dozen or more red-jacketed riders were zipping around like bees, leaving gaping holes in their coverage and risking needless collisions.

Lahlil hated fighting amateurs. There was always the chance they'd do something stupid enough to catch her off-guard.

<I don't see Anakthalisa,> said Jachad.

<That pile of boulders, on the western side.> The structure was more like a tower than a pile, and there was nothing natural about it. A flat slab on top made a kind of dais, on which sat a high-backed Norlander chair with a distinctive six-sided seat: Anakthalisa's throne, apparently. She had half a dozen Red Guards surrounding her and the terror-stricken Shadari woman by her side, free for now but clearly expecting the torture to start again. Oddly, her back was turned. Options rolled through Lahlil's head, arranging themselves like marbles on a game board. <Can you use your powers while on the triffon?> she asked Jachad.

<Triffons don't like fire.>

<We'll fly in low, straight at the witch. Once we're close enough, you hit her with everything you've got. It won't matter if we crash after that.>

<You'll be killed, by the fire or by the crash, but I could survive. You won't be able to uphold our bargain to kill me if you're already dead,> he pointed out, showing concern only for the order of their

deaths and not the deaths themselves. <I say we land and you get as far away as possible before I attack.>

Lahlil hesitated, but she had nothing better to propose. <All right. We need to get through these triffons first. I'll try to fly around as many as I can. If there's a fight, lie down flat.>

They had been spotted: a triffon broke toward them while they were still over populated streets. A chase would tire her own beast, so better to engage and remove one piece from the board. She heard people shouting below as she tightened the reins and flew to intercept. It was possible they were voicing support for her—or maybe for her opponent—but they were probably just angry that yet another war was going to drop things on their heads.

Lahlil drew her sword and balanced her feet at the front of the stirrups to give her the most maneuverability, but her opponent didn't even draw his own sword until after Lahlil began her attack run—and he didn't realize his harness was too tight until he tried to stand up and couldn't get out of a crouch. His shout of fear feathered into the wind as the triffons pulled back their wings and slid by. He parried her first stroke at the wrong angle and propelled her blade into his shoulder all by himself. She slashed his neck, just to make sure he was finished.

Another triffon came up behind her as they flew over a well-yard; she veered deliberately into his path and the inexperienced rider hauled on the reins in a panic, making the beast buck, pumping its wings and waggling its blocky head in fright. Lahlil dropped behind them and patted her hand up Jachad's thigh until she felt his knife. She took a moment to weigh the weapon in her hand and gauge the wind-speed and direction, then pinched the point between her fingers and threw. It spun end-over-end before plunging into the guard's back.

<You took my knife,> said Jachad.

<You weren't using it. Check your harness again,> she said, gingerly coaxing a little more speed out of the triffon. <There's more of them up ahead. This might get rough.>

Seeing two of their comrades killed had inspired more of the Shadari to break ranks and by the time Lahlil neared the edge of the city, three more were closing in on them. At least they were smart enough to realize fighting her one by one would only get them all killed, so they were intent on boxing her in and forcing her down.

<I'm going to twist them up. Hang on,> Lahlil called to Jachad as she tucked her mount into a dive, then banked into a sharp turn to trick the three triffons into wheeling around in pursuit. The force lifted her out of the saddle but the harness held. Two of her pursuers broke off to avoid a collision, but the third stayed right on her tail. She pulled up the reins to level off—and nothing happened. Her weary beast didn't have enough energy to counter the force of the dive and the temple was getting much too close, much too fast. The rain lashed at Lahlil's face as she tried again to pull up, keeping the pressure steady despite the situation so the triffon wouldn't roll or buck. Finally it pumped its wings and they swooped upward again, the weight of their sudden ascent pinning Lahlil to the saddle.

The Red Guard behind her must have waited too long, or maybe pulled up too sharply: his triffon bowled through the guards stationed around the base of the ruins and struck the rocky slope like a blunt arrow.

Even before they leveled out, Lahlil could feel their triffon's right wing dragging. <This mount is done,> she told Jachad as she watched the other two Red Guards wheeling around and lining up to attack. <We'll never get through to the temple with it. We're going to have to get a replacement.>

<In midair?> Jachad asked.

<I've done it before.> Never with someone else, but he didn't need to know that. The triffon on her left was on the small side but lithe and flying steadily even with a novice at the reins. <Loosen your harness enough that you'll be able to slip out of it, but don't take it off until I tell you.>

Lahlil's straps were already hanging loose enough for her to draw her arms out and then hook them around the leather, but one of the riders had spurred his triffon into an attack run, leaving her little time to finish her preparations. She unhooked all the clasps on her cloak except the top one and made sure her boots were loose in the stirrups. Then she opened the buckle on the lap-belt.

The Red Guard stood up, black-bladed sword at the ready. The distance between them contracted until both triffons snapped in their wings, then Lahlil ripped the cloak from around her neck and threw it over the rider's head.

Even as she shouted a warning to Jachad, she was leaning as far out over the other triffon's side as possible, ready to grab for the secondary pommel—but the wet leather slid out from under her fingers and for an airless moment she overbalanced, losing the stirrup on her left. A slice of sandy beach appeared in her vision in the space between the two triffons, but she threw all her weight over and grabbed again, this time getting enough of a grip to belly-flop onto the saddle and swing her leg over.

She twisted to get out of the way of her cloak, which was flapping in her face as the still-blinded rider struggled to rid himself of it, and wedged herself up against his back. Holding him tight, she unfastened his harness, ignoring his muffled pleas and curses, and before the last strap flapped lose in the breeze, she rammed her knife into his neck. Blood sprayed over her as she steadied herself in the saddle before tipping the body over the side.

<I'm coming to get you,> she told Jachad, buckling herself in, cursing when she found the stirrups set uncomfortably high. It took her a moment to find Jachad—his triffon had clearly decided to fly back to its stable since no one was telling it otherwise.

<Okay, Jachi, take your harness off now,> she told him. <When I say the word, you're going to jump over to me.>

She spurred the triffon on, charging straight for Jachad as if she intended to attack. His red hair stood out in the landscape of gray on gray and she fixed that image in her mind, that bright spot in the midst of the darkness. As soon as both beasts drew in their wings, she leaned toward him and yelled for him to jump. She got a fistful of his jacket and her arm collided with his chest; he didn't so much jump as fall toward her, but he managed to latch on to her arm, then he got his foot up on the saddle and propelled himself over to her as the triffons finally slipped past each other. He kept a strangle-hold on her neck, and her chest burned with the lack of air as he tried to get his foot over the saddle and into the stirrups.

<I'm in,> he said as he released her at last, leaving her gasping over the pommel. The buckles rattled behind her as he strapped himself in.

<Good.> She steered a course in between two Red Guards heading toward them from opposite directions, and as they closed in, she kicked her new mount into a burst of speed and then banked to the right as sharply as she dared. The steady beating of the wings behind her turned erratic—then came the shouting.

"Shof help us," Jachad breathed as one of the triffons shrieked, followed by a man screaming in agony.

Lahlil looked behind her and saw exactly what she'd expected: in his eagerness to reach her, one Red Guard had turned straight into the other and his triffon had scraped its claws through the other beast, practically tearing the rider in two. Then its tail had snagged on the injured triffon's wing, tangling them together. Their massive bodies collided and the still-living rider found his leg being continually crushed between the two great beasts as they bucked madly.

Lahlil had already dismissed them from her mind and was flying at the next attacker in her line of sight. The man in the saddle had broad shoulders and a good reach and he looked more comfortable with his sword than any of the others so far. She let him have the first blow as they passed, then used the momentum of the parry to swing around to slice down at his midsection. She missed, and he had time to nick her across the ribs with the preternatural speed of his black blade before the triffons pulled them out of range. The wound was nothing, but in the moment she took to check it, another rider came at her from the west, his hunched posture betraying his nervousness. She coaxed her triffon into attacking on his non-dominant side and as he twisted, his sword flailing in an attempt to get at her, she seized his sword arm and pulled him in closer so she could drag her blade across his throat.

The broad-shouldered guard was creeping up right on their tail now. Lahlil turned her head to check his position and caught a glint of fire in Jachad's eyes. This was taking too long. If he couldn't hold on to his power long enough for them to get to Anakthalisa, they'd both die for nothing. She wrenched the triffon around and shouted at Jachad to get down, then dived underneath their opponent. As they came up the other side, she slashed at the triffon's tail hard enough to cleave the bones apart. The beast bucked wildly, squealing in pain, and the rider dropped his sword so he could cling to the saddle. The black blade hovered, twitching, as the Red Guard tried to call it back to him, but he couldn't muster the concentration. The sword shrank as it fell and he went after it.

There were only four triffons left. She could handle that: lead them away, double back and get to the witch before they could do anything about it—

<Lahlil.> Jachad gripped her shoulder and she turned to see another half a dozen triffons flying straight toward them. She growled and thumped her fist down on the saddle: Jachad's hold over his powers wouldn't last long if she had to take them all down. They had run out of time.

Then the man on the lead triffon stood up and gave her a friendly wave.

<That's Lem, Daryan's lieutenant,> Lahlil breathed, allowing the tension to seep away as she slowed their flight. The triffons streaked past her, making for Anakthalisa's guards, except for Lem himself, who swung his beast around to fly alongside hers.

"What do you need?" he shouted over to her.

"Keep them off our backs."

Lem clapped his hands together and shook them in her

direction, which she assumed meant he understood, then he let out a completely inappropriate whoop and sped off after the others, while she swung toward the east so they could approach the temple from the water. Timing was critical: the witch would be watching for them, so they had to land before she could strike them down.

High tide loomed. The beach had all but disappeared and the waves were rolling and crashing right up against the dunes. Lahlil saw something twitch out on the horizon and shut her Shadari eye for a better look. A fleet of ships—three, maybe four— listed heavily in the rough waters.

<Can you see those ships?> she called back to Jachad, but he didn't answer.

The triffon started to slow as they got closer to the temple, tossing its head and trying to pull up and away from the obstacle, but Lahlil threw herself forward over its neck and dug her heels in. The triffon stopped its attempts to climb, but its wings wobbled and it dropped unexpectedly; she didn't even have time to shout a warning to Jachad before its belly was scraping the rocks. Its tail set off a landslide, sending boulders and stones plummeting into the sea while they bounced over the uneven surface until the beast managed to dig its claws deep enough to slow its progress.

Lahlil jumped down before the triffon had stopped completely and ran straight at the tower. Heat soon washed over her as Jachad overtook her, flames writhing in his hair and sparks dripping from his hands, raindrops hissing into steam where they fell on him. He was a magnificent threat, yet the old woman didn't even turn around to face them. Lahlil felt a stab of trepidation and called out, <Jachi, do it now!>

Flames engulfed him as they had in the throne room, only this time there was no ceiling to hem them in and the pillar of wild-fire twisted up into the clouds, terrible and ungoverned. Then Anakthalisa turned around to reveal a baby sleeping peacefully in her arms.

Oshi.

Jachad cried out and dropped to his knees, hugging himself to pull in the flames the way he had on the pier at Prol Irat. Ribbons of flame unspooling along the ground forced her to back away for higher ground. She couldn't get near enough to do anything to help him.

"You see now, don't you, Lahlil?" asked Anakthalisa, smiling down at them. "You see how this was meant to be? You didn't see Jachad in your vision because he *won't be there*. He has to die, Lahlil."

"No."

"Come now, child. You know you won't let Jachad hurt me while Oshi is under my protection. Even the Nomas himself understands what you have to do. He knows he was never meant to wield power of this magnitude. It's time for you to let go."

"You're right." Lahlil stepped a few paces further away from Jachad. "Let go," she told him. "Kill her."

Jachad didn't object, or ask if she was sure. He just opened his arms and let the fire burn.

Chapter 25

Isa insisted she could walk on her own, but two steps later she was reaching for a broken column. Her left shoulder spasmed like someone was pounding nails into it. Her right hand flailed for support, missed and came away with a bloody scrape across the knuckles. Finally the world tipped her over into Rho's arms and he held her against him through another burst of agony.

The attack left her spent and useless, panting into his chest. He had to carry her to the triffon.

<You'll be all right. We'll get you through this,> Rho promised. Nothing but cool, soothing blues rolled through her mind, which didn't make any sense. He should have hated her for what she'd done. Daryan did. So she shut her eyes against the embarrassment and let him lift her up, then tucked herself against his chest to make herself less of a burden while he negotiated the broken rubble.

<I'm getting a little tired of this rain,> he said after he skidded yet again. <Still, I suppose it makes a nice change from the constant threat of a fiery death.>

<I wish it wasn't so cold.>

The concern he'd been trying to hide from her broke free for a moment, probing her with sharp fingers until he pulled it back in. <You're too warm; that's why it feels so cold. It won't bother you once your fever goes down.>

<Who died and made you a physic?>

It was a childish joke and she hadn't expected him to find it funny, but neither had she expected to feel him pushing some gleaming edge of grief back into its corner. <I don't have to be a physic to know you have a fever. Now stop jabbering at me, I need to concentrate on where I'm walking so we don't both end up with our brains on the outside.>

She could barely endure the humiliation of being hauled up into the saddle like a sack of washing, but sitting down was so much better than standing.

<I need to check the harness and then we'll go,> Rho was saying. She knew it wasn't the first thing he'd said, but she hadn't really heard the rest, being too preoccupied with the bone-deep ache that had taken hold of her limbs and the blurriness at the edge of her vision. She wished he would hurry. There were people all around her, watching her, rejoicing to see her so helpless. She knew she was hallucinating when Iratian faces pushed through the Shadari, screaming at her; when they disappeared, leaving only a little Abroan girl with blood seeping into the collar of her blouse. Blood's Pride was in her hand, slick with something, water, it was raining, it was just water, it was just water—

<Isa? Take a breath. Good. Are you ready?>

<Where are we going?>

<I think the mines would be best. I know the caves around there from my time as a guard.> He took up the reins and whistled. <A stone floor should be more comfortable than most of the inns I've slept in over the last few months, and I won't have to wrestle Lahlil for the blankets.>

She would have laughed, except thinking about caves made her think about Falkar, and thinking about Falkar meant remembering his sickening screams of panic when she held his face down in the mud. <Anywhere but the ashadom.>

Rho tried to distract her with inconsequential details from his travels as they flew. She wasn't really listening, but the patter of words helped to stop her from drifting off.

<Where are you going? Rho!> she called out as he suddenly hauled on the reins and the horizon took a sickening swing. He didn't answer, but his distress tangled around her until it felt like he was dragging her down into a pool of fire. They passed right over the beach and kept going, straight out to sea.

The water below them looked warm and soft, in contrast to the rain beating against her skin like a wire brush. It was strange that after a lifetime of nightmares about falling, now she wanted to slash the harness and let herself drift down into the dark, where she could float, bodiless and alone—except she wasn't alone. Frea's silver helmet swam in front of her, the wolf's head gleaming. Her sister's ghost, dead-eyed beneath the slits, had risen from the deep. Frea had come to snatch away her coward's death and replace it with one of pain and blood and fire. A black-bladed knife cut through the water and Isa screamed and screamed for Rho to help.

<Isa! Wake up!> His anger flowed into her, strong and scalding, bringing her back to consciousness as Aeda tilted into a landing spiral. <I know Eofar's your brother but don't even *think* about defending him. There is no possible way he can justify this.>

They were circling a Norlander ship with the Eotan wolf's head sigil flying from the central mast. *Eofar's ship.* Three other vessels dotted the waves behind them. How could her brother be here?

Rho tore himself out of the harness as soon as they landed on the deck, leaving her to fend for herself. The wet leather straps refused to thread back through the buckle and she'd only managed one when a high-pitched whoop startled her badly and she looked round in time to see Dramash streak out of one of the cabins and knock Rho onto his backside with the force of the collision.

<What have you *done*?> Rho's voice boomed in her head as he scrambled back up, but he wasn't talking to her or Dramash, who was tugging on his cloak and babbling out a litany of questions. <I *trusted* you! You were supposed to keep Dramash in Norland. That's all I asked. Do you have *any idea* what you've *done*?>

<Rho, calm down, for Onfar's sake. Let me—>

Isa's brother staggered backward past her and fell to the deck, blue blood leaking from his nose. Norlander soldiers grabbed Rho and tackled him to the deck, holding him there while Dramash kicked and punched at them.

"Leave my friend alone!" the boy screamed at the Eotan soldiers. "He's Rho! He's a good person!"

<Let him go,> Eofar echoed wearily. He stood up slowly, holding a finger under his nose and tilting his head back to stop the bleeding. <It's a misunderstanding, that's all. I can handle it.>

"It's all right, Dramash," Rho said to the little boy after the Norlanders released him and stepped back. "No one's going to hurt me."

"Eofar said you might be here but you might not be," Dramash said solemnly, "but *I* knew you would."

Rho got back to his feet but other than that he didn't move. Dramash finally let go of his leg but remained plastered to his side as the rain flattened his curly hair and soaked into his Norlander-style clothes. Eofar didn't move either and the tension between the two men stung Isa's exposed nerves like salt.

<You need to turn these ships around now—*right now,*> said Rho.

<Not until you explain what's got you in such a panic.>

<He's right, Eofar,> Isa broke in. <Dramash is in *terrible* danger—you have to get him away from here before it's too late.>

Her brother finally looked up at her. <Isa? What's wrong with you?>

<That Shadari witch was drugging her,> Rho answered for her, which made her angry. <I *told you* something was wrong with Isa. She's stopped taking the drug and her body is less than pleased about it.>

<Then don't you think she should get down from there and out of this rain?> Eofar shot back. <My cabin is right over there. And—> He paused for a moment, looking back and forth between them. <—I'll give the order to turn the fleet around.>

"Come on, Dramash. Let's get inside," Rho said, thanking Eofar only with a blunt burst of fury. But he still came to help her down, even with Dramash attached to his hand like a ball and chain. Once again she submitted to being tended to like a helpless child, only this time she had an audience of Norlander soldiers who stared at her with that familiar mix of disgust and curiosity. Rho took her arm without asking and slung it over his shoulder before circling her waist with his other arm, and the two of them stumbled toward Eofar's cabin like drunken lovers. Dramash raced ahead to open the cabin door. She had to shut her eyes when the movement of the waves took her over, rolling, rolling, pulling her down. Frea had gone down into the water. Her cape had pulled her under and Isa had watched her sinking, down, down.

The disorientation lessened when they got through the doorway into a cabin twice the size of Nisha's on the *Argent*. Rho eased her down onto a quilted blanket of bright blue silk before removing her sword and boots and swinging her legs up onto the bunk.

"Are you sick?" Dramash whispered loudly, peering down at her from the side of the bunk.

"Yes," she answered and watched his frown deepen.

"I was sick," he confided to her. "I was sick for a long time. I was so sick I wasn't ever hungry and that's why they said I could go back home. I liked the snow at first but it wasn't fun after Rho left. No one except Eofar ever talked to me and he was always busy. He's a king now, but not like Daryan—he's a *real* king."

"I'm sorry you were sick," Isa told him as she shut her eyes.

<I'll be back,> said Rho, right before the door slammed shut behind him. He must have gone no further than the other side of the door, though, because she could hear every word as he laid into Eofar.

<Ani has been turning over the Shadar to find Dramash. If she gets her hands on him now, she'll take over and rule like a tyrant—which is *exactly* why I told you Dramash needed to stay in Norland instead of coming with me.>

<Look at Dramash. Go on, I want you to really *look* at him,>

258

Eofar said tightly. <He was wasting away in Norland and the physics could do nothing for him. He kept saying he wanted to go home. What else was I supposed to do?>

<I *told* you I needed to make the Shadar safe for him before he came back,> said Rho, but his righteous indignation was cooling. <How can you even *be* here? You're the emperor—you can't leave Ravindal without abdicating.>

<I'm king, not emperor, and guess what: I changed the rules. It turns out Gannon's daughter and I see most things the same way. I left her in charge as regent so I could keep my promise to Daryan and bring men to protect the Shadar.>

<We can't let Anakthalisa have him, Eofar. *We can't.*>

<We won't.>

Their words continued to ebb and flow, punctuated by more excited chatter from Dramash and softer answers from Rho, but Isa quickly lost track of the conversation. The rocking she had once found soothing on the *Argent* now disoriented her and she couldn't tell down from up. She wanted to sleep but the best she could manage was a disturbing half-waking where she couldn't be sure what was real and what wasn't. The darkness behind her eyelids began to fracture. When she drew her next breath, nothing happened. Her body had forgotten how to breathe.

Her mind exploded in panic.

She was lying on her mother's tomb with the sun burning her arm into a blackened, bloody mess. Daryan, her imaginary friend, couldn't save her. The agony stripped away everything she wanted to believe about herself, shattering every illusion. Everything but the pain was a lie; it would swallow her whole and leave nothing left. No one else would come to stop it because no one else cared. They knew she was wrong *inside, not like a real Norlander. They were ashamed of her. They would be glad when she was dead.*

Someone was holding her down. She struggled against them, flailing away as soon as they released her, jamming her forehead into the corner to hide from the memories gathering around her in ever thicker ranks. The things she had done—If she knocked her head on the wall behind her, she could drive the thoughts away. Maybe. For a little while.

<Isa! Isa, stop doing that.> Rho's presence in her mind made no sense; it was wet and filling her head with the color of blood. <It's going to be all right. For Onfar's sake—Stay still, you've made yourself bleed.>

The nightmares kept trying to fight their way out of her, screaming all her faults at her, waving her bloody arm in her face like a flag and laughing at her. She must have lost more time, because the next thing she knew, Rho was sitting beside her on the bed, unbraiding her hair so it could dry.

<Rho?>

<Right here.>

<Daryan gave you the last bottle of the medicine, didn't he?>

<Yes. It's in my pocket.>

She recalled Daryan's bitter remarks: *Rho, who will obviously do anything you want, no matter how stupid it is.* <Give it to me.>

He said nothing; there were no refusals, no objections. He'd already taken out the stopper before he fit the cool glass into her palm and waited until she had closed her fingers around it before moving back to give her some room.

She poured it out slowly, keeping her hand as steady as she could while she watched the drops break apart and scatter over the varnished floor. Air bubbled up inside the bottle, filling the space; cleansing it. She didn't have the strength to hurl the bottle far enough to smash the thick glass, but she let it drop and listened to it roll away with the rocking of the ship.

The convulsions took her then, pulling her muscles so taut she was sure they would snap, leaving her wrung out and helpless. Rho spoke comfortingly and swore in turns as the pain racked her again and again. In between bouts she became aware of him half-sitting on top of her and wiping her face with a cloth. She went from shivering so badly that she bit her tongue to feeling so hot she tore off the blankets, and then tried to do the same with her clothes before the coolness seeping in from his weight above her and his hand on her arm calmed her down. The spasms finally slowed and then stopped altogether, but still she could only breathe in sharp gasps.

<Breathe with me.> Rho grasped her chin and turned her head so that she could see him through her watering eyes, then took her hand and settled it over his chest. At first she lost the rhythm and ended up gasping worse than ever, but then he sat behind her and settled her back against his chest, rocking her with his exaggerated breaths.

<Much better,> he said finally, shifting a little behind her to stretch his neck. Every bit of her ached and she had all the strength of a blob of warm wax but she hoped the worst of it was over. She felt languid and at ease, draped on top of him, when he wrapped an arm around her waist and rested his chin on her shoulder, silent and steady. <We've turned around,> he told her, <but we're fighting the tide and the bad weather. They're worried about running out of supplies before we can get to a port.>

<We had to do it. We're better off going down than letting Ani get hold of Dramash.>

<As awful as that prospect is, I agree with you. And by the way, you and Dramash are welcome to all my rations. Sailing and my stomach are still the bitterest of enemies.>

<I was afraid of the pain,> she blurted out. His breath continued to drift across her neck in an even rhythm, but he didn't say anything and that made it easier. <I remember what it felt like when my arm was burning and I was afraid of having to live through that again. My arm was gone but I was *still* in pain and no one believed me—they just decided what I was feeling wasn't real and gave me fake medicine. No one *cared*. I had lost my arm and everyone acted like it didn't even matter—except for our people, who hated me for it and said I'd cursed them by surviving.>

He didn't reply to any of that either but she could feel him taking it in, examining it, turning it this way and that. <And then Ani was kind to you and took the pain away.>

The tears came easily since she didn't have the strength to hold them back.

He knew she didn't feel entitled to forgiveness, so he had given it to her without waiting for her to ask. She wasn't cruel enough to reject a gift like that, no matter how undeserving she felt.

<I *hate* having one arm. I hate that simple things are hard now. I hate the way people look at me. I hate being afraid something will happen to my other hand. I hate it when people help me without being asked but I hate it when I'm struggling and no one offers.>

He squeezed her fingers. <That's a good start.>

For a moment she let herself rest, listening to the muffled sounds from the deck and the creaking of the timbers. She wondered where Dramash had gone, and how they had persuaded him to leave Rho's side. Rho leaned into her shoulder again and she relaxed into the contact. It was familiar from all the time he'd spent teaching her to fight: the way he'd press up against her back as he walked her through the moves, guiding her arm; nudging his leg between hers to set her feet into the right position; his hand on the small of her back correcting her posture as she lunged.

<Will you go back to Norland now?> she asked him.

<I don't know,> he said. <Eofar said he brought Dramash back because he was sick, so it might not be any different if we go back. And then there's the plague. I haven't really had time to think about it but it's obvious the quarantine's failed. I'm *really* hoping Daryan and Lahlil can defeat Anakthalisa.>

<You don't have to stay with me. You could go back and fight with them. We may still be close enough to shore to fly back.>

He reached over to stuff one of the slippery silk bolsters behind his lower back. <I can't leave now. I only just got comfortable.>

As if to purposely taunt them, the ship gave a tremendous roll to one side, throwing everything to the floor that wasn't secured and squashing them both against the cabin wall. Rho's fingers bunched into her shirt and she grabbed him by the collar as a heavy book swatted her leg. At the same time part of her mind was thinking, *We're going to capsize*, another part was in denial, saying, *I'm not a sailor and this is probably perfectly normal.*

<Hang on!> said Rho, bracing himself against the opposite side of the bunk. The ship began to slowly rock the other way, but the speed increased and by the time the floor was level again they rolled off the bunk together, only coming to a stop when they hit the other wall. <Dramash,> Rho cried, <he was on the deck—>

He grabbed hold where he could and dragged himself to the door. Isa could barely think with the fear screaming off of him.

<Don't, Rho!> she shouted after him as he wrenched it open, but he had realized how suicidal it would be to go out on the deck and instead stretched himself across the doorway and yelled the boy's name out into the wind. She had to wait for the ship to tilt again before she could throw herself at him and grab on to the doorframe herself, but she didn't even have the strength to stand and once again ended up on the floor.

<Eofar!> she called out, spotting him on the opposite side of the deck, his arms wrapped around a post of the wheelhouse. Dramash was pinned in front of him. She had to call him twice before he looked over at them and the open door. The ship rolled and the force tried to pull her down again, but Rho got his boot down on the tail of her shirt and she managed to cling on to the doorway. When the ship got close to leveling off again, Eofar scooped up Dramash and pounded toward the cabin. Rho, leaning out, grabbed them as soon as he could and dragged them in before he slammed and bolted the door behind them.

"Are you all right?" Rho asked Dramash, checking him over.

Dramash, wide-eyed and breathing hard, nodded, for once at a loss for words.

<It's Ani,> Isa said.

<How?> asked Rho. His face abruptly turned green and he clapped a hand over his mouth. <She doesn't have any power over the water, does she? Please tell me she doesn't.>

<The sea floor,> said Eofar, still shaking from his ordeal on the deck. <There must be enough ore there for her to control it like

she did the sand on the beach. We've got to evacuate. The boats will be useless in these waves but we have enough triffons to get everyone to shore. Wait here.>

"Dramash, Isa, hold on to that table. It's bolted to the floor," Rho told them.

Eofar came back in almost immediately and said, <Rho, you take Dramash on the triffon you came on. Isa, you'll come with m—>

A terrible memory was washing over Isa and she grabbed Eofar's arm. <There's something I forgot,> she told her brother. <I heard Ani talking to some of her Red Guards. She found out the Nomas are camped not far from the Shadar. They're—they're supposed to bring Oshi to her. She didn't say why.>

The ship rolled again, but all Isa could feel was her own horror reflected back at her: a black sludge that choked her airways and flooded into her eyes and ears.

Eofar's response came down like a fist. <The witch has *my son*?>

<What do we do?> asked Rho.

<We get him back.>

<Then I'm coming with you,> said Rho. <Isa should be strong enough to fly a short distance. She can take Dramash and they can hide somewhere until we've taken care of the witch.>

<All right,> said Isa, only to be slapped with their combined disbelief. <You're right: I'm too weak to fight. I'm not going to put you in danger by making you protect me.>

<Well. Good,> said Rho, still not quite believing her. <Any ideas how we get off this damned ship without being flung into the ocean?>

<The sailors have rigged up ropes everywhere and your triffon is still tied up on deck, so Isa and Dramash don't have far to go. We'll make sure they're safely away before we get ours from the stable-deck.>

He made it sound simple enough, but the reality was nearly unendurable once they were outside. She was too weak to walk unaided and Dramash wasn't much better, and since Rho had started throwing up every time the ship hit a new swell, Eofar had his hands full. And all the while the ship kept pitching violently, sending objects and people careening about all over the place. Watching the triffons taking off continuously from the deck below was making her feel even dizzier.

By the time Isa and Dramash were strapped into Aeda's saddle and Eofar had unhitched her, she had to summon what little strength she had left just to sit up straight and hold the reins.

She felt a little better once they were in the air and her brain no longer felt like it was being bashed against the sides of her skull. The cool rain and fresh air revived her after the stuffy cabin, and she and Aeda knew each other so well she hardly had to touch the reins. She remembered Rho's intention to hide in the caves and couldn't think of any better place to go, so she pointed them west and tried to relax enough to let some of the throttling ache drain out of her muscles.

She didn't know what sparked the idea—she hadn't been thinking about Ani; she hadn't been thinking about anything but how tired she felt. She knew only that it would work.

"Dramash," she called back to the boy clinging to the saddle behind her, "I need to ask you something."

Chapter 26

Daryan and the militia had nearly reached the temple when the drums started. The first beat thumped him right in the chest like a blow from an open palm, hard enough to shake him. It wasn't a single drummer, either; the cadence echoed back from the well-yard and the surrounding streets; short and simple, enough that after two repeats it compelled his gait, his breathing, his pulse into a single rhythm. People came out to watch them march past, pointing from their doorways, clearly trying to mask their fright with pride for the sake of the children watching. Many grabbed the closest thing to a weapon they could find and muscled their way into the procession. Daryan led them down the center of the street, keeping out of the deepest mud so he could set the fastest possible pace. His feet were already stinging with blisters from his waterlogged boots but he wouldn't allow that or anything else to slow him down.

Lahlil and Jachad made a formidable pair, but Daryan was not going to entrust the Shadari's future to anyone but the Shadari.

"I want to talk to Binit," Daryan said to Tal, marching along beside him clutching the grip of a battered short-sword. The steward nodded and fell back, and a few moments later the man himself elbowed his way past the few other palace officials who had survived the massacre.

"The gods know we've had our differences," Daryan said to him, noticing a man old enough to be his father emerging from a nearby house. He shifted a long pike to his shoulder, nodded at Daryan and joined the ranks. "But when Anakthalisa appeared, you didn't toady to her or believe her promises. When I called for the militia, you came. Faroth would have been proud of you. Harotha, too."

Binit wet his lips even though his face was already dripping with rain. "Well, I—Thank you, Daimon."

The street opened up into yet another flooded well-yard and someone shouted, "Daimon?" A figure popped up over the heads of the marchers, then Hesh's boots banged down on the well-cover. As soon as he spotted Daryan he hopped down again and pushed his way forward. "I got them all together—the rezzies—and anyone else I could find. I think it's about a hundred."

"Good. We really need them—"

"Only they're not sure they want to fight for you."

"They're not being asked to fight *for me*. If they don't want to fight for the Shadar, they can fight for themselves," Daryan said calmly, steering Hesh around an abandoned cart with a broken wheel stuck in the mud up ahead. "Why do you think Omir specifically tried to blame the asha murders on the resurrectionists? Because you're a threat to the witch, probably the greatest threat besides me."

Hesh stopped walking to think about the question, and then had to skip ahead when the people behind knocked into him. "How could we be a threat to her?"

"Because you didn't wait around for someone else to tell you to care for the dead, and you didn't ask permission. You saw something that needed to be done and you did it. Anakthalisa can't tolerate that kind of independence because it makes her *unnecessary*. Believe me, she sees you as a threat."

Hesh laughed without even a trace of sarcasm. "Well, if you were trying to make me feel important, it worked. I'll talk to them again," he promised and waded into the gutter to head back the way they'd come.

Shortly thereafter, the resurrectionists appeared from the

alleys armed with the tools of their trade: pickaxes and shovels, crowbars and iron rods. Hesh reclaimed the place at Daryan's side, this time with a sickle swinging from a loop of twine around his belt.

A growl of sound settled under the drumbeats and the stomping of their makeshift army. "Was that thunder?" asked Hesh, and then said immediately, "I don't think that was thunder."

"It sounded like a tremor, didn't it? But I didn't feel anything." Daryan listened for the sound of the temple ruins collapsing, but there was no crash and no dust-cloud. Either an earthquake or Anakthalisa was coming for them; in either case he didn't want to waste any more time.

So Daryan ran, not away from his responsibilities but toward something he needed to do, and because he was their daimon, two thousand Shadari citizens ran with him. The houses thinned out and the mud gave way to wet sand and dunes furred with beach-grass as he led them north, to the temple, to the symbol of their enslavement and their liberation, the Shadar's crumbling testament to the fragility of freedom.

The Red Guards formed a double line around the site. They were all armed with swords and many had shields as well. Omir had told him he'd recruited close to fifteen hundred men for the Red Guards, and that number took on a new significance for him when he saw them together and blocking his path. He focused on the weapons and not the faces and names of people whose loyalty he had never before had reason to doubt.

Daryan hopped onto a pile of rubble and turned back to his followers as they halted, staring expectantly at him. They were soaked to the bone, but their eyes were bright with a mix of defiance and nervousness. "We're here for Anakthalisa, not the Red Guards. Get past them, get up to the top of that hill and do whatever it takes to make sure Anakthalisa never spills another drop of Shadari blood."

Then his army gasped and Daryan whirled to follow their pointing, seeing the dark clouds above the temple streaked with gold.

Fire roared atop the ruins, lashing and writhing like something alive. Jachad was attacking—and that meant Anakthalisa's attention would be elsewhere.

He wrenched his sword out of its sheath and swung it aloft. "Attack!"

His army roared and he charged, propelled forward by their faith in him. His first two opponents came and went in a blur; a total of three blows were exchanged with a Red Guard before Daryan simply ran past him; another reeled into his path after an exchange with someone else and Daryan dropped him by hitting the back of the man's head with his pommel. For a moment he had a clear path—then another of the soldiers sprang in to close the breach, boxing him in.

"Zamar—you don't have to do this," said Daryan, yanking the man's name from his memory. He was one of the guards Omir had chosen for the raid on Bima's house. "You can still fight with us."

The guard flashed him a look of pure disgust and attacked, and Daryan knew he was in trouble from the first blow. He barely saw the man's arm move and his parry was less a calculated move than a panicked instinct to protect himself, successful only because of the quickness of his black sword. This man could have beaten him handily on Daryan's best day, and now he was fighting wounded and exhausted. Daryan managed to block a few more blows, hoping he wouldn't run into anyone behind him as he backed up, failing to find any opportunity to strike back. Then he tripped, twisted his ankle and fell, dropping his sword in an attempt to get his hands underneath him.

Zamar froze, apparently caught completely by surprise—that can't have been something that happened in training—so Daryan lunged forward, grabbed his front leg and yanked it as hard as he could. The Red Guard lurched, trying to keep his balance, but Daryan clung on, he couldn't put his foot back down and finally he toppled over. Daryan stomped on his hand to break his grip on his sword and kicked it away far enough that Zamar couldn't call it back to him.

269

Drawing his knife, he knelt down, straddling his opponent.

"Traitor!" Zamar screamed, catching Daryan's wrist to stop him driving the knife into his neck. Daryan had the leverage, but his shoulder made him too weak to keep this up for long. "Anakthalisa will destroy you," the guard snarled.

"I'm not going to let that happen."

The man's face flushed scarlet. "We know what you really are. You sold us out to the Dead Ones—you're working for them."

At least now he knew how Anakthalisa's acolytes had converted so many to their cause. "I made an alliance with Eofar Eotan to save the city, which is not the same thing."

"They enslaved us and you want to pretend it never happened," he spat. "The Blessed Mother will make them *pay* for what they did. She would *never* ask us to forgive them."

"Neither did I." Not in so many words. But how many times had he stressed that Eofar and Isa were their allies? How often had he brushed off Binit's insistence that Falkar and his men should be tried and punished for their time as oppressors?

Zamar took advantage of his distraction to shove the knife away, but Daryan recovered in time to land a solid punch with his good arm in return. The man's nose crunched under his fist and blood spurted over Daryan's chest. The blow left Zamar dazed enough for Daryan to scramble back for his sword, then he bolted past the prone guard. It wasn't until he started scaling the ruins that he felt the pain blossom again in his shoulder: another stitch or two must have torn open.

The first time his breathlessness forced him to stop, he turned around to assess the battle. There were pockets of sloppy, ugly fighting, as much against the impossible footing as each other, ranging over the slope. A riot of bodies filled the streets below the temple as the militia and the Red Guards, the ranks on both sides swelled by civilians, struggled to stop each other. People fleeing their homes with their children in tow worsened the confusion. Motionless bodies already filled the streets, but he could see some compassionate souls dragging the wounded inside their homes.

So many on both sides had already fallen . . . but his objective had been to get through the line and he was not the only one to succeed.

He started up again, struggling for solid ground. He lost a glove when he caught a finger between two stones, and the rock he'd braced his foot on came loose and knocked him back down several yards. The temple thrumming beneath him at intervals told him Jachad and Lahlil were still battling. He hadn't realized how far west he'd come until he looked up and found one of the temple's exposed rooms dead ahead of him.

This was the landscape Daryan often saw in his nightmares: his life smashed to bits, then jumbled up into piles that made no sense; crags leading into rooms and corridors awash in scarlet. The wall he stepped through had been sheared away and one of the others had collapsed, leaving this slanted structure. A pile of broken stone littered the center of the room in a kind of bowl shape; otherwise it was empty except for a bird's nest of some sort . . . but of course he knew it wasn't a bird's nest, because he'd known which room he was in from the moment he pulled himself up onto the floor. That pile of rocks had been Isa's bathtub. That collapsed wall was where the door into the corridor used to be, where Rahsa had spied on him kissing Isa for the first time. The crushed bit of tarnished brass in the corner? That was the lamp that had been knocked over during that fateful earthquake. And the bird's nest rustling on the floor was the torn-up remains of his first attempt at *The History of the Shadar.*

He picked up the closest page within reach and scanned the meticulous rows of characters, blurred and faded as they were. He could have recited the passage from memory.

I have asked if the gods have abandoned us or if we have abandoned them. Maybe it is neither. Maybe gods grow old like everyone else. Maybe they are like the elders whose time for work has passed, who sit in front of their houses in the sun, watching the street with cloudy eyes and calling the children by the names of long-dead playmates.

A grunt and the squeal of a boot made him turn just in time to see Zamar coming at him with his black blade tightly controlled, despite how much pain the broken nose must have been causing him. Daryan dropped the piece of paper and with both hands on the hilt, blocked the blows. The guard hammered at him, forcing him back step by step around the broken bath.

Daryan didn't attempt to strike back; he knew he didn't have the strength. He used all his will to keep his sword aloft, but the muscles clenching in his abused shoulder would never withstand another blow. When his back hit finally hit the wall, he knew it was all but over. "Anakthalisa is not a god," he proclaimed, not sure why he said those words in particular.

"The Blessed Mother is *our* god!" screamed Zamar, speckling the floor with his blood. "She is a Shadari god. You'll never—"

Lem's sword came through Zamar's chest, changing his next word to a gurgle. The guard looked down at the point sticking out of him like he didn't understand what he was seeing, and then, to make it worse, he tried to *push it back in*, slashing his hands to ribbons before Lem pulled the blade out and the man finally collapsed against the side of the bathtub, blood steaming as it pooled beneath him.

"Well done, distracting him like that," said Lem as he wiped his blade off on his trousers, as if Daryan had saved his life instead of the other way around. "I wasn't even sure you'd seen me there."

"What are you doing here?"

"My job," Lem grinned, before nudging the man with his foot. "Zamar, huh? He's always been a scabby prick of the first order: the kind who finds the weakest guy and lays into him for fun. Ha! I'll bet that bloody nose must have hurt like sh—uh . . . hurt a lot."

The room shook with another impact from above and dirt hissed down all around them.

"We need to keep going," Daryan said. He sheathed his sword and they helped each other to traverse the narrow ledges around to the south side of the ruin, where the ground looked to be more stable. The fighting was creeping up higher now as more and more of their supporters found openings, while those Red Guards who had given up holding the first line were trying to regroup behind the vanguard.

"Do you hear that?" Daryan asked. It sounded like the rain had suddenly turned to a downpour, but he could still feel the same steady fall as before.

"Oh, shit. *Shit shit shit,*" muttered Lem, and only then did Daryan look to the sea.

The wave was barreling toward the city, racing effortlessly up to the dunes and cresting them easily. He didn't immediately appreciate the size of it, at first thinking he and Lem were high enough to be out of danger, but they watched with horror as the spray arched over their heads. Lem seized him just as the wave swept them up and they clung on to each other, completely helpless to do anything but tumble wherever the water took them. They were pushed under, but bobbed back up again in time to grab a breath before another surge pulled them down again. Lem kept hold of him as it happened again, and then again, and each time, Daryan could hear screaming before the water came roaring back into his ears again and drowned it out.

Finally his back came up against something solid, and then Lem was hauling him out of the salty water. He wouldn't have been surprised to have found himself on the other side of the city, but they'd only been knocked back down the hill.

"You're all right, Daimon," Lem panted, flopping against the stones, ignoring the water pouring down from above like a spring. "You're all right."

Daryan shook the water from his ears and tried to comprehend how such a disaster could have happened in the blink of an eye. The wave had rolled right over the city, leaving water everywhere. Bodies floated through streets turned into canals; the living screamed for help while they desperately tried to get to safety, or reach anything floating by. Flotsam merged with household objects as the water robbed anything it could carry. People climbed out onto their roofs through the chimneys, and Daryan looked at the tarps and thought of people drowning underneath because they had nothing with which to slash their way out.

"The tremor we felt before; this was Anakthalisa. I don't know how or why, but she did this."

"Daimon," Lem said slowly, sitting up and squinting out over the water, then, "No. *No*—Daimon, tell me that's not what it looks like." He pointed to a black splotch like a dark stain on the horizon: dereshadi, dozens of them, riding in razor-sharp formations. "*Sons of maggots*," he sputtered before thrusting his sword into the air and plowing through the rocks like he wanted to take on the whole Norlander army alone. "Coming back now we're helpless again, like the pants-shitting cowards you are, eh?" he roared at the sky. "Come fight me, you dog's-ball lickers! Ass-faced filth! *Shit-weasels!*"

Daryan pushed his arm down. "Lem! They're not invading."

"They're not?" Lem blinked.

"No—look at their tabards. Those are wolf-heads: they're Eotans. Eofar's kept his promise."

Daryan let himself linger, just for a moment, to watch the dereshadi landing all over the city. The beasts were large enough to keep their heads above the water in most places and the Norlanders immediately started throwing straps and ropes in the water, helping people climb aboard or getting them on to roofs. One Eotan man jumped into the water to rescue a woman with a child clinging to her neck; another clambered up on a roof to slash though the tarpaulin and help the people inside climb out.

Daryan could see some people screaming and throwing things, or trying to get away, but most looked happy enough to take a Dead One's gloved hand if it meant being spared from drowning.

Lem let out a surprised snort. "*Well.* Never expected to see something like that. I guess we'll *have* to be friends with them now."

"No," said Daryan, thinking back to Zamar's words, "this doesn't erase all of those years of slavery. It's a start, but that's all. Now, let's get up there before Anakthalisa comes up with some other way to kill us."

They turned back toward the summit and started making back the ground they'd lost, fighting the wind and the chill of their wet clothes, and trying to breathe through the sting of the salt water lingering in their sinuses. The tinny sound of swords clashing in the distance gained momentum as the battle resumed. Lem stayed by his side, pushing the pace with his longer legs. At some point Hesh turned up on the other side and took up his flank without a word.

The battle line pushed up behind them. From time to time, Lem or Hesh would stop to help someone in trouble, then run back to Daryan while he counted each fireball that streaked across the sky and every groan of the rocks beneath them. The rain eased off a bit, but the bruised sky darkened and the moisture thickened the air instead of cleansing it.

He understood now that the point of Anakthalisa manipulating the Dead Ones into invading the Shadar thirty years ago had been to humble and break them. She had killed all the ashas so no one would have the power to defy her. She had wanted to be greeted as a savior—no, *a god*—on her triumphant return, and so she had decided the best way to guarantee their unquestioning faith in *her* was to rob them of all faith in themselves.

All things considered, it had been a terrible plan right from the start.

Chapter 27

Isa spurred Aeda on over the massive wave rolling beneath them, terrified they would be caught by it as spray filled the air around her, but Aeda finally caught a gust of wind and pulled them up into the rain. The wall of water moved away from them as they turned south, running up onto the beach and right over the dunes that were supposed to block its path. The water looked black as it tore through the streets, running like rivers of ink and staining all that it touched.

She expected Dramash to make some sort of excited comment, but when she swiveled around to check on him, he looked stricken. "I think we should hurry," he said, cutting her off as she asked if he was sure he still wanted to do this.

"All right," she told him, and adjusted their course to take them straight to the temple. Every moment it took them to get there was another moment Ani could hurt more people.

First, they had to land, and that meant getting past the other triffons already circling the ruins. She had no idea whose side any of them were on, and Aeda was tired, but the opposition was sparse enough that she thought she could probably evade them. The Shadari were fighting their way up the slopes, leaving bodies of all descriptions dotting the field. The fighting hadn't reached the top yet, but it wouldn't be long. She had to get there first.

A fireball streaked like a comet across the top of the ruins and then abruptly burst apart. Aeda shied a little but Isa urged her on. She needed a better view of what was happening up there.

<Isa!> Rho's voice slammed into her head like a brick. <What are you doing here? You're supposed to be taking Dramash to the caves!>

She'd been so focused on the temple that she'd missed the fact that she'd caught up with Eofar and Rho. <I know how we can defeat Ani.>

Finding *any* place to land was not going to be easy. Ani had installed herself and her entourage on a towering heap at the northwest corner, on a "throne" that looked suspiciously like one of her family's dining chairs. The prospect of climbing up to it made Isa want to weep with exhaustion, but the hill was much too small for Aeda to land there.

Another fireball arched up, and this time Isa was close enough to see rocks hurtling in from every direction and crashing together just in time to block the fire before it could reach Ani. Rock met flame in a wild burst of destruction and Ani immediately retaliated, dredging up a wall of rubble and hurling it at Jachad, who pushed back with a wall of flame. The rubble began to glow, rippling behind the heat and bleeding ribbons of acrid smoke. Jachad drew the fire back to him and the rock fell with a sound that Isa couldn't place, until she recalled the time she had knocked over her mother's treasured vase.

Glass, Isa realized. *Sand and fire make glass.*

Between them, Jachad and Ani had transformed the top of the ruins into an otherworldly landscape of red glass, from chunks as smooth as river rocks and large as millstones to brittle tendrils branching up like stalagmites. It was dripping with rainwater and every spark Jachad conjured made it glitter like the jewels in the crown of some mad king.

<I know what I'm doing,> she told Rho, still demanding answers of her. <You and Eofar need to stay back or you'll ruin it.>

<Isa, you tell me *right now* what you're planning,> Rho threatened. He was angrier than Isa had ever known him, but she couldn't worry about that now. Suddenly Eofar flew across Aeda's path, not close enough to crash but enough to force her to slow.

<Stop that,> she called back, standing up in the stirrups to see if they were turning to come back, which they were. <I'm not going to tell you.>

<Why not?>

<Because if I tell you, you'll try to stop me.>

<You realize how much worse that sounds, don't you?> Rho was more than ready to throttle her, but she could also feel him trying to calm himself down. <You've been through a lot and you're not thinking clearly. Turn around now and we'll talk about it.>

They were near the temple now and the Shadari triffons were starting to take an interest in them. One wheeled in her direction, but Isa immediately banked to match and then pulled up over Eofar's triffon, crossing paths to confuse them.

<I am thinking clearly,> she told Rho, <and Dramash agrees my plan will save lives.>

<Dramash? *Dramash* agrees with you? Isa, he's a *child*!>

<I was four when I realized Lahlil shouldn't have been locked up in a room like a criminal. I was right, but no one listened.>

<Isa,> Eofar began, but she cut him off.

<No, Eofar. You're the one who brought Dramash back to the Shadar. Did you think he wouldn't face any consequences, coming back to a place where he's caused so many deaths?>

<Isa, I can't—> Rho stammered, panicked now. <We have to keep him away from that woman—her vision—>

<Forget her vision.> Another Shadari triffon joined the first and now both were heading toward them. Any fight right now would finish her, so she drove straight for Ani, flying with as much speed as she could coax out of Aeda. The air behind her moaned as Eofar brought his triffon into pursuit.

<Isa, don't you dare!> Rho warned her.

She stood up in the stirrups again to see past the glare of another attack by Jachad. <I said, *forget the visions.* Of course Ani thinks she saw herself conquering the Shadar: that's the only future she can imagine. But I'm the one who made the mistake of bringing her here, and I'm not going to let that happen.>

At Isa's command, Aeda tilted into a tight landing spiral. Wings, tails, heads, faces all blurred by as her brother foolishly followed her down. Another flash of light flashed into her eyes, kicking the pounding headache back up to unbearable. Aeda faltered and dropped out of the spiral into a swooping turn before Isa could crack her lids open again without flinching. They had swerved right between Ani and Jachad and a plume of flame was heading straight for them. Isa tried to pull up, but for once Aeda would not listen and instead they dropped down with an abruptness that made her stomach bounce. The fire arched over their heads, close enough to feel the heat.

"Dramash? Are you all right?" she cried out, while Aeda's heavy feet were still crunching down on the glass. She prayed there wouldn't be any more fire as she threw off her own harness, then hastily freed Dramash, all the while wondering what would happen if Aeda decided to bolt while the straps were half-undone. But they got to the ground safely, even if Isa's knees buckled the moment she tried to stand.

<Isa, what are you doing?> Lahlil called out to her, running toward her through the puddles of glass pebbles.

<She's lost her mind, that's what she's doing!> Rho called back incoherently.

Dramash patted Isa's shoulder, careful to touch only over the fabric of her cloak. "Should we go now?" he asked, pointing up.

Ani on her crooked dais was looking down at them and smiling.

Eofar and Rho thumped down to a graceless landing right behind Aeda as she told Dramash, "You go ahead." She unbuckled her sword-belt and let Blood's Pride fall to the rocks, then tossed her knife on top of it. "I'm coming."

"Dramash!" Rho yelled aloud as the boy scrambled up the slippery rocks like a little goat. "Dramash, stop—stay right there. I'm coming to get you."

Isa started after Dramash, pulling herself up behind him, one laborious hand- and foothold at a time. It was a miserable climb, with the red mud continually slipping under her feet and loose rocks coming away in her hand.

<Lahlil, *stop them*!> Rho shouted, running toward her with his white cape flapping behind him and Eofar at his heels. <Isa, you can't do this!>

"Please don't come any closer," Ani begged them, leaning down from her cockeyed throne, gently bouncing Oshi in her arms. She looked heartbroken: red eyes, pale cheeks, trembling lips. Her tears mingled with the rain on Oshi's swaddling. For the first time, her advanced age made her look *old*; she reminded Isa of an emptying hourglass. "You've forced me to do *terrible* things today. Don't make me do this one as well. This innocent child should not be punished for your pride and ignorance—but I will do it if you leave me no choice."

<Rho, don't!> Eofar pleaded and cut in out in front, stopping him in his tracks.

"Isa, please," Lahlil called out to her, but she didn't move from Jachad's side. Molten lines and whorls traced themselves over the Nomas king's skin and his face showed the strain of keeping his power banked down.

Then Isa realized Lahlil had spoken to her in Shadari instead of Norlander, which made no sense, unless—

This was going to work.

"You had your chance to join Ani and me," Isa yelled back down to her sister, climbing as fast as she could. "You chose Jachad. You almost turned me against Ani, but your tricks won't work this time."

Isa had left her glove on Eofar's ship, so her fingernails were broken and her palm was bleeding by the time she reached the top. Her legs felt like seaweed and she managed to stay on her feet just long enough to get a look at Oshi. A flush of warmth covered her nephew's cheeks and his hair was tamped down, either from sweat or the rain, but he looked completely healthy. His tiny fingers were curled into fists and his little bud mouth was open.

Isa collapsed to her knees, which added a few more degrees of warmth to Ani's smile.

Lieutenant Tamin had taken up a strategic position next to Ani, more than ready to defend her if Isa tried anything.

"Dramash," said Ani, turning to the child, "I knew you would come back to me."

"I explained everything to him," said Isa, still trying to catch her breath. Down below, Eofar was clinging to Rho's arm to keep him back, and Lahlil had taken up a stance directly in front of Jachad, warning him off while this played out.

"I told him his own people banished him to Norland because they were afraid of his power—and that Rho hates him for killing his friends and only ever pretended to like him."

"Yes, that's quite true," Ani said to Dramash. She dropped Oshi into Tessa's arms, unconcerned with either of them now that she finally had what she wanted. Tessa hugged the baby to her and tried to get away, but she managed to crawl only a few feet before her strength gave out. Oshi began to cry, but none of the Red Guards made any attempt to help them.

"I'm going to make sure no one deceives you again, child. Together we have the power to do that, and so much more."

Out among the ruins, a member of the militia crested the ridge and threw himself pell-mell through the field of glass, making straight for the dais. A Red Guard followed in hot pursuit and leaped on him from behind. They grappled wildly as they rolled through the dangerous shards. Further to the west, a Red Guard stumbled backward, trying to fend off a man with a sickle and a woman with a boat oar. Soon the temple would be overrun with fighters.

"Can we start now?" Dramash piped up.

"Of course," Ani laughed, pulling him into a grandmotherly

hug. Then she took out the bottle, the very sight of which made Isa shudder. "Take a sip, child. The taste may not be to your liking but you needn't drink more than a few drops."

The boy looked up at the old woman uncertainly and Isa burned to strike the thing out of his hand and tell him to run to Rho as fast as he could go. But that wasn't the plan, so she waited while he pulled out the cork, took a sip, made a comical face—and absently handed the bottle to Isa, who slipped it into her pocket.

Ani drew Dramash's hand toward her and pricked his palm before joining their hands together. Isa saw the moment the connection took: Ani's bird-like chest swelled and she breathed out like the air escaping from a long-sealed tomb. Her smile transformed into something beatific; Norlander painters would have surrounded her head with dots or dashed lines of gold paint.

The ground began to shake; a fissure opened next to Jachad and Lahlil and immediately pulled wider. Jachad lost his balance and fell, with no control now over the flames that sparked and flared out from him. Rho and Eofar ran toward them to help, but they wouldn't get there in time to save them from being swallowed into the bowels of the temple.

"Lahlil never gave up on her little Nomas king," Ani mused as she watched. "She still won't abandon him, even though she knows he must die. Loyalty, child, is a gift beyond price. One either has the capacity for it, or one does not."

Isa made the mistake of looking into Dramash's eyes and seeing the emptiness there. She had to remind herself that Dramash was an asha; he was strong. *Now, Dramash. Do it now*, she thought. *She can't reject power: it goes against everything in her nature. Make her ascend.*

The breach took Jachad, and Lahlil went with him. Eofar threw himself at Rho and tackled him to keep him from diving in after them.

Tamin's men suddenly fanned out to defend their little hill as a whole troop of fighters crested the top of the ruins, coming on with a full-throated battle roar that she never expected to hear from the Shadari. She knew in her gut that Daryan would be among them; she wouldn't let herself look at their faces.

Ani's Red Guards came charging up right behind them and in an instant the battle exploded into chaos. Fighters slid on the glass, falling and breaking bones, slicing flesh or impaling limbs. Others fell into the cracks or were pulled down; black swords effortlessly cut down barely-armed herders and millers, hacked into fishermen. Blood slicked the glass without changing its color.

"Isa, my child," Ani said to her, "we are left in an unfortunate position, you and I."

Isa bowed her head; it felt so very heavy. "I should never have left you."

"And Daryan?"

"You were right about him," she confessed. "He never loved me. He never cared about my pain. Only you did."

Ani sighed as if the truth pained her as much as it did Isa. "I would like nothing better than to be merciful, but you challenged my authority in front of my acolytes. You must understand how dangerous that is. Look down there: look how many have been hurt and killed because they continually resist what is in their best interests. Oh, child," Ani carried on, "if you understood how badly it hurts me to know they would rather destroy themselves than simply accept my love and protection."

Isa no longer had the strength to keep her eyes open. *Dramash. Please.*

"They should have learned their lesson by now, but Daryan and his traitors have corrupted them," Ani went on. "The corruption must be purged, and then we will start over. Now hold out your hand, Isa."

She turned her palm up without opening her eyes, vaguely remembering the balm the old woman had spread over her wounds while they were traveling. Instead, something hard scraped at her open cuts.

"Why?" she heard herself whisper, looking down at the rain

pinging off the plague stone in her hand, leaving the silvery veneer untouched.

"Since loyalty is not in *your* nature, I am giving you the opportunity to perform one last act of service, to redeem yourself."

Isa lurched up, clutching the stone in her hand as if it was something precious and not an instrument of death. All the strength that remained in her abused body flared up, bright and hot. The infection had already entered her blood through the cuts in her hand. It was too late to save herself.

Dramash. Please.

Then Isa ran, shoving past Ani's guards and skidding down the hill, letting the fall do the work that her limbs could not, well aware that she was one twisted ankle away from breaking her neck. She made it to the bottom in one piece and then ran in the direction of the sheerest drop. Ani's bottle was still in her pocket but she had no way to get it to Lahlil to accomplish the last part of her plan. She didn't even know if her sister and Jachad were still alive.

Glass crunched and snapped as she raced past the fighters pushing steadily in the opposite direction. The edge neared. Her legs were moving on nothing but momentum now and she expected them to carry her—and her plague-infected blood, and the stone—straight off the cliff and into the sea. But her instinctual self-preservation proved too strong: she ground to a halt with her boots one step from the drop, winded, half-blind and barely able to stand, but with enough agency left to drop the stone into the sea before it could be used again. In a moment, her legs would give out. All she needed to do was make sure she fell forward when it happened.

<Isa!> Rho called out in terror.

The ground beneath her fell away and her stomach dropped as the ledge on which she'd been standing broke apart and fell toward the churning sea. She shut her eyes and thought of her sister Frea, somewhere below the waves, waiting to drag her down.

Then something caught at her throat and she was choking, suspended in midair. This was not the way she wanted to die. She flailed and pawed at the thing holding her but the noose only pulled tighter—

—and a moment later, a hand clapped down over her arm and hauled her up. She lost track of everything for a moment except the pounding in her head and the omnipresent pain. Whatever had stopped her fall was soft and cool and Rho was calling out to her, asking if she was still alive, pleading with her to open her eyes. She wasn't sure about the former and she couldn't comply with the latter.

<Isa, *wake up*. Come on, now, I know you're still alive. What were you thinking, getting so close to the edge? You know perfectly well this whole place is ready to come down.>

Rho thought she'd fallen by accident. He'd *saved* her.

<Isa, please. Tell me what's going on. Lahlil and Jachad fell down a hole, Ani has Dramash and I don't know what to do.>

She managed to crack one eyelid open, but regretted it instantly when the rain stung her eyes. People were moving nearby in a confusion of boots and blood—and there, lying just out of reach, was the bottle. It must have fallen out of her pocket. Rho released her hand when he felt her trying to pull away and she flopped toward it.

<This? Is that the stuff Ani gave to Dramash? Do you want it?>
<Lahlil . . . >

<You want me to give it to Lahlil?> Rho guessed immediately, and she could have kissed him. <All right, I can do that. She's down a hole with a man *on fire* but of course I can do that. Why did you hand Dramash over to Anakthalisa? What was the plan? Because from what I've seen so far, it isn't working, and I am about to slash my way up there and get him back.>

<No,> she said, racking her wandering mind for a way to tell him in as few words as possible. <He has to give his power to her— make her a god—>

Rho's shock splashed over her, icy-cold. <Why on Onfar's balls would we do *that*?>

<Ask Lahlil.>

She felt him dithering for a moment but she couldn't see any more; she couldn't even tell if her eyes were open or closed.

<Stay here,> Rho said, which he must have known was ridiculous since she obviously couldn't move. <I'll come right back, I promise. And keep away from the edge this time, *please*?>

He took the bottle and ran off and Isa lay back with her face turned up to the rain, unable to distinguish her own erratic pulse from the boots pounding past. She had done the best she could; now the others would have to take it the rest of the way. They still had a chance. Lahlil had survived every other calamity the world had thrown at her and she would survive this one, too. Dramash might be just a boy, but he still had the capacity and courage to hope after experiencing tragedies that would have sent most grown men spiraling into madness.

And Rho . . . he had refused to abandon her even after the way she had treated him. He had trusted her with the safety of the person who probably meant the most to him in the world, even after it looked like she had failed. He had saved her life when that cliff could have crumbled out from under him too. He had held her hand—

Her gasp of horror pulled her bolt-upright and she looked down at the silver slime oozing over her scratched palm and burrowing into the cracks. *He didn't know!* He hadn't seen Ani give her the stone, or he hadn't understood what it meant. She forced her feet under her until she got enough purchase to draw her knees up, and then she concentrated on uncoiling her spine, vertebra by vertebra, pulling herself up until she could turn around and stumble after him. One of the Red Guards stepped into her path and she *screamed* as she gathered the strength to tear Blood's Pride from its scabbard before remembering how she'd disarmed herself, but the man shrank back from her in horror anyway. The sky rumbled and the ground groaned and the glass reflected the forked lightning and Isa kept going until she could see Rho's lean back bending over the fissure where Lahlil had disappeared. But before she could cry out to him, to warn him, darkness passed over her like a raven's wing and brought her down, soft and fluttering, into the void.

Chapter 28

The gray sky shrank down to the size of a coin as rocks fell in around Lahlil. She and Jachad had fallen into an old corridor, landing in a thick sludge of powdered stone and mud and water. Cracked walls canted up on either side. The temple groaned around them, gnashing its teeth as it swallowed more rock and red glass.

"Jachi? Can you hear me?" she shouted into the glare where Jachad sprawled, muddy water boiling under his hands. Lahlil breathed shallowly against the noxious odor. They'd asphyxiate soon if the fire kept eating up all the air.

She checked as much of the walls as she could reach, tapping to test them for solidity, looking for a way to climb up that wouldn't bury them further. The drop wasn't that high; she could pile together enough rubble to climb out. She started rolling the largest rocks to the most stable part of the wall.

"We fell," said Jachad.

"Anakthalisa tried to bury us," she corrected. She needed to get them out before the bad air took them both. "We're going to climb out."

"I can't be here," he said. His voice sounded hollow, and not just because of the rock walls surrounding them.

"I'm getting us out," she promised. "Just wait a little longer."

"Lahlil," he said, and this time his tone demanded that she stop and look at him. She knew he'd been afraid of small places all his life and this was his second time being buried today. "The fear—it's making it harder for me."

"You can hold it together," Lahlil insisted as she piled on another rock. Another big chunk crashed down from the fissure, so she heaved it right onto the pile. "We were close to defeating the witch until Isa showed up. As soon as we get out of here we'll finish this."

She felt the heat at her back before she turned around but when she did, only his eyes were still burning. "Give me your knife, Lahlil."

"Why?"

"Because you took mine."

She tried looking at his mouth instead of his eyes, thinking that would be easier, but the lines were too hard, too uncompromising. "No."

"You swore to me."

"We're not there yet," said Lahlil, even though her lungs were beginning to burn from the lack of air. The breach above them was still out of reach. "Stop arguing with me and let me finish this."

"If we both die here, Anakthalisa will succeed. I won't allow that. The best chance to defeat her now is for me to end here and for you to finish the fight."

"*Not yet,*" she said again, pressing her hand to his chest with the intent of pushing him away, but ended up clutching his jacket instead. "I didn't get where I am by giving up."

"And where are you, Lahlil?" Jachad asked. The lilt in his voice sounded so much more like his old self that she swallowed back a sob. "Buried under a temple by an ancient witch with a demigod who's about to erupt."

"With you," Lahlil whispered. "I'm with you."

Pressure squeezed her lungs and this time she couldn't help but cough. She moved her hand to his shoulder as she struggled to breathe and he supported her for a moment, but then he stepped back away from her as new flames dripped from his hands and warmed the air to stifling.

"It's time," Jachad told her, all emotions stripped from him once again. "Give me the knife."

She drew the blade and watched the firelight curl around the sharp edges. The tip was glowing like a star. Then she shoved it back in the sheath and drew Strife's Bane instead. "I'll make it as clean as I can."

"I know; I trust you. But you need to hurry now."

Beheading would be the quickest and least painful death she could give him, but there wasn't space enough to ensure she could do it in a single stroke. The next best option was the way Norlanders killed prisoners on the battlefield: a sword plunged straight down through the back of the neck, severing the spine.

"Turn around and kneel down." The voice was Lahlil's, but she would have sworn the words had been said by someone else. He followed her command, twining his hands together in front of him, flames circling in ribbons around them. He knelt with his head bent, the gold chain of the sun-god medallion shining among the freckles on the back of his neck, his red hair curled around his shoulders. She remembered the desert sun picking out the different shades, how it shone, and threaded her fingers through it; then she stroked the side of his neck, sliding her thumb along his jaw, as warmth seeped back into her numb fingers. His head dipped further and he angled his chin enough to fit it into the hollow of her hand, to press his lips to her fingers.

"I love you, Jachi," she said.

He didn't say it back; she thought he was concentrating too hard on not immolating them both before she could finish. More rocks pattered down from above, followed by a rush of rain. Lahlil arranged herself into the appropriate stance and raised her sword.

<Lahlil! Are you down there? Can you hear me?> The gray light disappeared and was replaced by Rho's dirt-streaked but still luminous face blocking up the opening. <Answer me—I know you're not dead.>

"Tell him to go," Jachad said softly.

<Rho, get back. You're not safe there.>

<I'm well aware of that, thank you. Now get over here so I can help you climb out.> Whatever he was doing up there sent more rocks pelting down. Jachad's shoulders were shaking with the effort of holding the fire back.

<Get away,> Lahlil ordered Rho, tightening her grip on the sword.

<Can't you ju—?>

The edge of the rift fell away in one big chunk, breaking up as it rattled down. One piece slammed into Lahlil's back, pitching her forward onto her elbows, and still the unforgiving debris crashed into them, taking every opportunity to rip and bruise. A torrent of rain followed the end of the onslaught. Lahlil freed herself from her half-buried state and looked up to see Rho still looking down, but from a significantly wider hole.

<Oh,> he said, blinking his silver eyes. The streaked sky surrounded him like a dirty halo. <Sorry?>

Jachad lay in a rubble-covered heap, unconscious but no longer on fire. She dashed over to him and felt his pulse beating steadily, despite a new cut on his forehead and a deeper one on his shoulder. His eye flickered when she carefully lifted an eyelid.

"Jachi," she called, jostling him gently. No response.

<Lahlil?> Rho called down, softly this time, his words vibrating with anxiety and regret. <What did I do?>

<You bought me another chance, you idiot,> said Lahlil. <Now help me get him out. Hurry.>

The cave-in had finished her work for her and she was able to hoist Jachad onto her shoulder and lift him high enough so that Rho could grab him. A little time passed before he came back for her.

<This way,> Rho said as soon as she climbed out. Fighting had exploded across the ruins, which had further destabilized the area. Several pits had opened up and more of the eastern edge had fallen away. No triffons were able to land now; only the victors

would be leaving. Rho led her to where some of the walls still stood and dropped down into a room which had once been a kitchen. He had propped Jachad up in one corner.

<Here,> said Rho, hurriedly digging something from his pocket that turned out to be a familiar glass bottle. <It's that stuff Ani gave to Tessa and Dramash to control them. For some reason Isa wanted me to give it to you.>

<Why?>

<*I don't know!*> Rho exploded in frustration. <Isa told me her plan was to have Dramash give his power to Ani and make her a god, and now I'm supposed to ask *you* why that wasn't the worst idea anyone ever had.>

Lahlil reached out to take the bottle from him but right before her fingers touched the glass, she saw the smudges and drew her hand back. <Isa gave that to you?>

Rho blanched at her tone. <Yes. Why?>

<When did you take off your gloves?>

<I left them on Eofar's ship when we abandoned it. Lahlil—>

<Rho,> she said calmly, even as whatever was left of the shell around her heart cracked like an egg, <look at your hand.>

Then she went to check on Jachad, to give Rho his privacy. "Jachi," she said, cupping his face and tipping it up to hers. A muscle twitched, but he clearly wasn't close to waking up yet.

Isa wanted her to have that bottle. The only reason would be for Lahlil to take it and be Jachad's anchor, the same way Ani was using Dramash. Jachad would be able to use her to control his powers and defeat Ani. Except that Jachad was now unconscious— and in any case, he would never agree to it after hearing Isa describe it as "violating."

Rho broke into her thoughts. <Do you have something to wrap this in?> he asked, holding out Isa's bottle. Lahlil tugged off her scarf and knotted it into a small sack; he dropped in the bottle without touching her or the fabric and she tucked the whole bundle into her pocket.

<If I wasn't indestructible, I would probably be a little worried

right now,> Rho said with forced lightness, pushing his wet hair back from his forehead and looking out at the battle. Lahlil ached to touch him in some way, just put her hand on his shoulder, maybe; but she knew he would be afraid of infecting her, so she didn't.

<Isa's terrible plan has obviously failed so I say we charge straight for Ani like the bloodthirsty high-clan warriors we are and go out with a bang Lord Onfar will hear from his celestial Hall. What do you think of that idea, Lahlil Eotan?>

<I think you've already earned your place at the Arregadors' table,> she said. She checked one last time that Jachad was still out cold, then drew Strife's Bane. <But if cutting Anakthalisa in half will get you a chair closer to the fire, I'm game.>

So they stormed out into the sea of broken glass side by side, matching strides until they met with the first resistance. Lahlil efficiently cut down any Red Guards who came within reach, even though resistance grew fiercer and more competent the closer they got to the witch. One man rammed a shield into her side, momentarily winding her before she stabbed him in the stomach. Another traded a few blows with her before she trapped his sword beneath hers, then broke his jaw with a kick when he knelt down to escape the trap. A bare-chested man grazed her leg before she bowled him over and impaled him on one of the jagged glass spikes.

She looked up at the dais and found Anakthalisa watching them, with Dramash as rigid as a pike beside her. Ani's veneer of maternal affection had vanished completely, exposing the raw, naked hurt of a rejected child. *This* was the face of the woman who had given Isa the plague in the midst of a self-pitying tantrum and passed a death sentence on every person in the Shadar because they didn't love her the way she thought she deserved to be loved. This was the woman who threw away her toys when they no longer amused her.

Which was why she didn't notice Eofar and Daryan liberating Tessa and Oshi just a few feet behind her back, right at that very moment.

A Red Guard whipped around and tried to stab Lahlil, regaining her attention. The jerky way he was moving made it clear that Ani was controlling his sword from afar. If he hadn't been carrying a shield—and cowering behind it, for the most part—Lahlil would have killed him at once; instead, she had to defend herself against wild hacks as he moved with a speed she couldn't match. She took a slash to the arm and a scrape across her ribs as glass shattered beneath her, cutting her flesh and sticking in her clothes. Finally she twisted around and stepped back in under the man's guard and punched him with the pommel of her sword. The impact knocked him backward, but she knew that wouldn't stop the witch, so she grabbed his wrist and bent his hand back until it snapped. The guard screamed in agony and finally dropped the weapon.

Ani was toying with them, of course; she didn't even need the Red Guards now that she had control over every black-bladed weapon in sight. Lahlil snatched up a shield as it rolled past her after Rho impaled its former owner. Rho had already acquired his own shield.

<We'd better hurry,> said Rho.

When she glanced at him and saw the silvery film in his eyes, she understood his urgency.

Another sword flew at her, this time with no owner behind it, and she deflected with the shield, and repeated her action when another came from the opposite direction. The third opened a cut on her side like the lash of a whip before she could get out of the way.

Then Rho set himself at her back, careful not to touch her, and that was better. Red Guards rushed them, a few voluntarily but most pulled by the swords they hadn't the sense to give up. She went for quick, killing blows whenever she could, slashing instead of thrusting, but the numbers were overwhelming. The shields helped, but they weren't enough. Time mocked her by slowing down each kick, punch, slash and thrust until it felt like she was leafing through the pages of a manual. She used her shield, her sword, her feet, any projectile she could find, and they were inching their way forward, but she was under no illusion that they would succeed this way. Once Anakthalisa grew bored of seeing them bleed from a thousand cuts, she would crush them.

Then Rho sank down, shaking and sick, the point of Fortune's Blight plowing through the dirt. The first phase of the plague was taking over.

<Rho—>

<Stay back,> he warned her raggedly.

One of the guards leaped in when he saw Rho go down and tried to stab him in the back, but Lahlil slashed the man's neck and used her shield to shove away a second who came with the same idea. She knew it was pointless to protect Rho when he was dying anyway, but she didn't care. He was flippant and annoying and a lodestone for trouble; he wasn't particularly smart or brave and he was a barely adequate swordsman, but no one was going to hurt him as long as—

<Rho.>

<Lahlil, I told you, don't come any closer. I've got to end this before—>

<Shut up and listen to me,> she snapped. <Dramash—you have to tell him to give up his power. Tell him he doesn't need to protect you any more.>

<Protect me?>

They didn't have time for this. <I thought Ani was toying with us, but it's not her. It's Dramash—he's struggling with her like he did on the Front in Ravindal, to protect *you*. Tell him to stop!>

"Dramash!" Rho shouted. His haggard voice ripped right across the din of the battle. "Let her have the power! You don't need it any more. You don't need it to protect us."

Lahlil took a chance to glance away from two more opponents and look up to the dais. The boy was looking right at Rho, so he had heard him. The wrinkle on his brow, though . . .

<Rho, get up.>

<I can't.>

<*Get up*, Rho,> she insisted, knocking back another foe. <Dramash won't stop thinking you need his protection while you're lying there like a one-legged dog.>

Rho groaned aloud and stuck his shield in among the loose glass, then used it to pull himself up to his feet. "Dramash! You see? We're going to protect you now. Let her have the power."

Suddenly all the glass pebbles shifted a few inches to the east, skittering over their boots.

"Please, Dramash," Rho begged. "You're strong enough without it."

The stones moved again, more violently this time. Lahlil felt like she was standing just below the water line as the surf slid by; for a moment her brain couldn't decide which was moving, her or the water.

Rho lost his hold on the shield and fell back down, silver tears glistening in the corners of his eyes. The only thing Lahlil could offer him now was a swift death, and she couldn't bring herself to do it.

Then Ani threw her head back with a shrill, bird-like cry of pure joy. Lahlil had witnessed all kinds of people slaking every appetite imaginable and she recognized the way the old woman shivered as Dramash's power flooded into her. She watched Ani drink it in, and the more she took, the greedier she became.

Dramash slipped his hand out of her grasp and stepped away.

Ani clung to the ecstasy for a moment, then felt the supply choke off. She turned in obvious confusion when she no longer felt Dramash by her side and then took a step toward him, her movements jerky and undisciplined. Blood still streaked her palm.

Lahlil felt the ground beneath her tremble, then lurch—and then a whole section of the ruin dropped away, tumbling down toward the city with a terrifying roar, sweeping up anyone unlucky enough to be caught in its path. Lahlil slammed Strife's Bane into the rock and hung on as the ruins continued to rock, the most violent earthquake she'd ever experienced. Cracks opened up in the city below, draining away the floodwaters but sucking up everything else within their reach. Red clouds billowed up on the western horizon as landslides crashed down the mountains with a sound like distant thunder.

And then she remembered what Jachad had said would happen if Ani used her power without someone to anchor her. *First she'll destroy everything around her,* he'd told them.

Then she'll become a god.

Anakthalisa's second cry had whole octaves of terror and rage resonating inside it. Dramash covered his ears before he finally fled down the little hill, but still the scream chased him, turning staccato as it shredded into unknown words that sounded like prayers and curses and cries for help all at the same time.

Ani was alone now, and no one was there to stop her from crashing into her borrowed throne and knocking it over. No one helped her up when her body twitched like a fish on a hook, or stopped her from stumbling over the rocks.

But *everyone* knew when she ascended. Lahlil had expected something dramatic: bright lights or booming sounds, a glimpse of something miraculous soaring into the heavens, but instead, she felt something massive shift violently out of their world and into another, leaving behind an emptiness like a missing tooth—

—and Ani's empty vessel slumped over the wooden chair. The rain fell into its unblinking eyes.

<Is it over?> asked Rho, his words leaving a damp trail of sickness behind.

<Yes, it's over.>

<Why do I still hear screaming?>

Because Jachad had risen. He paced slowly through the ruins, heralded by the screams and pounding feet of the people who fled before him; by the crackling of glass as it formed and cooled in the driving rain. He was surrounded by a light brighter than anything other than the sun itself, and the sun never had such colors as these: not just red, yellow, and orange, but blinding white and ice-blue flares, flickering tongues of purple and olive.

Lahlil took the wrapped bottle out of her pocket, popped open the cork and drank it all down.

"Jachi," she called out, the lone figure walking toward him instead of running away, "you need to let me in."

His face remained blank behind the inferno.

She kept moving forward even as the heat pounded her, wave after wave, drawing the moisture from her body until every inch of her skin was bathed in sweat. "I found a way to keep my promise, Jachi. But you have to let me in."

The flames parted for her but then closed around behind. She didn't mind; she had no other place to be. Her clothes began to smolder but they didn't matter, nor did the pain in her palm when she slashed it with her knife, nor the way her fingers blistered when she reached for his hand.

The connection pulled at her the moment their blood mingled: a golden thread, strong and needle-sharp. Then Jachad gave a *tug*, and Lahlil understood why Isa had described this experience as a violation: it hooked into something so deep inside her that she felt flayed, split open until all of her demons crawled out, blinking, into the light. She forced down a breath of heat-soaked air and focused on the thread, following it to its anchor point: the latch of an iron door where she had locked away her vulnerability and left it there to rot. He could have knocked that door down with a thought, but he wouldn't—so she opened it for him, and found that what she'd imprisoned there had thrived on her neglect. It flooded out of its cell, tendrils unfurling as it rioted through her, seeking him out. And when it found him, he opened to it: not taking, but receiving; not grasping, but accepting.

She could feel the strength coursing out of her and she gave it gladly, except for the little she needed to stay lucid. Slowly, the flames died out, smoke rose up to meet the rain and she felt like she could float up with it, until she raised her head enough to look up at Jachad. The wonder in his sea-blue eyes—the reverence, the devotion—left her breathless.

"Lahlil," Jachad said gently, folding to his knees beside her, "I have to go."

"Go where?" she asked, but her voice was so weak she was afraid he couldn't hear her.

He pulled her to him, making sure their hands stayed connected. "I have to ascend. You have to let me go."

"Why?" She moved her head against his chest until she could hear his heartbeat, loud and strong. Her own was fading.

"You'll die if I keep using you like this. Then I'll be as much of a danger as I was before, and you won't be here to stop me."

"Jachi, don't go. Don't leave me."

"Someone has to stop this plague, Lahlil. It's too late to contain it, and it's not just here in the Shadar."

"But only cold can kill it," she protested, taking too long to dredge up the breath for each word. "You're not cold. You're fire. How can a sun god stop the plague?"

"By taking the sun away," he whispered in her ear.

"No," she said, tangling her fingers in his hair and pulling his head down. Everything had gone blurry and soft and her thoughts were soft too, and *she needed him*. "Don't go."

"*You* would."

"No," she said immediately. "I could never leave you."

"Then maybe that's why this is my task, and not yours." He held her a little tighter and pressed his forehead to her hair. "Let me go."

"Come back when it's done," she countered.

"I don't think that's possible."

She pulled herself out of her lethargy long enough to lean back and look into his eyes. "The impossible is *what I do*. I'll hold you here, Jachi. You do what you need to do and then *you come back to me*. Do you understand?"

"Lah—"

"Swear! Swear you'll come back."

He pressed a kiss against her forehead. "I swear."

Lahlil pulled the scarf from around his neck and bound their clasped hands together. She needed to use her teeth to pull the knot tight. "There. They won't pull us apart. Not until you come back."

The last thing she felt before she passed out was the jolt as the golden thread snapped.

Chapter 29

The first time Lahlil woke, it was dark and cold and she couldn't see anything. She moved her left hand and felt the glide of silk against the back of her fingers and Jachad's rough skin beneath them. His hand was still warm. They were outside, she realized, but there were no stars overhead, and no fire. Someone was singing, very softly, and gently pulling a brush through her hair. She fell back to sleep with the brush-strokes keeping time to the music.

The second time she woke, it was snowing hard, small, crystalline flakes filling the sky. A makeshift Nomas shelter, just poles and canvas, was keeping them safe from the snow. A campfire glowed nearby and the smoke perfumed the crisp air. Someone had set a lamp on the ground and by its light, she could see Jachad lying beside her. Their hands were still bound together. She couldn't tell whether her inability to move was due to whatever was happening to her or the heavy blankets piled on top of her.

At some point Daryan, who was sitting by the fire, noticed that her eyes were open and began shouting. People crowded around her, asking questions in three different languages, but they all sounded like they were speaking underwater. She decided that if she couldn't communicate she would be better served by going back to sleep, so she did.

The next time she opened her eyes it was to the sight of brightly striped sailcloth over her head and Jachad in the cot next to hers, still holding her hand. She was certain she was dreaming until she glimpsed Rho through the tent-flap, talking to Mairi. He was bandaged in a dozen places, but clearly neither dead nor dying. She had the sense that time had passed, but it was still dark, still cold, still snowing. She thought she had even more blankets piled on top of her than before.

<You're awake,> said Rho, ducking inside and coming to sit down beside her.

<You're alive.>

<How dare you question my indestructibility?> Rho declared. <It's been snowing for the last two days. We were able to cure everyone.>

<Isa?>

Worry prickled through him. <They tell me she's recovering, but she's had a terrible time of it. The withdrawal nearly killed her and then the plague on top of that did her no favors. I was sure we'd lost her.> He was fussing, she realized, and he must have noticed as well because he admitted, <Mairi says she just needs rest.>

"So does Lahlil!" Mairi hollered from somewhere near the fire. "You people don't understand she can't go on like that! She'll die if Jachi doesn't wake up soon and stop draining the life out of her. She needs to save her strength."

Lahlil thought that sound reasoning, and since staying awake felt like it was using up a great deal of strength, she went back to sleep.

The next time she woke, it was because of a strange warmth in her hand. She snapped her eyes open, expecting to see Jachad twisting flames around her wrist. But Jachad's bed was empty and the warmth she felt was a ray of sunlight poking through a gap in the canvas.

She heard the sound of a baby gurgling and Eofar appeared in her sightline with Oshi in his arms. <Yes, she *is* awake,> he sing-songed to the oblivious infant. <How are you feeling, Lahlil? Do you want some water?>

She felt like she'd swallowed a mouthful of sand and she had dozens of questions about how the battle had ended and what had happened to everyone, but there was only one thing she could ask her brother right now.

<Can I hold Oshi?> she said.

He couldn't have needed more than two steps to reach her cot, but every instant, every heartbeat, weighed on Lahlil's nerves. He lowered an arm to help her sit up, which left her feeling like she'd run a league, and then spent another moment settling Oshi with kisses and reassurances before finally handing the baby down into her waiting arms.

She looked down into his golden eyes while he batted cheerfully at her face and pulled her hair. When she heard the sounds of someone approaching the tent, she was more afraid to look up than she had been of anything in her life.

"I had a feeling you'd woken up," said Jachad as he strolled in. He cleared his throat when he saw Oshi in her arms, and rasped, "The vision?"

She nodded, but she had forgotten how to do anything else like speak or breathe. Eofar helpfully took the baby from her so Jachad could open his arms and pull her to him, cradling her head as she buried her face in the crook between his neck and his shoulder.

"It's all right," he reassured her, stroking her hair. "I'm here. I'm fine. Well, if you need a lamp lit, I'm your man, but I used up the rest of my powers smiting Anakthalisa. That's what it's called, you know: smiting. Mairi thinks my powers will come back eventually, but what does she know? She makes these things up and then pretends like we all should have known that all along. I can't wait to get her back on the *Windward* and out of my hair. Speaking of my hair, Callia cut your hair, and mine, too. She told me I looked like a beggar because she's a very rude person. I'm not sure I want you associating with her."

Lahlil finally released him so she could lean back and look into his slightly watery eyes. "Jachi, are you *drunk*?"

He swallowed hard before leaning forward to rest his forehead against hers. "You didn't wake up," he whispered, like a confession. "I thought I'd taken too much from you. I'm sorry. I wanted to be here when you woke."

She kissed him, tasting the wine on his lips as he kissed her back, sweet and undemanding.

"It shouldn't have been possible, you know," he told her, tracing the scar at the corner of her mouth. "You shouldn't have been able to tether me like that, let alone for days. What made you think you could?"

"You told me you could always see me, no matter how far away you were," she said before kissing him again. "From now on, all you'll have to do is open your eyes."

Chapter 30

Isa pushed back the blankets and sat up when Rho came in. She was fed up with being stuck in bed. She'd managed to walk all the way around the tent that morning with Eofar and had only needed to lean on him a few times. She *wasn't* helpless.

<You see, I knew you would be in a bad mood tonight. That's why I brought you this,> he said, carelessly tossing her the plum and making her lunge to catch it.

<Where did you get a ripe plum in the middle of a half-destroyed city?>

<I will take that information with me to my tomb,> Rho vowed. <Why would you need me if you could get your own plums?>

An instant later she could feel his awkwardness as he regretted the joke, but she didn't understand why. He was probably worried about suggesting she couldn't take care of herself, but she knew he hadn't meant it like that.

<Any sign of Dramash's powers coming back?> she asked.

<No, none,> he said. <He's said from the very beginning that they wouldn't, but we were afraid it was just wishful thinking. Your plan was *beyond* brilliant, Isa. We defeated Anakthalisa and Dramash can live a normal life.>

<Thank you for trusting me.>

Gratitude had always made him uncomfortable. He paced

around the tent for a moment; picked up a cushion and examined the embroidery; turned it over in his hands.

<So, are you going to stay in the Shadar with him?> she asked.

<Somehow I don't think having a Norlander for a father is what Dramash needs to re-integrate,> he said, finally tossing away the cushion. Isa didn't think he'd realized he'd referred to himself as the boy's father. <Daryan said he would take him in, look after him. It'll be better for him if I'm not around. Less confusing.>

<Will you go back to Norland?>

<I don't know.> He wandered over and sat on the floor by the foot of her cot, kicking his long legs out over the carpet. <My step-brothers still have control of our estates and the Arregadors at court are insufferable. I may go back to Prol Irat, get lost there for a while. It's a good place for it. Assuming the whole city didn't burn down after we left.>

<I may not stay either,> she said, and instantly felt guilty. She shouldn't talk to Rho about this before she discussed it with Daryan. <I was born in the Shadar and I've fought for it, but it's not my home. The *temple* was my home, but that's gone. I might go back to Norland with Eofar.>

<Oh. I—To Norland? That's . . . I wasn't expecting that,> he stammered.

<You think I shouldn't, because of my arm?>

<No,> he said, then repeated it with more emphasis, <*no*. I'm only surprised because I assumed that after you'd sacrificed so much for the Shadar, you'd want to stay.>

Isa looked out through the tent-flap to the people beginning to gather at the camp's community fire. <That's what I'd thought, too.>

<Well, if we're all heading in the same direction, we might as well travel together. That's how your sister and I became so inseparable, you know. Adversity tempers steel—is that the expression? I thought it was something like that, but it doesn't make sense, does it? I must be missing something.>

<Rho, you're babbling.>

He thumped his palms down decisively on the rug and levered himself up. <I am, yes. And now I'm going to leave so you can get some rest.> He leaned over the bed to kiss her cheek.

<Come back later?> she asked.

He held her hand for a moment. <You don't have to ask.>

Ridiculously, she did fall asleep again, and didn't wake up again until Daryan cleared his throat outside the tent-flap, waiting for an invitation to enter.

"You're looking much stronger," he said as he sat on the rug next to her cot. He said the same thing every time he came to see her. She wasn't sure who it was meant to convince.

"I walked around the tent today. It's ridiculous, I know, but a few days ago I couldn't even manage that."

"It's not ridiculous at all. After what you went through . . ." He trailed off, looking down at her hand but not touching her. The last traces of the drug had left her body long ago and her body temperature had returned to normal. She couldn't help but think of that brief moment when they could touch each without pain for the first time, and how she had been so numbed by Ani's drug that her memories of it were less distinct than most of her dreams.

"I've been thinking I might go back to Norland with my brother," she said.

His body language shifted, but not with surprise. "I thought you might be. Eofar mentioned it."

"There are a lot of people like me in Norland—the 'cursed'—who are being thrown into a world that doesn't know how to treat them. They're being hounded and abused. People are still being set out, in spite of the law. As the emperor's sister, I could have an influence."

"You could help a lot of very vulnerable people, Isa. I understand. I do."

"It feels like it would give some meaning to this," she said, lifting her maimed shoulder. "Not that I think it happened for a reason, only that I would be doing something where I was useful *because* of it, rather than in spite of it. I want that; at least for a while."

Daryan nodded and looked down at his hands. "I've been think-ing a lot about what you said at the palace, when you asked if I would have let you die if that had been your decision. Well, you were right: I wouldn't have. I would have found some way to do it without your consent. The thought of it makes me ill."

She moved over a little in the bed so her leg brushed against his back through the blanket. "You can't know what you *would* have done. I think it would have been awful for you, but you would have done the right thing in the end." Now it was her turn to look down at her hand, at the new scars forming along the lines of the deeper scrapes. "You said I left the Shadar because I didn't trust you, and you were right. I was too miserable to see that you were becoming a real leader. I'm sure there's no one in the Shadar who doubts it now."

"Binit is still a bright purple pain in my arse," he admitted, "but you're right. It's not the same now. Do you think—?" He stopped mid-sentence.

"No," she answered anyway, "I think we would have both been unhappy, and too stubborn to admit it. In the end we would have hurt each other very badly."

He bobbed his head, no doubt thinking like her back to that night on the ridge where they'd decided to stay rather than flee together. "Are we ending this?"

The tears came suddenly and silently, a balm in the cooling air. She wanted to take it all back, but she knew in her heart it had been over the day she came back to the Shadar, if not before. "Yes. I think so."

"I still love you," he said.

"I still love you, too."

He looked at her, then at his feet. "But this can't work."

"No, it can't," she said, and there was an unexpected stirring of relief at finally admitting it out loud. "We both deserve more than we could give each other, the way things are."

He stood up. "Eofar said repairs on the ships are going to take at least another month, so there's no rush to say goodbye. I was hoping, when you're feeling better, you could help to translate between the Shadari and the Norlanders on the rebuilding crews. Eofar and Rho have their hands full."

"Of course. I'd like to be useful."

"I know it doesn't seem like it a lot of the time, but many Shadari do recognize all you've done for us."

"Thank you. I'll try to remember that."

For the first time, he noticed the plum sitting next to her on the bed. "I didn't know you liked plums."

"Rho brought it. He caught me stealing them from the refectory in the temple one night. He loves to remind me how he didn't turn me in."

Daryan's smile looked a bit off, but he turned away before she could get a better look at it. "Now that you—Lahlil," he broke off as her sister entered the tent. "No, don't go. I was just leaving. I'll see you both later."

He left them alone, which immediately became awkward. Her sister had visited a few times but only with other people present, and she'd said very little. Isa figured she was angry at her, and she had a perfect right to be, after everything Isa had done.

Lahlil walked over to Blood's Pride, glared at it, then took the sword and weighed it in her hand.

<Why didn't you try to stop me when I brought Dramash to Ani?> Isa asked. <Rho and Eofar did.>

<I knew you had a plan.>

<And you *trusted* me? After everything I'd put you through?>

Lahlil put the sword back on its stand. <I believed in you. You said once before that I owed you that. You were right.>

She'd take the time to savor *that* later, but right now she knew her sister was working up to say something difficult for her.

<It wasn't your fault,> Lahlil said at last.

<What wasn't?>

<What happened to Mother. She put you on that triffon instead of standing up to Father. And she didn't love me more than the rest of you, she just felt guilty. She wanted to make it right, but she went about it all wrong.>

<Maybe we take after her that way.>

<Maybe we do.>

Lahlil left as abruptly as she'd come, but this time Isa didn't mind. She felt tired but not weary, and suddenly her future didn't look like something to be simply endured; like a never-ending struggle. Her life needn't be only about *trying*; it could be about *wanting* as well, and Isa had never given herself permission to want before.

And right now, she wanted a plum.

Chapter 31

Daryan didn't make it out to the fire until long after dinner, but plenty of people remained.

The communal fire had been necessary when the sun had disappeared for four days and no one had enough fuel to keep warm. It had become part of their modest routine; something to look forward to at the end of a difficult day, which was the only kind they had at the moment.

Hesh had his arm around the same red-cheeked girl as the night before and neither of them were talking much, but Daryan could feel a strange atmosphere of contentment and anxiety buzzing between them. Lem and Tessa were the first to notice Daryan's arrival and beckon him over; Tessa was still chuckling over some story his bodyguard had been telling. Seeing them so comfortable with each other made him remember Lem speaking admiringly of Tessa's freckles. He thought of making an excuse in case he was intruding, but it was Lem who apologized and got up, saying he needed to talk to a friend who had just arrived.

"How are you, Tessa?" Daryan asked, feeling the first pleasant surge of heat from the fire as he settled down beside her.

"I'm about as well as can be expected," Tessa said lightly. "One day at a time. I've got most of my strength back, I think."

"Is there anything I can do for you?"

"I would like something to keep myself busy, if you could see your way to giving me some kind of task. There not being much laundry to do at the moment and the palace shut down forever . . ." She didn't try to hide the pain; she simply took a moment to let it roll over her. "When things get too quiet, I remember the court-yard."

"Ah," he said. "It's funny you should say that. I've been waiting for you to get your strength back before I asked, but I want you to be my chancellor."

Tessa hummed happily. "If that's what needs doing, I'll oblige, and gladly. What does a chancellor do?"

"You'd be the highest authority in the Shadar next to me."

Tessa burst out laughing and shoved his knee. "Go on with you! Really now. What is it?"

He laughed with her for a little while, then sat there, waiting for her to catch on.

"You're mad."

"Tessa, I'm really not. I need someone with common sense. Someone who will be compassionate and considered; who will never act from greed or false pride. Why would I go looking for someone else when I have you right here? If you want to help people and you want to be busy, then take the job. Trust me, nei-ther one of us will regret it."

"Of course I trust you." She said it offhandedly, like it was never in question, and that warmed him more than the fire. "Let me think about it. I don't want to jump into anything."

Daryan laughed. "You see? You've just proved my point."

"What point?" asked Hesh, looking up at their laughter.

"That your mother is very wise."

"Well she's a terrible cook," groaned Hesh, then blushed. "Don't say I didn't warn you."

Daryan's laugh sounded a little false in his ears, so he stood up as soon as he saw Eofar wandering along behind the fire with Oshi lounging against his shoulder. The baby was wide-awake, although his father was stumbling along half-dead. They had passed around a story that Eofar had fathered Oshi with a Nomas woman in case anyone suspected that Harotha was Oshi's real mother. Daryan knew the deception was necessary, but he could tell how much it pained Eofar to have to keep that secret even now. Maybe one day they'd be able to tell everyone the truth.

"Can't get him to sleep?" Daryan asked.

"No," said Eofar. "I thought the fire might make him feel sleepy."

"Maybe he's hungry?"

Eofar leveled him with a decidedly un-Norlander glare. "He's *not* hungry. He *doesn't* need changing. He's *not* ill. He's just—*awake*, and he won't let me put him down."

"Give him here," said Tessa, scooping him out of Eofar's arms and taking him for a stroll around the fire, prattling to him and introducing him to the people they passed.

Eofar flopped down next to him and looked up at the stars. "I think the rain is gone for good."

"If we're lucky, we'll finish the clean-up just in time for next year's rains," Daryan said, only half joking.

"You'll get it done long before that. It's only been a week and people are already moving back into their homes."

"Eofar," said Lahlll, coming around from the other side of the fire with Jachad by her side. She was carrying Strife's Bane in its scabbard. "I was looking for you," she said, sitting down next to him and laying the sword by his side. "I want you to have this back."

Eofar bumped his hand over the silver triffons, thumbed the jeweled red eyes. "It's yours by right. You're the oldest."

"I don't have anyone to pass it on to," she said, shifting her gaze to Tessa, who was holding Oshi up so a group of her friends could make silly faces at him. "You do."

"You're taking Oshi back to Norland, then?" asked Daryan.

"It might not be the wisest decision, but I can't leave him again.

313

The people who will have a problem with him already hate me. But Norland is changing. Ironically, people are less narrow-minded because of the empire. Our whole generation has spent more time outside of Norland than in it."

Daryan nodded a greeting to Tessa when she came back and handed the sleeping baby back to Eofar, who made himself comfortable by the fire, cradling his son. Lahlil and Jachad dropped down beside them and settled back to back, heads lolling together.

Tessa sat down next to Daryan, then stretched out on her stomach, resting her chin in her hands. He could tell from the little frown lines between her eyes that she was thinking about his offer.

He sat back up in surprise when Isa came out to join them, close enough to Rho to lean on him if necessary but walking under her own power. For a moment he was going to congratulate her, then thought better of it, deciding she wouldn't want that kind of attention. She sat down next to Eofar and he put his arm around her so she could rest her head on his shoulder. He'd been a good older brother to Isa until his doomed relationship with Harotha pulled them apart.

Rho made himself comfortable on Isa's other side and watched Dramash play with a group of other Shadari children his own age, all of them gleefully enjoying the fact that no one could be bothered enforcing bedtime.

The conversations dropped off one by one, but the fire continued to exercise its magnetism over them and no one left, even as the hour flowed on toward midnight. Daryan had a thousand things to do, but he wanted to gift himself this moment before they went their separate ways: all of them together for the first and last time, sharing a silence. He'd come to associate silence with danger. For most of his life, silence had meant Dead Ones were nearby and he mustn't make a noise or he would be punished; it meant the loneliness of empty corridors and empty rooms; of being avoided because he was the daimon and *different* from everyone else. It meant the inside of a tomb or a caved-in mine or the bottom of a landslide.

This silence was different. It was rich: full of the said and the unsaid; of promises kept and those still to be made. This time, the silence was complete.

Acknowledgments

Thanks goes to the usual suspects, which serves to prove how little I left the house during this book's creation. Of course, thanks and huge amounts of credit go to my editors, Miriam Weinberg and Jo Fletcher, for their saintly patience and encouragement, and for coming to my rescue with a metaphorical compass and baggy full of trail mix when I trekked down the wrong path yet again. I also have to thank Jo for catching the eye-opening array of British euphemisms I blundered into. My family, particularly my stupidly wonderful husband, Lou, for never once asking "what I did all day."

Thanks to my agent and (young) fairy godmother, Becca Stumpf, even as she moves on to bigger and better things, which she absolutely deserves. And never forgetting my soulsister Lisa Rogers, who knows what she did, but that's our secret and you'll never drag it out of me.

About the Author

Evie Manieri has a degree in medieval history and theater from Wesleyan University. She lives with her husband and daughter in New York City.

Twitter: @EvieManieri
Facebook.com/manieri.evie